The Dressmaker of Paris

About the Author

Georgia Kaufmann was born and grew up in North London. She studied Social Anthropology and Demography at Cambridge, LSE and Oxford. For most of her twenties and early thirties, she managed to live elsewhere, with a preference for places beginning with B: Brussels, Belo Horizonte, Brighton and Boston, amongst others. Since 1995, she has lived in London, exchanging her career as a demographic anthropologist to bring up her children and write. She currently lives within cycling distance of central London with her husband, two daughters and a cat. *The Dressmaker of Paris* is her debut novel.

GEORGIA KAUFMANN

The Dressmaker of Paris

HODDER &
STOUGHTON

First published in Great Britain in 2020 by Hodder & Stoughton
An Hachette UK company

2

Copyright © Georgia Kaufmann 2020

The right of Georgia Kaufmann to be identified as the
Author of the Work has been asserted by her in accordance
with the Copyright, Designs and Patents Act 1988.

A CIP catalogue record for this title
is available from the British Library

Hardback ISBN 978 1 529 33602 3
Trade Paperback ISBN 978 1 529 32286 6
eBook ISBN 978 1 529 32288 0

Typeset in Plantin Light by
Palimpsest Book Production Limited, Falkirk, Stirlingshire

Printed and bound in Great Britain by Clays Ltd, Elcograf S.p.A.

Hodder & Stoughton policy is to use papers that are natural,
renewable and recyclable products and made from wood grown in
sustainable forests. The logging and manufacturing processes are expected
to conform to the environmental regulations of the country of origin.

Hodder & Stoughton Ltd
Carmelite House
50 Victoria Embankment
London EC4Y 0DZ

www.hodder.co.uk

To my mother,
Elisabeth Michaela Ida Anna Lorenz Kaufmann,
without whom this story could not have been told

I

Stone

Is that the time, ma chère? I'm going to be late. I am, for once, floored. No, it's not the weather – New York is never inspiring in November, even at the best of times. Nor is it that this winter's collections are so boxy and drab. It's that I can't think of anything appropriate to wear. Don't look so surprised, ma chère. I might know what to wear to a White House dinner or a fashion show or a board meeting, but such events pale in comparison to the importance of my engagement tonight.

Please stay, ma chère. It will calm me – and this meeting will affect you too. It may change our lives. But there are some things I need to sort out first. Leave those papers, please. It's my will, I was just checking it. I'm only sixty-three – it is not in my five-year plan to die! – but as you know, I like to be prepared. As I said, this appointment is important.

You know the story of this house, don't you? The one thing we didn't change when we reorganised the living arrangements was this bathroom. I've never met a businessman who did not count the pennies. Frivolous spending is not the habit of people who have earned their wealth. Any choice I make is informed by style, of course, but more so by understanding structure, materials and function. In designing clothes or a room or indeed anything, the material is a primary choice. In all things the craft is to understand the fabric and materials first, to know their strengths and weaknesses. The choices I made in this bathroom create the atmosphere.

Do you know what this is? The whole bathroom is clad in

marble. Naturally this is Italian, not just because I come from there but because Indian marbles are porous and polish so poorly that, despite their unrivalled beauty, they are not practical in a bathroom. Good design makes beauty from materials appropriate to the task. This marble is both impermeable and beautiful; see how it seems almost alive with rivulets of pink, red, grey and white flowing over each other? It took a lot of effort to source this palest, pinkest Arabescato Orobico Rosso marble. I can't tell you how many slabs I examined in how many stone warehouses to find such a pale one. Later, nothing would induce me to risk ruining this marble just to shift it upstairs, so here we have stayed. It is different from the master bathroom upstairs; there, I envisaged something stately and muted. The whole notion was to show that Mr James Mitchell was not a flashy, showy upstart, but rather someone with class. There was no question of having Carrera marble. All that white in one room? That would be like buying haute couture for the label rather than the design, tailoring and fabric. That is for people with money and no taste.

I am rambling. I am so nervous, I feel sick. Come, come. What was I saying? Ah yes, I remember: Breccia Oniciata, that's what I chose for the bathroom upstairs. It's a sleek beige marble with flecks and streaks of white, pink and lilac. Just as you have to choose the right stone for a tile and the right fabric for a dress you must select the right look for a meeting. If I am going to a business meeting, I need to consider how much I want to impress, how much to seduce. If I intend to impress with my business acumen and power the moment I walk in the door, I'll wear Dior or Yves Saint-Laurent. If I want my creative spirit, my artistry and capability as a designer to overwhelm, I choose my own Dumarais clothes. Or if I want to beguile, make people feel at ease with my femininity and then hit them with my business nous, I'll model some Chanel pieces. All this I can accomplish in the time it takes me to enter a room and walk across it. But not tonight.

This is ridiculous, ma chère, have you ever seen me dithering over what to wear? I've never thought my wardrobe excessive before. The problem is that I am so scared and desperate, I have to make the right impression, but I don't know where to begin. Usually I start with the fabric, ma chère, always the fabric. I learnt that from the first time I cut a pattern. The same pattern in wool or silk or cotton, or the same fabric cut bias or along the grain, and you have a different outfit each time. The fabric works at a subliminal level. Cotton means summer, summer means being relaxed. Linen is similar but more refined – it takes confidence not to mind the creases. Wool means winter, cosiness and protection from the cold. Silk is for every season and always means opulence and luxury. And as for nylon and polyester – well, nylon has its role in hosiery but under wraps is where it should stay.

I left home – a home in which, incidentally, there was no shower and we bathed just once a week, on Sundays before church – with the proverbial nothing, other than a battered suitcase containing only two outfits and some underwear. From that, relying on hard work and talent, I created this. So, every day, every single day, I go into my bathroom and ask myself: what do I need to look like today? Who am I going to meet? What do I need to achieve? I start with my make-up and hair before I dress and then, when I have perfected my look, I am ready to go out and perform to the best of my abilities. I leave nothing to chance. I would have made an excellent girl guide.

I am lucky – a combination of my natural form and lessons in deportment and posture at Dior means I look good in almost everything. I cannot do otherwise; even in jeans and a T-shirt I look elegant. If you have style, you have it regardless of what you wear. But tonight? I have no idea about what would be appropriate, what would work. I just don't know.

I need to tell you a story. A long story. My story. Only then will I know what to wear, how to prepare myself. You'll be able to help me.

★

It all started with my mother, of course; everything starts with your parents. It took me a long time to understand that people get things wrong, whatever their good intentions, and it is often the unintended consequences of their actions that leave the deepest imprint on a child.

It is not just a fable; we really did have very little when I was a child. Italy was a poor country in the 1930s and up in the Alps people had little money. Most were subsistence farmers. Skiing and walking holidays were a thing of the future. There was not even a toyshop in Bressen, the market town in the main valley that led down to Meran and Bozen, the biggest towns in South Tyrol. There was just a small selection in the back of the clothes shop. Up in Oberfals, the only toys we had were made of wood and carved by the farmers on the long winter nights.

When I was eight my mother gave me a painted wooden doll for Christmas. She was unclothed but, in my child's mind, she was lovely. I played with her all the time. I named her Elisabeth after the little English princess whose father had just become king. I already knew how to sew and knit. We all learnt early – not for pleasure, but as a practical, necessary skill. So, I collected scraps of old serviettes, tea towels and cloth remnants and sat in the evenings, when my mother did not need me in the Gasthaus, making a wardrobe for my princess doll, large stitch by large stitch. It is hard to imagine now what my first foray into clothes design was like, but at the time I was pleased with my handiwork. I made her a dress that had a lacy blouse front, which came from an old doily. I sewed white cotton underpants and a vest for her. I knitted her socks, which would not stay up, and a cardigan. When the news of the impending coronation of the princess's father filtered through from the *Dolomitten*, the regional newspaper, I cut the scarf, royal blue with tiny yellow flowers, that went with my dirndl and made my doll a long, trailing robe for the ceremony.

At first, I kept her at home, but gradually I began to take her out with me, first to church and then in my satchel to school.

She barely fitted in – the tips of her feet poked out of one corner – but I felt that a future queen needed schooling, too. It was the week after the King of England's coronation in May when I was showing my friend Ingrid Stimpfl how Princess Elisabeth had processed behind her father. We were wondering if we could somehow make a fur trim for her gown – Ingrid's father had brought a rabbit home for stew the week before and she thought the pelt might serve for ermine. Ingrid was talking while I smoothed out the train behind the princess, then she fell silent, mid-sentence, and as she looked over my shoulder her face closed. I turned around.

Rudi Ramoser had snuck up behind me. Although only thirteen, he was tall and heavily set with a farmer's muscles. He was handsome, blond and blue-eyed, his natural swagger buoyed up by the fact that his father was the richest man in town and brother-in-law to the mayor, Herr Gruber.

'*Du, Gitsch!*' Rudi shouted at me. 'What are you playing with?' He sneered as he took a step closer to me.

'My doll,' I said, looking up at him and standing my ground. I was used to bullies.

'That's a doll?' He sniggered and looked around to see if anyone was looking. 'A piece of wood, more like.'

He was bigger than me; he did not want the doll, but he wanted to get at me. I had seen that look in my father's eyes when he was drunk. I had learnt to stay away. 'She's mine,' I said, finally taking a step back. 'I'm not afraid, you're just a *Raudi*.'

'She's Princess Elisabeth.' Ingrid Stimpfl was a sweet girl, but not too bright.

'Princess Elisabeth.' He reached down to take her, but I held her tight against my chest. 'Let me see,' he said in a low snarl as his fingers wrenched mine off one by one and he crushed them in his grasp.

When he had twisted her from my hands, he turned and walked away. 'I'll let you know tomorrow what I want – if you want her back.'

Ingrid began to whimper. My hands were striated white and

red from the force he had used to yank them off Elisabeth. I bit my lip. He was not going to make me cry.

My parents did not spend much time with us. My mother ran the Gasthaus Falsspitze, the only bar and restaurant in Oberfals. She worked very hard (I suppose that was something good that she passed on to me). My father was as dissolute as she was forbearing. When the bar was open, she was busy but approachable, though we all knew not to interrupt her when she was cooking. She seemed to lose herself in the rituals and routines of chopping, grating and stirring. There was a meditative rhythm to her movements that I used to love to watch.

When I ran into the kitchen that afternoon, breathless and confused, she was making *knödel*. All the stale bread from the day before was heaped in a pile in front of her and a large knife was swinging in her hand as she chopped it into small pieces for the dumplings. You could almost tell the time by what stage she was at in the cooking. It must have been just gone three.

'Mother.' My uncertain voice tried to reach her. I remember being caught between my anxiety at losing the doll and my fear of interrupting her.

Her blade swung up then down, chop.

'Mother!' I called louder.

She looked up. The knife chopped through the stale bread. 'I'm busy.'

Tears spurted from my eyes. 'Rudi Ramoser has stolen Princess Elisabeth.'

'Who?' she asked after a long, distracted pause.

'My doll. The one you gave me for Christmas.'

She put down her knife and stared at me. 'So, get it back.'

'But Mother, he's thirteen. He's bigger than me.'

'Rosa, it's just a doll. I'm too busy for this.' She picked up her knife again.

The next day Rudi Ramoser was waiting for me when I came out of school. He was leaning against the wall opposite talking to some other boys but broke away from them when I came out.

'Do you want your doll back, Gitsch?' His big blue eyes looked innocent but his voice was taunting.

'Yes,' I said, determined not to show any fear.

'Meet me by the bridge. At three o'clock.'

The Gasthaus was in the centre of the village and the road to Unterfals and St. Martin led out from the square, crossing the river Fals as it left the town. After school the streets were empty; children were tasked with errands and chores while mothers prepared supper and the men were still at work. I knew everyone in each house that I walked past. I stared at the fresco of St. George on the Koflers' house. They were very proud of it. I realised that I should have asked Ingrid or my sister, Christl, to come with me. I was warmly dressed in my hat, gloves and scarf and my tightly knitted jacket but nevertheless, I was shivering.

I heard the sound of Rudi and his friends before I got to the bridge. They were down by the side of the stream, which was full with the spring melt. They were throwing stones across the water. I stopped to look around at the top of the mud path leading down to them. Elisabeth was neither in his hands nor on the ground.

'Where's my doll?' I shouted in dismay.

'Here.' He pointed up in the air. He had strung Princess Elisabeth from a tree hanging over the riverbank.

'I can't reach that high.' I fought back my tears.

'I'll get it for you,' he said.

I stared at him. He did not move. The water rushing over the boulders was sending up a fine spray that gleamed in the weak spring sunlight. I pursed my lips: bullies do not respect weaklings, I was going to stand my ground.

'But you have to do something for me first.'

The other boys had stopped throwing stones and were standing around him now, huddled like sheep. I came down the path slowly. It was slippery. He was a head taller than most of the boys, and I was smaller than all of them.

'I want her back,' I demanded.

'You have to earn her back,' he said, his face creased with a mean sliver of a smile. There were patches of snow on the meadows above the treeline. We were alone and out of sight.

I stared at him, wondering what he could want. I had very little, and certainly nothing a boy could want. I was sure that he was not a reader, he would not want my books. 'How?' I asked after a few seconds.

'Well . . .' He smiled at his friends. 'Lift up your skirt.'

The boys laughed.

'What?'

'Lift it up,' Rudi repeated. 'We want to see, *Gitschele*.' He was looking at me intently, and some of the other boys were smiling, but Michael Stimpfl, Ingrid's cousin, was looking at the ground. In school we stripped down to our pants and vests for sport but this felt different, I didn't know why. But I could see no real reason to refuse. His blue eyes were burning into me. I reasoned that they had all seen knickers like mine in school and I wanted Elisabeth back, so I lifted my skirt. The boys all laughed again, and I felt my face burning. Trying to mask my shame, I dropped the woollen dress and it settled back against my thighs.

'Now give it back to me,' I pleaded.

'I ain't done,' he jeered. 'I didn't say stop. This time, lift up your skirt and then drop your pants.'

I stared at him. We never did that in gym. Not even in front of the other girls – when we went to the toilet, there was a door to hide behind. I was certain that this was wrong, even sinful. I had made a mistake giving in to his first demand, and like any bully he had no reason to stop now.

'No,' I said, straining to look taller than I was. 'I did what you asked, now give me back my doll.'

'You won't get it back, unless you do as I say.' He stepped forward and tried to grab me.

The rock under my feet was slick and shiny and I slipped as I backed away from him. His hand closed like a pincer around my arm and began to drag me up. I grabbed a loose piece of stone and, twisting in his grip, hit him as hard as I could. Blood spurted from his face and he shrieked as he released me.

I landed on the ground and then scrambled back up the bank and ran. I kept on going until I got to the Ramosers' bakery. The mayor, Rudi's uncle, a portly, complacent man, was leaving as I ran into the shop. I dodged past him and came to an abrupt stop, overwhelmed by the thick, sweet, yeasty smell. Herr Ramoser, Rudi's father, looked over the counter at me. My dress was dirty, my knees were grazed and bloody, and my face was stained with tears.

'Rudi stole my doll,' I cried. 'Princess Elisabeth. He made me . . . and he still wouldn't give her back, so I hit him with a stone. I think I've killed him.'

Herr Ramoser fixed his shocked blue eyes on me.

'What did she say?' Herr Burgermeister Gruber said from behind me. 'She's killed Rudi?'

'I just wanted my doll back,' I said, trying to explain.

'What have you done to my son?' Herr Ramoser bellowed.

'She hasn't done anything,' Michael Stimpfl said as he squeezed in past the mayor. 'It was Rudi. He wanted to do things to her. She's only eight. It's not right.' He took a step towards me and pulled Princess Elisabeth from inside his jacket. 'Here, take her,' Michael said.

I snatched Princess Elisabeth from him and pulled her to my chest. Her clothes were wet and torn and I could feel their stiches coming apart. A huge sob burst out from me.

It was only when I got home that I realised I was still clutching the stone. I held it up to the light to examine it. Oberfals rested on poor, thin soil that seemed to slide off the rock underneath. Now I know that it was schist. It is made of millions of tiny flat plates of mica, like thin sheets of plastic, interleaved with quartz and feldspar sprinkled with hard crystals of garnet. Schist is not hard like the limestone that marble is made from. It is soft and flaky. Back then, I loved prising the leaves of mica apart with my nails.

It was a stroke of luck that the piece I had grabbed had a

chunk of dark red garnet poking out from it. If the rock had been pure mica it would have just glazed off his face and he would have caught me again. Instead, Rudi would always bear the scar over his left temple where I had buried the dark red nugget. It's all about choice; even a stone, if it is fit for purpose, can serve you well.

2

Toothpicks

When I am nervous, like now, I smile. It takes effort to set my face in calm repose when my instinct urges me to flash my teeth. I wonder if it is an ancient reflex to stress; the difference between baring teeth in a smile or fangs in a snarl is not so great. Of course, my teeth are white and strong. I brush and floss them religiously. I have tried all the techniques in my time: dental tape, dental floss, noisy oral irrigators, floss strung between two prongs like a mini slingshot, and these new minuscule wire brushes colour-coded for their size (the larger for the healthier gums, the smaller for the more inflamed), each like a shrunken version of a brush for baby milk bottles. It takes time and patience, my jaw stretched open in an eternal 'aaah' while I clean each crevasse, tooth by tooth, around my mouth. The benefit, of course, is that I still boast all my own teeth and they shine milky white like mother-of-pearl inside a shell. When I was a child, life was simpler. We used toothpicks.

Every morning after breakfast, before school, I would go to the store cupboard in the kitchen and pick up a carton of toothpicks. My job was to refill the salt and pepper pots on each table and stow the toothpicks in little wooden boxes. It was the custom for everyone to pick their teeth absentmindedly after they had finished eating, while they washed down lunch or dinner, or my mother's famous strüdel, with a drink. It was a discreet but public ritual.

Now I would consider it vulgar to pick my teeth in public. I floss here, in my private lair. As a child, living in a Gasthaus, the distinction between what was public and what was private was unclear. It made me more protective of my privacy. I do not think that I was truly aware of the public arena, the power of spectacle until the end of the summer of 1943. Children growing up in a war have nothing to compare it to, it is just normal. It was only much later that I came to understand how the South Tyrol, my homeland, had been badly stitched on to Italy after the First World War when the Austro-Hungarian empire was unpicked. Trying to fit originally Austrian, German-speaking, Alpine South Tyrol on to Italy was like me trying to sew a teddy bear's arm on to Princess Elisabeth.

Since I was eleven, families had agonised over the choice between being German or Italian – to opt in or out. The two fascist nations had made an agreement that cut through the fabric of daily life. The young men had to choose between signing up to Hitler's Nazis or Mussolini's Black Shirts. It tore families in two. Those who opted to stay were denounced as traitors, those who chose to go to Germany were vilified as Nazis. Men would disappear quietly, conscripted into one or the other army, the families giving as little away as possible. We kept things close to our chest – we were mountain folk and talked of the weather, late snowfalls and summer storms that threatened the crops, not our disgraces.

And then in September 1943, everything changed. The Allies pushed Mussolini north where he set up his puppet state of Salò in Lake Garda, and the Germans, unable to resist, marched into my homeland, the South Tyrol, and declared it part of Greater Germany. It solved that dilemma of opting in or out but was in a way more confusing than ever. My parents moaned that they had been born in Austria, lived in Italy and were now in Germany, without ever having moved from Oberfals.

It was mid-morning when we had first heard the distant bells tolling in Unterfals and then in St. Martin below us. Herman Egger, the bell ringer in St. Martin, played the same melodies week in and out; we were so familiar with his chimes that we knew he would never have created this cacophony willingly. The clanging, discordant crash of metal on metal sounded a beat that we all instinctively understood. It was the panicked forewarning of worse to come.

Fräulein Petsch, our teacher, ushered us out of school, urging us to get home without delay. My sister, Christl, and I followed Herr Maier, the postman, across the square and battled against the stream of men leaving the Gasthaus. My mother was standing by the door, which she closed and locked as soon as we were in. Laurin Maier walked across the deserted room to his usual table, greeting old Herr Holzner as he passed. Herr Holzner always took half the morning to totter to the Gasthaus and most of the evening to hobble home, and my mother must have realised that it would have been cruel to send him on his way. She told me to serve Herr Holzner a tankard of beer and *semmelbrot* and *speck*, while she closed all the shutters. As she drew the last ones by Herr Maier's table, the gloom thickened. The postman looked up at her as she turned from the window and they talked briefly. She did not ask him to leave.

He came every day at this time for his lunch and to read the newspaper. He was a rare creature in our valley: an unmarried man. To me he seemed old, but looking back now I guess he must have been in his forties. He was a strong man, tall and well-set, but his bulk moved easily as he walked up and down the valley paths. My mother told me to take him his beer while she went back into the kitchen to fetch his lunch. Herr Maier opened his copy of the *Dolomitten* and started to read, sipping his drink. Christl and I sat playing with the beer mats until she came back with his goulash soup and bread. Then she shooed us upstairs.

Whatever emotion the bells' clangs caused, curiosity was by far the strongest for us children. It was a month before my sixteenth birthday and the furthest I had ever been from our village was the twice-yearly day trip we made, before and after the snows, down our valley to Bressen. The town sat across the bridge straddling the fast-flowing river Etsch, where our own narrow valley, Falstal, joined the larger, flat-bottomed Vinschgau Valley below. We would hitch a ride on the back of the brewer's dray cart and ride down behind the empty caskets of beer. My mother bought our summer dresses in the spring and our winter clothes in the autumn. I was lucky. I was the eldest girl and always got something new; my sister only ever got a new dress if my hand-me-downs were worn beyond repair. We would wander the streets of the town admiring the frescoes painted on the walls advertising the sentiments or professions of the owners. I could never go into the Gasthaus without first stopping to admire the image of St. George, his legs straining up in his stirrups as he drove his spear down into the dragon coiled around the horse's stomping hooves. The flames from the dragon's mouth shot up towards the eaves. Away from the fire, cherubs hovered over the door, garlanded by grapevines, looking down at approaching customers with satisfied smiles. After we had made our few humble purchases, we always lunched and watched my parents drink beer courtesy of the patron (this being also the brewery for the beer they sold at home). We knew nothing about life in town and little about the world beyond our valley.

The soldiers who were marching into our lives came from far beyond Bressen, from over the mountains, from another country – they were Germans.

Our Gasthaus stood on a corner of the square closest to the end of the valley. From Oberfals the road climbed steeply until it terminated at a fence and a stile. When my mother joined us upstairs she opened the windows and pulled the shutters in, leaving them on a latch so that we could see out through the crack that ran vertically between them. We peered out through the gap, listening to the sound of muted voices and footsteps carried up from the square, and waited.

People began to congregate in the square below us. It was easy to see who: the ambitious, the disaffected and the hard done by. The Grubers stood next to the Ramoser family – Rudi and his brothers in lederhosen, his sisters in dirndls – all of them in their tightly knitted Sarner jackets, ranked in size, and waving swastika flags. Herr and Frau Demetz, the grocers, the Koflers, the Hallers, the Obristins and the Mahlknechts came, one family after another. The men wearing farmers' blue aprons were the ones whose land holdings were too small to provide for big families. The parents and older children had to take on extra work on the bigger, fatter farms. They came with their scruffy clothes and hungry looks and stood in the square, waiting for change.

We heard the sound of the engines from the road that snaked up Falstal from Vinschgau before we saw them. First two motor-bikes, then three trucks and a single large Mercedes drove into the church square. The vehicles parked in a neat row. Uniformed men spilled out of the trucks, carrying bags and equipment, and there was momentary chaos. In just a few seconds, they had filled up a space that usually stayed empty except for the meandering of stray cats and dogs, and the widows going to and from the church in their black vestments. Then the square was quiet again. The soldiers had formed themselves into tidy blocks and were standing to attention either side of their commander.

I knew why they had come. Although Oberfals lay at the dead end of the valley, there was a thin, straggly footpath that took you over the mountains into Switzerland. For years already it had been the escape route for anyone who wanted to slip away from German rule.

The Hauptmann waited, arms behind his rigid back, flanked by his uniformed men. Herr Burgermeister Gruber emerged from the crowd of onlookers. The mayor appeared to shrink as he walked towards the Hauptmann, his gait uncertain, his head bowed. We stayed huddled around the window and watched as Gruber came to a stop and tried to puff himself up to welcome the Hauptmann, who stood as still as the statue of St. Martin in the church down the valley. I stared, fascinated and frightened in equal measure. We had seen Italian soldiers once or twice in Bressen but they had been casual. This array of military vehicles and the German soldiers standing rigidly, their rifles pointing skywards, was a chilling display.

No one ever knew what words passed between them but it looked as if the Hauptmann, when he inclined his head down to our rotund mayor, slowly drew all the pomp and confidence from him, so that when the mayor nodded then turned to the gathered villagers, he was utterly deflated. Even from our window I could see that his normally ruddy and complacent face had paled and his jowls looked like pallid fat. His die had been cast; he would do everything that the Germans asked – calmly, quietly, but soullessly.

'*Meine sehr verehrten Damen und Herren,*' he began, his voice flat. 'Who will help us provide accommodation for the Feldwebel and these fine young soldiers?' When no answer came, he turned to the soldiers. 'May I suggest you eat in our excellent Gasthaus while we arrange the billets?' He led the Hauptmann in our direction, while Herr Ramoser took the sergeant and two soldiers elsewhere. We rushed downstairs. Without hesitation, my mother went to open the door.

'Rosa,' she said, her voice low. 'Go and clear Herr Maier's table.' She took a deep breath, turned the key in the lock and shaped her face into a welcoming mask.

It was only then that I realised the postman was gone. He must have slipped out through the back door. I rushed to his table then stopped. The shutters had been opened – he had been watching. He had left some of his goulash and half of his beer. The toothpick holder was turned upside down. All the toothpicks lay on the pale green tablecloth, in two neat piles. It looked as if Herr Maier had picked up the entire bundle and broken it in two. It would have taken a lot of force to do that. Some of the wooden tips were stained red with blood.

3

Talcum Powder

Now that I am dry and the cream has soaked into my skin, I feel refreshed. The next step is talcum powder, the first beauty product most people wear. Mothers dust it between the toes of their babies, into the creases between their little folds of fat, to keep the flawless skin soft. Smell this, ma chère, it is the sweet aroma of infancy. It does not come in cut-glass vials, but simple cardboard cylinders. But make no mistake, the choice of talcum powder is as important as that of perfume. No matter that no one sees where you use it, a puff between your toes or, on sweltering days when perspiration can threaten to ruin the shimmer and flow of silk with a dark patch, just a touch under the bra, a light dusting down over the shoulders. But it must be good quality: too scented and it will clash with your perfume, too coarse and it will show. Talc must smell clean; the powder must be fine enough to become translucent, not white like chalk. I have two talcum powders: one is infused with Bulgarian rose oil, for days when I do not go out, and the other, I must confess, is baby powder.

During the war, after the arrival of the Germans, talcum powder was just one of many goods on an ever-growing list of desirable but unobtainable items. Squeezed between the Allies' liberation of Southern Italy and the German stranglehold on the north, we depended on the packages that well-wrapped men left in the wooden barns in which the cows sheltered overnight on the high summer pastures. The narrow path into Switzerland over the pass was widened and deepened by the passage of so many weary feet travelling along it. Not just those of the smugglers but also those of the scared and hungry fleeing from the Nazis. There was so much that was forbidden, so many things it was better not to be.

As soon as he had finished eating in our Gasthaus, the Hauptmann left the village, leaving the sergeant in charge. That evening, the local men sat with beers and cards untouched on the tables. The conversation was excited and fearful, full of the afternoon's events. History had come to us.

Around seven o'clock, the sergeant and his men came into the Gasthaus and looked around. The village men stared at the intruders then at their beers, and a novel hush descended on the crowd. Herr Maier's table was empty and the sergeant and his two soldiers aimed for it. As they moved through the room a faint, foul odour drifted behind them.

Normally I would go and wait on tables, but this time my mother beat me to it. Her voice carried back to me behind the bar. She was not unfriendly, but no warmth tinged her voice either. I heard her name the familiar dishes and tried not to look at the soldiers. The sergeant was a vast man, as fat as he was tall – his bulk was invasive. The two soldiers seemed barely older than me. One was thin and nervous-looking, the other was a proto-typical Aryan god. He outshone all the village boys. Both seemed rigid, sitting tensely upright as if they were forcing themselves to sit still. I sent my sister over with the box of toothpicks. She came back with a look of revulsion on her face. 'He stinks,' she said, wrinkling her nose.

And so, unknowingly, Feldwebel Schleich took over Herr Maier's table. The postman lived in St. Martin and normally stopped off in our Gasthaus on the way to make his deliveries all over the valley, climbing treacherous paths in the winter up to the farmsteads that clung on to the snowy slopes, and running down with the rain when August thunderstorms watered the fields, flattening the late summer hay. Until the day the Nazis arrived, he had taken his lunch every day at the table furthest from the door. From there he had a fine view of the whole square and the clients as they came in. Farmers, down in the valley for stocks and goods, would nip in to the Gasthaus for a beer and a quick word with the postman to see if he had any mail for them. His daily lunch must have shaved hours off his afternoon treks as the farmers from the upper slopes, recognisable by their faces scoured and polished by the sun and wind, and wearing the traditional blue aprons and felt hats, came to his table to greet him and then stuffed their own and neighbours' letters into their apron pockets before they started back up the steep slopes. But after the arrival of Schleich and his soldiers, a week passed before Herr Maier came back.

But now, Schleich had taken the table as his own. He would come in, shove the table out and settle his bulk heavily on the wooden bank that ran the length of the wall. Then he would grab the menu and squint at it with his piggy eyes, his skin stretched and pink. My friends and I began to call him Sergeant Stinker. Wherever he went the foul smell announced his arrival and trailed after. After a while, we decided it was exactly like the stench of rotten cheese.

Then Laurin Maier was there again, at his usual table, asking for goulash and *knödel*. Everyone greeted him as he came in, and it took him five minutes to get to his seat. He had just started his beer, enjoying that long pause that beer drinkers seem to share after the first gulp, when the sergeant's silhouette blocked out the light at the doorway. Schleich saw the postman at the table as soon as he crossed the threshold and he stopped still. His face gave away nothing. Then he made his way deliberately towards the table, followed by the two young soldiers, as always.

'This table is mine,' he said in his sweet, sing-song Swabian accent that was so out of keeping with his immense mass.

Herr Maier looked up at him and reached for his beer. 'I think you'll find that it's Frau Kusstatscher's table, but as a loyal customer I have been sitting here for years.' He took a long gulp, his eyes never leaving the sergeant's.

The soldiers standing behind the sergeant looked as if they wished they were elsewhere.

'*Spieß?*' the tall, handsome private began. His name was Karl

Heinz Köhler, the village tongues had told us. Schleich stiffened and put his hands on the back of the chair facing the postman.

Herr Maier tore off a piece of bread and dipped it into the thick red sauce in the bowl in front of him. He leaned forward, lifting the bread to his mouth, and spoke clearly. 'As I said, I've been sitting here for years. This is my place. Of course, I cannot object to you using it when I'm not here but, for now, I'd be grateful if you would move away. My goulash is getting cold.' And then he took a bite out of the dripping bread.

Everyone in the room had heard the postman's words, and the sergeant knew it. He reached his hands to his belt, where we all knew he had a pistol. Then the thin, scraggly soldier leaned forward and whispered something in the sergeant's ear. There was a long silence while whatever the lanky private had said trickled into the sergeant's mind. It worked. The soldiers turned to go. No one knew the soldier's name that lunchtime, but by evening we were all singing the praises of Private Thomas Fischer.

But at the door the sergeant paused and looked over to the postman, as if about to speak. I was at his table giving him the beer my mother had sent with her compliments. As I made my way back to the bar, the sergeant stared at me in a way that turned my innards over. He had an odd face: pink, scrubbed skin, small, sharp blue eyes set in the bloated expanse of his jowls, and a hint of shaved ash-brown hair showing beneath his military cap. He looked more like a baby than a man, but when his eyes fell on me I felt his all-too-adult hunger. These days I can deflect unwanted lust with an effortless shrug, or with a glance invite more attention. Back then, I was unprepared for the stark desire, and unsettled by it.

Life settled back into a semblance of order after that. Herr Maier would come two or three times a week and then he sat at his table. On the other days he could be seen tramping around the high farmsteads, making his rounds. Every day shortly after the church bells had sounded noon, either Köhler or Fischer would come into the Gasthaus, stop at the door, glance at the table and the bar, and then leave. If the table was free they would return with the sergeant; if the postman was there they would lunch at the Streitbergers'.

Looking back on that period, what I find most remarkable is how easily we adapt to outrageous circumstances. Be it a military coup taking a stranglehold on a democracy, or a friendly invasion, soon it becomes normal, soon we forget there is another way to live. There were a few men like Laurin Maier who drew a line and held up against the bullying of the sergeant. The rest kept him happy, plied him with beer and cakes (we learnt quickly that he had a sweet tooth) and went about their business.

For us children, life continued as before, our time split between school and helping at home. My mother forbade me from joining the new Nazi Jugend group that Private Köhler had set up. All the other girls at school talked about him incessantly, but my mother said she needed me in the bar. Instead, I saw him almost every day with Fischer and the sergeant. I had quickly learnt to serve the food from across the table to the sergeant; to come any closer was unbearable.

Serving those three taught me most of what I needed to know about men. The sergeant would fasten his eyes on me as soon as I started making my way towards him. He stared so hard that I always felt like he left a slime trail of lust over me. Köhler was all smiles and winning glances, but he never bothered to learn my name – he just wanted to be adored. But Fischer was different; he alone seemed to see the discomfort I suffered. Within days he was addressing me by my name, he never omitted to say 'please' and 'thank you', and whenever the sergeant went to touch me, somehow Private Fischer's hand would be there between us. My mother saw nothing of this and my father was usually too drunk to see anything past the next bottle of beer.

Everyone in Oberfals knew that my father was a drunk and a bad card player. Everyone also liked to keep on my mother's good side. In the Gasthaus, people let him win and then he would go off and buy a drink (my mother tried to control his drinking by insisting on him purchasing his booze like any other customer). Schleich, it turned out, also played cards. For the first week it was with the sycophants, the mayor, the Ramosers and other fools. When he was playing he seemed to shrink. He hunched over his belly, the cards jammed into his sausage-like fingers, intent on the game. He did not seem brilliant, just methodical, but one by one his opponents found excuses and dropped away. Within two weeks, no one would play him.

It started with just one small game. After the soldiers left one night, Schleich stayed and nursed a beer for the longest time, staring at me as I collected glasses and dirty plates, cleared the waste and replaced the tablecloths. My father had the look of a parched man, sitting nervously at the bar, his empty beer glass stained by the drying foam. My mother had left it there, a sign that he had drunk enough.

I never saw how it happened but the next time I came in from the kitchen, my father was sitting with Schleich dealing out the cards. Schleich lost, bought my father a beer, and then lost again. He did not play again for a few days. Then they played again. The first day Schleich won narrowly, the second day my father trounced him and then they were playing every night. Even then Schleich lost most of the games. It didn't take long for my mother to realise that my father was going down to St. Martin at lunch time and drinking in the Gasthaus there, spending his winnings.

And then abruptly my father's winning streak stopped. He had been to St. Martin in the afternoon and was now regaling all the regulars with the gossip from the bigger village. He barely seemed to notice his cards until after a few rounds, when he fell silent. The heap of coins we had become used to seeing on his side of the table for the last few weeks was gone; instead, Schleich was arranging neat piles in front of him. He did not slaughter my father in an instant, but dragged out the torture over the whole evening, the coins jumping from one side to the other. But anyone could see that they always returned to Schleich. Each time my father won them back, his confidence would inflate and he would wager even more. Some of the regulars were standing around the table, sipping in silence. I was tired but I could not drag myself away from the spectacle. My father was slouched in his chair, gripping his cards; his very posture said 'loser'. Schleich, in contrast, had heaved his mass as straight as physics allowed, his vast bulk attentive, his thick fingers holding the cards delicately.

'Your luck has turned tonight,' Schleich observed as he closed the fan of his cards.

'It'll come back. You wait and see,' my father said.

'Well, if I were you, I would stop now.' Schleich fanned out his cards again, one by one.

'No. Let's play.' My father glanced at the neatly sorted piles of coins. 'For it all.'

'And what will you wager?' Schleich asked casually, aligning the edges of his cards.

'What do you want?' My father's voice was thick.

'Oh, not much. Just a roast chicken.'

'What? That's all?' My father sat up, relieved. He smiled, clearly thinking that Schleich was an even bigger fool than he had realised.

'Just your plumpest, juiciest one,' Schleich said, staring straight at me.

I fled into the kitchen.

The next day, my father woke up late. After breakfast he went into the kitchen and looked for his blue apron.

'The cows need milking,' my mother told him, her eyes fixed on her cooking.

'Not now.' He paused, and I could see sweat glistening on his brow. 'I'm going to get a hen,' he blurted.

She finally looked up from the stove and fixed her attention on him. 'What do you want that for?'

'Schleich.'

'What?' She put the peeler down and stared at him.

'He won a roast chicken off me,' said my father, trying to sound as if this was ordinary, and darted out the door.

In those days the houses were still built traditionally, the ground floor doubling as a barn for the animals, the living apartments on the upper floors. The front entrance that gave on to the square was the bar and restaurant, and an entrance off the side led into the warm barn where we kept our cows, pigs and hens. My mother started after him into the corridor that led to the stable, Christl and I trailing behind her. By the time we were in the barn my father was holding Trudi, my mother's favourite, by her legs and she was squawking loudly. She was a young hen, with a glossy coat of speckled brown feathers, a prolific layer – a big egg every day without fail. She was also the plumpest hen in our small flock.

'Not Trudi,' my mother pleaded, looking around wildly at the other screeching hens. 'Take Lotte, she's getting on.'

He brushed past us all out into the utility room where my mother kept an axe and a wooden chopping block, the bird flapping wildly.

'He won my juiciest one,' my father said, studiously avoiding my mother's eye. He held Trudi, who was still protesting, down on the block.

'Are you mad? You lost all your money and then you bet my hens?'

Trudi screeched and flapped her wings.

'I nearly got it all back,' my father said, his voice barely audible over the hen's cries.

'Nearly! You lost everything.'

For a moment a flash of guilt showed on his face, but just as swiftly it was replaced with pride. 'A man has to pay his debts.' He glanced at my mother before defiantly lifting the axe and swinging it down hard, and the barn finally fell silent. 'It's a question of honour.' He dropped the headless bird on to the floor where it ran around silently tumbling over and up again.

'You fool.' She looked at the flailing bird and then him. 'Don't you understand, Norbert? Schleich is playing you. He will always beat you.'

But as my father started to win again he forgot about the last game, about the clear pattern that everyone else saw. Each time he had a winning streak his luck would turn – and still he played. In time, he lost all his treasured possessions: his felt hat, the beautiful walking stick his father had carved for him, his accordion, his hunting knife. On those nights they would play until three, four in the morning. The next morning we would wake to the sound of my mother's hissing fury as she tried to shake him out of bed.

One night they even played for my mother. My father laughed about this the next morning as he pulled the cow's udders with uncharacteristic gentleness, remembering how well he had played, how he would never let that Sergeant Stinker touch his woman. My mother stopped speaking to him. And Schleich stopped playing, saying he had lost interest. He was losing too much. My father pestered him repeatedly until, disinterestedly, he agreed to play again.

One night, in late November – I don't like to remember the date – I was woken by my father's hand shaking my arm.

'You've got to come with me,' he mumbled, pulling me to my feet.

'What's the matter?' I muttered.

'Nothing. Be quiet.' He pulled harder. The whiff of the stale, acrid alcohol seeping through his pores penetrated my groggy state. I got up and clutched my shawl around my shoulders.

'It's one of the cows,' he muttered. 'I need your help.'

We went down through the bar and then along the cold stone hallway to the barn.

'I lost again,' he blurted out as he turned the door handle and pushed the heavy wooden door open. He put his arm around my shoulders and herded me in. 'It's a question of honour,' he said, and then shut the door.

Look, ma chère, I am shaking. Still now, all these years later, I don't want to open the door to that memory. I have never wanted to tell you the next part, ma chère, but the rest of my story won't make sense unless I do. You will never understand unless you go through that door with me. Forgive me and stay with me.

I stood in the dark, confused. What had honour to do with an ailing cow – and why had he even been with the cows in the dead of night? My sense of smell must have been heightened as I waited for my eyes to adjust, because a nasty odour was cutting through the familiar, thick, sweet smell of the animals. The strange stench was foul and cheesy, and made my stomach curdle with dread.

My heart began to race and I peered around as distinct shapes and shadows began to emerge from the dark. There was someone crouching by one of the cows. And then it all made sense. It was Sergeant Schleich. He was kneeling next to a cow, his hand tight around her teat. Thick white rivulets ran down from his open mouth.

'What are you doing here?' I hissed. Even then, I was still fearful of disobeying my father and making a noise.

'Taking the cream,' he said as he heaved himself to his feet and took a step towards me.

Of course, I tried to get out but he moved quickly, surprisingly fast and agile. He shoved me aside and slid the key my father must have left him into the lock and turned it. He held up the key out of my reach before depositing it in his pocket. His hand flipped up the bottom of his jacket and he casually loosened his holster and took out his pistol.

I opened my mouth to scream.

'Quiet, my pretty,' he panted. 'You don't want your father to get in trouble with your mother, do you?'

'Please,' I begged. 'Let me go.' I heard my father heave and vomit in the hall and then the faint sound of his footsteps retreating. The sergeant yanked up my arm behind my back and then pushed me, the gun in the small of my back, towards the hay spilling out from the rack.

I could not fight him off. I had no chance: he was just too big. But I could bite and scratch. I ripped at his shirt with my short nails and bit him hard. He had breasts and folds and layers of swollen flesh, which absorbed all my force as I pushed against him. He was the most solid man I have ever seen. He held me fast against his belly; I could not breathe, I thought I would suffocate.

In the end I stopped fighting. I was overwhelmed and over-powered. I knew that he could easily kill me. I shut my eyes and tried to pretend I was somewhere else but his smell intruded with each breath. There is a word we used in the mountains, *schirch*, which would translate into High German as 'ugly', but it encompassed so much more. The sergeant was *schirch*. It was not just his whale-like lard but his repellent sour-sweet smell that I could not help but breathe in as he forced himself on me. I strained my face towards the sow and squealing piglets in the stall next to us. And somewhere in there, in the dark, on the hay, it occurred to me that he needed to use talc. That the smell came from under all the folds of fat, the places that he could not wash and dry well; that it was the smell that sometimes came from my belly button; that if only he had had a mother who had dusted him with talcum powder and love, he would not be doing this to me now. Oh, ma chère, that was the worst night of my life and all I could think in the end was how people need a good mother.

4

Soap

You see that I have several soaps here. One for my basin, one for my bidet and one for my shower. For my hands I always choose handmade soaps made from animal and vegetable fats. A good soap has beef tallow as a base, olive oil to make it gentle on the skin, and coconut oil to help it lather well. The rest, the aromas and colours, is window dressing. Of course, the way a soap looks and smells is important, ma chère – of all people I would not dispute that. But what my skin feels like afterwards is more important. If my appearance is my work of art, the softness of my skin is my masterpiece. Ask a blind man: touch is the queen of the senses. For my bidet, of course, I choose a soap with a musky smell and for my shower my soap is unscented. It would not be good to mingle the scent of soap with my creams and perfumes.

During the war we had no such luxuries. Sometimes we were lucky to get a batch of soap from Rome or Milan but it was a scarce commodity. Bathing had always been a brave affair, even in more plentiful times: we stood with flannels over a creamy white chipped washbowl and rubbed ourselves clean in the cold air in winter and the warm air in summer. When the Germans annexed our little world, the supplies dried up. Retrospectively, that is no tragedy now that we know what 'animal' fat the Nazis used for their soaps.

My mother had made soap before the war, as an occasional whim that reminded her of her mother. During the war it became another one of her many inescapable tasks. Every time any of us went out into the woods, if we found branches of birch, the only local hardwood, on the ground we would bring them home to be burnt to ashes. And if my mother came back with pieces of oak or chestnut from her trips into the valley, she would beam with triumph.

My sister and I were tasked with sweeping cold ashes from the hearth and dropping them into a special barrel raised on a stone platform. When it was full my mother would nag my father until he could be persuaded to tend the ashes, pouring the rain water that she collected in another barrel over them. Liquid lye, a brown, caustic fluid – we soon learnt not to touch – soon began to leak out of the trough at the bottom into a waiting bucket. Christl and I scraped every piece of beef and pork fat off the customers' finished plates. We stored the rotting fat in a large milk urn. When she was ready, my mother would start by boiling up the fat in a vast metal pan with some water, skimming off remnants of meat and bone. Then when the lard was liquid and running clear, she would add the lye. We laid out the wooden moulds for the soap bars in long rows on the kitchen worktops. Each mould was unique, carved by the village men during the long winter nights. She never added scent. The soap she made was smooth and firm. We used it in the kitchen for washing up, in the pantry for our laundry and in the bathroom for our toilette. Our clothes, our pots and pans and ourselves all shared the same waxy smell. But it did its job, it kept us clean.

It is fair to say that I was unbalanced for a while after the sergeant raped me. He left me there in the stall with the pigs, too numb to move or cry. Unlike the actual act, which I can remember all too well, the hours after are a blur. I don't know how long I lay like a discarded doll on the straw, but sooner or later I made my way through the bar back upstairs and into our bathroom. I soaped and washed myself again and again, filling bowl after bowl with water, using flannel after flannel, wetting, soaping, lathering and rinsing again and again, bruised and shaking, barely able to stand. The blood and semen had come away with the first wash, but I could not stop. It was not just his sweaty, pungent traces, but the memory of him on me, on my skin, in me, that I wanted to wash away.

That was how my mother found me: standing naked in the bathroom by the basin, a washcloth in one hand and a small, worn bar of her soap in the other. She did not seem to see me, the only thing she registered was the fragment of soap in my hands. 'What are you doing?' she exclaimed, not bothering to hide her annoyance. 'I only put that out yesterday.'

I've never understood why she did not see the tears staining my face or notice that my skin was mottled with bruises or that my body was trembling. Instead, she moved past me towards the basin and turned on the faucet. She did not even look in the mirror. She was, as always, too busy or too blind to help me.

'Well, are you going to get dressed or not,' she said briskly, snatching the remainder of the soap from me and washing her own face and hands. 'Get yourself ready and come down. It'll be busy today.'

I did not go down, but went to bed. I did not get up for the next three days, just lay there, exhausted but unable to sleep, unwilling to eat, crying on and off. My mother brought soup, touched my brow and frowned. I did not see my father once.

On the third day, after the restaurant had closed for the afternoon, it was as if a fireball shot through the house. My parents were in the kitchen but their shouts shook the timber floors and walls. My mother's screams mingled with the metallic clang of pots and pans. And then there was silence. A long silence before a door opened and closed, followed by the sound of my mother padding up the stairs. The footfall stopped outside my room, the door handle turned a tiny bit. I'll never know if she was trying to compose herself after her anger, or whether she was overcoming her guilt, but I used the time to turn my back to the door. Finally, the door squeaked open.

'I'm sorry,' she said in a choked voice I had never heard before. 'I should have known.'

I stayed silent, just listening to her heavy breathing. After a while she sighed and then said, 'I'll get your father to oil that hinge,' and then she went back down the stairs to tidy the kitchen.

*

She did not insist on me helping for a few weeks after that. I became a recluse, rereading the few books we had or simply staring at the wall, trying hard to wipe my memory clean. My mother had told me that the sergeant would no longer be allowed in the Gasthaus, but it still took a while before I was able to come down again. When I did, I was astonished by a radical change. The postman was no longer sitting alone but was deep in conversation with the hitherto quiet private, Thomas Fischer. I asked my sister about it and she said that they had been eating together ever since the sergeant and Köhler had stopped coming in.

That day I did not serve but merely stood for a few minutes behind the bar, watching people for signs. I wanted to know if they could see what my mother had not. A few regular customers asked me if I was feeling better, pleased that I had recovered. Their easy questions convinced me that they knew nothing; I had not realised how worried I was about what others would say until relief flooded over me. As I climbed back up the stairs, I realised that the noise and the bustle of the bar was better than the silence of my bedroom. The next day I began to work again.

It did me good. The endless orders of bread, beer, wine, *speck* and *knödel* temporarily blocked the lingering smell of the sergeant from my mind. At lunchtime as I went to Herr Maier's table and greeted him, I felt the beginnings of a smile pulling at the corners of my mouth: this was the one man in the valley who had stood up to Schleich.

'Rosa!' he cried, putting his newspaper down. 'You're back.' He sat up straight and gave me a look of deep warmth and understanding, then stood up and leaned forward across the table, hovering close to my ear but careful not to touch me. 'He'll pay for what he did to you,' he murmured. As soon as he spoke, he stood back up straight and looked me in the eyes.

The notepad was shaking in my hands. The shame was so intense that I wanted to flee. But as I met his gaze I realised that he was not repelled by me, but was regarding me with sympathy. I gripped the notepad tightly, trying to gather myself. I hoped no one else was looking. The idea that someone knew and was on my side was overwhelming. The best I could do without crying was to nod, and he nodded in response, sat down again and picked up the newspaper as if nothing had happened.

'A beer and the *griessnocken* with *steinpilze*,' he said, his voice returning to its normal tone and volume.

I tried to turn away but found that my body would not move; I could not face the rest of the customers.

He looked up. 'Rosa Kusstatscher,' he said. His face was as calm as a mountain pool, but his voice was firm. 'Go now, take the order, try and do as you always have. The pain will fade and I will sort out the rest. I promise you. Just pretend everything is normal and slowly it will become normal again. You had better go now, people are beginning to look. Go.'

He touched my hand lightly and that jolted me from my shock. '*Griessnocken* and beer?'

'That's right. Oh, look, Fischer has arrived. I can order for him. He has the same every day, don't you, private?'

Fischer stopped next to me. 'Fräulein, I'm glad to see you are feeling better.' He clicked his heels together and bowed his head, as if he was greeting someone worthy rather than a soiled waitress. 'Some water and spinach *knödel* for me, please.'

The postman smiled. 'He's a vegetarian – the only soldier in the Wehrmacht who has no appetite for killing.'

'No, you're wrong,' Fischer replied. 'I just can't abide slaughtering the innocent. The rest get what they deserve.' His voice was low and gentle as if the words were intended only for me. It dawned on me that these two unlikely companions had become co-conspirators, that they sought justice for me. I tried not to cry, but I know my face creased up and my lip quivered.

'Thank you,' I managed and then forced myself to walk back to the bar. Pretend, he had said, and then it would become real. I would pretend, I could do that, I thought, as I yelled the order into the kitchen and busied myself with the beer and water.

*

Of Schleich I heard little. Apart from telling me that he was banned, my mother did not mention him again. My father stayed away for over a month and when he came back my mother kept him working in the kitchen and with the animals. The evening he was permitted to return to the bar, he was warmly greeted by the other men. My mother rang a knife against the beer glass she was holding.

'Gentlemen,' she called over their babble. 'You may welcome my husband back, but if one of you so much as lets him sniff your drink, you will find yourself unwelcome here.'

She was as good as her word. The following week Hans Kofler, always a simpleton, chanced his luck and tried to share a jug of beer with my father. My mother upended the beer over the two men and simply ordered, 'Out.' It was months before Kofler dared to come back, and after that my father dried up for good.

On New Year's Eve, Schleich returned. It was a bitterly cold evening. There were no stars visible in the sky, which was heavy with snow and wedged in between the dark, frozen peaks. The townsfolk gathered in the icy square, crunching the fresh snow, which was falling fitfully, under their boots. Father Matthias led a procession from the church and then, as he did every year, lit the first firework. Having since witnessed the explosion of light and sound on Copacabana Beach in Rio, I know how meagre this display in Oberfals was. But back then, at just sixteen years old, it was exciting and magical to hear the harsh cracks echo across the valley, to see the snowy rooftops of the buildings and the swirling flakes falling from the sky briefly lit up in glory.

While I was staring, oohing and aahing, I must have drifted from Christl, the only person in the world to whom I had told everything and who protected me like one of her goats. I was standing at the back of the crowd staring up when my whole body spasmed involuntarily and I retched. I was bewildered – it came from nowhere, I had not been feeling nauseous at all. Then the unmistakeable stench of Schleich cut through the aroma of pine smoke and cordite. My heart was pounding even before his heavy hand grabbed my shoulder. My terrified scream was lost amongst the crowd's shrieks and gasps as a rocket split the night sky into green and yellow cascades of shimmering fire. He clamped his other hand over my mouth and tugged me back into an alley.

'Happy New Year, *mein Schatz*,' he grunted as he shunted me against the wall and pinioned me with his weight. He began to fumble with his free hand at the fastenings of my coat. I tried to bite his other hand but he jammed his fingers into my mouth so all I could do was tear at his sleeve to try and stop him suffocating me.

Then, suddenly, the pressure eased off and even though his fingers were still in my mouth, I could breathe.

In the flash of light of a rocket bursting overhead, I saw the barrel of a gun jammed up against Schleich's temple. A quiet yet authoritative voice spoke.

'Let her go, Spieß,' it said. 'You don't want to be doing this again, do you? Not with all the townsfolk here. They're drunk, they'd string you up, and I would not be able to protect you. You don't want unnecessary trouble. The Kommandant would hear about it. Let her go.'

Schleich slowly withdrew his fingers from my mouth. He rubbed the saliva off on my shoulder and vanished wordlessly into the night.

'You're safe now,' Thomas Fischer, the vegetarian private, said as his fingers touched my elbow. I was trembling. I started to back away but he grabbed my gloved hand and held it fast. 'He'll never harm you again. I promise you.'

The next day at lunchtime, Thomas Fischer and Laurin Maier were so deep in conversation they did not notice me approach their table to take their order.

'*Grüß Gott*,' I said, trying to sound as natural as I could. 'Pretend everything is normal and it will be' had become my mantra. 'Rosa,' the postman said. 'Thomas has told me about last night. Don't be afraid. We'll make sure nothing happens to you ever again.'

Thomas Fischer finally looked at me. 'Fräulein Kusstatscher, I promise you, Schleich will never trouble you again.' He smiled and his Prussian propriety melted. I realised I had never seen him smile before.

Over the following days, Thomas Fischer arrived for lunch before Herr Maier and stayed after he left on his rounds. He asked me about life in Falstal, about myself, my family – never prying, simply curious – and fed my growing curiosity about his own background, his interrupted studies at Leipzig University, his family. I thought about him more and more and found myself smiling shyly into the bathroom mirror when I brushed my hair in the morning.

One day, in late January, Thomas asked me for an afternoon walk, and we took the track the postman always took. Along the way up the slippery path, we passed a cave. Thomas was interested to hear of our childish games there; I had always ended up as an Indian losing to the Cowboys. I told him about how I had hated hiding in the cave as it was always cold, damp and dark. A little further on, the trees gave way and the trail crossed a snowy expanse. We stopped to admire the view.

To my surprise, Herr Maier appeared, striding towards us, coming back down from his deliveries. He asked if I didn't mind waiting for a moment to look after his postbag; there was something he wanted to fix and Thomas was just the man for the job. We were just beyond the trees when they left me.

I clambered on to a rock jutting out of the snow and sat down on Herr Maier's postbag to cushion myself from the cold stone. Oberfals lay below me and I could see each house distinctly. Our house on the corner of the square with the big yard at the rear was one of the largest. From my rocky outcrop it looked clean and sparkly; there was no way of knowing what went on in each of these tiny, model homes. The sky was clear of clouds and the sun was beating down, baking me like a stuffed muffin in my many layers. I closed my eyes and rested my head on my knees and drifted off.

It was the light brush of Thomas's fingers on my arm that

woke me. The blue of his eyes were so deep in the afternoon sun.

'Has Herr Maier gone?' I asked blearily.

'Yes.' Thomas's cheeks were flushed and his eyes were shining strangely.

'Is everything alright?'

Thomas hesitated. 'Yes . . . that is, no. That is, I want to ask you something.' He looked back down the path then directly at me. He blushed. He opened his mouth to speak, looked down at the valley and lifted his hand distractedly to his mouth.

'What do you want to ask?' I asked after a while.

'Can I – I mean – would you mind – no, would you like me to kiss you?'

'Oh,' I said, taken aback with delight and fear at the same time, and feeling my cheeks burning. 'I've never kissed anyone before.' The memory of Schleich rubbing his lips against mine, trying to force his tongue through my clenched teeth, broke into my thoughts, but I pushed it away. That had been no kiss.

Thomas frowned as if he could sense what I was remembering. 'That's fine, I can wait. Maybe one day you will. It's just that I think you are wonderful.' He blushed again, and looked down towards St. Martin in the valley.

'Me, wonderful?' I mumbled as another hot blush rushed over my face. I was not used to any praise but his serious eyes regarded me steadily and I realised he was not joking. Over the past weeks as I had thought about Thomas more and more, I had come to the conclusion that he was the finest person I had ever met. He seemed to become more handsome each time I saw him and every day I was grateful for his kind attentions to me – but I had assumed he merely pitied me. 'I'm nothing, I wait on tables and . . . you know,' I petered out, and we both knew what I was referring to.

Thomas held out his hands towards me and after a few seconds I put mine in his. 'I know that you are like a Valkyrie – you're so brave. You don't even know how strong you are. What you survived would have crushed most people.' His eyes were ablaze with indignation and passion.

Only then did I finally accept that this was not pity. He liked me. I had come to adore his earnest face, his blue eyes, his kindness, but I had never dared hope for this.

'Thomas,' I said, smiling as I tentatively tilted up my face to his. 'Kiss me.'

For the rest of the day I could think of nothing else.

That night, Köhler burst into the Gasthaus. I did not know if he was simply following orders or if he was siding with his boss but, like Schleich, the handsome soldier had not been back since the night of my rape. His very presence made the hubbub die away so that all our customers turned to him. I watched him from behind the bar as he asked if anyone had seen the sergeant.

Until then, the mere mention of him had been enough to make me tremble, but after an afternoon spent in the embrace of Thomas I felt different, somehow immunised and happy again. Köhler's words barely touched me; I merely registered a small relief that Schleich was, for the moment, gone.

Two days later, having led the searches for him with Köhler, Thomas reported him missing. The police came up from Bressen, asked questions and left. The Hauptmann came back in his black, slush-bespattered car and stood in the square interrogating Thomas and Köhler. When Thomas came in at lunchtime, he was wearing a sergeant's insignia on his shoulder.

Many years later, a tiny headline drew my attention to the foot of the international pages one Sunday: 'Soap Man Found in Italian Cave'. The reporter wrote how children playing above the remote mountain village of Oberfals, in northern Italy, had crawled into the cave through a new fissure and come across the gruesome discovery of a corpse. When the local police and villagers had rolled back the boulder blocking the cave, a soapy smell gushed out. The body was lying at the far end of the cave, covered in a hard waxy crust, a rope on the ground next to it. He was identified as the German soldier Sergeant Wilhelm Schleich, who had vanished during the Second World War. A murder enquiry had been launched.

It is funny how love and fear make us blind. I had not noticed that the cave had been sealed, neither that afternoon when I came down from that walk hand in hand with Thomas, nor any time after. The route Thomas had us walk, the 'coincidence' of meeting the postman on the path, Thomas finally having the confidence to kiss me, and then Schleich's absence – it all suddenly added up. At this remove, I wonder how I had been so blind. I'm still not sure if it was innocence on my part, or whether I subconsciously decided not to see. Nevertheless, even decades later, the realisation winded me.

The newspaper fluttered like a trapped bird in my trembling hands as I read how – like the lard that we scraped from the pork – Schleich's ample blubber had, in the cold, damp, airless cave, saponified into grave wax. At last he was clean: he had been transfigured into a bar of soap.

5

Cotton Wool

Cotton wool is extraordinary stuff; so soft, so absorbent. Herodotus vouched that it was softer and whiter than lamb's wool – and if you have ever handled unspun wool as I did as a child, you would agree with him. And to think that a cotton boll – all fluff, seeds and lint – can be turned to so many uses. We spin it into thread, make jeans, T-shirts, sheets and tents from it. We use it to make coffee filters and paper. In the bathroom alone we use it for wiping, cleaning and sterilising. This glass jar is always stuffed with snow-white balls of the softest spun cotton wool. I use them to apply toner and make-up remover and, occasionally, alcohol.

In Oberfals, my mother kept a thick wad of cotton wool rolled up in the bathroom. When we fell over, she would inspect our graze, unroll the wad and cut off just enough to clean the wounds. When I was thirteen and had my first period, she took me into the bathroom and showed me how to wrap a slab of cotton wool in muslin and stuff it in my underwear. Other girls were given towelling rags, which they would rinse out before tipping the bowl of bloody water over the geraniums in the window boxes. My mother had no time for extra work – it was quicker to throw the soiled wool in the fire.

In early 1944, I began to have an uncomfortable feeling in my stomach. My breasts swelled up and I felt heavy and bloated as I always did before my period – but it did not come. When I went into the kitchen to fetch an order, the smell made me gag.

'Rosa,' the postman called as I started to clear the table beside his. 'I want to talk to you.'

His food was what he had ordered, his breadbasket was full,

the cabbage salad looked untouched and he had already eaten one of his three *knödels*. 'Is there anything wrong, Herr Maier?' I asked.

'The food is perfect, Rosa, as always,' he said, picking up his knife and fork, 'but I wanted to know if you're alright. Is anything wrong?'

'No, I'm fine.'

He flicked his eyes at my stomach and then speared a *knödel*. It was the same as any *knödel* that my mother had ever put on his plate. I liked helping her make them. We rolled the bready dough around in our palms every afternoon; yesterday's stale bread moistened into a gluey mass with milk and egg, mixed with the thick, creamy flesh of wild mushrooms – *steinpilze* or *herrenpilze* – or spinach and cheese. My favourite ones concealed a rich treasure of pork crackling in the centre, which when you bit into it would spill hot, juicy fats on to your tongue.

Maier took his knife and sawed the *knödel* in two. The white halves split apart, exposing flecks of red and brown: *speck* and *steinpilze*. Each half lay in a puddle of blackened butter.

'Excuse me,' I gagged, cupping my hand over my mouth.

He looked up at me and nodded gently.

'It's the smell of the butter,' I explained, although I had always loved the smell of burnt butter.

He sighed and leaned back in his chair. 'Have you been feeling sick a lot?'

It was not the first time, not even the second or third. I closed my eyes and tried to control my impulse to retch. 'Yes.'

'All the time?'

'When I wake up, when I'm hungry.'

He raised his eyebrows quizzically.

In that moment, I saw suddenly what I had not seen, what I had been too frightened to see – today we would call it denial. I had managed not to notice the changes in my body but under his scrutiny it was too obvious to ignore.

'I'm pregnant, aren't I?' I said, gripping the chair in front of me.

'I think so. I've been worried ever since November. I thought your dress looked a little tighter, and your nausea – well, I think it is a safe guess.'

Not only was sex outside marriage a cardinal sin, but unmarried mothers were a disgrace, shunned and scorned. I began to panic. 'What shall I do?' I pleaded.

'Does your mother know?'

I considered his question. She was my mother, she should have known, but there was no sign that she was aware. 'She hasn't said anything to me.'

'But does she know?'

'No,' I said bitterly as I realised that she had not even noticed that I had stopped using the cotton wool, despite her keeping tight control of her stocks. 'Of course not, she's too busy.'

Ma chère, don't look so shocked. Have you never heard of girls giving birth in school toilets, and no one noticing? As it happened, no one really could have been certain I was carrying a baby until I was in my third trimester. I was toned and strong from running around all day. And my mother – well, like with so much, I guess she did not want to know. It would have opened such a can of worms. It took me many years, ma chère, to understand my mother's inaction and blindness.

Herr Maier was more sympathetic. He stared across the room at the swing door leading into the kitchen. 'Don't tell her, Rosa. It would break her,' he said, setting his knife and fork down on the plate, next to the neglected *knödel*. I followed his eyes. The men were still drinking and talking in the bar. Behind the frosted glass of the window shadows were moving in the square. The world seemed the same but it was utterly changed.

Suddenly, he sat up straight. 'You can't stay here,' he said.

'Here' was the only place I knew and the idea of going anywhere else terrified me. 'Why?'

'People might put two and two together, and with Schleich's disappearance . . .' His face was set and determined. He shook his head. 'No, you have to go.'

I cast around, desperate for a solution. 'I could get married?'

'To Thomas? It would just implicate him.' At the time I assumed he meant 'implicate him' as the father, but now of course I realise that the postman was worried about the discovery of Schleich's corpse and the murder being attributed to Thomas.

'You really think I should leave?' I asked.

'Yes, there's no other way.' He shrugged and sighed again. 'You're coming over the pass with me – and soon.'

Herr Maier gave me a week. He said that the snow and ice were just passable and we had to go while I could still climb. It did not take me long to pack. I owned so little.

Every afternoon I found an excuse to go for a walk. Thomas would meet me on the edge of the village and each day we took a different route. But it was the same whichever way we went. As soon as we were in amongst the trees, he would push me against the nearest trunk and kiss me. We kissed with large white clusters of snow falling over our coats, with the sun's light making the snowy carpet around us sparkle. Looking back now it was so chaste; we were bundled in winter clothes and coats so that only our faces were bare, and it was too cold to explore anything else. Only our lips could touch. Each kiss was like feeding an addiction, I only wanted more.

On the last night, at the appointed hour after the house had fallen silent, I crept past the cattle, past the stall where Schleich had raped me. It was the first time I had been back in the stalls and my fingers trembled as I opened the door. Thomas was waiting. He stepped in and took me in his arms.

'Not here.' I pushed him off. 'This is where . . .'

Thomas blanched. 'Of course,' he said, 'I'm sorry.'

I bolted the door with difficulty. When I turned around he was stroking one of the cows between the ears. I took his hand and led him past the cattle into the quiet of the house.

'Your boots,' I whispered as he entered the hallway. He took them off and followed me upstairs, clutching them to his chest. We crept past my parents' room. Christl's was opposite mine. When I began to open my door, the sound of metal scraping on metal pierced the quiet, and we froze. I cursed my father for

never having bothered to oil the hinge. No
ushered Thomas into my room. And then fina
in my bedroom.

I could not move. I had dreamed about this n.
frightened and overwhelmed. I stayed with my l
door and he took a step towards me.

'Rosa,' he said, and his voice was so gentle a.ıu cautious I
could barely hear him. 'We won't do anything you don't want to
do.'

I pressed back harder against the door.

'Do you want me to leave?' He tilted his head.

'No,' I gasped, shaking mine.

He came closer and reached out for my hands, interlacing his
fingers with mine. 'You need to sleep. Let's just get into bed and
hold each other.'

He sat down on my bed and took off his coat, his jacket, his
socks, his shirt, leaving only his long-sleeved military-issue vest
on. He kept his head down when he stood up and unbuckled his
belt. He unbuttoned his trousers and slid them off. He did not
look at me once, but I could not take my eyes off him. My heart
was pounding in a maelstrom of fear, excitement, desire and
embarrassment. He stood in his undergarments, the white cotton
long johns and long-sleeved vest, hesitating, a sheepish smile
playing over his face.

'It's cold,' he said, lifting up my duvet and slipping in underneath it.

I took a step away from the door, then stopped. I wanted to
pull my cardigan and dress off and join him but was paralysed
with embarrassment. He must have sensed my shyness because
he rolled over to face the wall. It was easy to undress then.

I lay down beside him, still in my long-sleeved vest and short
johns, and pulled the duvet over me. He did not move but I
could feel the heat radiating from his body. I put my hand tentatively on his hip then rested my fingers on his soft, worn cotton
shirt, so aware of his hard and bony hip underneath. I brushed
my fingers over the fabric around to his chest and his muscles

...ened under the material and my touch. I stopped and listened to his breathing, and he to mine. I pushed myself higher in the bed and nuzzled into the back of his neck. His smell was sweet and sweaty, and I pressed my lips to his skin then whispered in his ear.

'Kiss me.'

Once we began it was hard to stop, hard not to giggle at first, and later almost impossible to not cry out as we fumbled under my single duvet, taking our remaining clothes off piece by piece, exploring each other's bodies. The moment we first embraced toe to toe, mouth to mouth, skin against skin, was a revelation. I had no idea that anything could feel so right.

We did not sleep that night.

When we crawled out of bed at five, it was still dark. I did not want to, but knew I had to write a letter to my mother. The first few times I tried my anger flooded like the black ink on to the paper. The torrent of words was unreadable. With Thomas's help, I cut it down to what was necessary.

> *Dear Mother,*
>   *When you find this, I will be gone. I cannot stay here, not after what happened last November. Don't look for me, don't come after me. I want to start a new life.*
>   *Give my love to Christl,*
>   *Your daughter,*
>   *Rosa*

I left the letter on top of the covered bowl of dough that she always left to rise overnight on the middle of the kitchen table. Thomas and I crept out of the house and walked to meet Herr Maier in the dark.

'Take care of yourself. I will come and find you when the war is over,' Thomas said before we kissed one last time and I forced myself to turn away. 'I love you,' he called out behind me. We left him standing on the bridge near where I had vanquished Rudi Ramoser. It was agony leaving him. I wanted to tell him how much I loved him but instead bit my lip to try to stop myself crying, but I could not halt the tears flowing down my face.

It was tricky climbing up the slippery tracks, and the wrenching morning sickness made me spew my way up over the icy pass. If anyone had wanted to track me, my flight was more clearly marked than the trail Hansel left behind him with his white pebbles.

What I had guessed at, perhaps always known, was that Laurin Maier was not just a postman. He was working for the Resistance, smuggling people and goods over the pass. He knew the twisted path up, over and down the other side like an old familiar friend. I was more breathless than I had ever been and cold despite my exertions. Nevertheless, he urged me on, up the path away from the narrow valley I had barely left in my lifetime. A few times I slipped and fell, scraping my knees. At the top of the pass we paused, and I turned to look back one last time.

'Do you think I'll ever see Thomas again?' I asked him.

'Rosa, in these times, nothing is certain, but I know that he loves you. If it is possible, he will find you.'

I could just make out the windows glinting in the winter sunlight far below. I was frightened by what lay ahead but felt no regret at leaving my parents. My father had betrayed me and my mother had failed to care for me. My only concern was for my sister, but Herr Maier promised to keep an eye on her for me.

'Come on,' he said. 'We've got a long walk down.'

My feet would not move – it was as if they had rooted to the top of the pass. I was sixteen. I had known too much neglect and misery and had just had my first taste of love. If I took one more step away, I might never see Thomas again. I was head over heels in love, and, ma chère, I honestly thought I would never love anyone else again.

At last the postman came and physically turned me around and soon I was stumbling down the far side of the mountain blindly, my eyes swimming with yet more tears.

We descended all morning, following a track along the river but breaking off to skirt past two villages. I was exhausted, hungry and nauseous when Herr Maier pointed up towards a farmhouse perched just below the treeline.

'We'll stay the night there.' My feet would not move. The farmhouse was not so far, but the incline felt insurmountable. He pushed me gently. 'Come on, they're good people. There'll be food and a bed.'

The next morning, the farmer got out his cart and was readying his horse to take me further when Herr Maier handed me a wad of letters.

'They're numbered,' he said, pointing at the top left-hand corner of each. 'I'm sending you by post. Each one has a name and address. The letter asks the recipient to look after you and to send you on to the next. It's how I get refugees out. These are people you can trust. They'll ask no questions and you should ask them none in return. They'll feed you, give you a bed for the night and send you on your way.'

I flicked through the bundle, stopping when I got to the last one, which was addressed to a Herr Professor Dr Heinrich David Goldfarb in St. Gallen.

'Who is this?' I asked.

'Ah, that was Thomas's idea. He was Thomas's professor.'

He took my small suitcase of clothes and stowed it on the cart. 'Here, you'll need this.' He thrust a small roll of Swiss franc notes into my hand.

As he took a step back, I threw my arms round him. For a second he resisted before folding me in a bear hug. I had walked away from my parents without a tear – perhaps even with some sense of freedom – but I could not say goodbye to Laurin Maier without regret.

'Thank you, I don't know what I would have done without you,' I said, trying to sound bright and confident. I didn't want him to worry.

'I wish you well, Rosa Kusstatscher,' he said gruffly. 'You've got your head screwed on, you'll be fine. Write to me.'

★

It took five days for me to travel the 150-odd miles to St. Gallen, catching trains, buses and lifts, sleeping at the addresses that the postman had written on the different envelopes. Each host gave me some food and a place to sleep, then sent me on the way to the next. I had barely been out of my valley before, yet now I moved from one strange house to another. But I felt no fear, nor any other emotion. I was so young and I had just been uprooted from everything I knew. Now, looking back, I think I was in shock. I was being passed along, like a package that Herr Maier had sent.

It was only standing outside a house on Dufourstrasse, the address on the final letter, that the dreamy feeling vanished. As at all the addresses before, I knocked and waited. The door was opened quickly by a waspish woman.

'Yes?' she said coldly, looking me up and down.

'Good day,' I said nervously. 'I'm looking for Professor Goldfarb.'

'Who?'

'Professor Goldfarb? He lives here. Look.' I showed her the envelope.

'He does not. We've lived here a while and I would have noticed a professor in the house. Try next door.' Without another word, she closed the door in my face.

I was overcome with nausea and just managed to get on to the pavement before I retched. There must have been a mistake. I could feel the bulk of Thomas's letter of introduction to his old professor in my hand. Maybe he had the wrong house number. I sat for some time on the wall that ran along the front garden, the iron railings cold against my back. The hope that had kept me going ebbed out of me and I felt lost and defeated.

But then I remembered that Thomas had called me a Valkyrie. *'You don't even know how strong you are.'* I scrabbled to my feet; I could not give up so easily. I was not going to let him down. I opened the next gate and strode up the garden path. I knocked on some twenty other doors on that road, but most of the people who came to the door said they did not know him. Two people said that if I meant the man who had been there for a while, he was gone. At some point I found myself walking downhill, back the way I had come. I had not prepared for this. Clinging to this envelope had let me believe that everything would be fine. It was not. I was alone, in a foreign country, and I knew not one person. Perhaps I was not the Valkyrie Thomas thought I was.

It was February. The snow was still on the ground; it was cold and already getting dark. I found a cheap hotel but had to pay extra so that they would ignore my lack of papers. The next day my money was running low and all I could do was buy myself a meal and stay in the warmth of the nearest Gasthaus until it closed. I'll never forget the fear that second night as I lay huddled in the cathedral porch. I was frightened of the dark, of being alone and pregnant, of having no money, and of the prospect of freezing to death. For two more cold days and nights I begged and even stole some rolls from a basket outside a bakery. The nausea from the baby was worse with the lack of food. They would not let me into the Gasthaus to eat on the fourth evening; I was looking shabby and haggard by then, and men began to look at me in a way that reminded me of Schleich.

The following morning, desperation drove me back to Dufourstrasse and I began knocking on every door again, starting at the first house. I reached the end of the street, crossed it and returned down the other side. It took me all morning and yielded nothing but an even greater sense of hopelessness.

I stood at the end of the road, trying not to cry. Then I martialled myself – there was no reason to assume he was not in the city, I should just knock on every door. But then I remembered that St. Gallen was not like tiny Oberfals. I might die of starvation before I ever found him, or worse.

I was desperate and my energy was fading. I knew that I had to find him soon or . . . I could not bear to think of the alternatives. I looked up the street one last time and slowly turned around, and then the solution presented itself to me. It was so simple, I started to laugh out loud. I might not be able to find where he lived, but if he had been Thomas's professor it meant that he taught at a university – I would find him where he worked.

I asked the next four people who passed me on the road where the university was. The first three seemed not to hear. The fourth was a young woman, who smiled and said, 'There isn't a university as such here. Do you mean the Handels-Hochschule?' She pointed out the way.

The business school was close by but it took me a while to find anyone who had heard of him and then they pointed to his building. I walked around the Economics department but was unable to find his name on any of the doors, so I knocked on the door of the secretary's office.

'Come in,' a thin voice called out.

I stepped in. 'Excuse me,' I said, using the same tone I would use to welcome customers in the Gasthaus. 'I'm looking for Professor Goldfarb.'

The secretary was a thin, middle-aged woman, hiding behind her typewriter in an office full of metal filing cabinets. 'Are you a student?'

'No.'

Her eyes narrowed. 'A family member?'

'No.'

'Then I cannot help,' she said shrilly. 'We can't just let anyone in here.'

All the fear, hunger and desperation that I had been trying to keep at bay overtook me, and I sat down on the chair facing her desk. 'I don't know what to do if I don't find him,' I said, then I could not stop the sobs escaping from my mouth.

'Excuse me,' the secretary said, her voice softer now. I looked up to see her standing beside me – she must have come round when I started crying. She stood over me, touching my shoulder. 'If it's that urgent, I'll go and see if I can find him.'

I calmed down and managed to quell my weeping but was still wiping my face when she returned with an unkempt man in an ill-fitting brown tweed suit. A few days of unshaved, grey bristle shaded his pallid skin. I stood up.

'This is Herr Professor Dr Goldfarb,' she said.

He squinted into my desperate face. 'Fräulein Polt says you are looking for me. Do I know you?' His accent was clipped and clear: German.

'No, but I have to give you this,' I said, waving Thomas's battered envelope in the air.

'Can I see?' I nodded and his thin fingers gently prised the envelope from my grasp. 'Your hand is cold. Your accent – you're not from round here?'

'No. I'm from South Tyrol.'

He studied me a moment longer, then he switched his focus to the envelope and read Thomas's tidy smudged loops, taking in his own name and the address. Then he turned it over to where Thomas had written his name and return address.

'Sit down and wait.'

Fräulein Polt showed me to a chair in the corridor outside her room then brought me a glass of water. I was tired and grateful to rest, but too anxious to sit still. I peered out of the window and watched men, young and old, walking along the paths that I had trudged up and down earlier. I tried not to think about what I would do if the letter failed in its purpose.

About ten minutes later, the professor came back. He was wearing his overcoat, his scarf was wrapped around his neck, and his hat was in his hands. He was carrying a briefcase.

'Rosa Kusstatscher?'

'Yes.'

'I have a lot of respect for Thomas Fischer,' he said, his voice formal yet soft. 'Come with me.'

As soon as I took in what he had said, I collapsed back on to the chair and cried.

The professor took me back to his house and straight into his kitchen.

'Sit down while I make you some hot milk and honey,' he ordered. 'Then we'll talk.'

There was a traditional tiled stove in the corner of the kitchen and I sat on the bench running around it while he prepared my drink.

'Here,' he said. I opened my eyes to find that my head was resting against the warm stove. I had fallen asleep. 'This is for you.'

He left me to savour the hot, sweet milk while he busied himself opening cupboard doors and drawers. I buried my nose in the cup and inhaled the thick, cloying scent, and for a brief moment I imagined myself in the kitchen with my mother. But I quickly banished the notion. I was here, I was safe.

As the professor moved around, I took the opportunity to study him properly. I had imagined a wrinkled, white-haired man, but he could not have been older than fifty. He was skeletal. I sipped my drink in a daze of a relief, still stunned at having found him.

'Here.' He pulled out a chair at the table for me. 'I don't have much but have some bread and cheese.'

I dragged myself from the warmth of the stove and joined him at the table. He had laid out a pungent pale yellow cheese on a platter with some gherkins and a few slices of rye bread. I took a deep breath and sighed. I was not going to starve or freeze to death, at least not that night.

He offered the food to me and helped himself. We ate in silence. When he had finished he put his cutlery down and wiped his mouth carefully with a linen napkin.

'Thomas Fischer was probably the best student I ever had – certainly my favourite. He has asked me to help you out.' He paused as he took in the empty serving platter. 'My word, you must be hungry. Let me get some more.' He stood up abruptly, pushing his chair back. 'There is a spare room at the end of the corridor. You can stay as long as you need to.'

The professor's house was full of books and showed few signs of domesticity. The only tokens of a life beyond his work were four portraits in silver frames on the mantelpiece. In the first, two boys in their early teens stood, swathed in large white shawls with dark stripes and tassels. In the second, a girl of about twelve stood in fifth position wearing her ballet skirt. There was another of the same three as small children with the boys in sailor suits and the girl in a stiff pinafore. The last one was a portrait of an angular-looking woman with a 1920s bobbed haircut.

He took me to visit his physician, Herr Dr Oster, who, after examining me, told me to visit once a month and sent me into the kitchen to ask his wife to prepare coffee for him and the professor while they discussed the latest news. Frau Dr Oster had drawn my whole story from me by the time she had laid out coffee, sugar, cream, cakes and porcelain cups and saucers on a tray. From then on, every time I came for my monthly visit, she would ply me with used baby clothes or ill-fitting maternity dresses she had coaxed from the doctor's other patients. With her help, I built up my own trousseau of sorts.

Every day I would walk around the pretty town with its austere Palatinate monastery and the Baroque cathedral with its twin black towers, enjoying the stolen glimpses of Lake Constance, which stretched out in the valley below, as well as the dark mass of Mount Säntis rising up out of the rolling hills like a wall behind me. I would come back with food and prepare lunch and dinner for the professor. While my mother had never paid me much attention, she had taught me how to cook, clean and work hard. The hot food pleased the professor and his clothes seemed less baggy as the weeks passed by. As for the housekeeping, I was not sure that he noticed but I cleaned and tidied with grateful zeal. It was an odd setup but, young and inexperienced as I was, I supposed I was lucky. The professor had accepted me, sheltered me and was barely aware of my presence. I felt safe. Every evening we would eat together, then he would retreat to an armchair in the lounge where he would listen to records and read while I honed my needlecraft.

The dresses that Frau Dr Oster handed over to me in neatly wrapped packages of brown paper and string were invariably too big so I began, cautiously at first, to alter them. And then something happened, as I sat night after night, my belly growing, letting out dresses that I had previously taken in: through trial and error, I learnt when to stitch tightly like tiny sutures, how to darn, tack and baste. I kept my seams tight with backstitches. I pulled the thread from my hems in frustration until a friend of Frau Dr Oster showed me how to do a slip stitch. There was one moment, an epiphany perhaps, when I had cut and pulled out all the threads holding together an ugly dress made from a gorgeous printed cotton and understood for the first time how the dress had been structured; how the gathering and pleats, the darts and shaping were the skeleton of the design. I began to understand what I could achieve with careful cutting and stitching. I transformed the shapeless sacks into elegant dresses. And in those long evenings I would wonder what to do with the child when it came.

Until quite recently, ma chère, young, unmarried women would go away to have their bastard, hand it over to a convent or hospital for adoption, and then creep home hoping that no one would notice. Single mothers were rare and lived in shame. Yet, I could not help being excited by the feeling of life growing inside me. I knew I should give up the baby – that's what women did in my circumstances – but as I sat sewing or walked the streets, I envied the other mothers and their children. But, I told myself, I had not chosen to be pregnant, and I loathed Schleich – I could not keep his child.

One day the professor came home early, while I was on my hands and knees scrubbing the kitchen floor, and it was as if he was seeing me for the first time. He stood in the doorway and almost shouted at me.

'Rosa, what are you doing, in your condition?'

I heaved myself back on to my heels. 'I'm cleaning, like I do every day.'

He took a step in. 'You do this every day?' he asked in a gentler tone.

'Oh, please, Herr Professor, please don't come in, not while the floor is wet.'

'I just wanted a coffee,' he said, but turned and left, lost in thought.

'I'll bring it for you as soon as I am done,' I called after him.

When I brought him the coffee, he was standing motionless except for his fingers, which were stroking the photos on the mantelpiece. I had never seen him even glance at them before. He turned as I entered and let his hand fall.

'Your shoes, Rosa,' he said abruptly. 'How old are they?'

'Oh,' I said, a little taken aback. 'Two years, I think. Yes, my mother was pleased last summer when my feet had stopped growing and she didn't need to get me a new pair.'

'Well, they've had it. I am sorry I took so long to notice. You need new ones.'

I looked down at them. I kept them polished but they were worn and scuffed and let the water in on rainy days. He was right, but I did not have money to repair them. The professor had given me so much already that I didn't feel comfortable asking for more. 'They're fine, professor,' I said.

'Nonsense,' he said briskly. 'I saw the holes in their soles just now.'

'But—'

'No buts. Tomorrow, we go shopping. I'm just not used to taking care of others. It was my wife's territory.' He turned the photo of the woman with the cheekbones and the bobbed dark curly hair for me to see. I had dusted and polished the frame many times and had often wondered who she was. It made no sense to me that he had never mentioned her or the children in the other frame, but I had never wanted to pry. I was glad he had broached the subject.

'Ah,' I said, 'she's very handsome.'

'Yes. She was.' He went and sat down in his armchair.

I went up to the photos and peered at them.

'Are these children yours too?' I asked after a long silence.

'I came here to get their visas. I had to come first, to get the paperwork in order. By the time I got back to Leipzig, the Nazis had taken them.'

'Oh,' I said, breathing in sharply as my mind grappled with what that meant. It is strange to relate now, but at the time I thought they must have perished in an accident. I was young, sheltered, even ignorant, and really had no idea what was going on in Germany. All that would come later; after the war it would be inescapable. I had had my fair share of pain in my short life already, but my first inkling of the loss, trauma and suffering of others was in the quiet of this living room.

'That's why you couldn't find me. I had taken a big house for us all, and that was the address Thomas had. When I came back, I moved to a smaller apartment.'

After a long silence I asked, 'What happened to them?'

'They're all dead.'

He was staring down at the carpet. I knelt down in front of him and took his hand. I could not find any words, could not fathom what he had lost, what the pain of losing his children felt like. The only comfort I could offer was my presence.

He did not retract his hand and we stayed like that for a long time.

'I wanted to be alone,' he said at last, 'but maybe the angels have sent you to me. You, with your endless sewing and cleaning and cheerfulness.'

I blushed and let go of his hand. 'Herr Professor, keeping house for you is the only way I can thank you for your kindness,' I told him as I got to my feet.

He shook his head. 'No, it is I who should thank you. And you need new shoes. Tomorrow, we will go shopping.'

In Bressen there had been three kinds of shoe on sale: work shoes, walking shoes and Sunday-best shoes. I had never had the opportunity to try on more than the two or three pairs that my mother deemed suitable. Here in St. Gallen, women could buy shoes for many different occasions in many different styles, and not just in black or brown. The professor was amused by my excitement but even more so by my opting for a pair of sturdy shoes rather than the more elegant ones – ever the waitress in me. But they were more chic than anything I had ever owned before, polished beige and brown two-tone leather with small leather laces. I was delighted with them.

That afternoon after lunch the professor came into the kitchen while I was making coffee.

'I bought something else for you,' he said, looking strangely sheepish.

'Oh, but the shoes are more than enough,' I said.

'No, this is different. It was when we were in the shop and I could see people looking at us and wondering. You see, you don't have one of these.' He held out a small package wrapped in white tissue paper. I took it. It was solid and light. 'Open it,' he urged.

Inside the wrapping was a small red box, and inside the box a plain gold ring. I looked into his face, confused.

'You should wear it,' he said, reaching up to massage the back of his neck distractedly. 'People will ask, they will notice. Many women have lost their husbands in the war. You should just tell people you are a war widow.' He stepped forward. 'Is this my coffee? I'll take it through now.'

When I walked out wearing my ring and my beautiful new brogues, I felt smart and elegant for the first time in my life. I liked the civility this encouraged in the townswomen, the discounts it won me from the market stallholders. The professor was not well remunerated – despite his title, he had an adjunct position cobbled together as a favour by colleagues – and I had to stretch the housekeeping money he gave me to feed us both, but a smile and my Tyrolean accent seemed to reduce the prices.

One day a woman, a few years older than me, stopped me in the street. She was pushing a pram with a fat baby in it, and her fur jacket was bursting open over a woollen dress that ill-fit her capacious bosom.

'*Gnädige Frau*, excuse me for asking, but where did you get that dress?' I was startled by her question and looked down at my dress. It had been a too-busy dress that I had altered, simply recutting it to offset the swirling emerald and black pattern, but left the original fancy black pleated fringe at the bottom.

'From Frau Dr Oster,' I replied. 'She was so kind as to give it to me.'

'I thought so. It was mine but I looked like a cabbage in it. You look wonderful. Did you alter it yourself?' She did not wait for my answer but snapped her bag open. 'Look, I live here.' She thrust a card in amongst the vegetables and newspaper-wrapped trout in the basket I was carrying. 'Come by, I have lots of dresses that need altering. I will pay, of course. Good day.' And then she strolled away down the pavement with her baby.

I stared after her. During that briefest of exchanges, she had not for a moment let go of the pram. She had reached down to pick up her handbag, which was lying on the tidily tucked-in blankets below the baby's feet. She had opened the bag and extracted the card with one hand, the other clasped firmly around the steering bar. Whatever she was doing or thinking, being a mother was central to who she was. She was attached to her baby by invisible threads. I let my hands rest on my round, hard belly. In that moment, the abstract idea that I was pregnant became a tangible reality. Until then I had failed to appreciate that, in this swollen belly, a baby was growing – my baby. It was happening, whether the war ended or not, and in four months' time I would give birth. I would either hand my child over to the nuns or become a mother. I watched her disappear down the street, pushing her pram. Under my hand, I felt my baby kick.

When she disappeared from view I picked up her card. *Frau Ida Schurter*, it announced. Until now I had survived on charity and goodwill, but I knew that at some point I had to start earning money. In her simple act of stopping me in the street, this woman had opened a world of possibility to me. If I had stayed in Oberfals I would have been expected to take over the Gasthaus from my mother. I had left and now I had to create my own future. I had to allow for the possibility that Thomas would not survive; he would not come and find me. I had to start making my own living – and how better to do that than by becoming a seamstress? This was something I could do.

My visit to Frau Schurter could not have been more of a success. She wanted me to alter two dresses to begin with. The first was

made of a satin cotton with a floral design, and I simply made
the adjustments she asked for. The second was a charcoal worsted
dress. The cut was – oh, ma chère, to say it was not flattering
would be an understatement. I took it upon myself to fashion it
into something that would not only fit her, but that would enhance
her. She was sceptical when she first saw it on the hanger, but
her suspicion turned to approval and then delight as soon as she
tried it on and glimpsed herself in the mirror. When she put the
notes and coins in my hands after that first job, the reality of
holding my own earnings, of the choices that afforded me,
momentarily stunned me. On the way home I purchased a small
paper bag of chocolates for the professor, the first gift I had ever
bought. The rest, though it was not much, I secreted in a sock
in my room. I had not expected or imagined that I would feel
elated, but I did.

Soon I was sitting day and night cutting and trimming, taking
in and taking out, lengthening and shortening, styling and fixing
her friends' and their friends' dresses. It was a crash course in
dressmaking and business. My needle skills were sharpened with
each new project, and my negotiating proficiency improved with
each new commission. Soon I was able to buy a second-hand
sewing machine. It took me several tries practising on scraps and
one unwearable dress, but once I had mastered it, I realised that
with my increased work rate, like Rumpelstiltskin, I could craft
gold. My fingers seemed to know how to cut and sew like magic
and the years of helping in the Gasthaus meant I knew how to
deal with people. I worked and saved, and began to dream of
setting up shop as a dressmaker. Every time I was paid I put
some money aside for the baby, some money for the shop and
bought a small luxury, like chocolate or a scented soap, for the
professor. I was happy.

The professor and I settled into a contented routine. He would
spend the morning at the Hochschule then, after coming home
for lunch and a nap, would pass the afternoon reading in his
armchair or writing at his desk. I would spend the morning

cleaning, washing, ironing, shopping and preparing lunch. Then in the afternoon I would visit my clients in their homes, measuring and pinning, sketching and listening, until it was time to return home.

In the evenings, the professor and I would sit together; I sewed and he read. Once he realised how little I knew of the world, he read the newspapers out loud to me. I came to understand the madness, carnage and effort propelling the armies to battle as I cut, pinned, ironed and stitched dress after dress.

One evening the professor noticed me wince. 'What's the matter?'

'The baby.' I grimaced. 'It's kicking.' Sometimes it felt like butterflies tickling me but other times, like this, it was a painful jab.

'Your baby is getting big and wants more room,' he said, standing up and stretching out his hand. 'May I?'

I hesitated. We were living side by side but we had never touched, apart from the night he told me about his family. 'Yes,' I said finally.

He rested his hand on my belly and waited. When the baby kicked he smiled, a warm, soft smile, and I smiled back at him. It was as if we had crossed an invisible line.

'Have you thought about what to do afterwards?' he asked. His voice was casual but there was an intensity to his gaze.

'I'm saving to open a dressmaker's shop.'

He stared at me. 'I see. That's a good plan. But I meant with the baby.'

'Oh,' I said, blushing at my mistake. 'No.'

He considered me for a long moment before saying, 'You don't have to give it up.'

Sometimes I would stop working and rest my hand on the taut, growing dome and wait for my tummy to bulge as the baby moved or kicked. I came to discern when it was asleep and to expect a flurry of activity when I lay down in bed. The growing sense of another being inside me became a salve against the gnawing loneliness I felt despite – or perhaps because of – the happy home the professor and I now maintained.

I bought a few baby clothes – just so I would not hand it over with nothing, I told myself. As the baby grew inside me I had to keep letting out my dresses and began to walk awkwardly, but still I had not decided where I would take it afterwards. When I was idle my hand would rest on my swollen belly; my hand seemed to express something I had not yet understood.

As my belly swelled I began burping from indigestion. I went to the pharmacist and while I waited for him to fetch his remedy, siphoning the antacid into a brown glass bottle, I watched the shop assistant take out a thick wad of cotton wool. She unrolled it, measured it, cut it and then wrapped it up for the woman she was serving. I hadn't seen a roll this thick for months, not since my last period.

The pharmacist handed the assistant the bottle of antacid for me. 'Do you need anything else?'

I pointed at the white roll. 'A metre of cotton wool, please.' I would need some to wipe my baby's bottom.

6

Aspirin

In any bathroom cabinet there is a division – as you can see when I open these mirrored doors – between our quest for youth and beauty and our fight against ill-health and slow, creeping death. As we get older the balance shifts; the proportion of the cupboard stocked with a rainbow of nail varnish, lipsticks, eyeshadow, mascaras, rouges, powders and foundation dwindles as the small clump of medicine bottles, tubes of ointment, tins and packets of pills grows. Oh, ma chère, this is the slow march of death, the conquest of the lipsticks by the white plastic medicine bottles; the retreat of Dior, Lancôme, Chanel; the advance of Johnson & Johnson, Pfizer and Procter & Gamble. But I have not swapped my lipsticks smartly sheathed in black for the drab white bottles of compounds and chemicals. They have not vanquished me yet.

There are a few, however, which I am never without: vitamin C, aspirin and penicillin. I learnt their importance long ago. Aspirin has been around a long time. When we humans were still wearing animal skins – that is, when were they first tanned, cured, fashioned and styled rather than just slung over the shoulders – shamans were using willow bark and leaves to treat pain and fever. Hippocrates used it four hundred years before Christ. Now we know that not only is it an anti-inflammatory and analgesic, it can also help mitigate blood-clotting. After my mother learnt that I had been raped, she made me take an aspirin. It was such a pathetic response. How an aspirin was meant to ease the pain of my father's betrayal, my humiliation or Schleich's violence is beyond my conception. Perhaps it was a symbolic gesture of someone trapped by circumstance. I'll never know, I never got to have that conversation with her.

On the morning of July 21st, 1944, the professor had rushed out early to get a newspaper, excited by a report on the radio about the assassination attempt on Hitler the day before. Everything I did that morning was slow. A dull, persistent backache had stopped me from sleeping well, and I was exhausted. But it was weeks before my due date and I was not worried. I was carrying the Rosenthal coffee pot to the sink with the utmost care, because it was one of the few items that the professor had brought all the way from Leipzig, from his wife's trousseau. A neighbour had saved it with a few other things when the Gestapo had emptied the contents of his family's flat.

Suddenly, a surge of pain came from nowhere. It overwhelmed me and I fell gasping to the floor. The coffee pot fell and smashed on the kitchen tiles. I collapsed on all fours and panted for air, watching the coffee run between the dark grains and the pieces of broken white porcelain. Perhaps it was my way of pushing my fear to the side, but I was more worried about the broken pot than myself. The pain subsided and I gathered up the broken shards and wrapped them in old newspaper to show the professor later. As I reached for a cloth from the sink, the second contraction slammed me forward. I clutched at the rim of the stone sink and breathed in huge gulps of air. This time as the pain receded, I felt warm, wet fluid streaming down my legs.

It is so hard to believe now, but I still got down and cleaned the floor before I staggered between contractions to the bathroom. At least that taught me that the pain was most bearable on all fours. I took off my underwear and put them to soak in the basin. I wanted to clean my legs before I walked to Dr Oster's, but soon I realised I was not going anywhere. The contractions came too fast, another one slamming in just as I recovered and tried to get up and leave. They just kept on coming. I squatted down on the bathroom mat and leaned against the bath for support, panting and resting and then bracing myself against the bath as the next wave of pain engulfed me. The urge to push was intense and overwhelming.

I don't know how long I had been there when I heard the professor calling me.

'Rosa! Are you here?'

Before I could answer, another contraction squeezed me like a vice. I tried to stifle my scream. I covered my mouth, acutely embarrassed: he could not find me like this. I was like an animal, panting and feral. I tried to move to the door to lock it but merely managed to shuffle around so that I was facing it.

His footsteps were loud, he was outside the door. He knocked and every sound, every sensation seemed heightened; each knock made me tremor.

'Rosa?'

I groaned.

'I'm coming in.'

'No,' I howled. 'No, you can't!'

'I must.'

He opened the door, took one look at the scene and backed out. I heard him pick up the phone in the hallway and summon Dr Oster. Then he was with me again, with a glass of water and a flannel to wipe my brow. I didn't even know that I was thirsty, but my sips turned to gulps as he held the glass to my lips.

'Did you know,' he said, as if we were drinking tea in a fine café, 'that in Africa women squat to give birth, and the red Indians too.' The glass was shaking in his hands as he pressed it to my lips.

I grunted.

'You're doing very well. You're so brave.'

'It hurts,' I groaned.

'My wife said that it was only one day. You will forget all about it tomorrow.'

I cried out as the next wave of pain hit. Then as I recovered, I snorted. 'And you believed her?'

'She did it again,' he said with a small smile. He stood up. 'I'll go and ring the doctor again.'

He left the room and returned a minute later, looking anxious.

'My sons were twins,' he muttered distractedly. 'They came out bang, bang one after another. So tiny, they shot out easily, not like Irma. She was a big baby – four and a half kilos.'

A contraction took hold of me and I pushed and strained. They were coming more rapidly now.

'That's right,' he soothed, crouching down beside me again. 'Breathe deeply. I don't think Dr Oster will be here in time. I think I may have to help.'

I nodded. I was beyond talking.

As soon as I gave my consent, he washed his hands and grabbed a clean hand towel from the cupboard above the boiler and knelt in front of me.

The pain had reached a new level. It was so intense that I could see it like an iridescent cloud of tiny white and blue knives piercing my innards. Whatever I am or was had retreated; my body was a vessel for the birth and I merely a remote observer. I looked down; a round dome, pink and grey with thin blond streaks, was protruding from inside of me.

'Rosa,' the professor urged. 'Just two or three more pushes.'

The next contraction came. I screamed and pushed. Blue-white light scythed through me. When the agony subsided, I was too frightened to look down. I was sure that I had been split in two.

'Look. You're nearly done!'

Between my legs I could see a tiny head plastered in a white paste.

'Rosa, when you push next time it'll come out and I must catch it.'

I nodded, pulling myself back into action. When the wave came, I screamed and pushed and when I opened my eyes, the pain was gone and the professor was holding my baby in his hands. His face was creased up with a wide smile. His eyes looked liquid. The baby started to cry.

'Oh, that's good. That's very good.' He laughed, wrapping it in the towel. 'He has very good lungs.'

'He?'

'Oh yes, it's a boy, a lovely boy. And I believe he's hungry.'

He handed me the bundle and I pulled him to me. He was tiny, pink and hairless and his face was screwed up in despair or shock, I didn't know which.

'Hello, little one,' I soothed.

He seemed to respond to my voice. He stopped bawling and looked up at me.

The professor washed my blood off his hands and covered me with another towel. 'I'll go and find out what happened to Herr Dr Oster.'

I inspected the baby's little face, steeling myself to find a miniature of his father – but all I could see were his eyes, which were deep, dark blue, like the mountain sky in summer. A wave of love and euphoria washed over me and in that moment I knew. The baby was not Schleich's bastard. He was my son.

I was not the only one to fall in love with him. For a week after his birth, the professor would not let me do anything, just rest and feed.

'I managed before, you know. I can manage now,' he would say at my protests, gently pushing me back into bed.

Whenever I left the baby sleeping and got up for a coffee or a bath, I would come back to find the professor gazing down into his cot; sometimes smiling, sometimes with tears trailing from his eyes.

'You know, Rosa,' he said after about a week, 'you can't call him "the baby" forever. He has a right to a name.'

'I know.' I sighed. 'But it is so hard.'

'Have you any ideas?'

'I thought of Thomas.'

'Like Thomas Fischer?' He stared at me then at the baby. 'So is Thomas . . .'

'Oh no.' I rushed to explain. 'He's not the father.'

'Oh?'

I had never seen the letter Thomas had sent; it had never occurred to me that the professor imagined that Thomas was the father. I wanted to be honest but since the painful confession to Christl I had not spoken about what I had been through and was struggling to say it aloud, to voice the ugly truth. 'I was raped by Thomas's sergeant,' I said finally. 'It was only after that, when Thomas was so kind, that we fell in love.' I bent forward and kissed the little creature on the forehead. 'I did not expect to love the baby. But now I see he's my son, and I don't want him tainted by that brute. He will never be his father."

'I see. I'm so sorry, Rosa, I never imagined . . .' The professor reached his hands out to me. 'May I?'

I handed the baby over to him.

'You know he's not to blame. He's innocent.' He planted his lips on the top of the hairless head. The baby stirred and he handed him back. 'What about your father or grandfathers' names?'

The baby was half asleep but his lips puckered and he started to suck at the air. I slid him back on to my breast.

'I think it's going to be Laurin.'

'Who?'

'Laurin. It's the name of Herr Maier, the postman who helped me escape.'

'Laurin Kusstatscher. I like it.'

My vague plans to give Laurin away were forgotten. The professor carried on reading to us, the war ended and hope returned. I sewed and sewed, and my savings were beginning to accumulate. For two years, whatever we three were, we were happier than my family in Oberfals. The professor loved Laurin, and Laurin loved him back.

Then in April 1946, the professor was invited to visit the newly reopened Leipzig University. I feared that he was going to be offered a job and tried not to think about what it meant for

Laurin and me. If he took a job, I guessed he would go back to Germany and I would be alone in St. Gallen.

The professor was very quiet when he came back and it was only after I had cleared the dinner away, checked on Laurin and joined him in the sitting room to sew, that he put his newspaper down and stared at me. I was hemming a skirt and was so tense the thread I pulled through snapped.

'I decided not to take the job, Rosa.'

I let the skirt fall into my lap and gathered myself, trying not to let my relief show. 'Weren't they good to you in Leipzig?'

'They could not have been better.' He sighed. 'They are desperate for me to rebuild the department, to restore what the war and the Nazis destroyed. They offered me the choice of new staff, a good apartment, a generous salary, everything. But . . .'

I turned the skirt around and repositioned my needle. 'But what?'

'But every time I shook a hand, greeted someone, I wondered: what had this person done or not done for the last few years? There is no going back.'

'So, you will stay here and I can stay with you and keep house,' I said, confirming what I wanted to hear.

He smiled at my rapid response. 'You would like things to stay as they are?'

'Yes, of course.' I looked up at him. 'Wouldn't you?'

The professor hesitated, then shook his head sadly. 'No. I can't stay here. I can't live in a crematorium.'

'But all that was in Germany.'

'It was all of Europe,' he said, his voice unusually hard. 'It's not just the ghosts of my family, but millions. I can't stay here where it happened. I want a different life, to start again.'

'So where are you going?'

'Palestine.'

'The Holy Land?'

He regarded me while I continued hemming, and although I knew I was doing it, I could not stop myself stitching too tightly.

It was a smock for a pregnant friend of Frau Schurter. My life was about to unravel and I was frightened, but still I sewed.

It was if he had caught a thread and if he pulled just a little more everything would come undone. 'When will you go?' I asked, my voice clipped.

'As soon as I can arrange it.'

For some reason the needle seemed stuck, I could not force it through. 'Without us?'

'That is the question,' he said, and his hands flew up to massage the back of his neck – something he always did when he was stressed. 'I have been worrying about you all the way back on the train. I don't want to leave you, but I cannot think of how to take you with me. You are not my daughter. And as much as I love Laurin, he is not my son.'

He paused, and my needle finally eased through and, despite my trembling fingers, I carried on sewing.

'You are not my family. But you have become like my family and you are all I have left to care about in the world. And then it occurred to me that if we married, you could come as my wife and Laurin would be my son.'

I left the needle pierced in the fabric. He was not looking at me but at his newspaper, then he put it down and stood up. He walked over to the mantelpiece and traced his fingers over the images of his dead children.

'When you arrived here, I never thought to love again. I had had my family and lost it. I wanted to dry up and float away like an autumn leaf. But you changed all that. I feel alive again.'

He turned and stared at me, his sharp hazel eyes ablaze, his face flushed. His grey beard had been trimmed in Germany and with his fine aquiline features, he might have been good-looking when he was younger. The crow's feet and wrinkles only amplified his smile.

'I can give both you and Laurin my family name and my protection. I know I am older than you, but not too old. We could be a real family.'

I could feel the blood draining from my face. He could not

be saying what I thought he was saying. A real family, man and wife. I owed this kind man so much – but surely not marriage. I forced myself to answer. 'I don't know what to say.'

'Don't say anything now.'

He took my hands and pulled me up gently. We stood face to face. We had not been so close since he had delivered Laurin. I did not want to offend him so I let it happen.

'Good night, Rosa.' He leaned forward and I closed my eyes. His lips were soft and warm when they met mine briefly. He smelt of travel, cigarettes and damp wool. 'Think about it. Tomorrow, I will start preparing to leave.'

He turned and left the room, and I collapsed on to my chair. My mind was reeling. The last time anyone else's lips had touched mine was when Thomas had said goodbye. He had promised to come and find me. He was a man of honour, and as long as he was alive I believed he would keep his word. I still loved him. I still felt his hands' tender touch on me when I closed my eyes at night, still cherished the memory of his kiss. But I had no idea how long I should wait, how long before I should give up. Ma chère, you should understand, more than two years had passed since I left Oberfals. I had written to Herr Maier once I had been settled in St. Gallen and he had replied with the news that Thomas had been moved on and had not left a forwarding address. It was nearly a year since the war had ended. And now, the professor had kissed me. The touch of his lips on mine had left me unmoved and confused. He had been nothing but gracious and kind to me, never taken anything, never demanded anything, but with his declaration, the way we had been living would not be able to continue unchanged.

The next morning, as I was unfolding Ida Schurter's latest fabric on her large formal dining table, I stopped to watch the boys. Max was pulling a string of wooden ducks across the floor while Laurin followed him, laughing every time the ducks quacked, and I laughed along with him. Laurin loved coming here. Then I realised that Frau Schurter was talking to me.

'. . . but anyway, it was the colour that I liked, such a deep purple.'

I fingered the cloth, forcing myself to focus on what she was saying. It was heavy silk satin, perfect for autumn and winter evening wear.

'What did you have in mind?' I asked her.

'You know, Rosa, I thought that I would leave that to you. Oh boys, not there,' she chided, taking Max's hand and leading him out of the room. The sound of the boys alternately crying and laughing carried down the hallway.

'Rosa, is there anything the matter?' Frau Schurter asked some time later, standing in the doorway, her gentle eyes scrutinising me.

I tried to give her an easy smile. 'No, why?'

'Well, I played with the boys, fed them and put them down for a nap and you've . . .' She walked to the table and lifted up my sketchpad. 'You've done nothing.'

I looked down at my sketchpad. Normally, after such a morning, I would have three or four designs for her to choose from. 'I'm sorry. I can't concentrate,' I admitted. I sat down heavily.

'I can see,' she said. She looked at my page. I had written two words – Palestine and St. Gallen – and drawn a big question mark between them. 'What's the matter?'

And then I told her. She listened, interrupting only to seek clarification, and I told her everything. As the words rushed out of my mouth, my thoughts became clearer. Telling her made it real.

'. . . so I could marry him and then we would be safe.'

She was silent for a moment, frowning. 'Safe, yes, but Rosa, you don't love him, not that way.'

'No. He's more like a father than a husband. It would just feel wrong.'

'Can you imagine being with him . . . properly?'

I closed my eyes and tried. Nothing. I thought of lying with Thomas that last night in Oberfals and immediately my stomach tightened. I thought of the professor again. Still nothing.

'No,' I said finally. 'But I am fond of him and I know he loves me and Laurin.'

Frau Schurter pursed her lips and frowned. 'You can't sacrifice yourself, Rosa.'

'But I can't think only about myself; I need to think about Laurin. He loves the professor.'

She shook her head. 'He loves you more. Look, he's a baby, he probably loves everyone he knows – Max and me, too – but that doesn't mean you can't leave us.'

She poured some coffee, then added the milk and stirred it. She offered a cup and saucer to me and I took it gratefully.

'Frau Schurter, what should I do?'

She put her coffee on the table and laughed. 'I can't tell you that. I was lucky – I had no ambition but to marry a good man with a good bank account. Ottmar is a bank manager, the man of my dreams.' She sighed and then looked at me and shrugged. 'The thing is, Rosa, you have something else: talent. You shouldn't be here in St. Gallen or in some field in Palestine planting trees. You should be in Paris. If you became successful there, you could be like Coco Chanel, a woman of means, and you could provide for Laurin and yourself without needing a man. I know it is a modern idea, but the war changed things. Women all over Europe did men's jobs, and there are widowed women everywhere who have to work.'

I stared at her, biting my lip.

'Of course, you couldn't go to Paris immediately,' she continued. 'You would have to start here, build up your clientele, maybe open a shop, make contacts first and then when you have more experience, move to Paris. You could do it. I'm sure.'

It was like a dazzling vision of a future I had never even dared imagine, like a candle being lit in the darkness. Suddenly, for the briefest moment in the flickering light of her vision, I could see a path, a way forward. Then, as abruptly as it had appeared, it faded, blown out by harsh reality. 'I can't,' I said, 'not with Laurin. It would be better for him to be in a family.'

★

It was impossible to sleep that night. Frau Schurter was right. I had a talent and, I realised, ambition. I had a surfeit of clients already. More and more of them wanted the dresses I made from scratch, not just alterations, and they trusted me to design them rather than copy them from magazines. I knew in my bones that, given the chance, I could succeed. The question was, where? I loved the professor as a father, mentor and guardian, but not as a husband.

It came down to two choices: either I stayed with the professor and gave Laurin stability and a good father, but sacrificed my own passions and dreams, or we took our chance on our own. I reasoned with myself that I had survived rape; letting the professor make love to me could never be that bad. I could close my eyes when necessary and maybe in time I would enjoy it, and we would be safe and cherished, albeit in a strange land. That seemed to be the sensible, rational solution, but my spirit revolted.

After playing out the different possibilities again and again, I knew what I had to do. I had left Oberfals on my own, now the professor could leave me alone here. It would not be as difficult, though I would have to find the way to make ends meet, pay rent, buy food and look after Laurin and me. I sat up the rest of the night going through the accounts I kept in an exercise book, calculating and recalculating my expenditures, growing profits and costs, estimating what I would have to take on without the professor, but whichever way I cut it, whatever I sacrificed as unaffordable luxury, I couldn't do it. It just would not add up. Without the professor's financial support I could not rent an apartment, meet all of our needs and afford to start up a shop. I needed to save and I needed more time to develop my skills. But the professor had made it clear that time was the one thing I did not have.

I turned over Frau Schurter's words in my head. I had dreamed about Paris before but never considered it seriously. The more I thought about it, the more convinced I became that Frau Schurter was wrong. It would take too long if I stayed in St. Gallen. No, I had to go to Paris first and throw myself in at the deep end, work and save, and then come back and set up shop. She was right about Laurin loving her and Max, and Herr Schurter being a good man.

Having made my mind up, I decided to act immediately. I knew that if I stayed, I would confide in somebody. And if I did, I would come to my senses and act rationally. What I felt was an impulse, a survival reflex. People talk now about fight or flight. My only fighting chance was to fly. I went into the professor's study and took a sheaf of paper. When there were no more words to write I drew off the golden band that the professor had given me when he bought me my shoes. The wedding ring looked so small sitting on the letter. I slid them both into an envelope.

I did not have long to pack as there was little time before people would begin to stir. I stitched a hidden pocket into my coat and stowed enough money that I hoped would see me through for a month and stuffed the rest of my savings back into the sock and wrapped it, along with Laurin's clothes, in a blanket and wedged the bundle on to the rack under Laurin's pram. Keeping Laurin quiet was my greatest concern as the professor generally woke to his cries, but thankfully he did not stir. As soon as we were outside, I wheeled the pram round to Frau Schurter's house. For a moment, as I stared at Laurin, my beloved son, I nearly faltered. He was a chubby child and with his thin blond hair curving round his sleeping face, he looked like a cherub on a church fresco. He was so beautiful. I kissed him goodbye, hammered on the door, then ran to the station.

The first westbound train left minutes after I boarded. Once the train had left the town behind, I opened the small suitcase that Herr Maier had carried over the mountains into Switzerland for me. In amongst my clothes I found what I was looking for: the small cardboard packet that Herr Maier had handed to me as we had left. 'Swiss medicine,' he had told me. 'Wonderful stuff, it cures most things.' Never in my life had I needed relief from pain as much as then, so I opened the packet and took out one of the small white tablets. I doubted very much that it could cure the searing pain that cramped me into my seat, but I let the sweet-sour taste melt into my mouth. Aspirin was known as a healer, a cure-all. I promised myself I would come back for Laurin.

The pain has never left me. I still have aspirin here in my cupboard.

7

No. 5

It might strike you as strange, but I always put my perfume on at this stage. Yes, ma chère, I am still unclothed but I like to dab it here, here, here, here and here. Always on both sides: symmetry is as important in scent as it is in appearance. Under the ears, the insides of my wrists and a dab in the hollow between my breasts.

Have you ever noticed how the same perfume can smell like a pissoir on one woman and like honeysuckle and jasmine on another? It is the magic that happens when the parfumier's concoction mingles with a body's own oils. I, for example, cannot wear Chanel 19. The looks of distaste, anxious sniffs and wrinkled noses on my first outings with it taught me that quickly. Years of trial and error are such that I have these few gallant companions. They are small, no? That is because I never buy eau de toilette, which is mainly alcohol, or even eau de parfum, which is only a little better. I only use parfum, which has the highest concentration of fragrance. My five dabs last most of the day and the higher concentration of perfume oils is kinder on my skin, compared to the cheaper, pungent alcoholic mist that evaporates in a few hours. And don't you think, ma chère, that – despite the outrageous cost – the few ounces of liquid are worth it? Like most good things it comes at a princely price in tiny bottles – like tiny crystal bank vaults. Look at the exquisite design, the colours and shapes, the way they throw the light; each one is a work of art.

Each one represents a mood, for me. Aspirin was not the only treasure that I kept in my small suitcase when I left St. Gallen. Prize amongst my possessions was my first adult gift, the first homage ever paid to me as a woman. On my birthday, the professor had given me the plain rectangular bottle with its no-nonsense crystal stopper, filled with Coco Chanel's first fragrance. I've never been without a bottle of Chanel No. 5 from that day to this. It is simply feminine, beginning with rich neroli then drifting through sweet jasmine followed by a strong, lingering hint of sandalwood.

Before Frau Schurter had made me think of it seriously, this perfume had let me dream that Paris was where my destiny lay. If I was to be a dressmaker, then I had to go to the capital of fashion. I planned to work in an atelier, somewhere I could learn more techniques, more stitches, how better to cut. And, like Frau Schurter, I admired how Coco Chanel had made it as a woman on her own terms.

In 1946, Europe was not the tourist destination it is now. It was in ruins, piles of rubble and skeletal buildings everywhere – like one sprawling scrap heap. Paris, however, was still magnificent, despite having been scarred by the German occupation. I walked that city day and night looking for work and somewhere to stay. Trash littered the streets and I had to sidestep dog excrement on the sidewalks every few paces, but every building I passed, however run-down, however shabby, was like a palace to me. I marvelled at the tall windows and the massive doors. I peeked in, past open shutters, at the elegant rooms with high ceilings.

The wad of money I had secreted in my coat became thinner day by day. I stayed in a cheap hotel near the Gare de Lyon, bought bread and cheese in the shops and drank water from the bathroom tap, but still my rate of spending frightened me. I had not forgotten those first days and nights in St. Gallen. I calculated that I had enough for two weeks. By the end of the first week I began to eat even less; one big soup a day in an inexpensive café where I could sit and rest.

From the moment I left the hotel in the morning until late afternoon and the fall of dusk I walked the streets in the Sentier district. It was in the quiet backstreets that the *fournisseurs* worked: the embroiderers, feather-workers, sequin sewers, button-makers, lace-makers, all the artisans in ateliers and workshops behind the closed wooden doors. I walked from door to door scrutinising the small brass plaques flanking them, names and companies etched out in the polished metal. I would ring a bell and ask for work, and time after time I was refused. Every day I returned to the hotel without hope. I was miserable. I had come to Paris dreaming that I would make something of myself and all I was doing was wearing out the shoes the professor had bought me. I had given up so much to fulfil my dream, and yet the more I walked the more foolish and hopeless I felt. I missed Laurin so badly, yet each day as I trudged from door to door, knocking, asking and being sent on, I reminded myself to be strong, like Thomas's Valkyrie, to keep going for Laurin.

At the end of another futile day knocking on doors, a spring breeze shook the young leaves on the trees in the Rue Tiquetonne as I turned the corner into Rue Montorgueil. From the few times I had been taken in to discuss work opportunities, I knew that often the studios were a long way up at the top of the buildings, where it was cheaper and there was better light, so I had learnt to knock, wait, then knock again and wait some more before giving up. I was about to turn away again from another unanswered knock, when the door opened a fraction and a sour-faced man looked me over. I was looking shabby by then but lifted my head and composed my face.

'Yes, what do you want?' he asked hesitantly, enunciating his words through a thick accent. His eyes were dark brown, his hair black, his nose sharp and long, his skin a shade darker than most Frenchmen.

'I'm looking for work,' I chanced in Italian. 'I'm an excellent seamstress, pattern-maker and cutter.'

He stared at me. I knew what he saw: not a compatriot, but a desperate, cheap worker.

'Come in,' he said, not bothering to be friendly or polite, 'I'll try you out.' He opened the door wide and pointed at the broad, curving stairs. 'We're at the top,' he said as he started up two steps at a time. Despite my hunger and fatigue, I raced up the stairs behind him.

As the summer heat subsided and the days darkened and shortened in the ever-colder atelier, the memory and terror of being hungry and homeless kept me bent over my stitches. The maestro only smiled when his clients came to inspect or commission work. The workshop specialised in stitching beads and sequins on to evening wear, and he had taken me in because he needed an extra pair of hands for the simpler tasks. His wages were pitiful but, in fairness, he provided me with a proper apprenticeship, giving me ever more complex work, and he allowed me to sleep on a cot at the back of the atelier. I worked hard but found little joy in the concentrated effort of sewing bead after bead on to other designers' patterns.

I spent my time alone and lonely but I was too lost in imagining what little Laurin was doing to seek company. I thought about him all the time – his absence was like a physical presence, like a phantom limb. Every week I would send a letter to Frau Schurter in St. Gallen, begging her to tell Laurin how much I missed him, how I loved him and how I would return as soon as I had learnt enough to set up shop on my own. Each week I folded the bulk of my earnings in between the sheets of writing paper, keeping only enough money to meet my needs. I never got a letter back; I never gave my address.

The workload increased before Christmas, as women ordered something special for the holidays. On Christmas Eve, I found myself working like any other day. I had been in Paris nearly seven months, but had made no friends I could celebrate with. It was a weekday and as the night closed in around me I tried not to think of Christmas. Last year Laurin had not really understood what was happening, but this year he would be excited. I imagined him gathering around a tree singing carols with the Schurters. I put my work down and walked the streets, looking in the bars and cafés at the happy lives others were leading around me. There was a general air of glee that felt to me like it went

beyond the usual seasonal festivities. It seemed to take forever
to climb the long staircase back to the workshop.

When I eventually reached the garret I was surprised to see
the lights on, as I had turned them off when I had left. There
was a noise coming from the kitchen and as I approached, the
maestro came out carrying two chipped tumblers and a bottle
of wine.

'Merry Christmas, compatriot,' he said jovially. 'I thought you
should not be alone tonight.' He put the bottle down on the
scarred table where I worked and shoved a glass into my hand.

I forced a polite smile on to my face. 'Thank you, but—'

'You should be celebrating?' He was speaking rapidly and his
face looked oddly loose. I recognised that look, I had seen it too
often on my father's face: he had been drinking. '*Buon natale!*'

He drank some of the wine.

I raised my glass to toast with him. '*Cin Cin,*' I said, without
taking a sip. 'I've just come back to get my hat and scarf,' I put
my glass down on the table. 'I've been invited to friends'. I'm so
sorry.' I took my hat and scarf from the peg behind the door and
hooked my string bag over it, then turned before I left. 'Merry
Christmas, maestro.'

I spent the next few hours walking the streets again, this time
in a big loop down to the Place Vendôme, where I watched women
in glossy fur coats step out of cars with their attentive husbands;
to the Place de la Concorde and back along the Seine, whose
flow seemed thick and sluggish in the night. When I returned he
was gone. He had left the empty bottle and glasses on the table
for me to clear away. I felt so alone. It took me a long time to
fall asleep. On nights like these I dreamed of Thomas and the
last night we had shared in Oberfals. I had no idea if he had died
or been swallowed up in Russia or East Germany.

I was not surprised that the maestro appeared again when
fireworks crackled over the gabled rooftops announcing the arrival
of 1947. It was ten minutes past midnight and I was already in
my cot when I heard the door open. It was so cold there that I
slept in a heavy cotton nightdress and bed socks, but still I threw

on a cardigan as I scrambled out of bed. We met in the kitchen. He was clutching two glasses and a bottle of champagne.

'Happy New Year,' he said, making to kiss my cheeks. I stepped back and moved so that the table was between us.

'Don't open it. I don't drink.'

'But, *bella*,' he laughed, 'this is champagne! It's New Year's Eve!'

'And I need my sleep,' I said, trying to keep the tremor out of my voice. 'You asked me to finish the order tomorrow and if I don't sleep, my eyes will be sore and I won't be able to work.'

'Ah, I forgot tomorrow is a holiday. You could lie in,' he leered, glancing at the dark doorway into the tiny storeroom where I slept.

'But we have an order to complete, maestro, and Madame Fournel will not be happy with us if we don't finish it on time. Maybe next time, she'll go elsewhere,' I said. I thought that the threat of losing his best customer would bring him to his senses, but he just laughed again.

'Ah, tesoro, you should relax more.'

'I was relaxed sleeping,' I said, struggling to keep my temper.

He started to tear at the foil wrapping the cork. I stepped around the table and grabbed the bottle out of his hands.

'I think you should go now, maestro. We would not want anything to happen that we would regret.'

'Ah, *bella*, what makes you think we would regret a little celebration?' He stepped forward, slipped his hand round my waist and pulled me towards him. I raised my hand high and stared into his eyes, which were inches from mine. His hands were sliding down my hips.

'Maestro,' I spat. 'I could smash this bottle on your head and then you would fire me. Or I could smash it on my own and go to the police and say you assaulted me.' He blanched and I took pity on him. 'I know you're not a bad man,' I continued, more softly now, 'you're just lonely, like me. But no one is ever going to rape me again. Do you understand?'

★

The next Saturday I spent the afternoon making a coat. I had saved enough for the fabric from the little money I kept and had laid it out on the large sewing table. Inspired equally by Chanel and the knitted jackets that the farmers wore at home, I cut out simple, straight shapes, losing myself in the rhythm of the scissors.

I had just begun to tack them together when someone thumped on the door. My heart started pounding. I peered through the peephole and recognised Madame Fournel. I opened the door for her and she pushed past me without waiting to be invited in.

'Is the maestro here?' She was breathing so hard that she could hardly speak. She was a heavy-set woman and the four flights of spiral stairs, grand and elegant as they were, had taken their toll on her.

'No,' I said. 'He won't be back until Monday.' The maestro and I conversed in Italian and my French was little more than mangled Italian, but Madame Fournel understood me.

'Oh, no!' Her face paled and the perspiration on her brow made her look ill.

'Here, Madame Fournel, please sit and rest,' I said, pulling out a chair by the table where I had been working. 'I'll get you some water.'

When I came back from the tiny kitchen – if a sink with a single burner next to it can rise to that name – she was no longer sitting. She was standing over the fabric of my coat, examining the cut-outs, moving them this way and that, inspecting my simple tacking stitches.

'You did this?' she asked, without looking up at me.

'Yes,' I replied.

'Really?' She glanced at me. 'Just you, no one else?'

I was worried that she thought that I was stealing fabric, or misusing the maestro's facilities. 'Yes. I do it in my spare time,' I explained. 'I saved for weeks to buy the worsted. It's not the best, but I couldn't afford better.'

Madame Fournel rubbed the fabric between her fingers. 'The design, the cutting and the sewing by yourself?' She murmured as much to herself as to me.

I relaxed a little and considered my answer. I did not want to get in trouble – people were so precious about designs – but I decided in favour of honesty. 'Yes, but I took my inspiration from Chanel – I love her work and approach. But I also drew on where I come from.'

'And where is that?'

'The Alps,' I said, then added, 'northern Italy,' not expecting that to mean anything to her.

'You don't have an Italian accent,' she said, looking at me thoughtfully. Then she returned her attention to my work.

'Your talent is wasted here,' she said abruptly after a long time. She stood up as tall as her stocky build would allow and turned to look me in the face. 'If I were you, I would go and pack now and leave this place.'

I just looked at her blankly. She was not making any sense.

'I'm offering you a job,' she said with exaggerated patience. 'I'll double anything your maestro here is paying you and give you a proper apprenticeship. You're wasted on beads and sequins.'

I was momentarily unable to respond or move, but the chance to work for a proper courturier was something I had longed for, and an apprenticeship was my dream. Besides, an escape from the maestro's pathetic attempts to bed me would be most welcome.

'Are you coming or not?' she said, and then took a breath as if to gather herself and continued more kindly. 'I'm in a hurry and we need to work this weekend. We have a crisis.'

'Wait five minutes, madame. I'm coming.'

Madame Fournel had not been exaggerating about the emergency. In the taxi on the way back to her atelier she explained that she was no longer working for herself but had sold her company and been absorbed into a new fashion house, and she had less than three weeks to finish off a new collection. She said she was desperate for skilled seamstresses and knew that I would flourish there. I was already overawed by my sudden departure and my first ever taxi journey and her short explanation did not prepare me for the change from the tiny atelier to the new workplace.

Number 30 Avenue Montaigne was not just a house, but a small mansion. The structure dominated an entire corner of the street. It was six storeys high, with the first five storeys bathed in the light from six enormous windows on each floor. Only under the grey mansard roof did the rooms shrink to human dimensions. The building was awash with workmen painting every surface white or grey. I stood at the bottom of the stairwell, my hand resting on the cast-iron banister to steady myself. A few years before I had been living in a simple mountain village and now I felt I had walked into the centre of the universe.

'Now, follow me,' Madame Fournel instructed as she carried the pieces of my coat like a swaddled baby in her arms. 'We have three weeks to finish the first collection,' she puffed as she climbed the stairs, pushing our way past people running up and down. I had never seen such an army of workers, and I had to concentrate hard not to be distracted. 'There are ninety dresses to complete.'

She stopped on a landing. In front of us a door opened into a large atelier. Dozens of women and some men were bent over material, standing around dummies, fastening pins, altering, sewing, cutting. For all the motion and bustle it was quiet and there was an atmosphere of fierce concentration in the air.

'I need more skilled seamstresses. I brought everyone with me when the maître bought my company and I've been hiring more, but we still don't have enough.'

At the end of the room a short, balding man was standing staring at a mannequin that was wearing an unfinished dress. Next to him stood a man and a woman waiting in attendance. Madame Fournel marched straight up to the group of four and I trailed after her.

'Monsieur Dior,' she said, and the man looked round. He had a soft, full face, thin lips and a sharp, angular nose. I had no idea who this man was, but I remember being struck by how sad his hooded eyes looked. Knowing what I learnt soon after, ma chère, he was probably just exhausted.

'Yes, Madame Fournel. What can I do for you?' He turned back to the mannequin again. 'As you can see, I'm busy.' The two attendants glared at Madame Fournel fiercely, and she drew herself up to her full height.

'Yes, I know. That is why I have hired this young woman.'

'Can she sew?' he asked, without even looking at me.

'Beautifully.'

His glance rested on me like a butterfly before moving swiftly on. 'Then she is yours.'

Madame Fournel was shaped like a barrel on thin pin legs and despite her ability to create the fabulous garments in which the swan-like mannequins stalked around the atelier, she always wore a simple navy suit. She was a veritable magician; when she took up her long tailor's scissors or threaded a needle with her chubby fingers, she worked miracles of dexterity and speed, fashioning wonder from limp fabric. She helped out wherever there was a need – and there was always a crisis that required her intervention. The madness of preparing for Dior's grand opening in mid-February kept all the workers in a frenzy of activity.

It had been Chanel's name and style that had drawn me to Paris; I hadn't known that she was living in Switzerland. Now, I found myself one of an army of eighty-five workers, toiling for this unknown designer. Someone was pouring money into this fledgling business, that was evident from the numbers employed, and soon it became obvious why. I had grown up in a world starved of excess by the austerities of war. Our lives had been cold and bleak for too long, we had made do and mended, altered and repaired. After all those years of meagre fare, there was an appetite for more taste, texture, beauty. Dior seized the moment. He offered us luxury, opulence and heightened femininity. He wanted us to tighten our belts as never before, cinch in our waists, pad out our hips and behinds. Like the intricate petals of a flower, we created Dior's *Ligne Corolle*.

It was a vision that I understood but struggled with as I sat stitching the yards and yards of material that had to be gathered into each skirt. I had learnt my craft cutting and trimming the hand-me-downs of more fortunate women than myself and now here I was heaving such an excess of wool and silk into skirts that belonged to the past, to the days before the First World War, clothes that with their sheer weight and girth forced women into decorous passivity.

Each day the material would be cut and Madame Fournel would share out the pieces to the girls. For the first few days my fingers ached as I worked harder and faster than ever before. It seemed that every time any of us put down a finished piece, Madame Fournel would appear.

'Ah, *bien fait*,' she would say as she scanned the sewing, her eyes running the length looking for even, perfect stitches. Or, 'Perhaps you could redo this little bit, ma chère, this is not your best work, *n'est-ce pas?*' Somehow she coaxed the best out of us despite the pressure and fatigue.

On the first day, Madame Fournel had found another seamstress, Juliette, who needed someone to share her rent. We lived in a cramped, cold attic room, but it was close to work and she was a wholesome country girl who was happy to teach me her language in the evenings. We worked too hard for much banter, but conversations flowed slowly up and down the long trestle tables where we sat four in a row bent over the heavy satins and crêpes that spilled on to our knees and pooled around us like molten lead. As each day passed, I found myself able to understand more and more of what my companions were saying and my Italian morphed into French. A few weeks later, as I hurried upstairs one morning, eager to get to work, chatting to my roommate, I realised that I had found my path, that I might make it after all, that soon I would have learnt what I needed and then I could return to St. Gallen to fetch Laurin.

The last two days before the show, barely anyone slept. On February 12th, 1947, the shop opened for the showing of the first Christian Dior collection. All the staff were feverish with excitement; we knew that we were part of something extraordinary. And yet there was a fear that it would be too much, that the world was not ready.

Indeed, our work caused a sensation. Dior was declared a

genius and his vision dubbed the New Look. We slept well that night, our sleep hastened by fatigue and the champagne that Madame Fournel had shared out between us.

After the dazzling opening, our work eased off. We had more time to chat and there was a happy buzz in the atelier as we began sewing the calico *toiles* of the new collection. Madame Fournel introduced me to an electric sewing machine. Having learnt the basics on my old Singer in St. Gallen, I quickly mastered it and began what felt like a love affair. With no work left to finish in the evenings she permitted me to stay late and sew for myself. At last I could finish the coat she had first seen me making. In time, I fashioned my own wardrobe using offcuts and scraps leftover from the dressmaking.

Late one evening in April, when the days were beginning to lengthen and the light lingered in the workshop, I was working on a dress. I was using crimson silk that I had cut out of a pre-war dress I had found in the *marché aux puces*. It was a heavy, rich satin with a bias cut. It had no label so I could not tell if it was by Schiaparelli or just inspired by her. Thankfully, it had been made for a large woman so there was plenty of fabric for me to reshape. I had unpicked the dress the previous evening and was now laying it out, thinking and imagining. When I knew what I was going to do, I picked up the heavy scissors that Madame Fournel had taught me to use and began to cut.

To this day I'm not sure what it was – perhaps I caught a fleeting shadow – but suddenly I had the feeling I was being watched. I whipped around but could see no one there, and I soon returned to my work and forgot all about it. I laid out the first piece for the front and started on the back. When I had cut all the pieces and laid the front on top of the bottom I stepped back, appraised my vision and nodded in approval. It would work.

'You seem very certain, mademoiselle, of what you are doing,' said a voice from the shadows. If I was startled by it, it was nothing compared to my anxiety as I realised who it belonged to. I stared across the atelier until the outline of a head, then shoulders and finally a body emerged from behind the highly gathered skirts of a tailor's dummy standing on a plinth. The figure was short and as he came towards me the light caught the smooth surface of his head. It was Monsieur Dior.

I froze. In the few months that I had worked at Avenue Montaigne, Dior had been transformed from an unknown designer to the new deity of the fashion world. The building was not just the heart of his business but was like a temple to this new god. We executed his designs, we followed his instructions and wishes to the letter, but we did not approach him. I was arrested and uncertain as soon as I understood that he had been watching me. Yet the interest on his face told me that he was intrigued rather than annoyed.

'You haven't even done a drawing?' he enquired.

'No,' I said, my heart racing. I was both terrified and excited, determined not to put a foot wrong. 'I like to play with the fabric until . . . I can't explain it, until I just know how to cut it. I'm sorry, maître, is this wrong?'

He laughed and walked forward. 'Madame Fournel hired you, didn't she?'

'Yes, maître.'

He came closer. 'And you made this, too?' he asked, indicating the dress I was wearing, which I had indeed made from rescued fabric. As I nodded he noticed my coat hanging over the chair next to me. He picked it up, turning it over with great care. 'And this?'

'Yes, maître.'

He hummed as he examined it. 'I had noticed you. You know how to move and carry clothes, but I didn't appreciate that you had also made the clothes themselves.'

'I love it. I love the rush of an idea, the vision of how it would fall or sit. And, of course, I can't afford to buy my own clothes, not ones I like.' The words gushed out of me in a torrent. He was regarding me curiously, and my flood dried up.

Slowly, a small smile turned up his mouth. 'It is interesting,' he said lightly. 'You cut and sew like a fairy tailor, you dress like a queen – but not in my clothes. You are taking Balenciaga's ideas to Schiaparelli's fabrics and all the while you are tickling my nostrils with Coco Chanel's flowery number. Have I made no imprint on you?' He paused and moved the cut pieces around on the table. 'There. We can't have a traitor in our midst. *Au revoir.*'

He turned to leave. I had lost my chance, my golden opportunity. He had called me a traitor. I would have to pack up my few possessions and leave. It would be hard to find another such a job. Maybe Madame Fournel would help me, she had contacts.

I watched him as he disappeared through the open doorway and the sound of his footsteps ceased. I wiped a tear from my eye. Then suddenly he reappeared and called across to me, 'I will not have my staff stinking of Chanel's No. 5, is that understood?'

And with that, he turned and left.

8

Miss Dior

Of course, you are wondering whether I have any of Dior's perfumes. And look – here is the original Baccarat crystal bottle of Miss Dior. Compare them. Chanel No. 5, all lines and simplicity, whereas Miss Dior is not even in a bottle; it's an amphora, shaped and curved with crystal drops pendants – it is the essence of the New Look.

Like the maître's dresses, this is not a perfume for the faint-hearted. Here, sniff. Close your eyes. Breathe. Isn't it magnificent, ma chère? But I am getting ahead of myself.

After my encounter with Dior that evening in his atelier, I was too nervous to go in the next day to finish off the dress. It was a Sunday, so I trailed around the Louvre and then sat for a long time on a bench in the Jardin des Tuileries. The sun was beating down and I had to open my coat. Bursts of pale, fresh green leaves were beginning to bud and blossom, erupting like cascades of fireworks, draping the trees in their spring finery.

Trees and grass reminded me of home. In Falstal, the mountains were cloaked in evergreen firs, pines and spruce; flowers grew wild, scattered over the meadows, hiding in the scree, and I could pick as many as I wanted to. Here the tulips stood to attention above the neat array of lesser flowers, martialled by Napoleon's architectural order. I suddenly yearned for the clean, sharp Alpine air and the silent sound of an empty valley. But I couldn't go back yet. If I returned now I would have failed, would have abandoned Laurin for nothing. I had to make leaving him worthwhile. I had more to learn.

I walked back over the Pont Neuf, ambling down past the Boulevard St. Germain until I could not bear my hunger anymore, and wandered into a café. I was still saving every cent I could to send back to Laurin and nearly left when the only seat the waiter could find for me was a window seat, which I knew would cost me extra. But I felt almost faint with hunger and, I persuaded myself, this would be my only meal of the day.

I enjoyed watching people go by, and of course, the thing I paid most attention to was their clothing. The women were still wearing the tight, practical styles that saw us through the war. Dior's new approach was still building up like the vast, towering white clouds that gather silently in the blue summer skies above the mountains, before a thunderstorm unleashes all its transformative lightning and energy. But for the moment, all seemed calm and unchanged.

As I chewed my last morsel of leathery steak, a couple stopped in front of me. Above the woman's elegant shoes, I spied the unmistakeable folds, the pleats in black wool that I had sewn, and my pulse quickened. When she came in, her escort lifted off her coat and revealed the fitted creamy-beige jacket with its peplum that exaggerated her slender waist. She looked like a swan amongst geese in her Bar suit as she followed the waiter to a table. Whereas the other women moved with efficient grace and precision, she moved slowly, swaying in her swathes of luxury. With her rustling skirt, her narrow waist and padded hips – all the handiwork of me and the other girls in the atelier – her femininity and elegance was almost *de trop*. All around the café there was a hungry look in the other women's eyes as she gathered up her skirt before nestling down on a chair. The folds of her skirt fell heavily, like the first squall. The storm had come and I wanted to be in its eye. If only I could stay.

When I walked in on the Monday morning after Dior had called me a traitor, I was not surprised to be told that Madame Fournel wanted to see me.

She had an office but she never seemed to be in there. She always left the door open as she moved around between us inspecting, encouraging and correcting. Her office was the place she retired to think, order, plan and, on a few occasions, dismiss people. She had always been kind and encouraging but I knew she could be fierce, and a sense of dread climbed up my throat. I straightened up and braced myself as I rapped on her door, determined to meet my fate with dignity.

'Ah, Rosa.' She looked up from the designs she was examining on her desk. 'Come in and shut the door.'

My heart was pounding in my chest. The day before, sitting in the spring sun amongst the Parisians, I had felt that I could become one of them – and now my dream might be over.

'Sit down.' She pulled the design towards her, folded it and placed it neatly on a pile of tissue paper. Then she shifted her chair closer to the desk and regarded me steadily. 'Now. I have heard—'

'I'm so sorry, madame,' I burst in. 'I didn't intend to cause the maître offence.'

She paused, looking a little bewildered. 'Offence?'

'Yes, the Schiaparelli dress, the Chanel perfume, the design – he said it was like Balenciaga and—'

'What?' she asked incredulously, her face unguarded and showing her astonishment.

'He called me a traitor!' I cried. We both stopped and looked at each other. Her aghast look melted into a smile and then she started to laugh.

'You've got it all wrong, so wrong. He was impressed and he's asked – no, instructed – me to teach you everything I know. Everything. And, Rosa, it will be my pleasure.'

Number 30 Avenue Montaigne was unlike any other haute couture house. Everything was in-house, nothing was outsourced, we were like a family – even our *mannequins* were unique. Usually mannequins, or models, as the English would call them, were all of the same long, willowy mould – but not with Dior. He liked to have women of different ages, different girths, different shapes; but what they all had in common was that they knew how to wear their clothes.

And now he had chosen me to be not just one of his mannequins, but also his trainee assistant. Madame Fournel told me
that he had rung her up on Saturday night almost delirious,
saying that he had found his muse. When she came in on
Monday morning she found a handwritten note outlining all
she had to teach me and by when. I dropped my head into my
arms, trying to hide the hot, relieved tears spurting from my
eyes.

Over the next few months I didn't have time to pause and
think. Monday mornings would start with a fitting for evening
and day wear. I still wore my own clothes day to day, but all the
while the rail of beautiful outfits made specifically for me grew
more and more crowded. Almost every week I sat in a different
section, at a new table. I worked with the men and women tasked
with making the *toiles* mock-ups of the maître's designs, the
pattern-makers, the tailors cutting the fabrics, the seamstresses
like myself sewing and assembling, the experts in beading, embroi-
dering, feathers and lace. At the weekends Madame Fournel took
me to her apartment for more lessons. She lived alone in a
run-down block in the 6th arrondissement and seemed to be glad
for the company. After a month she asked me whether I would
like to move into her spare room.

When she opened the door of my new room for the first time,
I was unable to cross the threshold. It was like a fairy-tale princess's bedroom. In one corner, to the left of the tall window, was
an antique bed, the headboard matching the gilted wardrobe,
scrolled into the wall, somewhere between single and double.
Stowed at its feet along the wall was a gilt and inlaid wooden
wardrobe and in the space facing them across from the window
was a small bureau and chair with an opulent golden velvet seat.
It was perfect.

'In you go,' she said, ushering me in. She left me to take it
all in while she bustled over to the windows. 'I forgot to draw
these.' She started to tug at the heavy damask drapes, which hung
in great swathes that pooled richly on the floor.

'Oh, please leave them,' I cried. I joined her by the window and fingered the curtains. They were made of a rich, amber silk. 'They are perfect like this. Did you make them yourself?'

'Of course,' she said, giving me a surprised look. 'I never use this room, but I like things to be right.'

I looked out of the window at my view for the first time. We were on the second floor just skimming the leaves of the trees lining the street. If I half-closed my eyes I could pretend it was a grassy meadow stretching out before me. I surreptitiously rubbed my face against the silk fabric, hoping she would not notice my tears. I felt like I had been rescued.

'Oh, Madame Fournel,' I finally managed. 'This is all so beautiful.'

'Yes,' she said, looking gratified at my obvious delight. 'It was a stroke of luck getting it all.'

'I can't thank you enough, for this, for everything.'

'Don't be silly,' she scoffed. 'Women should look out for each other, that's all. It's like all this,' she said, sweeping her hand around the room.

'What do you mean?'

She walked over to the bureau and pulled out the chair. 'Why don't you unpack while I tell you?'

'Of course, but it won't take long,' I said as I lifted up my battered suitcase and placed it on the bed. It was no longer empty but full of the clothes I had made. The new wardrobe was still hanging at work in the Avenue Montaigne for the moment.

'You see, during the war, just there opposite me, in that building there was an . . . establishment.'

I paused in the middle of hanging up a dress, my interest piqued. 'A what?'

'A brothel.'

'Oh.' I went to the window. 'There?' A chill passed through me.

'Yes.'

'It looks . . . normal.' I stared at it. There had been many times when I was looking for work when men had offered to 'buy me a meal'. It would have been so easy to have ended up in such a place. I began to unpack my dresses, feeling a little less exuberant now.

'I like to be polite, so I always greeted the madam and the girls – you know, "*bonjour*". They stayed open because they serviced high-ranking Nazis – at least, that is what I deduced from the large cars and SS drivers waiting down below every night. At some point, they fell out of favour. Monsieur Lambert, from the patisserie, said that it was because a Kommandant's wife contracted an unpleasant disease. Whatever, they were all arrested and all the furniture was thrown out on to the pavement.'

I glanced down, imagining these beautiful furnishings piled up like trash. I knew what it was to be chancing fate on the streets, and shuddered. 'That's terrible,' I said.

'Yes, and a waste,' she said, then her tone brightened. 'So, I paid young Pierre – you'll meet him, the concierge's son – to carry it all up here.' The furniture all seemed very elegant to my untrained eye – and costly, I guessed from my hours spent in the flea markets. These pieces were princely in comparison to the junk I could afford.

'They must have been very beautiful girls, to afford all this,' I said quietly.

'I found the madam's accounts in the bureau, and they certainly earned it. But it did them no good. They were all sent away to camps.' She joined me at the window and fingered the amber curtains.

We knew enough about the camps by then for us to both pause. 'Did you ever see them again?' I asked.

'Yes.' She sighed. 'About a month after the war I saw the madam leaning against the wall outside. She had come back to see if there was anything left. I invited her up to eat and then wrote her a cheque for the furniture. Obviously not the shop price,' she said, 'but enough to get her back on her feet. She could not thank me enough when I gave her back her account books. An independent woman like that should not have been made to suffer in that way.'

In my world, women were still meant to grow up and get married.

I still hoped that I would go back to St. Gallen, find Laurin and resume some sort of family life. But as Madame Fournel talked of the brothel owner as just another independent woman, with such sympathy, I realised that I had more in common with them than with Ida Schurter. I finished unpacking in silence, trying to comprehend what this revelation meant for me and my destiny.

When the room was tidy and the suitcase stowed on top of the wardrobe, I joined Madame Fournel again at the window.

'Didn't it bother you how she earned her living?' I closed my eyes, fearing her response, fearing what she would think of me if she knew everything.

'No, Rosa. I've never been married, and from what I can see, women have to struggle to be independent. They can use their looks to marry or whore – to me it's the same – or they can use their brains to work hard. I respect that. She might have been a prostitute herself once, but the madam had no more looks; all she had was her graft and brains. Her accounts told her story – she was sharp and generous.'

'Thank you for everything, madame.' I bit my lip. 'Their fate could have been mine.'

'Never,' she snorted. 'That was never going to be your fate; it's why I liked you. You are beautiful – ' she threw out her hands in a gesture as if to say 'of course', then continued – 'you could have taken that path – and it's not easy either – but you chose a different struggle. It was your work and skill that got you the job with me, and the glimpse of your talent that has excited Monsieur Dior. He has mannequins enough not to need your beauty; that is just the icing on the cake.'

From that moment on, for the first time since I had left St. Gallen, I did not sink into pining and misery every minute I wasn't working. Instead, I worked with Madame Fournel at home, going over fabrics, patterns, stitches. However busy I was, though, however exhausted and excited, every night as I got into my ancient bed and felt its covers settle over me I would reach for my pen and paper and compose a little more of my weekly letters to Frau Schurter and my beloved Laurin. I was still spending little money and had saved by moving in with Madame Fournel so was able to send even more than before along with each letter. Every week I thought of giving her my address, but my fear of being found before I was ready was greater than my desire to hear news – or maybe it was that I was frightened what I would do if I realised how much I was missing.

One radiant June morning the doorman at 30 Avenue Montaigne informed us as we shed our summer coats that the maître was expecting Madame Fournel and Mademoiselle Rosa in his office. Madame Fournel was pleased – she gripped my elbow and whispered that it was time.

We climbed the stairs spiralling up to his floor and then walked until we reached the big double doors at the heart of our little world. They were open and Dior was sitting at his desk, the day's newspaper spread in front of him. I had barely seen him since that evening in the winter. He greeted me when we passed in the corridors, but never stopped to talk or enquire how I was getting on. All I knew was that he was busy.

'Ah, Madame Fournel and her protégée,' he said, a grin curling his lips. Just like that night I could not read his tone, though I suspected him of irony. 'Rosa, welcome. Join me.' He rose from his chair and began to walk towards the doors that led into an adjoining room, his studio.

He stopped in front of a tailor's dummy and turned to me with an air of gravity. 'Rosa,' he said, catching me in his intense gaze. 'Do you feel ready?'

'Yes,' I said gravely, then on impulse, I added, 'although I'm not quite sure what for.'

For a split second I thought I had offended him, but then his face puckered, and he barked out a throaty laugh. He pivoted to the dummy. 'I'm unhappy about this dress,' he said, brushing his hand over the white cotton toile. The skirt was wide but not as voluminous as the pleated skirts of his first Bar suits. The bodice was slim-fitting and had the same tidy collars as the jacket from the original suit.

'It will be in black silk, but I can't get the flow right.' He sounded irritated and frustrated. 'You have a feel for Schiaparelli and Balenciaga. What do you think?'

I glanced at his face. Dior was asking me, a nobody, what I thought. I was stunned. I turned to Madame Fournel, who smiled as if to say 'go ahead'.

'Well?' Dior said.

I took a deep breath and began to walk around the dress, pulling the material, inspecting the pleats and darts, examining it from every angle. This was the test that Madame Fournel had been preparing me for. The closer I looked, the more certain I became that I could see what he wanted, what the dress needed. I took a step back and flashed a glance at Madame Fournel, who gave me another encouraging smile. This was my chance and I realised that I had to give it my all and not hold back.

'This cut, maître, would be too severe.' My heart was pounding and I knew I was gabbling. I paused to slow myself down. Dior was listening intently and showed no sign of anger at my implied criticism. 'What you gave the world last year was femininity, softness, curves. This collar and these tight sleeves – they are for working women, and such a woman doesn't wear your dresses. Look here, you could let the sleeves drape. And the neckline, let it be loose and flowing, let the silk do its work. Don't pull it into a straitjacket.'

'Ah ha. You mean something like this.' He scattered sheets of paper over his desk as he searched for one in particular. 'Voilà!' He held up two sketches on one sheet. The first was of a full-length medieval dress with long draped sleeves and a low neckline, which was transposed in a neighbouring sketch to his Bar silhouette.

I studied them for a moment. 'Yes,' I said, pausing to deliberate. 'But both necks are wrong.'

'Christian?' Madame Fournel interrupted us.

'Yes,' Dior said impatiently.

'Can I get back to my work now?'

'Yes, Madeleine.' He flashed a smile at her. 'Thank you.'

★

And that was it. You can see that dress we first worked on now in the Met. It was not ready until the next winter season. The rapport between us, however, was immediate; we were motivated by the same drive, the same compulsion to achieve perfection. From that day on he used me as his design assistant, as well as one of his mannequins – when I went home that night I was surprised to find my new wardrobe had been taken from the atelier and was hanging in the gilt cabinet inherited from the brothel. He never came up with an official title for me, but I was his muse and helpmate. We laughed and argued, we agreed and disagreed, but I pushed him to greater and greater heights.

Dior had become an overnight sensation and he was deluged with invitations for dinners and soirées, trips to the opera or theatre, and he began to take me as a companion. After a few events he added English lessons to my timetable, so that I could converse with the rich Americans.

Madeleine (Madame Fournel and I were now tutoying) would wait up for me and help me hang my dresses and skirts up as I disrobed. Sitting together at the kitchen table, each of us clutching a hot, sweet cocoa, she would question me insatiably about who I had met, the politicians and financiers, the diplomats and the moneyed rich, the fine gentry, the Americans in exile.

In late August Dior returned from his summer break on the Normandy coast near Granville, where he had grown up. He looked relaxed and rested, ready to work but still in a playful mood.

'Rosa. Tonight you will come with me to dine. It'll be dreadful industrialists and scientists and I'll need you there to keep me sane.'

I sighed. These dinners were truly dull, but I understood why he took me: to show off his masterpieces. 'What's the occasion?'

'Reconstructing the economy. I've become an expert on that, too, it seems. All I know is how to make women into flowers!' Suddenly he wrinkled his nose. 'Speaking of which, you're still wearing that perfume.'

I grinned. 'Only because I have no choice, maître.'

Dior was having his own perfume developed and had spent a lot of money spraying scents in the shop floors of the building to try their appeal out on his clientele. But still I used No. 5. Each of his attempts at a perfume were either too much, or not enough.

I had been fitted for the most glamorous evening dress I had ever seen a few weeks before and we were both excited about its debut. It was a new line he was working on, tight silk on the bodice, a slimmer skirt with a bustle draping down from my derrière. Even though it was one of his own creations, even though I knew his interest in me was of course only professional in nature, I knew how good I looked when Dior drew in his breath as I came down to meet him. *'Pas mal,'* I heard him mutter under his breath.

The evening began with the great and the good of industry, commerce and science milling around in awkward little groups. Some of the men were rich, some were famous and a few, like Dior, were both. The women were dressed well. Although only a handful wore Dior's gowns, they began to cluster around the maître as soon as we walked in – but so did the men. Dior had novel ideas for business and especially exports and he was as fascinating to the men as to their wives. He had his eyes on the American market; I knew that plans for the opening of a store in New York were in hand. He understood that his already iconic name was an opportunity to mint gold – and, ma chère, people flock to gold. After I had ritually complimented the women on their attire and listened modestly to their praise of mine, I moved around the room weaving in and out of conversations. My job was to be seen, to be a mannequin, to sell his vision. The world was at Dior's feet, and where they trod, my elegantly shod feet followed.

But that night, they hurt. I was still not accustomed to the shoes Dior would have me wear. All my life I had worn sensible footwear: lace-ups I could walk up mountain paths in, boots I could survive winter snow in, brogues I could wait tables for a whole day in, that let my feet rest between strides. The shoes I wore now were pointed, high-heeled pumps, as painful as they were chic. I could not stride in them but had to take small, delicate steps, and soon I needed to sit down. I turned away from the crowds and moved towards the windows. I leaned against the windowsill, taking some of the weight off my feet, and looked out at the view of grey rooftops. I must have sighed loudly because barely had I let the air pass through my lips when a man's voice summoned my attention.

'However bad a party it is, it can't be that bad.'

My head whipped round. The man facing me must have been the youngest in the room. His face was not fat and overfed like most of the other guests and his suit was shabby. He was certainly not an industrialist. 'No,' I said coolly. 'It's not the party. It's the shoes.'

He looked down at them. 'Feet naturally splay,' he said, ignoring my frostiness. 'Your shoes come to a point. The heel is high and tips you forward. It alters your posture and gait. Have you any idea how much pressure you are subjecting your foot to? It's like walking around carrying an elephant. Fashion!' He grimaced theatrically. 'You must be mad.'

I raised my eyebrows. 'I would have thought it rather impressive that I can carry an elephant across the room and look graceful.'

'Touché,' he said with a big grin then turned his head as the bell tolled for dinner and a butler summoned us in. 'After you,' he said, still smiling. 'Let me watch you carry your elephant.'

I was used to people watching me – I was, after all, a mannequin – but I knew that this man was not interested in the gown or even shoes as I turned away from him and headed to the table. I straightened my back and tried not to swing my hips too much.

I was not sure if I was pleased or annoyed when I proved to be sitting with him. He sat down next to me and handed me the place card, which read: *Charles Dumarais, Chief Chemist, Research Division, Coty.*

'Dr Charles Dumarais, pleased to meet you,' he said, extending his hand.

'Mlle Rosa Kusstatscher.' I gave him mine and then turned to introduce myself to my other neighbour.

Throughout the soup course I tried to devote all my attention to the middle-aged banker on my right, but I was aware the whole time that Charles Dumarais was making the attractive lady on his left laugh. I tried not to care.

Then, while we were waiting for the deft waiters to present us with the langoustine, he leaned over and whispered, 'I think you managed very well. No one else here is aware of your elephant.'

I masked my amusement and ignored his remark. He was unlike anyone else I had met at these dinners; it alarmed me. I retreated to safe ground and asked the same question I asked of most people I met at these gatherings. 'So, what is it that you do, Dr Dumarais?'

His dark brown eyes dimmed. 'Needs must. I make smells.'

'What do you mean?' I asked, my curiosity catching fire.

'Just that,' he said. 'I manufacture scents for perfumes.'

'Are you good at it?'

He looked at me long and hard, as if to gauge whether I was serious. 'Let's just say I'm better at making perfumes than you are at carrying your elephant.' I sat back, both shocked and refreshed by his directness.

'You have a high opinion of yourself,' I said, returning the volley.

'No,' he said, 'I'm just being honest. I am a good scientist with a sensuous nose.' He picked up his wine glass and inhaled deeply.

'Surely you mean sensitive?'

'No, sensuous,' he said. 'You see, I can't tell you which château this wine comes from, but I can tell you that the soil was thin and gravelly, that the sun was hot and fierce, the grapes were baked intensely; you can smell and taste the heat. And the wine is smooth and oily – there is a lot of alcohol. This is a wine from the south. But I don't know its name. It's not about knowledge, but rather sensing provenance, the essence of something.'

My experience with men was limited. I had learnt how to deal with drunken approaches. I had seen how other women smiled but kept their distance from powerful men. I had fallen in love with my earnest Thomas. Dr Dumarais, however, was like a boy back in the schoolyard. He was showing off, trying to impress me. He was flirting with me and I knew instinctively what to do. I smiled. 'So, in short, you think you are talented?'

He shrugged. 'I'm the best,' he said as he took another sip of the Châteauneuf-du-Pape. He cocked his head and watched my reaction, so I took a moment to consider. The words were arrogant, but he was not showing off. He seemed to be just being factual.

'Well,' I said slowly. 'How would you like an impossible challenge?' I tried to look serious.

'That depends. Who would set the challenge?'

'Me.' I was failing; a smile was spreading across my face.

'In which case,' he replied, beaming, 'yes, probably.'

'I need a perfume. That is to say, we need one.'

'We?' Our eyes met and I felt a rush of heat flush over me. 'Who is we?'

'Christian Dior and myself.' I did not want him to see my blush, so turned and gestured down the table. 'That's him, talking to the lady in green.'

'You want me to make a perfume for you?' I could feel his eyes drilling into me. I dared not turn back. 'That would be easy, Miss Dior.'

9

Arnica

As you can see, Miss Dior and No. 5 are not the only two perfumes I own. Over the years I have been lucky enough to receive other fragrances. Not all to my taste, I must admit, but a gift is a gift that needs to be cherished for the spirit in which it was offered. In any case, I have found that all but the most discerning man could be cuckolded by another man's scent purporting to be his. For the most part, ma chère, it is enough just to display the bottle prominently on my dressing table and wear another, more suitable choice.

Ah, it is the large bottle that has caught your eye behind the shiny crystals and poisonous shades of my collections. That is indeed a special bottle. See that heavy amber liquid. Now, inhale deeply, draw in beyond the alcohol – a smell of resin and hay, of mountains. It is arnica steeped in schnapps. There is nothing better to heal swellings, strains and bruises. Of course, picking wildflowers is illegal now, but when I was still living in Oberfals my mother would send us out to pick the flowers. I found it deeply satisfying to snap off the lemon-yellow blooms from the stems.

Each flower head is made up of a host of tiny trumpet-like florets packed densely across the central disc, and this was ringed by a dozen or so thin, scrappy petals. The outer petals came off easily, but it was hard to shred the trumpet blossoms in the centre. We would fill a basket with this sunburst of heads and then take them back to my mother, who would force them in the bottle of schnapps she had set aside for the purpose. I know you won't believe me, but this very same bottle has been with me since I was first given it in 1947. But I'm jumping ahead of myself.

Thomas Fischer had come into my life slowly. He had arrived, uniformed and unremarkable, with the other German soldiers in Oberfals and then gradually, through his behaviour, he had stood out and caught my attention. His kindness had won me over little by little, so when he had asked me for that kiss on the rocky outcrop and first brushed his lips against mine, the realisation that I loved him had settled like snow blanketing the world. Until that evening, nothing and no one had made my love for him melt.

Meeting Charles could not have been more different. The next morning I woke early, giddy with excitement. I remember putting my make-up on that morning and then taking it off as I could see I looked lovely without it; my eyes were ablaze. In the end I put on only my lipstick, hoping that no one would notice.

But Dior had an eye for detail.

'You're distracted?' he said when I had failed to respond to a question. 'And no *maquillage*?'

I could not help smiling as I said, 'I'm sorry.'

'Do you want to tell me so that we can concentrate on this design?'

'Well,' I began, struggling to control my excitement. 'I think I have found the right man for our parfum.'

'Ah, so that's what you were talking about last night.' Dior turned away, a flicker of a smile on his face. 'So, what is the plan?' He examined the folds on the model's dress.

'Well, you know the director at Coty, don't you? Can you persuade him to second Dr Dumarais to us?'

He regarded me over the model's head. 'Is he any good?'

I shrugged. 'I have a hunch that he will do you justice.'

He moved around the model. 'I think it is the wrong fabric. You were right.'

'When am I ever wrong?'

He chuckled. 'Alright, let's follow this hunch of yours.'

Dior was not one for delay. It took only a few weeks to nego-tiate an arrangement with Coty but time seemed to drag in the interval. As soon as the necessary agreements were drawn up,

Dior told me to liaise with the chemist. I had to send Charles a letter explaining his brief. I set to work immediately, yet I could not write it. Whatever Dior's secretary read back to me seemed wrong; too formal, too much detail, too pompous. In the end I picked up a pen and wrote:

> *Dear Dr Dumarais,*
> *　Make a perfume for me.*
> *　Yours sincerely,*
> *　Miss Dior*

His reply came two days later – not that I was counting, ma chère. I just knew the large, thickly inked, loopy scrawl had to be his, and I fumbled opening it. Inside the envelope was a handwritten questionnaire – no cover note, just two pages of questions. He wanted to know all my likes and dislikes: my favourite flower; my preferred breakfast, lunch and dinner; red or white wine, dry or sweet. I answered all the ones I could – how could I compare tennis to skiing when I had never picked up a racquet? – and tucked it in another envelope, also without a covering note, and had one of the office boys deliver it.

On his return the boy handed me another note and complained that Dr Dumarais had made him wait in his laboratory while he had read my answers and penned his reply. I opened the note and read:

> *Steak au poivre or with sauce béarnaise or sauce archiduc?*

I put the note on my desk, sent the boy away and spent the day as usual.

But that night I lay in bed oscillating between the intense richness of a béarnaise sauce with its tart kick of tarragon, the heat of large flecks of black pepper, and the mellow, comforting smoothness of the creamy mushroom archiduc sauce. I tasted each sauce in my mind, I considered texture, aroma and hunger. Pepper was exciting and spicy but a short-lived sensation; mushrooms were soothing and substantial. Thomas had been a vegetarian, he loved mushrooms.

When Thomas came into my mind, I gave up all thought of sleep and sat up, turning on the lamp beside my bed. I had never consciously given up hope of seeing him again, yet as I thought about it, I realised that the *idea* of loving him had slowly but surely replaced the *feeling* of loving him. I didn't even know if he was alive or dead, if he had ever gone to St. Gallen to find me or met someone else and forgotten all about me. It was over three years since I had said goodbye to him, two years since the war had ended. Perhaps it was time to let the precious memory of him go.

At eleven the next morning I rang a café near Charles Dumarais' lab and had a steak béarnaise delivered to him. The following day I received a note saying that he would invite me to test the perfume when it was ready. The note was attached to some wax paper that was wrapped around a slice of ripe brie, so ripe that when Madeleine and I unwrapped it that night the cheese oozed over her grey and white marble dish.

And then silence. I had not expected a perfume to be developed and distilled in one day, but after a week I was becoming restless. Each morning I dressed with deliberate fastidiousness, just in case. My hunger grew by the day so that when at last a note was delivered to my office, I barely had time to tell Dior where I was going before I found myself on the street, still throwing on my jacket as one of our doormen hailed a cab.

I had never been so far outside Paris as the Coty factory in Suresnes. It was on the banks of the Seine just over the river from the Bois de Boulogne. All through the long journey I stared out of the window. The taxi left me outside the large gates and I approached what seemed more like a mansion than a factory. The receptionist had me escorted by a morose janitor, who led me to the second floor and pointed down a corridor, grunting that it was the third door on the left.

I went to knock but hesitated, then turned the knob, opened the door and plunged into his lab. I wanted to see him *au naturel*. Initially my eyes had to strain to see him as the blinds were pulled closed over the great windows and the lighting was poor. As my eyes adjusted to the gloom, it was as if I had stumbled into a sorcerer's cave rather than a modern scientific laboratory. Bunches and branches of trees, flowers, shrubs and herbs hung suspended in neat rows from the ceiling. Bottles, tubes, vials, burners, flasks to generate and condense steam, separators, vessels to receive precious fluids, pipettes and red rubber hoses stood in crowds on the tables alongside an array of tiny bottles with gold, amber, yellow, green, brown and clear liquids. Yet there was no chaos; it was like watching a finely tuned orchestra playing a gypsy dance. Charles was at the far end, sitting with his back to me and – from his air of concentration and small, jerky movements – writing, his pen moving rhythmically like a conductor's baton in a passage of allegro. There was a tiny vial on the desk next to his papers.

For a moment I could not move. I knew with absolute certainty that my life was about to change. There was nothing to base this knowledge on – a conversation at a dinner party, a few notes, an exchange of food and then silence – but I knew. I closed the door behind me.

The room was quiet and the linoleum failed to silence the tap of my elephant heels on the floor, yet Charles did not turn around. As I walked down past the glass constructions laid out on the dark wooden tables full of bubbling, steaming and dripping gases and liquids, I felt as if my senses were being extracted and condensed into this moment. The tiny movements that had indicated that he'd been writing had stopped and he shifted in his seat, his spine stiffening. I slowed until I stopped just behind him. I reached out towards his shoulder but then, before my fingertips could touch his frayed collar or his pale neck, I retracted my hand.

'I suppose that must be it,' I said. 'On the desk.' My voice sounded shaky, not calm and measured as I wanted. I took a step back as he started up from his chair and turned to me. His large, dark eyes refracted the little light the lab offered, and I could sense that his desire for me was as equal and palpable as mine for him.

'Yes. It is,' he said casually, twisting around and taking hold of the ampoule. 'I think I've captured you. Be careful with it. It is all I have for now.'

He dropped the tiny bottle into my outstretched hand, without touching my skin. I prised the stopper off and breathed it in. The scent so familiar to you now, ma chère, was, at that first ever inhalation, extraordinary. It has been much copied since, but back then it was unique and it was the essence of me. That first heady rush of trees, the chypre, evoking moss on the forest floor, and the release of resin as I crunched on the pine cones high in the mountains of my childhood; and then came the sweet jasmine smell of a young girl in love, my time with Thomas; and the sweetness was tempered by the lavender and neroli, the young woman I became; and finally the rich base notes of moss, sage and patchouli announced the strength and resilience of this woman standing in front of this genius, this man.

'You have done it.' I let my breath escape in a sigh. 'I knew you would.'

As I tried to nudge the stopper back into the tiny vessel, my fingers suddenly clumsy, he leaned forward, almost nuzzling my neck, but did not touch me. Instead, he hovered so close I could feel his breath and then he sniffed. He inhaled deeply. I pulled in air as if I would faint, breathing in a smell of olives and cheese, a sweet, musky scent from his curly hair. The urge to bury myself against him was so intense I had to force myself to breathe out. Then he sat back on his desk, smiling.

'Yes. I've got it right.'

I must have looked dazed or unsteady; I was certainly quivering because he took the vial off me and held out his chair, his eyebrows raised in a question. I shook my head. 'You sit in the chair, I'll sit on your desk,' I ordered as I tried to gather myself.

He shrugged but obeyed. My reasoning was simple: nothing was so enticing as elegantly crossed legs, and this opportunity to dangle my silk-stockinged calves in front of him was not one I was going to miss.

'The perfume is perfect. We'll take it and start manufacturing plans immediately.'

'Yes. Yes.'

'And I'll get our lawyer to draw up contracts.'

'Fine. Are you done?'

I panicked. Was he going to dismiss me, now that our work was done? 'Well, yes,' I said, wondering if I had read him wrongly.

'Rosa, all that is trivia,' he said, gesturing at the vial of perfume and the lab. 'You know that, don't you?'

I felt a blush sweep over me. 'Yes,' I acknowledged.

'We have more serious things to talk about.' His voice took on a serious tone, but he smiled.

'Such as?'

'Why I haven't kissed you yet, for one.'

He used the informal *tu*, not the formal *vous*. The certainty that had propelled me until then transmuted itself into something as solid and real as gold. I wanted to slip into his arms, but something held me back. There was something deadly serious underneath his flirtation. I must have shown my tension.

'Aren't you interested?' He pulled himself back in his chair and sat up, distancing himself from me. 'Have I got it wrong?'

'No, no. You haven't,' I said hurriedly, emphasising the intimate *tu* form. He smiled and relaxed back into his chair. 'So why haven't you?' I asked.

'Because a gentleman would never kiss a lady, not until they have been on at least one date, and not until he's obtained her permission.'

I dipped my head in a mock bow. 'From this I deduce you are a gentleman?'

'Indeed.' At this point our smiles were so wide that the shine off our teeth must have made the lab brighter. 'Mademoiselle Kusstatscher, would you care to join me on Saturday night at 8:30 p.m. at Le Grand Véfour?'

I hesitated, not because I was undecided, but because I had heard of this restaurant, its exceptional cuisine and precipitous prices, and for the briefest of moments the idea of me, Rosa Kusstatscher from Oberfals eating at the Le Grand Véfour seemed more outlandish and unbelievable than the realisation that Charles Dumarais was as taken with me as I was with him.

But as you know, ma chère, a lady must keep her cards close to her chest. I simply said, 'Yes.'

Dior took control of my appearance. This was to be the first public outing of the new parfum, which he called 'Miss Dior' after me – although the legend has it named after his sister. He always insisted on perfection, but on this night he wanted me to be superlative. I think he was rather chuffed by the combination of the success of the scent and the little intrigue that formed in its concoction. For once he decided to underplay it. He settled on Maxim's wool crepe and silk velvet cocktail dress from his first collection.

'But, maître,' Madeleine argued, 'you know what the Véfour is like, it is so over the top, all the art décoratif, the gold, the painted columns and the chandeliers. She should wear this one, at least it is an evening dress.' She picked up a black one that had a silk gauze veil flowing over the figure-hugging dress beneath it. The straps were garlands of velvet leaves climbing over the shoulders, to the naked back, while the front was demurely covered with a spread bouquet of flowers. 'She would look like a goddess or fairy in it.'

'Precisely, Madeleine, precisely,' cried Dior. 'We want him to fall in love with Rosa, don't we? We don't want her to be part of the décor, we want her to stand out!'

Chanel might have invented the little black dress, but Dior's response was sublime. The skirt was not as grand as the full gathered *corolle* of the Bar suit, but the waist was tightly cinched in over a hip-hugging skirt that gave into a modestly gathered bloom. It had two practical, large pockets and the top had a deep, square-cut décolletage that was masked by an oversized bow, as if I was a present all wrapped up and ready for Charles. When I walked into the restaurant with its multicoloured flowery carpet, Pompeian frescoes and adorned ceilings, I saw instantly that Dior was right: less was indeed more. I could not help noticing heads turning as I walked past, ten minutes late – Madeleine had been insistent – but I was surprised when Charles failed to get up. I stood by my chair and waited. I have never seen a man struck dumb before but this clever, oh-so-confident pharmacist was, ma chère. If you ever have such a moment of triumph, treasure it; they are rare indeed. A waiter appeared behind me and pulled the chair out for me. Only then, as if woken from an enchantment, did Charles half-spring out of his chair, far too late.

'Mademoiselle Kusstatscher,' he said in a choked voice, 'I can't decide. Are you a work of art or a fairy-tale princess?'

'Dr Dumarais,' I chided, 'we're both old enough not to believe in fairy tales. As for the art, well.' I smiled. 'I am wearing it.' I gestured to my dress. 'And, of course, another masterpiece,' I said, holding out my scented wrist towards him.

He stood and leaned across the table, his face hovering just over the white skin of my arm, and inhaled. 'Ah. Perfect,' he whispered, looking into my eyes. He sat back in his chair as the same waiter materialised and lifted a bottle of champagne that Charles must have had waiting and filled our crystal goblets.

'To the future,' he said quietly, lifting his glass.

Needless to say, the food was better than anything I had ever eaten but, sadly, I was so wound up I could not finish any of it. Charles, it turned out, was not a big drinker, which – after my father – was appealing. We were still drinking the same bottle of champagne with our dessert. Our conversation danced from trifles to dreams. We told each other that we were both alone in this world: his family had died during the war, I had left mine behind. He wanted adventure and travel, I wanted to learn everything from Dior. Our curiosity about each other was matched and there was a solemnity underlying the flirtatious remarks and ripostes.

When we left, we started walking down the beautiful colonades then through the Jardin du Palais Royal, past the Louvre until we reached the Seine at the Pont du Carrousel, talking all the while. We slipped down on to the riverbank on our left and seated ourselves on one of the stone benches that lined the embankment.

We sat close but not touching, as our ceaseless conversation abruptly dried up.

'Was this business or pleasure, Charles?' I asked after a silence that felt more and more loaded.

He took my wrist, pressing his nose against my flesh and inhaling the scent on my skin. 'What do you think?' he asked as he let my hand go.

I could not think. It was the first time he had touched me. I felt a charge radiate out from where his fingers had held me tight.

'I think it was not business,' I said. My desire to take his hand and bury my face in his palm, to sniff him in turn, was over-whelming.

'We agree, then,' he said.

'In which case,' I began, trying to resurrect my capacity to string more than a few words together, 'I just wondered if the gentleman was going to ask permission – well, you know how things should go.'

He doffed an imaginary hat. 'The gentleman will take that liberty after he has discussed some other matters with the lady in black.'

'What can be so urgent?' I asked, trying to sound unaffected.

He hesitated a moment, clearly struggling with himself. 'It's nothing and everything.' He inched towards me and slid his hand down my arm to meet my waiting fingers. For a moment, we said nothing, our hands just exploring each other's. I could not understand; we clearly were drawn to one another, what could be so pressing that he would only hold my hand? There could not be many more romantic spots for a first kiss than by the Seine. I waited.

He stared straight ahead at the moving water of the river. 'If there is one thing I've learnt over the last few years it is that nothing is certain. But despite that,' he said, turning his face towards me, 'I feel certain about you. About you and me. If I'm right and not mad then you need to know this now.' He stopped and held my gaze, and it took all my strength not just to lean forward and press my lips against his. His face was etched with a combination of pain and shame as he continued. 'What you need to know now, however presumptuous it may seem on my part – but something tells me it is not – is that I cannot, will not, ever have children.'

I blinked. 'You can't have children . . . does that mean—?' My eyes inadvertently glanced down.

'Oh, nothing like that,' he said, giving me a look that made me blush. 'The plumbing all works.'

My mind was reeling, trying to understand the gravity of this news. My thoughts were like the grasshoppers we used to trap in our hands as children in the long summer grass, bouncing off the inside of my head. He had effectively proposed – why else would he tell me about not wanting children? Even as I wondered at why he did not want them, I realised I didn't care. I wanted to be with him, come what may. Whatever his reason, I could wait until he was ready to tell me. But as quickly as the happiness washed over me, a wave of dread followed in its wake. He had said he would not have children – but I had a child. But I could not hide the truth from this man if I were to be his wife.

'Then I have something to confess, too.' I had to take a deep, steadying breath. It's not like now, ma chère – a young, unmarried woman didn't admit such things lightly. But I forced myself to continue. 'You see, I already have a child, a little boy. He's in Switzerland.'

'With his father?'

'No! I have nothing to do with him.' I hesitated. His honesty gave me the courage to speak. 'I was raped.'

He inhaled sharply. 'The war?'

'Yes.' Our hands were still interlaced and it was as if they were having a conversation independently of us. I watched the water as it flowed past. 'It was hard being alone. I thought it would be better if I came here and made something of myself, then returned for my son. I left him with a good family. I send money back every week.'

Charles got up and coughed, his eyes fixed on the river. I felt sick, thinking that he must be disgusted by me, a ruined woman and not the unplucked flower he had imagined.

He took a step and turned to face me.

'Rosa?' he said. 'I have one more question.'

I steeled myself; I could survive this, even if it was where we would say goodbye. 'Of course,' I said.

'May I kiss you?'

The joy I experienced in that moment was indescribable, ma chère. I didn't answer but leaped up to him and our lips met. Soon we were clinging to each other tightly, his arms wrapped around me. We broke apart, breathless, and his hand cupped my head to his chest.

'This is good,' he said. 'You shall go and get him. I can't give you a child but if you have one already, we can have a family. See, we're meant for each other.' His grip loosened enough for me to turn my face up to his, and our lips met once more.

Charles was nothing if not decisive. He refused to sleep with me before we were married. It was no prurience on his part; I think he wanted to maintain the ecstatic pleasure that we derived just from seeing each other. But neither of us could bear to wait too long so he told Dior that he had four weeks to make a wedding dress for me. Dior relished the challenge and sketched out a dress immediately and personally oversaw its fabrication. It was almost as if he had run around the atelier and gathered all the tulle together, wrapped it around me in a ballerina skirt and then draped a sumptuous satin silk Bar suit jacket over it. He modified it so that it appeared in the 1948 collection as 'Fidelity' – it was what he wished us in his greeting card.

'That leaves just the question of what we should wear, Mme Fournel,' Dior said as he tucked in a final pin, 'when I give her away.'

I swivelled to see him.

'Keep still,' the maître scolded. 'May I perform that honour?'

'Of course,' I said and flung my arms round him. *'Merci pour tous.'*

Charles took little interest in the flurry of preparations but made only one request: that I return to St. Gallen and fetch Laurin so that we could start our family at once. I telegrammed the Schurters to tell them that I was coming.

When I stepped off the train at St. Gallen in late July, I felt like royalty. When I had told Dior where I was going he had insisted that I dress in the working samples and report back to me on their impact outside of Paris, so I was wearing clothes from the next collection. It took no more than three or four of my delicate steps before a porter materialised and offered to carry my suitcase. Three years before, unwordly, frightened and pregnant, I had been deposited on a nearby street, in my worn clothes, with little money and only a letter to guide me. I had been terrified and alone. Now I had purpose, security and a head full of plans and dreams. I felt certain that I could achieve anything.

I did not go to the hotel. My urge to hold little Laurin in my arms again was so overwhelming that I gave the taxi driver Frau Schurter's address. I had only one change of clothes and a nightdress for myself but the rest of the case was stuffed with presents for the children, as well as a complete Dior suit and an evening dress that I had made myself with Madeleine's help. It had been good to keep myself occupied while I was so feverish with excitement at the thought of seeing Laurin – to stop myself obsessing over how much he had grown, whether his hair was still blond, what he liked to eat. I had added two centimetres all the way round the dress, confident that the measurements would have increased from those I still knew so well. I was sure Frau Schurter would be more matronly, more generously proportioned.

By the time I reached the door to the Schurter house and rang the bell my heart was pounding. It was a heavy wooden door and I strained to hear anything from inside – the sound of Frau Schurter's heels clicking on the parquet floor, perhaps. But there was nothing but a long silence before she opened the door.

'Fräulein Kusstatscher. Come in,' she said stiffly. I flinched – she had used to call me Rosa.

I put out my arms to hug her but she stepped back and I flushed with embarrassment. She let me pass and then shut the door behind me. We scanned each other. She looked wonderful; the two centimetres I had added had been unnecessary. I knew what she was looking at – a Parisian lady, Miss Dior, not the waif dressed in hand-me-downs that she remembered. No wonder, I thought, she was treating me differently.

'They're in the garden. You'll want to see him.'

We walked back through the house, which seemed unaltered since I had last been there, through the kitchen. She opened a door leading on to steps down into the garden and as she pushed the door wide, the sound of children playing flooded in. My heels were not designed for anything more extreme than sidestepping dog muck on a Parisian boulevard and I had to concentrate walking down the steps and then on the rough, muddy path. It was only when we came to a halt at the edge of the lawn that I looked up and saw two little boys playing with a hobby horse and a small tricycle. A pram stood at the edge of the grass with a plump baby propped up looking at them. We stood unnoticed, watching them take turns, squabble and squeal with delight. I knew at once which was Laurin, he had blond hair like me – and, I had to admit, Schleich.

My baby was a little boy. Words failed me. I was flooded by guilt and joy. In the end all I could utter was a banality. 'He's so tall. He's as big as Max.'

'Yes, people ask if they are twins.'

'That's ridiculous!' I said.

'Really?' Her voice had a sour tone I had never heard in her before.

I crossed my arms and squeezed them tightly. 'And the baby? I didn't even know that you were pregnant.'

'I was not getting fat like you thought, that was Vreni. I was about three months pregnant with her when you left.'

'That must have been hard.'

'Yes, my family grew from one child to three in six months.'

'I had no idea,' I said. Her generosity in taking Laurin in, when she was already pregnant, made me feel ashamed. 'I'm so sorry, Ida. And grateful,' I said, trying her first name. 'I couldn't look after him, not on my own, not then, and I knew you would give him a home.'

'It was hard at first, Fräulein Kusstatscher,' she pointedly replied, using my surname. 'He cried so much. Max saved him, he loves him. We all do now. He's one of us.'

'Thank you,' I said, humbled.

'You did the right thing,' she said, more gently now. 'Perhaps not in the right way, but you did. He's wanted for nothing. You were so young. Now look at you – you couldn't have become this – ' she dragged her gaze back from the playing children and swept her hand over me – 'with him around your ankles.'

'You were right, too. I would never have been happy here; I had to make something of myself. And it was a struggle, really hard at first. And then I got lucky. But I know how much I've missed.'

'You have. That was the price, and you'll never get it back.' Her tone was not cruel; she was simply stating the truth.

Then the boys started running towards us shouting, 'Mummy! Mummy!'

I stared at the little face that was looking up at me as he ran over the grass. His golden curly hair was messed up, his cheeks were flushed and his blue eyes were filled with curiosity.

'Mummy! Mummy!' they both cried again.

I knelt down, ready for his embrace, my heart pounding. But then Laurin ran straight for Frau Schurter, ignoring my outstretched arms. He clasped her skirt tightly and leaned against her leg. Max stopped next to him.

'Laurin,' I said, 'it's me!'

He slid around her skirt, out of my reach, hiding from me. I stood up awkwardly.

I had imagined this moment so many times. In all my dreams I sank to the ground and scooped him into an embrace, and he had clung back to me. In none of them had he not recognised me; in none of them had he clung, frightened, to his 'mother'. I bit my lip, unable to say a word.

'Mummy,' said Max, 'why is the lady crying?'

'That's rude,' Frau Schurter said. 'Say hello, both of you.'

'Hello,' said Max.

'Hello,' Laurin echoed, giving me a curious look. We stood for a moment in painful silence.

'Well, come in, children, let's show Fraülein Kusstatscher the cake we made her.'

The boys ran ahead at the mention of cake and Ida picked up the baby then led the way back in. The boys were sitting at the table, no doubt in their usual places, and I took what I supposed was their father's seat. Laurin and Max were either side of me, and little Vreni was in a highchair next to her mother. Frau Schurter served them slices of buckwheat cake with a dollop of loosely whipped cream, which they wolfed down between great gulps of raspberry squash.

'So, Laurin and Max, how old are you two?'

'He's nearly three,' Max replied, holding up three chubby fingers. 'And I'm just four,' he said, waving four fingers this time.

'And Vreni?'

'She's eight months old.'

'She's our baby sister,' Laurin announced. There was not a shadow of doubt in him, in his sense of belonging. He had shown me his place in the world in his few words.

'I see,' I said, forcing myself to continue smiling. 'Am I right in thinking it will be your birthday in a few weeks?'

'Yes.' He beamed. 'I'm going to have a party.'

'That will be nice,' I said, and each time he spoke it felt like he was piercing my heart.

'Yes.' He glanced at Frau Schurter.

'Who is coming?' she encouraged him.

'Eric, Anton, Klara and Matthias are coming. And my cousins, Moritz and Helga.'

His cousins; he meant Max's cousins. There was a silence while I tried not to become the crying lady again; I focused on the milk in my coffee, which was swirling in spiral patterns where I had just stirred it. After a while the milk and the coffee became one, and I was able to speak again.

'That sounds lovely,' I said, wearing my smile in the same way I had learnt to at soirées with Dior.

'And Mummy's making a cake,' Laurin squealed with excitement, his face lighting up even more.

There was a silence again, and I cast around for something to say. 'I've brought presents for you two.'

'Mummy, she brought presents!' the boys shrieked with delight.

'And some for your mummy.' I went to get my suitcase, relieved to have just a few moments alone.

After they had opened their little parcels, Laurin and Max rushed off to play on the stairs with the slinkies I had given them. Vreni was napping in her pram. Frau Schurter left her parcel unopened. Instead, she put a thick photo album in front of me. I could track Laurin's growth over Christmas, the boys sledging with her husband, Ottmar, in the winter and their summer holiday on Lake Constance. In every photo my eyes were drawn to the boys, the inseparable boys.

'I've rung the hotel and cancelled your reservation,' she told me when there were no more photos left. 'You should spend more time with Laurin, so he gets to know you again.'

I spent the rest of the afternoon on the floor with the boys, playing with the American wooden cars and yellow trucks that I had also bought for them, then snap and jigsaws. It was only when the children had been put to bed that Frau Schurter and I sat down to eat with her husband. We ate the bread, cheese, cold meats and gherkins of my past and drank an ever-emptier bottle of wine, talking. I had never met Herr Schurter before and he was, as I had hoped, a steady, kind man, the manager of the second biggest bank in St. Gallen, an older man who felt himself blessed with his wife and family. We talked about the war, about reconstruction, about Paris, my job, my impending marriage – about everything but Laurin, not until Frau Schurter had cleared the table. They would not let me help. We listened to familiar sounds of plates and cutlery coming from the kitchen while Herr Schurter played with his silver napkin ring and the linen rolled inside it. He made no attempt at conversation. Frau Schurter came back into the room and hovered at the door.

'I suppose, Rosa, now that you're getting married you have come for him?' He plunged in without any warning.

I smoothed my hands over my skirt and forced myself to meet his eye. 'That was my plan.'

They exchanged swift glances. 'Of course,' he said. 'We thought this was why you had come.'

'It will be very hard to lose him,' Frau Schurter said, sitting down heavily. 'Max will be devastated.'

'When are you leaving?' Herr Schurter tried to assume the air of a calm bank manager, but he was tapping his wooden board with his knife. His face was pale.

Now I could not meet his eye. 'I'm leaving tomorrow,' I said quietly.

'Tomorrow.' The chair screeched against the floor as Frau Schurter pushed it back. 'I suppose I should go and pack his things,' she managed, before collapsing back down with a stifled sob.

'You can't. You can't just turn up here and take him.' Herr Schurter stood up and started to pace, then gripped the back of his chair. 'He doesn't even remember you. That's what Ida told me.'

'Yes,' his wife said weakly. 'He asked me who "that lady" was.'

'I wrote to him every week,' I said defensively, but even as I said it, I realised how pathetic it sounded. They had fed, held and cosseted him; they had a relationship with him. I had sent him paper he could not understand.

'I read the letters to him, of course I did, but he was only two! Do you think he understood what they were?' Her pale skin flushed red. I had never seen Frau Schurter lose her composure before.

'And at the beginning, when we talked about you he would just cry. So, we stopped,' her husband said.

'He copies Max in everything. When he started calling us Mummy and Daddy, it seemed cruel to stop him, like it would make him feel less loved. We did not know when – ' Ida took a breath before she continued, her face fiery red but her anger icy – 'or even *if* you would come back.'

'Why did you never give us your address?' Herr Schurter asked, failing to hide his exasperation. 'Then at least we could have discussed things with you.'

They were right, I had no defence and I knew it. 'I don't know,' I said, looking down at my feet. 'It was stupid of me.'

Herr Schurter picked up his napkin and ring again. I began to fold mine, while Frau Schurter dabbed her eyes with an embroidered handkerchief. We all had a lot to digest.

'He's a lovely boy,' Frau Schurter said after a long while. 'We wanted to make him feel loved.'

'He doesn't just feel it, he *is* loved,' Herr Schurter said with finality. 'We've shown him more love and constancy than you and all your fine dresses ever did.'

I felt a prickle of anger at the injustice of this. 'It was your idea, Ida. You told me to go and make something of myself. To make enough money to become independent and look after him.'

'How dare you blame me!' she shot back. 'I said you should start here, start small and work up to Paris. You ran away the next day and left Laurin on our doorstep!'

'I was young. I was terrified and I thought I could make enough money faster without him.'

'Enough. What's done is done.' Herr Schurter said, reaching for his wife's hand. She gripped his tightly. 'You went to Paris to make your fortune and you left Laurin with us. Was it worth it?'

'No. Money isn't enough,' I said finally. 'But I wasn't doing it just for the money; I was trying to build something, so that I could look after Laurin.'

'And the price you paid for it is that he loves us now,' he said.

'I know. And you love him.'

'Yes, we do,' Ida said.

'But . . .'

'But what?'

'I am his mother. He is mine.'

The next morning I did not flee St. Gallen before dawn like the last time. Instead, the Schurter family, all four of them, came to the station with Laurin and me after breakfast. We trooped down the platform in silence until I found the carriage with my reservation. We stopped dead. Herr Schurter was carrying the small suitcase that Frau Schurter had packed for Laurin. He did not put it down.

I took Laurin's hand. 'Are you ready for an adventure, Laurin? We're going on the train. Say goodbye to everyone.'

He looked at me and back at the Schurters, his little forehead creased with worried lines.

Frau Schurter dropped down on her haunches. 'Come and give me a kiss.'

He pulled his hand out of mine and ran over to her. 'Mummy, I don't want to go,' he said, his lip wobbling. 'I want to stay with you.'

'No, Laurin, you must go with her. Like I told you this morning, she is your real mummy and she is going to take you to a new daddy.'

'No, you're my mummy and daddy. Max is my brother, Vreni is my baby.' The little boy started to bawl. He wrapped his arms around her legs and sobbed.

I knelt down next to him and begged, 'Please, Laurin, come with me.' He shrank from my touch and yelled as if I had hit him.

Ida tried gently to prise him away from her but he just clung more tightly. Max ran over and flung his arms around Laurin and shot an angry glance at me. Herr Schurter's face was white, his lips pulled thin and taut.

As you know, ma chère, I like to steal a scene, to make a dramatic entrance, but this was the most piteous spectacle I have ever lived through. I was crying, Frau Schurter was crying, Laurin and Max were bawling as only children know how to, and even Vreni joined in. Only Herr Schurter was tearless. Yet his quiet voice cut me to the quick even more than Laurin's cries.

'If you love him, do the right thing by him.'

He put the suitcase down, turned on his heel and walked off down the platform. I watched him go, my dreams shattering before my eyes. The right thing is not always what it seems. Sometimes the wrong thing is the right thing. I am not one for biblical stories, but I like to think that the story of the baby, the two mothers and King Solomon came to me then. What brought me to my senses was that Herr Schurter was choosing to walk away rather than make Laurin suffer more. He was putting Laurin first, and all I was thinking about was what I wanted. I wanted to have a family with Charles, I wanted to have what Laurin had already with the Schurters. It was a terrible realisation that in order to be a good mother, unlike my own, I had to give selflessly. I had to give Laurin back to his family.

'Herr Schurter!' I cried. 'Ottmar! Come back.'

I knelt down in front of my son and Frau Schurter. 'Laurin, you can stay,' I said, smoothing down his blond curls. 'I won't take you from your family. You belong here with them.'

I stood up. Herr Schurter was breathless after hastening back.

'You will have to adopt him,' I said, more curtly than I meant to.

'Of course,' Frau Schurter said immediately.

'I'll get my lawyers on it today,' Laurin's father said.

The colour had returned to Herr Schurter's face. Ida bent over and hugged Laurin, who was still wrapped around her legs. She whispered something in his ear. After a moment's hesitation he let go of her, went to Vreni's pram and pulled out a brown package from under the blanket at the foot end.

'Laurin wants to give you something,' Ida said.

I knelt down to face my boy for the last time. He approached me slowly and did not come too close. His face was flushed and blotchy; he examined my bloodshot eyes.

'Mummy said that you were crying so much because you hurt.

This is good for hurts. We picked the flowers.' In his small hands he held out a brown paper bag and inside it was this very bottle full of arnica flower heads trapped in Swiss spirit.

The next night, back in Paris, I made Charles take me to his bed, before our wedding. It was only in binding myself to him that I could begin to mend the rupture that I felt tearing me apart. There are some bruises that arnica cannot heal.

IO

Tweezers

A single hair can ruin hours of preparation. It is not that the hair stands out, necessarily, but it will subconsciously distract from a perfect presentation. You see this one, ma chère, it lies three millimetres below the arch of my eyebrow; that will never do. That is where I highlight. Can you imagine a hair meandering across my shimmering mother-of-pearl eyeshadow? Once, just once, when I first arrived in Brazil, I permitted my eyebrows to be waxed, but never again. The arch was too high, the skin red, sore and stretched, and I hated subjecting my face to the whims and unpredictable skills of someone else. I prefer to concentrate my own mind and fingers on the task in hand. This pair of tweezers, my tweezers, is all I need. We have to work with our nature, not destroy it. That was something that I learnt from Charles.

The night that he stayed with me, that first time, we barely slept. Eventually hunger drove us into the kitchen to see what Madeleine had in her cupboards. We stood at the window, one sheet wrapped around both of us, feeding a ripe camembert to each other. I would like to say that the moonlight was dancing over the gleaming rooftops and that we stood bathed in a pool of blue light, but as I recall the night was dull. A heavy, thick cloud hung drizzling over Paris. But I remember it as if it were incandescent.

And yet, happy as we were in each other, the sadness of leaving Laurin was so palpable that Charles treated it almost as a third person in the room. When I had licked the last morsel of cheese from his fingers, he held me tight against him. I was fascinated by the black curls of the hair on his chest. Thomas, the only other man I had made love to, had been slight and hairless. Charles was not tall but compact and stocky, and he was naturally strong. Dark, tight curls covered his chest and he needed to shave twice a day if he wanted to look smooth-skinned. My face was chafed from rubbing so much against the shadow of a beard that seemed to coarsen as each minute passed. I teased a tight, black hair out between my fingertips and closed my eyes to listen to his heart beating inside his chest.

'Rosa,' he said softly, drawing me out of my reverie. 'I have an idea. After we're married—'

'We are man and wife now,' I interrupted with a kiss.

'Legally, I mean.' He paused, his lips seeking mine. 'After we have registered our marriage, I think we should go away.'

'A holiday? I'd love to go to the Côte d'Azur.'

He shook his head. 'No, another country, permanently.'

My instant reaction was to say no but then I asked, 'Why?'

'To start a new life, to put our pasts behind us,' he said, kissing me again. 'So you don't have to think about Laurin all the time.'

I stared out over the rooftops and the colourless night sky and sighed. 'So I won't be tempted to go and spy on him in St. Gallen, you mean?'

'Yes. Maybe. I think it is always better to move on. It's what we do.'

'I'll think about it.' I burrowed my head into his chest and inhaled. This was what happiness smelt like now.

I did think about it and the more I thought, the more I realised that he was right: it was what I did. First I had left Oberfals, then St. Gallen and now I would move on from Paris. If I stayed there something would die in me; I would be constantly yearning to return to Laurin. Yet as I visited lawyers who drew up papers that went back and forth to St. Gallen, I had to accept that I would have to forfeit the right to contact him. It would be up to Ida and Ottmar Schurter what they chose to tell him, and their lawyers let me know that they wanted him to feel no different from the other children. They regretted the pain it would cause me, but they requested that I ceased all contact. I had to stop writing, never visit and even my money would not be welcome but would be returned to me.

When, finally, I had the papers in front of me, I read them, picked up the pen, held it, put it down. I could not sign. The lawyer brought me a glass of water and a handkerchief but I sat unable to move for a long time. It was the single hardest action I have ever taken. In the end, I forced myself to take up the pen and sign away my baby. The lawyer's gold-nibbed fountain pen could have been a knife, and the black ink blood, for the pain it caused me.

Charles and I had been married the week before, a tiny affair at the local mairie followed by lunch with Christian, Madeleine and Charles's assistant, and since then we had been sharing the small bed in Madeleine's flat. His bedsit room barely had enough space for him, let alone all my dresses, and Madeleine seemed to enjoy our happiness. She took to playing cards with her neighbours and grumbling contentedly that I was always late for work now. But the night I signed the papers, for the first time since I had returned from St. Gallen, her absence, her delicate gesture, was unneeded. I turned away from Charles when he slid into the bed beside me and faced the wall. He leaned over me and I could feel his eyes upon my face as he waited.

'It will have to be somewhere far away,' I finally managed. 'Very far.'

He folded his body around me, copying my jack-knifed form, and reached his hand over to clasp mine. 'I thought so,' he said, planting a gentle kiss on the top of my head. 'Very far.'

After Charles let it be known that he was seeking employment elsewhere, a barrage of battered airmail letters arrived offering lucrative posts in an array of exotic locations. It was then I learnt that not only did he have a nose for wine and perfumes, but that his Ph.D. had been a brilliant and elegant treatise on anaesthetic esters, and he had published enough before the war to win him a singular reputation. We knew nothing about Brazil, only that Charles had been offered a prestigious job in the chemistry department of the university in Rio de Janeiro – and that, crucially, it was a long way from St. Gallen. In Brazil, the academic year started in February so we had no time to lose organising ourselves. We arrived in Rio the week between Christmas and New Year.

We booked into the Copacabana Palace Hotel, not because we could afford it – we could not – but because it was the only Brazilian hotel we had ever heard of. Despite the astronomical prices, we did not regret it. The hotel was a Parisian building transported on to a palm-fringed beach. It was furnished with Brazilian hardwood furniture – I would learn a new lexicon, Jatoba, Cumaru, Ipe, Maçaranduba, in the future – but as a newcomer I simply walked around trailing my hand over the rich, burnished woods, admiring them. Our room had a small balcony overlooking the curving beach that stretched between two forested headlands; to the north the Pão de Açucar, the fabled Sugar Loaf Mountain, rose up above a green promontory, and to the south two vast, dark brown granite rocks nestled one against the other, the entwined Dois Irmãos, or Two Brothers, less famous than the Sugar Loaf but more dramatic as they rose from the jungle-clad lower slopes. And in front of us the sea, the Atlantic Ocean reaching all the way to Africa and further to Europe.

For the first two days we were barely able to move. The heat and humidity sapped our strength and we spent the days drinking caipirinha cocktails by the pool and wandering along the sand in the morning and evening. On the last day of 1947, we sat on the beach waiting for the sun to dip into the waves, then returned to the hotel to dine. After our evening meal I showered again – the gentle fans in the restaurant had not been enough to keep the sweat from running in rivulets between my breasts; Dior really had not mastered clothes for a hot climate. I came out of the shower and found Charles rummaging through his suitcase.

'I can't find my suit,' he said as he tossed half of the clothes on the floor. 'The linen one?'

'It's in the wardrobe,' I told him. 'Why do you want it now?'

'We're going down to the beach,' he said, looking up at me and smiling like an excited boy.

'It's ten o'clock. And dark.'

He located his cream linen suit and levered it off the overstuffed rail. 'Look out the window.'

The night before, the beach had just been a shadowy place beyond the light cast by the street lamps lining the Avenida Atlântica. Now, a swarming mass of ghostly white moved under the palm trees and on to the sand.

'The concierge said that people dress in white to welcome the new year with peace and harmony,' Charles said as he buttoned up a white cotton shirt. 'That's how we'll start our new life.'

It had begun to rain, and the droplets were so fine that they seemed to just hang in the air. The almost full moon was obscured by the softly scudding clouds but the beach was not dark. There were so many candles lit in makeshift shrines embedded in the sand or held in the swaying arms of the white-clad devotees, and everywhere fires crackled and sputtered in the rain. We moved between the singing crowds, and people grabbed our hands and pulled us into their dances. Slowly, we made our way closer to the crash of the waves. Our bare feet trod on snuffed-out wax sticks and flowers. Flowers were everywhere – on the ground, in people's hands, on the shrines. As we came to the steep incline that led down to the surf, we saw a woman standing at the top of the slope. She was young, dark, with long black hair flowing loosely over her white dress. Later, as I would become familiar with the subtleties of Brazilian racial hierarchies, I would have described her as a morena. Her hands were hanging limply from her otherwise rigid arms and her eyes were shut, her head folded back. She was groaning like an animal in pain. Her companions were holding her tightly as she moaned and swayed, trying to break away from them. She gave a cry and collapsed into a bundle on the sand. Her companions gathered round her; they seemed casual and calm. My head was buzzing with a supercharged mix of excitement, confusion and even a little alarm.

I tugged Charles's hand and led him stumbling down to the sea. People were standing at the water's edge throwing flowers into the dark sea as the surf crashed onto the beach, the drenched blooms scattered on the sand. Everything was new to me – the thick, humid night air, the swarming mass of bodies in white, the rhythmic sound of the drums battering my ears. The crowd was unlike any I had seen: young and old, rich and poor, black and white, and every shade in between. This was not just a new year, a new beginning – it was a new world.

And then the fireworks began. In Oberfals, a few rockets echoing across from one side of the valley to another had been enough to thrill me, but here in Rio as the year rolled over, the showers of light lit up the beach and the clouds above as far as the eye could see, as if a ribbon of gold and fire had been drawn across the sky. The crowd stood with their heads craned upwards, oohing and aahing.

Charles wrapped his arms around me and I felt strangely delirious. New Year's Eve meant snow and ice to me, yet we were standing in warm rain in light summer clothes, hot and sweaty. When I left Oberfals I could not have imagined that I would ever leave Switzerland. Yet not only had I passed through St. Gallen, but I had also conquered Paris. It was exactly four years since Schleich had threatened me for the last time as the Silvester firecrackers had sparked around me, and now I was on Copacabana Beach in Rio de Janeiro letting sand fall through my fingers. Yes, Laurin was gone, but the war was over, Europe was far away and our future stretched out like the flower-strewn sand ahead of us, lit by flashes of brilliance. A huge wave of hope splashed over me as we climbed back up to the road.

We crossed the Avenida Atlântica, buffeted by the stream of people moving along it, and returned wordlessly to our room. We stripped and showered yet again. It was pointless: by the time we left the bathroom, little beads of sweat were already starting to re-form. We went out on to the balcony to look down at the white throng still celebrating. I leaned against Charles, my head pushed back against him, and a drop fell from his chin on to my shoulder.

'*Mon amour*, you're dripping.' I laughed. 'Go and have another shower.'

He did not respond, and I felt another drop.

'I'm sorry,' he said, moving back into the room, and his voice sounded strange. I followed him in, dismayed to find that it was not sweat but tears that were running down his face.

I put out my hand to him but he took a step back. 'What's the matter?'

'This – everything.' He swept his hand in an expansive gesture that took in our whole lives. 'I don't deserve it.'

'What do you mean? Aren't you happy?'

He turned towards me, caught me in his arms and pressed his lips against mine in a hard, desperate kiss.

'Oh, God, yes,' he said when he had broken away. 'I love you. But I don't deserve this. I don't have a right to such happiness.' He released me and walked back out on to the balcony. His face was etched with the pain I had seen a shadow of when he had told me that he could not have children. He leaned over the balustrade. He was standing in the only place where he could be alone so I took the hint and retreated to our bed.

I must have fallen asleep because when I felt his hand tracing the lines of sweat running over my skin the night air was quiet; the singing on the beach had faded away. I opened my eyes. He looked so sad. I had never seen this mood in him before.

He kissed me. 'You never asked me why I can't have children,' he said so quietly that I had to strain to hear.

'No.' I took his hand in mine. 'It was for you to tell me – in your own time.'

'I want to tell you now, otherwise I'll never be able to.'

'Later,' I said, pulling him to me.

It is funny how kissing and making love are a language all of their own. The same actions, tongues interlaced, touching, fusing, can be quiet, loving, gentle, angry and even violent. Most of the time when we came together it was as if Charles and I were driven by the same desperate need to merge and force our flesh into one. But the same movements and gestures could take on compassion, sympathy and tenderness. It was as if each touch, every caress, was a balm, an ointment smoothed on unspeakable wounds.

Afterwards, he lay on the bed next to me staring at the ceiling as I leaned against him on my side, my arm stretched over his chest, his arm hooked over my back, his semen sliding down my belly, mingling with the ever-present sweat.

'My name Dumarais is French,' he said, just as I was drifting off to sleep. 'You think that I am a French man?'

'Yes,' I said, surprised, 'of course.'

'So did I.' He paused. 'And indeed, my father was French. My mother thought she was French. But in 1940, when the Germans invaded France, my mother and I ceased to be French. The only thing that mattered about us was that we were Jewish.'

'Oh.' I reached for his penis. It was soft and sticky and at the end it was smooth and naked. 'I had wondered.' My experience was not great and it had been dark in my bedroom when I had given myself to Thomas, but I had noticed the difference. I had just accepted it along with the difference between a thin, lanky smooth-skinned boy and my muscular man. But now the penny dropped. 'So you're circumcised?'

'Yes. Even if I never thought about it, even if I thought of myself as just another French kid, as far as the Nazis were concerned that was as good as having the mark of the beast printed on my forehead.' He stared at the ceiling for a long time and I pulled his hand towards me and pressed my lips against it. I had never knowingly met a Jew before the professor, and living with him had taught me that he was just another human. The loss of his family and his sadness meant that I was well aware of the Holocaust. I dreaded what I was about to hear.

'We escaped to the south when the Germans came to Paris, but the Vichy regime was no better. We stayed with friends, moving all the time, ever more desperate. My father tried everything, but he could not make us disappear. The authorities did that. Eventually, we were rounded up. My father's efforts had been in vain and we – my mother, my sister and my wife and son – were all were transported to Drancy on Christmas Eve in 1942 and then on to Auschwitz in January 1943.'

'You were married? You had a family?' The pang I felt for Laurin was so strong, but at least he was alive.

Charles was struggling. He stared at the ceiling fan whirling round and round, a liquid line of salt and water streaming down his cheeks, and bit hard into his lip. I kissed him on the forehead and took his hand.

'What happened to them?'

'My mother, my wife Françoise and Louis – he was still a baby, just fourteen months old – were selected.' He closed his eyes. 'My sister and I were not. They went left, we went right. Left, right. Death, life. My mother, Françoise and Louis were dead within hours. We didn't even get to say goodbye.'

He turned away and I nuzzled his neck.

'And your sister?' I asked, already knowing the answer but still dreading it.

'She had it hard. We were separated, I tried to save her food. But it wasn't enough. By the time we were liberated she was so thin, she died from dysentery a week after.'

It was hard for me to comprehend. I had chosen not to say goodbye to my family. They had only ever disappointed me, made me feel unloved. He had never mentioned his parents without tenderness and affection. He had never mentioned his wife and child but I was not angry. I understood, it was a pain that he had buried. I knew that nothing could comfort him.

'I'm so sorry,' I whispered. We lay without moving. I knew he was not finished but I could not imagine what more was to come. It was not like now, ma chère, when we have books, films, TV series and documentaries about the Holocaust. The survivors and victims had not found their voices yet.

Charles sighed. 'I try not to feel guilty about surviving. It's hard.' His hand fell on to the mattress beside me as he took a few deep breaths. 'So, I walked to the right and, given that I was a chemist, I was put to work in a chemical factory. It belonged to IG Farben.'

'What did you have to do?'

'We made rubber, mainly. Then they put me to use in their

labs. Bayer bought prisoners to test drugs on them. Rosa – ' his voice cracked – 'I saw things there that I still can't believe. Once or twice I had to take concoctions they ordered to Block 10, where they conducted medical experiments. That I was starved, beaten, filthy, sick and emaciated was nothing. I survived. But what I saw men do to other men, to women and children. It was horror beyond imagining. Do you know Bosch, Hieronymus Bosch?'

I shook my head.

'He's a painter. I'll show you sometime,' he said. 'His paintings conjure fear and revulsion. When most people look at them, they feel those things, then they turn away and the feeling goes. I live with that feeling suffocating me all of the time. It has never truly left me.'

'What happened to your father?'

'When the war ended, I found my way back to Paris, to our old apartment. He wasn't there. But the concierge told me that he had committed suicide on Christmas Day of 1942, the day after we had been deported.'

He cried then. Like a broken dam, he was washed away by great, heaving sobs. I did not say a word, just held him until he was quiet, until he stopped shaking.

'I could never bring another child into a world that could do this. Never. Do you understand?'

I kissed his shoulder, wet with our tears and sweat. It broke my heart – part of me had toyed with the idea of persuading him to change his mind – but now I understood. 'Yes,' I said.

I woke before him on the first day of 1948 and lay watching him sleep, relaxed and at peace. He opened his eyes and smiled at me.

'You're still here.'

I smiled back. 'Always.'

'It's funny. After last night, I thought I would feel worse today, but I feel different – lighter.'

'What do you mean?'

'It's like I've had a shard in my heart these past years. A constant ache. But right now, this second, it's gone.'

'You've being hiding so much pain, mon amour. It had to come out.'

'Last night, the way you listened . . . it was like the way my mother used to gently tease out a splinter with tweezers.'

I stroked his hair. 'She must have loved you very much.'

A year later, on New Year's Eve, we spent the evening on Copacabana Beach again. This time we understood what was happening; the *candomblistas* dressed in white were offering flowers to Iemenjá, queen of the sea, the goddess of fertility. They lit candles, sang and danced in praise of her, some of them going into trance-like possession. Despite having learnt conversational Portuguese to a certain level, we still did not understand their chants since the words were bastardised Yoruba, *candomblé* being the surviving remnants of the old African religions that the slaves had brought with them across the Atlantic long before. After the fireworks, which seemed even more spectacular than the previous year, we walked back along the beach towards Leblon. It was a suburb in the making and we had rented a small house on a side street leading from the waterfront. If I leaned out of the balcony, I could see the ocean stretching into the distance at the end of the road. You wouldn't find anything like that now; it was replaced by an apartment block long ago.

When we got back that night, we stayed out on our veranda looking up at the alien night sky. Although I knew so few constellations in the northern heavens by name, it was only in Brazil that I realised just how familiar those stars were. Every time I turned my eyes to my new southern skies, I felt lost and disorientated. I could not have told you, ma chère, what was different, just that it was. Charles nudged me as I stood gazing up at the fierce, strange stars. He was holding a box out to me.

'Christmas was over a week ago,' I said.

'I know. Aren't you going to take it?' He started to retract his hand.

I held out my hands and he dropped the box into my palms, smiling. It was wrapped in soft, handmade paper that was secured with a golden ribbon. I untied the ribbon and uncovered the box. Inside, nestling on crumpled white tissue paper, was a pair of gold-plated tweezers. A large C was engraved on one side and an R on the other.

Look, ma chère, the letters are still there. Some things never fade.

Nail Varnish

You've always liked the rainbow of little bottles lined up in this cupboard. Nail varnish is a necessary finishing touch to any outfit. Of course we can read more into it. Chipped nails may speak of work and washing up, while glossy, unblemished nails can be misread as a symbol of idleness, or understood as a sign of wealth. And as for slapping on one colour and shielding your hands for a week, that is a ridiculous idea. As a waitress in my parents' Gasthaus and as a seamstress in Paris, I thought it enough to file my nails once a week and then varnish them for special occasions. Since then I have learnt that polished nails signify effort and just that, polish. Each day, just as I choose a lipstick to match the outfit I will wear, I paint on the matching nail varnish.

Whenever I strip the old varnish off with acetone, I soak my hands, paring back water-softened skin to expose my moons, then rub in oils before I revarnish. And varnishing is no easy thing. Drying and hardening between each layer lies at the heart of good nails. There are no shortcuts; it takes time. So, strange as it may seem, I often decide what I shall wear the day before and prepare my nails at night watching TV if I am at home. Otherwise, I prepare my nails in the first hour in the morning when I am making phone calls. Of course, I do not have the time now, not for this of all meetings – it's all so last minute – and I still have no clue what I'm going to wear.

Time should never be an issue when it comes to appearance. Of course, I understand that not everyone can dedicate themselves to this art of beauty to the extent that I do, but I accept no excuses for myself. My own teacher in this particular matter was so exigent herself that I could not fail her. I mean, of course, Graça. It's funny to think that my most enduring relationship is with her, and she started off as my maid. Of course, I noticed that Brazilian women did not feel dressed without lipstick and nail varnish, but it was only through Graça that I began to understand the true importance of this to them.

Graça came to work for us in our third year in Brazil. She was a shy, modest young woman, unusually tall and willowy for a Brazilian, who padded around the stone and wooden floors of our house in her bare feet like a sylph. Every morning she would arrive before we woke up and open the shutters and windows to let the sea breeze billow through the house before she closed them again in a vain attempt to shut the heat out. We would come down to a find a fresh posy of flowers arranged next to a breakfast of freshly squeezed orange juice and a slice of lime ready to squeeze over the firm orange flesh of two halves of papaya, from which Graça had already scooped the dark, round seeds. We would eat the fruit and still-warm bread with *maracujá* jam as we read the newspapers and sipped our coffee, while Graça moved about discreetly, cleaning and tidying behind the scenes. From the day she started working for us, she became indispensable for the smooth running of my life.

I was very busy. Naturally, I had made a stir at the first few social occasions we had attended when I let it slip – casually, of course – that I had been trained by Dior himself and was, in fact, his muse. Ladies would congregate around me like humming-birds around a nectar-laden flower, beseeching me to make them dresses. Within months of arriving I was making gowns, skirts and suits. Within two years I was running a busy fashion house. My style and connection with Dior were enough of a sensation, but even the grandes dames of Brazilian society who shopped in Paris came to me because, unlike Dior and other Parisian haute couture designers, I was using fabrics that could be worn in the tropics: silks, fine cottons, linen. I started to experiment with the new fabrics rayon and viscose. From the moment I stepped off the plane in Santos Dumont airport and felt the thick, humid, hot air gushing over me, I knew that Dior's love of excess, of metres and metres of heavy fabric, simply would not work here. I had to take his New Look and mould it to the demands of the environment.

We had arrived in the southern hemisphere's summer and I imagined that the abundance of the fruit and the flowers would fade. But when winter came in Rio I learnt that it was hotter than a summer in Oberfals, and no less green. My initial instinct was to choose a riot of colour but I quickly learnt that my clientele did not favour the travesty of their style that Carmen Miranda was propagating. My ladies of Rio, thousands of miles from Paris, yearned for sophistication. Like their sisters before them who had sent their dirty clothes and linen from Manaus – a city sitting on the greatest source of fresh water in the world – 'back' over the Atlantic to be laundered in Portugal, how much more so did they want their clothes to be modern and elegant rather than 'tropical'.

At first, Graça was shy with me; it was more than a year before we had a proper conversation. Indeed, I barely saw her; I was hardly at home in the day. Little by little, though, through sheer necessity, she began to speak. Then we began to share confidences, almost in passing. She learnt the names of my biggest clients and our friends, as I told her whose glass she was clearing away, why that particular pillow was so ruffled. And gradually I learnt that she came from the *roça*, the rural hinterland, and found the big city rather frightening. She was living with a cousin in Dona Marta, a favela made up of a series of shacks that clung precipitously to the mountainside rising above Leme.

Rio de Janeiro grew up around the southern rim of Guanabara Bay. If you stand under Christ at Corcovado, the Sugar Loaf Mountain squats below at the narrow neck of the bay, a jagged natural harbour reaching some twenty miles across. It looks like a gargantuan termite mound and is one of many black-red granite rock masses that rise up out of the pale sand and remnants of the coastal jungle. The colours are so intense – the blue of the sea and the sky, the green of the trees, and the pale sun-bleached yellow of the sand. The rich paid to be close to the beach and took all the flat land running along the seafront and forced their cleaners, mechanics and workers up into the steep slopes under the sheer cliffs. Dona Marta was one of the oldest favelas, its entrance a single road that wound tightly up the mountain. Shacks built from unfurled oil cans, discarded doors and corrugated iron were crammed haphazardly on either side. As Graça took us the last stretch on foot on to her cousin's house, I glimpsed the priceless view of islands floating like jewels in the blue waters of the bay, which the *favelados* enjoyed over their washing lines.

Graça should have been a beauty. With another start in life she would have walked tall, dressed in sharp, fine suits, tailored trousers and sleek skirts. As it was, she was like a crumpled banknote. She wore her hair short and pulled back tightly over her head, clamped down by pins and cream. Oftentimes she wrapped a scarf around her head – not in a fetching bandana-style with a coloured silk square, but with a ragged scrap of faded cotton, torn at the edges and tightly, practically knotted. I only saw her in her work clothes, which were simple and old, the shapeless blouses hanging over square-cut A-line skirts that swamped her skinny frame. Her long, angular limbs look starved, not slim. Her arms and legs, always moving, lifting and sweeping, dusting and polishing, wringing and hanging, were sinewy and tough. It was hard to see any beauty in her then.

At that stage I was too absorbed with Charles and myself to notice anything. Not that there is much to tell: happiness, to anyone other than those experiencing it, is dull. Yet they were my golden years, quite literally. Every morning we walked on the beach before or after breakfast and on weekends we would lie on the sand until the heat became too intense, and we were permanently tanned. The meteoric rise of my business along with Charles's position at the university had our coffers overflowing. I secured an old city store and renovated it and, like Dior, I had my creations fabricated on the floors above the shop. It had been very cheap in such an unfashionable area, but my store began to revitalise the street. We travelled within Brazil, following the Amazon from Belem, near its mouth, deep into the jungle beyond Manaus. We stood over the thundering Iguaçu Falls, spied on wildlife in the vast swamps of the Pantanal, worked our way up the string of colonial cities along the coast and toured the ancient mining cities of Minas Gerais, with their tiny baroque churches festooned with more golden cherubs than was imaginable. We bought loose gemstones: diamonds, rubies, sapphires, emeralds and amethysts, as well as semi-precious stones that I had never heard of before: aquamarine, beryl, citron, peridot, topaz and the magnificent tourmaline – and the gold to set them in. Back in Rio, I had them made into spectacular jewellery that I myself designed. That led to a second business.

When I left St. Gallen with the plan to make good in Paris, my hope had been to run my own shop. Now I had two successful businesses, it was as if I had chanced upon the fabled treasure of the dwarf mountain king from the fairy stories of my youth, visible only on the pink glow of sunset. I feared that our happiness would be as ephemeral as the sunset. Within three years I had bought a house on the Avenida Atlântica in Leblon. In the early fifties the traffic was minimal and we could cross the road and be on the beach in seconds. Charles was absorbed in his teaching and research and happily accepted the comfort we lived in, without really noticing it. But – because, ma chère, there is always a but – every so often the thought of Laurin would launch itself against me like a mad fury. But even then, despite my crying and wailing, Charles would never give in. He would not have children. You must think it strange, ma chère, that I accepted his decision. Over the years I have wondered why I did not just get pregnant 'by accident'. I suspect that, at heart, I did not think I deserved to be a mother. I never forgave myself for losing Laurin and, ultimately, I wanted to respect Charles's decision.

One morning, when I was on my way out to my office, I was thirsty and headed for the kitchen to get a glass of water. I remember that I was in a good mood: a new design had come to me in the night and I was working it out in my head. I have always loved the rush of creation. I opened the fridge door and took out the jug of cooled, filtered water that Graça refilled every morning and poured myself a glass.

It was only when I had stowed the jug back in the fridge that I realised I was not alone. Graça was sitting on a stool by the kitchen door at the end of the line of cupboards, her back against the creamy tiles, her eyes shut and her face wet with tears.

'Graça,' I cried, 'what's the matter?'

She rubbed the tears from her cheeks with her apron. 'It's nothing,' she said, pulling herself to her feet.

'No, there is something. Is there anything I can do?'

'I'm fine.' She tried to force a smile, picked up the duster she left on the worktop and left the room.

I stood swaying on my stilettoes for a moment and then listened to the tap of my heels on the marble floor as I walked to the front door, as if I was listening for an answer in Morse code. I watched her closely after that.

Her face showed it the most. She had always been unobtrusive but now she became barely visible. Her eyes seemed to shrink; the irises became a dull brown and lines of red blistered the yellowed whites. Her skin should have had a honey-brown sheen, but fatigue sapped her colour and forced a sallow pallor over her visage.

And then one Monday she did not come to work. I was worried; she had never been sick, never simply not turned up. Once, she had missed a day to take her cousin to the doctor, but she had sent the teenage daughter of her neighbour to help us out. The next morning, I heard her working but she was elusive, leaving rooms just before I entered them as though she had some kind of sixth sense. On the Wednesday morning breakfast was laid out but she was nowhere to be seen. I searched the house until I found her polishing the floor of our guest room. It was already immaculate – it was not used often – but it was somewhere that I would not usually go. She was hiding from me.

'Good morning,' I said, trying to sound casual, as if I had not hunted her out. 'Are you alright?'

'Yes, senhora,' she muttered without looking up from the cloth on the parquet floor.

'Are you better now?'

'Yes, senhora.' She continued polishing the beeswax into the burnished wood.

Bruises are harder to see on dark skin yet, as Graça stretched out her hand and her blouse pulled back, I caught sight of purple-black marks on her arm. I knew that she would not turn around. My father used to beat Christl and me when he was drunk. We used to skulk in the house until the bruises could not be seen because we were ashamed. Anger bubbled up inside me like a volcano but I forced it down; it was better to leave her alone, for the moment.

The next morning Charles and I got up earlier than we had in years, brewed coffee and sat at the kitchen table waiting for her. When she opened the door and saw us waiting, she froze long enough for us to see the livid bruising over her face, her swollen eyes, her cut lips and the burnished marks on her neck.

'Oh, Graça!' I sprang to my feet and grabbed her hand. 'Who did this to you? You can't work. Have you been to the hospital?'

Her mouth opened as if to answer me, then closed, silent. I felt a hand on my shoulder; the touch of Charles's hand on my skin still always stopped me in my tracks.

'Rosa, Rosa. Go to the bathroom and get the white spirit and ointments, and maybe some plasters and bandages.'

When I came back, Charles was pouring fresh coffee into cups while Graça sat hunched over, looking down into her lap. I put the medical supplies down in a heap on the table and then perched on the chair next to her. We had never sat together before. Charles served the coffee then rummaged through the pile of bottles, bandages, tubes and plasters. He picked up an ointment and then, turning her face up with his finger, set to work silently, smoothing in the antiseptic. I tore off a piece of cotton wool from a wad and uncorked Laurin's precious arnica bottle.

'You are not alone, Graça,' I said, looking at her. 'You have us. No one has the right to do this to you.' Graça's eyes pivoted to me, her face still under Charles's scrutiny. 'We'll help you.' I soaked the cotton wool with Laurin's precious arnica tonic and handed it to Charles, who wiped all the bruises he could see on her arms, neck and face. When he was satisfied, he sat down.

'Now Graça, tell us: is this the first time?' Charles asked. I could tell from the coolness of his voice that like me he was seething but trying to mask it, trying not to agitate her.

She shook her head.

'I didn't think so,' I said. 'Just never so bad before.'

Her eyes were fixed on the table, and we waited. When she looked up her eyes were fiery, her face set.

'Senhor Charles, Senhora Rosa, I will go and not come back. I shouldn't bring such shame to your house.'

'Ashamed!' Charles's angry cry escaped from his mouth. 'You should not feel ashamed.' I reached for his arm and he went on more calmly. 'The person who did this should. Not you.' He went and leaned against the sink and filled a glass of water.

Graça relaxed back into her chair.

'Charles is right, Graça.' I took her hand in mine. 'It is not your fault. Please tell us who did this?'

She pulled her hand back and then she started crying. In the tropics, a rainstorm has no precursor of drizzle. One moment the sun is beating down, then the sky darkens as grey cloud swoops over and there is a deluge. Graça's tears spurted violently as she sobbed. I tried to put my arm around her but she held back from me. Then, all of a sudden, as if the wind had blown the cloud away, she fell quiet, rubbed the tears from her face and sat up.

'It's Sé.' She spat his name out in a hiss. 'My cousin's fiancé. She's a good woman, strong. She won't sleep with him until they are married but they have been saving to build a house for three years. It started a while back . . . he says that if I want to continue living with Gabriela and him when they are married, I have to start . . . paying rent now. He says if I keep him busy he won't leave Gabriela.' As she spoke the fingers on her right hand began to flex and retract, the long nails scraping the polish off the opposing fingernails.

'Most of the time I just avoid him, but sometimes when he knows that Gabriela is out he comes to the house, drunk. I would never let a man in the house if I am on my own. It's not right. But I can't say "no" to him and anyway he comes in even if I do. Usually I manage to talk him down or run away but last Friday he had been drinking *pinga* in a bar.' She glanced down at her ruined nails and clamped her left fingers over the right. 'He came in angry, so angry, and grabbed me by the throat the moment he walked in. I could smell the cachaça on his breath. I fought him. I fought him bad. And I got away.

'But it's awful at home now. I can't tell Gabriela what has been happening and he won't come round because he's so badly grazed. Soon she'll get anxious and start asking questions.' She held out her fingers as if for me to admire her long, well-shaped nails, the striated red veneer of which was chipped, leaving flecks of white at the tips. I imagined how the varnish had flaked off where she had dug her nails into the brute's flesh.

I took her hand and kissed her fingers in approval.

'Where does he work?' Charles was leaning against the sink. His voice was deadpan but I could see from the way his knuckles were white where he gripped the basin rim his anger had not abated.

'He works at Maluf Exports somewhere in the Centro,' Graça replied.

'Not for long. We're going there.' There was a determined, angry look on Charles's face now.

'We can't,' Graça said, glancing from me to Charles and back, a look of panic in her eyes. 'Gabriela will find out.'

'Are you mad?' The words burst out before I could stop them. I took a deep breath and paused; I could not let my anger at him vent against her. 'I'm sorry, what I mean is: think. Do you want this to happen to her? What do you think he'll do once they're married?'

'But senhora, he loves her.'

'And no doubt he told you that he loves you too.'

She nodded. 'He says I'm driving him crazy. I don't know

what to do.' Her misery and desperation reduced her voice to a whisper.

At that moment I knew what to do. I sprang to my feet. 'I'm going to get myself ready.'

'Senhora Rosa,' she said, scraping her nails again, 'I don't think you should get involved in this.'

'Why ever not?'

'It's not something you can understand. It's my business. It's so ugly.'

'Graça,' I said, taking her hands again and forcing her to meet my eyes. 'I know more about this than you can imagine.'

She stared back at me, her bruised face showing the steel that had fought that man off.

'I swore a long time ago I would not let men get away with this sort of thing,' I went on. 'Not if I could help it.'

She did not move from the chair but shook her head as she said, 'I'll lose my honour. It's best if I do nothing.'

I watched her for a moment, then asked as gently as I could, 'Do you know anyone at his work?'

'No.'

'Then it doesn't matter. What matters is that he gets stopped.'

She touched the tips of her fingers into an arch as if in prayer. Her swollen, puffy eyes were closed.

'We'll leave in ten minutes.'

She blanched. 'Senhora Rosa, I can't go to town like this.'

'Oh, that's fine, you'll fit my clothes, I'll lend you some.'

'No, no. I mean like this.' She stretched out her fingers, displaying the scratched and ruined varnish. 'I can't go anywhere like this.'

This was an epiphany for me. Every woman, everyone, wanted to look their best. It would take me a while to work through it completely, but I had come into fashion through my ability to sew, to create clothes. And – I am ashamed to admit – I took looking good for granted. Foolishly, I had assumed that everyone could look the way I did if they wanted to. I did not then understand that circumstance clothed people. Graça was exerting the little control she had over her appearance, and she would not go into town with chipped nails. She taught me far more than I her.

'Oh. Wait a minute.' I only had two bottles of nail varnish then, a pillar-box red and a salmon pink. I fetched them and a beige linen dress and jacket, which I thought would complement her skin tone. She studied the varnishes.

'The pink,' she said finally.

When she had changed into the linen dress and jacket, we sat together at the kitchen table while I removed the old varnish and then painted her nails a refined, elegant pink. Charles paced around the kitchen, his anger and outrage written all over his face, then he disappeared upstairs. Graça seemed soothed by the beauty ritual. She sat still while her nails dried, her bruised and savaged face strangely at peace. I realised that for her, nails were like the right choice of shoes; they were about being ready to face the world. Without them she felt undressed but with them, even battered and beaten as she was, she had her sense of self. The next day I went out and bought myself the beginnings of my collection.

12

Razor

Ah, ma chère, now we come to the question of body hair: to be or not to be hairy? It was a little like nail varnish. In Oberfals the soft down that covered my youthful arms and legs never bothered me. In St. Gallen I only exposed myself once or twice on Sunday trips to the lake, but all the women had body hair. Swathed in lovely clothes, I never went bare-legged in Paris. And Charles never complained. He used to bury his nose in my armpit, nuzzling me like a dog; he said that the fine hair trapped my perfume, that the parfum he had created for Dior was second only to it. And compared to a man like him, I was as smooth and hairless as a boto, the pink Brazilian dolphin.

Although we rarely exposed our limbs except in the high summer days, and though the sun-bleached hair barely showed against my tanned skin, in Brazil, hair had to be made invisible. If you had money there were many ways to depilate but for those with little, peroxide was the cheapest – though least successful – option. Nails and lips were to be coloured, always. And skin a perfect tan, always. No one ever said anything at clients' pool parties when I lifted my arms to the waiter's tray to take a glass of champagne freshly flown in from France; no one ever commented as they scanned my legs while I played volleyball on the beach. But gradually, I became aware of how hairless the women were; how – according to their aesthetic – I was misguided, too *macho*. And then the word *depilação* seemed to be everywhere, on shop windows, posters and flyers, advertising that vital service, depilation: the removal of hair. My first attempt at depilating myself was on a whim. I took Charles's razor from its stand and tried to shave my legs and under my arms. It was a massacre worthy of Norman Bates.

So, the question became not whether to but how to. If you ever had any illusion that beauty was easy, ma chère, I am sure I am helping to dispel that. Hair removal is a fine example. From India through Iran to the Arab lands, our sisters twist and pull fine cotton threads, so fast that they whip the unwanted hairs out. Other women in the Middle East prefer to roll a sugar paste over their legs; the hairs get stuck into the mass and torn out in batches. Here in New York I have avoided electrolysis – I cannot imagine why anyone would choose to send an electric current shooting up their hair. It has always seemed too painful and time-consuming. I've tried depilators, more an instrument of torture than a beauty aid, the rotating blades screaming and whirring as they snatch resistant hairs, taking an age to work up your legs, yanking unceasingly as they go, a long, rolling wave of pain.

As for the creams, the noxious fumes are enough to tell me this is not right, that it can't be good for the skin to smear on something that rots the hair away so quickly. Another chemical solution, which I experimented with in Brazil, was lathering on hydrogen peroxide foam. It made the hair on my legs pale and wispy. Then one day when I was discussing how to bleach different fabrics and the damage that bleach made on silk and linen, I realised I should not be using it on my skin. Eventually, I took the plunge and entered a *salão de depilção*. I shuddered as they spread hot wax over my skin, but at least with waxing the pain is over in an instant.

These days I use the tweezers that Charles gave me for plucking the stragglers under my eyebrows, and wax for the legs and bikini line. And I take Charles's razor every day to the hollows under my arms, where he used to inhale me.

Charles was particularly attached to his razor. It had been his father's before him and it was one of very few possessions that he had from his childhood. A family friend had taken a small case of their belongings to the concierge of their pre-war apartment block in Paris, guessing that if any of the family were to survive the concentration camps, this is where they would return. Like the professor and his portraits and porcelain, Charles kept his few mementoes of his lost life close to him. I never asked him how his father had killed himself, but sometimes as I click a new blade into the gold and ivory holder, I think about how easily it glides over my skin and how effortlessly it would draw blood.

Much as Charles would not dwell on or talk about the past, he was trapped by it. His decision to have no children was a response to what he had seen, and equally his abhorrence of any kind of violence compelled him to act. He had already seen what happens when good men do nothing.

On the morning we confronted Graça, Charles disappeared upstairs while I painted her nails. He came down clean-shaven and dressed in his smartest suit before joining us at the table. We watched in silence while she held out her hands, fingers spread across the table like pink starbursts on New Year's Eve.

'I'm ready,' she said after a careful inspection of the rose-quartz nails.

'I'll go and flag a cab down,' Charles said.

'No. I don't think you should come,' I said in a neutral tone.

'What?' A scowl transfigured his face.

'Come on, mon amour, you're too angry.'

'Of course I am. I want to beat him to a pulp,' he shouted. 'I want him to pay.'

'Exactly. That is why you can't come.'

'Graça?' he implored her. 'Talk some sense into her.'

I exchanged a glance with her.

'If you go, there will be a fight,' I said. 'Then he'll go home and beat up someone who is weaker than him.'

'Yes, senhor, she's right,' Graça said quietly. 'He'll thrash Gabriela.'

Charles said nothing.

'Charles,' I said. 'You are better at cleaning wounds, and you know that I'm good with people. I can make sure this man never does it again.'

Finally, Charles nodded. 'You're both sure?' We both nodded. He walked to the door. 'I'll hail a cab for you.'

A few minutes later he kissed Graça on the cheeks and hugged me before we stepped into the cab. Graça sat stiffly in the back of the little VW beetle as it took us along the seafront. She stared out of the window as we swung left at Urca under the shadow of the Sugar Loaf Mountain. It dawned on me that she had probably never been in a car in Rio before. As the taxi moved through Botafogo, Flamengo and Glória, then veered left into the old town centre, I rehearsed what I was going to say to her tormentor. When Schleich had raped me, my parents had done nothing to comfort me, nor support me. I was not going to stand aside meekly as they had done.

When he dropped us off, the taxi driver gestured vaguely in the direction of a maze of cobbled streets and dilapidated colonial town houses. It took us a while to find the building where Sé worked, but when we finally did, we were shown on to the floor where rows of women sat bent over long trestle tables, working in quiet concentration. Rather than waiting where we had been left, I started walking along the tables looking over the women's shoulders. They were examining, sorting, packing and wrapping gems. A few tapped their fine, varnished nails on typewriters.

'Excuse me, Senhora, can I help you?'

I turned around slowly, half-regretting that I had not worn an old Dior suit – it would have fluttered beautifully. I had chosen to look regal in one of my own creations, a cobalt silk dress and jacket. A plump, short man, his suit one size too small at the waist and two sizes too long in the leg, was standing in front of me. He wiped his brow with a big white handkerchief.

'I am Rosa Dumarais, of the Maison Dumarais,' I said. I am not a tall woman and I was still only in my mid-twenties, but at Dior's I had learnt how to stand, how to draw myself up and impose myself on a room. I held out my hand. 'Maybe you have heard of me.' It took him a while to understand but eventually he took it and kissed it.

'Paulo Maluf, at your service.' He dipped his head slightly.

'Ah, Maluf as in Maluf Gem Exports,' I said.

'Yes, I am the owner.' He puffed his chest out and pulled his shoulders back, though there was nothing he could do to prevent his trousers still pooling around his ankles.

'I have a proposition to make for you.' I scanned the workshop. 'Is there somewhere we can talk?'

'Yes, of course, please follow me. My office is—'

'May I leave my assistant to look over the work of your women?' I fixed my eyes on him, so that he understood that it was not a question.

'Senhora?' Graça's voice sounded alarmed. She had shadowed me as we walked up and down the trestles, and dressed in my beige dress and jacket she looked as if she was indeed my assistant, not my housemaid.

'Please, would you survey the different stones and settings.' I hoped she would understand that I just needed to be alone with Maluf, that this was a charade. She stared at me with a baffled expression that turned to comprehension. Her eyes seemed to light up and I was struck by how beautiful she was.

Graça finally nodded and turned to the array of trestle tables. The women's hands were still moving through their automatic motions but I knew that everyone was listening to me. I was certain they had never seen anyone turned out and fashioned like me in the flesh before, nor for that matter a black woman as well-dressed as Graça.

Senhor Maluf stalled, unsure if he should lead the way or follow behind me to his office. His hand suggested the direction, so I strode, as I had learnt as a mannequin at Dior's, to the door and waited for him to open it and conduct me in. Once sat behind the cluttered expanse of his battered wooden desk, he relaxed. I perched on the wooden chair opposite him and surveyed the room. Like the factory, everything was old and faded. He was employing about thirty women on the floor, and I guessed from the faint sounds of movement coming through the ceiling that there were other offices or workshops on the floor above. He was keeping his head above water, but only just. He needed business, he needed orders. In the attic with the Italian maestro

I had learnt how to adorn fabrics with sequins, feather, lace and gems. Gems were expensive and laborious to affix. But they had cachet. There was a deal to be made. In the few seconds it took to deduce all this, my plan was clear in my mind.

'So, Senhora Rosa, to what do I owe the honour of this visit?' He picked up a pen, striking what he must have thought was a masterful pose as if about to write something down.

'The thing about fashion, Senhor Maluf, is that it is an art form. And art is a work of inspiration. I woke up this morning and thought that this season's collection would be called *Cintilante* – it's going to be brilliant and sparkling; scintillating. I want to saturate my fabrics not with sequins, but real gems. I need to find a reliable source of good quality, well-priced stones.'

'I see,' he said, looking a little perplexed.

'Do you know anything about fashion?' I asked, and he looked blankly at me. 'Have you heard of me?'

'Forgive me, senhora, no.' He flushed a dull red at the admission.

A wedding ring flashed on Maluf's pudgy fingers. I smiled. 'I see you are married. Do you have daughters?'

He nodded.

'May I suggest you ring your wife and ask her if she or your daughters have heard of the Maison Dumarais?'

I sat back as he dialled then spoke to his wife.

'Isabela, what do you know about the Maison Dumarais? Why? Because Senhora Dumarais is with me right now.'

His face went from red to white and back to red as his wife spoke on the end of the line. I could discern an excited stream of sound. By the time he put the phone down, he was regarding me with awe.

'I believe that your wife knew of me?'

'Yes. She did.' He stared at me for a moment. I let him think. 'Did you say saturate?'

In that moment I knew I had him. I could see him doing the sums in his head. There was a febrile glint in his eyes as he tried to imagine what this could mean.

'Yes, I imagine I would be ordering a lot. If the right conditions were met. Obviously, the gems have to be good enough and the prices have to be right. Would you be interested?'

'Absolutely.' His lack of guile was charming and explained why his business was just bumping along.

'There is one other small matter that I would like to discuss. It concerns one of your employees.'

His face paled and I surmised he had been stitched up before.

'Senhor Maluf, this is not what you imagine,' I said, smiling my reassurance. 'Indulge me by listening to me, that is all, and then we'll draw up a contract.'

'Just listen?' The poor man looked crestfallen; he thought I was playing him.

'Yes, just let me tell you a story.' At first, he listened politely but distractedly – no doubt running the numbers through his mind again – but as I went on, he focused then began to look uncomfortable, tapping his desk with his pen in agitation.

'I'll sack him at once,' he said as soon as I had finished. 'Let me call for him.'

I shook my head. 'No, that won't do. No one will know what he is capable of, and he will carry on somewhere else. Imagine this happening to your daughters.'

'So, you want me to have him . . . disposed of?'

'No, God forbid!' I cried, genuinely shocked.

He looked relieved, and I knew then he would have done it. Although I was not sure if his motivation would have stemmed from moral outrage or his desperation to win my business.

'No, I want you to keep him here. Where you can watch over him. Out there he will go free, the police will never pros-ecute him. But here he will be in a virtual prison. Here everyone will know about him, what kind of man he is, and he will know what kind of reference you will write for him if he ever tries to leave. It'll be a life sentence, and if he is not an idiot he'll be a model worker for you. Graça is outside talking to your women, they will all see her bruises. When we have left, I suggest that you take him out there and make him tell them what happened and why you are keeping him. Let him live with his shame.'

Senhor Maluf stared at me as he pondered my proposition. After a while he stood up and said, 'You're smart, Senhora Rosa. Wait a moment, please.' He went out on to the floor.

He returned a few moments later with a young man in worker's overalls. His rolled-up sleeves and open neckline exposed a fine, strong physique. He would have been hard to fight, yet the cuts on his face and hands showed Graça's resolve.

'Senhora Rosa, this is José Ribeiro da Silva.'

I rose from the chair and deliberately scanned the man from top to bottom, all the way from his tight, dark curls, over his scarred face and down to his tattered espadrilles. He eyed me back, clearly enjoying the attention.

'Senhor Maluf, I'll be right back,' I said and promptly left.

Graça had seen Sé arrive and had retreated to the far corner of the shop floor. He probably had not even recognised her dressed in my clothes.

'Come. He can't hurt you. I've pinioned him.'

'I don't want to come.' This was the first time she had ever refused me but her look was not of defiance but terror. I took her by the hand, but still she resisted.

'You must,' I reasoned with her. 'Otherwise you will live in fear of him. He has to see that you are not to be touched.' I kept pulling her hand until she finally let me lead her into Maluf's office. She barely stepped into the room, closing the door behind her and leaning against it. Her hand was on the handle, ready to flee at a moment's notice. Sé glanced at her then looked away briefly before turning back to stare at the lady in the beige linen suit, his face tightening as he recognised her.

'Da Silva, don't look so surprised. Did you think Graça had no friends? She—'

'Senhor Maluf, I—' Sé interrupted me, addressing his boss.

Maluf cut him short. 'Shut up and listen to Senhora Dumarais.'

'Graça told us what happened,' I said, my voice hard as diamond. 'You tried to rape her. You beat her when she resisted.

I've seen her bruises. What kind of man does this? She deserves your protection – not because she is your fiancée's cousin, but because she is a woman. Graça has nothing to be ashamed of; she should be proud of standing up for herself. But you, you should keep your head down. You're no man.'

'Senhor Maluf.' Sé's voice had become whiny and panicked. 'Don't believe a word the senhora says.' He looked at me defiantly. 'Who is she to accuse me? I've never met her before.'

Senhor Maluf's disgust and resolve were written large on his face. He smoothed his hands over his desk. 'Don't try me, boy. I can see the bruises on the lady's face and neck, and the scratches on your own. You'll listen to Senhora Dumarais if you know what's good for you.'

'Thank you, senhor,' I said graciously, then turned to the cowering bully. 'You should know that Senhor Maluf wanted to sack you, but I have persuaded him to keep you on here where everyone will know what you are. Of course, you can choose to leave, but both Senhor Maluf and I would write references to your new employer telling them what we know. And, of course, we could visit the police.'

'Or you can keep your job,' said Senhor Maluf, 'where I will watch your every move.'

Sé puffed himself up and opened his mouth. I wondered if he was stupid as well as cruel, if he would react with bluster and anger, but then he closed his eyes and pursed his lips. He fixed his eyes on the floor and seemed to deflate. When he looked up again and nodded it was clear that he realised he was trapped. I smiled at Graça. We had won.

Charles drove us up to Dona Marta, where we packed up Graça's few belongings. That same day, we moved her in with us. All the old houses had servants' quarters at the back of the house off the kitchen and she settled in there happily. Don't look so appalled, ma chère, it was in fact a big step up for her. It was cleaner and bigger, she had her own bathroom with running water and a flushing toilet and, after two days, new bedroom furniture and a mattress she chose herself. In contrast, her cousin's shack had been little more than one room with a flimsy partition along one side for her bed and use of a communal pit latrine and a standing pipe outside for water. The inescapable, pungent smell had shocked me most of all.

Inhaling sweet fragrances is one of life's more sensuous pleasures. The day after we had returned from Dona Marta, the memory of that stench made me seek refuge in the thick, rose-like white pikake flowers in a vase on my dresser. Some scents are delicate and ephemeral, difficult to absorb. Like meditation, the very act of reaching for the pleasure banishes it. It was much harder to shake the unwanted odour of misery. So, there I was buried in the vase of blossom, intoxicated, when something struck me that I had never understood until then.

Graça used to have a constant, slightly musky odour: her *cheirinho*. It was the aroma that seeps out from the pores with work and fatigue, not from sport and pleasure. Sweat has many smells, many emotions: fear is bitter; fatigue is dull and musty; and excitement is acrid, not sweet as it should be. Graça had always smelt as if she had been standing for hours on buses full of swaying bodies, packed and exhausted from too little sleep, too much time spent journeying, everyone leaning against each other in Rio's molten air. And then she would arrive and change from her travel dress to her work clothes, slipping from one identity into another, and start to work. As she walked around the house, the pungency of the favela bus would trail behind her.

I straightened up, pulling my face from the petals' allure, and waited, listening. Graça was somewhere working or unpacking. I hunted her down to the entrance hall where she was polishing the mirrors. A woman should never leave her home until she has checked her appearance at least twice, from all angles: back, front and sides. I had four full-length mirrors (as I still do – a pair for each check) and a small magnified one at face-level by the door, for my last-minute lipstick check. Graça was polishing away, ignoring her own image, seeing not herself but stains and specks.

'Stop,' I said.

She hesitated then stopped.

'Look,' I said.

She looked.

I asked her softly, 'What do you see?'

She scrutinised the mirror in front of her, looking at the glass, not the image.

'Senhora, I have not finished polishing yet,' she replied, dabbing at a spot fretfully. 'Surely it will shine better in a few minutes.'

'Oh, Graça,' I exclaimed. 'Look properly!'

She stared ahead harder still. I decided that patience was the order of the day. It would take a while. So, I posed in front of the other mirror and inspected my appearance. I was wearing a ripe-peach silk outfit. It must have been autumn, probably May. The tropical autumn, the time of abatement after the intense, cloying Rio summer. I idled away some minutes, shifting from toe to toe to let gentle undulations ripple my silken skirt. I posed as I had learnt at 30 Avenue Montaigne and regarded my silhou-ette, patted my compact belly, checked my hair.

'Senhora?' she said tentatively. 'You want me to look at myself, not the glass?'

'No,' I said. 'I want you to *see* yourself.'

'Oh.' She dropped back on her haunches. 'Oh.'

Her face was still battered and bruised; her right eye was puffy, only half open. Her hair was scraped back and pinned down. The shapeless blouse she was wearing had been washed so many times that the pattern was indistinct, the white had turned a drab grey. The green of her slack skirt was bleached from being hung out to dry in the fierce Brazilian sun. Her skin was dull and tired. She stared and stared, not moving. After a while she settled back on to her heels and sighed.

'What do you see?'

She turned and smiled at me but there was a sad look in her eyes. 'I don't see what you see, senhora, when you look at your-self.'

'I'm not asking about what I see. What do you see?'

Fixing her eyes on her reflection, her voice thickened with each word she spoke. 'I see bruises. I see worn clothes. I see a battered, poor woman.'

'I want to change that,' I said, moving to stand behind her and resting my hands on her shoulders.

'Change?' She laughed wryly. 'Senhora, I can't change. You asked me to see what I am. This is what I am.' A tear rolled down her cheek.

'Do you think I grew up like a princess in a castle?' I knelt down beside her.

'Yes,' she said, shifting her eyes to my reflection. 'You have no idea how hard it is for me.'

'Perhaps I don't, but I didn't grow up in a palace. Far from it.' I took a breath. I realised that I was going to share my secrets, my history, with Graça. It felt like a big step. 'I had a father who beat me, a mother who neglected me and . . . well, it got so bad that I ran away from home with nothing when I was sixteen. I walked the streets, worked with my hands like you, sewing, and I made myself. I decided then that no man was going to ruin my life again.'

She carried on staring at my reflection. She was nineteen, I was twenty-four; she was innocent, I was married; she came from the countryside, I had seen the world. But as she kept her eyes on me, I could see that she was beginning to understand that despite all our differences, we were just two young women.

'Stand up.' I held out my hand. 'Please.'

She pushed herself up off the floor stiffly and stood in front of the mirror.

'Look at you: you are tall and slender; you have great legs – you're like a gazelle.'

'I'm too thin,' she said, smiling.

I, too, scrutinised her in a way I never had before.

'Nonsense. You have such wonderful bone structure.' She had high, chiselled cheekbones and a fine nose. She reminded me of someone, but I struggled to think who.

'My grandmother was Indian.'

'Ah, that explains your curls.' She kept her hair up or in a scarf, but I had seen her comb through the long ringlets. 'You are beautiful; it's just hidden away. You're going to start over from today.'

'What do you mean, senhora?' she asked quickly.

'Come.' I took her hand and led her to my bathroom.

The bath stood gleaming, thanks to Graça's efforts, on its brass feet amongst the blue and white Portuguese tiles. I turned the taps on. Graça remained at the door clasping her hands in front of her. I scooped a handful of bath salts from the bowl and tossed it into the water.

'Senhora Rosa,' she protested, rushing into the room at last. 'Let me do that.'

I held my hand up and she stopped. 'No,' I said. 'Today I'm going to wait on you. No discussion.'

Graça looked uncomfortable so I cast around for something she could do. 'Alright, could you fetch me a glass of hot milk with a spoonful of honey?'

'Yes, of course, Senhora Rosa,' she murmured and vanished from the room. The bath was full by the time she came back carrying the glass of honeyed milk on a silver platter with a lace doily.

'Thank you,' I said as I picked up the glass and tipped its contents into the water.

'Senhora!' she exclaimed, outraged.

'It's not wasted; don't worry. It's well spent.' I turned the taps off. I was sitting on the rim of the bath and she edged back to the threshold.

'Graça. No one can be happy unless they love themselves. You have to cherish yourself. Looking good helps, having the attention of a worthy man helps. But it must begin here.' I lifted my hand to my face and slid it down over my chin and rested it on my chest, right above my heart. 'The secret weapon of any woman is her skin and her smell. Both must be soft, elusive and gentle. Cleopatra bathed every day in goats' milk. You may find this a little excessive,' I said, gesturing to the bath, 'but this trick was taught to me by my great-aunt Bertha. She was a mountain woman. Her skin had braved the harsh winters and strong summers, but even as an old woman it shone like a polished stone, so taut and soft. A glass of milk and a spoonful of honey, she would say, taken the right way, keeps a woman young and beautiful.' I took her hand and tugged her into the room. 'Graça, *this* is the right way. It's time you enjoyed a soak.'

She hesitated and then stepped forward. 'Are you sure, Senhora Rosa?'

'Yes. Now get in, and do not get out, nor move, nor even soap yourself until I get back. Just get in, lie there and dream. Please.'

And with that I patted my hands dry on a hand towel, reached for a large, fluffy bath sheet from the stack and handed it to Graça. I closed the door behind me and listened. For a moment there was silence and then I heard a quiet splash. I smiled and left.

I have no idea what she did or thought in those first twenty minutes of luxury. But when I knocked and came back in with a glass of lemonade for her and placed it on the rack suspended across the bath (which held my Sunday cocktails) she barely stirred. Her eyes had glazed a milky white and then I realised who she reminded me of: Nefertiti, the Egyptian queen. As she became aware of my presence, she stirred and threw me a dazzling smile that I had never seen before.

People assume that if you grow up in poverty that you are used to it. I knew from my own experience that however usual misery is, it never ceases to be intolerable, whereas comfort feels natural and easy. It was only chance that had deprived her so long of this.

'May I sit down?' I asked.

She nodded dreamily. 'Of course.'

I perched on the rim. She was lying low in the water, her feet resting on the end. A golden fuzz of bleached hair shimmered as it dried against her chocolate skin. She looked as contented as the rich women relaxing after being cosseted and pampered in the beauty salons of the Zona Sul, although evidently she had never experienced such treatments. I leaned across and levered

Charles's razor blade from the lion's paw scallop shell I had brought back from the beach. It was perfectly sized to keep the razor in and even had built-in drainage ridges.

'You will feel reborn when you get out, Graça,' I said as she opened her eyes, 'but there is one last touch. Newborn babies have the smoothest skin. Take this, but be careful, it is very sharp.'

I handed her Charles's razor. I wanted her to step out of the bath like Venus emerging from the sea. Together, we were erasing the past.

13

Sleeping Pills

There is one problem with going out late – at least as I get older – and that is that I get tired earlier. Gone are the days when I could party all night, stay up until dawn and go for a swim on the rouged beach with the orange sun slowly heaving itself out of its Atlantic slumber before I downed my fresh breakfast juice and went on to my office in the crumbling old centre of Rio. There I had a chaise longue, covered in a rich amber raw silk, where I could nap between phone calls, meetings and design work.

In those days, I didn't need these at all. See, ma chère, it's the only unmarked bottle. An inconspicuous white plastic bottle. I always tear off the label of these, I would never want to facilitate their misuse. It is a long time since I've had to use sleeping pills. Taken in small, irregular quantities, barbiturates can be helpful but used wrongly they are dangerous and addictive. I started using them after a conversation with Graça that prevented me sleeping.

One morning, as she gave me my coffee she blurted out, 'What is the matter with Senhor Charles?'

'Nothing,' I said, barely registering her question. But as she went about her business, I found myself unable to put her question from my mind and a feeling of unease settled deep in my stomach. When I had finished my coffee I went back upstairs to our bedroom and stood in the doorway, looking in. Charles was still in bed fast asleep and I crept into the room so as not to wake him. It was not so much a thought as an instinct that made me drag the sheet off his body and look. I examined him not as his lover, but as his wife. I had never fathomed how a man who spent his days huddled over laboratory benches, lifting and filling tubes, could maintain such fitness. He was naturally strong and muscular and was rarely ill. Charles's olive complexion, dark curly hair and warm brown eyes had adapted to the Brazilian clime well. He never sunbathed, but the little exposure he gained from plunging into the Atlantic waves and playing on the beach had lent his skin a healthy bronzed hue. He always glowed.

Change is hard to see when you are close up to it so I made myself scrutinise him the way I examined the mock-up of a dress. Charles had dropped weight. His arms and chest had lost bulk, his once-thick thigh muscles were slimmed down. As his chest filled and collapsed with each breath, I could see his ribs. I ran my finger down the skin of his arm, which was no longer soft, but rough. He was pallid. My finger found a small patch of blue nestling on the back of his knee and then another mottled patch inside his thigh.

I kissed the bruise and traced the length of his motionless leg and up his back, ever more alarmed at the sight of minuscule, damaged blood vessels, erupting into tiny bruises masked by his fading tan. Charles rolled over on to his stomach, displaying the speckled marks of tiny purple lesions dotted over his back. His arms and torso were covered with discolourations.

Charles stirred and then went back to sleep. It's over thirty years ago but when I stop and let myself, I can still remember the feeling of confusion that overwhelmed me as I sat on the bed next to him. The sense of certainty and security I had lived with for a decade was shattered in an instant.

Some time ago I bought some Meissen china, an old set but one I could use, and once in a while a plate would break, or a bowl would disappear – chips, cracks, losses – until about a year ago I realised that I did not have enough left for a simple dinner party. It was just like this with Charles. I had not noticed until it was too late, had failed to detect the early warning signs. As I sat there staring at him, a pattern emerged, suddenly so clear to me I couldn't imagine how I hadn't seen it before. It had begun with him occasionally not feeling like taking our morning walk along the crashing breakers and frothing foam, and then more often. At the weekend he stopped joining in the beach volleyball. He began to cancel tennis matches. Without me noticing it, he gradually withdrew from physical activity. He was always tired.

The next few weeks were filled with visits to doctors and specialists, and a growing sense of panic. Eventually, Graça could stand it no longer.

'Senhora Rosa,' she said one morning as I sat unmoving, staring at the papaya she had prepared for my breakfast. 'I've been thinking. Your medicine is not working. This thing, they cannot stop it. Maybe it has nothing to do with them.'

'What do you mean?'

'Medicine can only work if the illness is natural. This thing Senhor Charles has, it's not natural.'

I waited, uncertain of what she meant; cancer was cruel but natural in my book.

'It's *Macumba*,' she said simply.

'Magic?' I tried not to smile.

'I know you don't believe it,' she said with dignity. 'In your country you don't have it, Senhor Charles told me, but here it's real. People, when they are jealous, when they don't like you or what you have, they go and see someone. They cast spells, they do these things, these rituals, and then you get sick and the doctors can never help you – not if the cause is magic – and then you die. Senhor Charles will die, senhora, if we don't do something for him.'

She had rarely spoken so much in one go and I sat looking up at her, stunned. She was right, I did not believe any of it. But neither did I have any faith in our doctors, who had conversation after conversation with Charles, full of technical, medical words and ideas, but helped him not one iota. It would not hurt to try, and I was desperate.

'What can we do, Graça?'

I had never travelled by bus in Rio and I stood jostling against a school of commuters, clad in their faded, over-washed clothes.

The orange skirt and white jacket had been a mistake; I looked like a clown fish swimming amongst mackerel. That was the first and last time, in many years, until today, that my wardrobe let me down.

I kept thinking about how foolish Charles would think I was being. But it was my choice to pursue this futile hope. A gentleman stood up in the crowd and offered me his seat, which I graciously accepted, and so we continued, Graça standing guard over me, her bag and mine bumping on my lap as the engine strained across the hot, flat plain north of the city centre. When we came to our stop I followed Graça into the favela beside the factories that squatted by the roadside.

The walk was short but interminable. High heels are not made for jumping over open sewers, fetid puddles and paths strewn with junk that even the poor do not think worth salvaging. It was a relief to reach the large wooden gate wedged haphazardly into a rough brick wall. Graça clapped her hands loudly and called out Dona Aparecida's name. After a long wait we heard the sound of faltering steps. The door opened and a stout woman, her face lined with deep creases, her black curls streaked with white, invited us in.

As we stepped into the shade of a mango tree, it was like entering another world. Behind us the dirt brown of the narrow alley ran between untidy lines of shacks, lean-tos and the occasional brick edifice, but hidden from the alley behind the wall was a mirage of green and quiet. Papaya trees sprouted inside the uneven wall, against which *chuchu* vines clambered, dangling their spiny green squashes; below them large green *couve* leaves waited to be picked and thinly sliced. An avocado tree was weighed down with huge, dark fruit; in a vegetable patch the carrot tops waved in the breeze and, somehow squeezed in, a cluster of maize was growing, the cobs still small and green. Clucking, scrawny chickens darted around. Stepping into this urban farmyard hidden in all the squalor of the favela, I felt a rush of hope; maybe Dona Aparecida did indeed have transformative powers.

We followed her into her house.

'Sit there,' she ordered, pointing at one of two heavy wooden chairs in the centre of the room and at the bed for Graça. I sat down. She busied herself making coffee. One side of the room was her kitchen: an old wood-fired stove, a large stone sink and side table, harvested carrots and pale green *chuchu* lying on a wooden cutting board. There was a pan of beans cooking on the stove, giving off the same garlic-rich smell that came from almost every house in Brazil in the mornings. The next wall was covered in shelves. On one shelf were all her cooking utensils, cutlery, crockery and aluminium pans scrubbed to a shine. Above sat a few tins and a set of jars arranged from large to small. This was the first time that I had seen this array of rice, beans, sugar, coffee and salt – as they are in most Brazilian homes.

Graça had settled on the bed that was pushed up against the wall facing the 'kitchen'. The bed was covered in a roughly woven cotton blanket, the kind I had seen men hawking by the roadside as I drove down Avenida Atlântica on the way to the beach or the city centre. A flap of material that looked like printed cotton hung over the top of a wooden crate under the bed: her wardrobe. It dawned on me then that this single room was Dona Aparecida's entire house. It was a sobering realisation. I felt like I had lost everything, like my heart had been carved out of my chest, but I knew looking around this home that I still had so much, so many things, so much comfort. I also knew that I would have swapped it all to have Charles back.

'Senhora Rosa,' she began when she had poured us coffee and a glass of water. She sat in the heavy wooden chair facing me; there was no table. 'From what Senhora Graça tells me, you don't really believe in the work of the spirits.'

I hesitated for a moment, not wanting to offend her. 'In my country, I had never even heard about them. We have the Church and that's about it.'

'The Catholic Church?'

'Yes.'

'So, you know about the devil and his demons?' she asked, and her eyes seemed to penetrate me.

'Yes,' I said slowly, thinking for the first time in years of Oberfals. I knew a demon when I saw one – I had seen the complete absence of goodness in Schleich's eyes. The last time I ever went to confession, I told Father Matthias that I had been raped. I wasn't sure if I had committed a sin or not. The priest had assured me that I had not; rape was the rapist's crime. It had been a relief to hear that, even in the eyes of God, the transgression had been all Schleich's.

'And the saints and the Holy Virgin?' she pressed.

'Yes, but—'

'It's all the same. Look behind you,' she commanded, and I swivelled in my chair. The wall behind where I sat was dedicated to the effigies of saints and deities clustered on a small shrine draped with a golden cloth; flowers and small offerings of rice and beans solicited their good will. The wall behind had been painted sky blue. 'Angels, saints, devils and demons. Our *orixas* and ghosts, they are the same as in the church, just by another name. Iemanjá is Saint Barbara, Ogun is Saint George.'

'I've seen the offerings to Iemanjá on the beach at New Year.'

'So you've seen how the *orixas* enter a body and take possession. Think, then how much easier it is for the spirits just to make someone ill, just tweak a little something rather than take control.'

I had never forgotten the sight of the possessed woman groaning on the beach in front of the Copacabana Palace Hotel that first New Year in Rio. Now I had become accustomed to sidestepping the little offerings of maize and chicken left on the streets, having been taught to avoid stepping on them as they would bring me bad luck. I was even used to the trances that I had seen many times since. But I had never thought this could affect me or Charles.

'I'm sorry, I want to believe. I just don't know how.'

'Senhora,' the medium said sternly, 'we are wasting each other's time if you don't believe. This is not science, but it is fact. Ever since I was a child I have been blighted with my vision.'

'Blighted? Surely it's a gift?' I wrinkled my nose at the sudden stench of an unpleasant aroma.

'It's a blessing to free people from malicious ghosts and spells but it's a curse to see the dead, it's a curse to have premonitions and be unable to stop what I've seen happening – and then get blamed for it.'

'Blame you?'

'Yes. When I was little I tried to warn my father from going to work one day. I begged and pleaded, but he went anyway. When he never came home, my mother called me a witch and never forgave me. After a few more warnings like that she threw me out.'

Another wave of the pungent smell assaulted my nostrils. I looked around but the only foods to be seen were the vegetables and beans bubbling on the stove. Perhaps something had been put aside to feed a pig – Graça had told me that was common practice in favelas.

'So, do you believe now?'

It took me a long time to answer. My head told me that this was nonsense. Yet something, perhaps her matter-of-factness or her lack of performance, made an impression on me. In any event, I surprised myself by saying 'yes' and realised that I meant it.

'Good. So, I assume you've come about the spirit?'

By now the smell had become so overpowering I was nauseous. I gagged into my hand and shook my head. 'No, I've come to get help for my husband. He's very ill.'

'So, this spirit is not your husband?'

I stared blankly at her. 'No.' I gulped.

'Senhora,' she said, as though it were obvious, 'you have a carnal spirit with you.'

A chill ran down my spine and I looked around in alarm. 'What spirit?' I shivered, feeling suddenly clammy. Another whiff of the unpleasant odour came with my next breath.

She sighed and settled back in her chair. 'There are many different types of ghosts and spirits. There are the mischievous ones, who haunt from afar. They are the imps, who loosen the tops of jars so that when you pick them up, glass and jam fall crashing to the floor. Then there are the thuggish rogues, whose pleasure lies in frightening you with sounds and apparitions. But the worst kind by far are the carnal spirits.'

'And that's what I have?' I could feel my defences going up; this was ludicrous.

'Yes, you have such a companion, senhora. I worried for you when you came in; I assumed he was why you have come.' The whole time she spoke, her eyes were fixed on something over my shoulder.

'He?' I glanced behind me but could see nothing, yet the pungent smell seemed to be thickening.

'A carnal ghost,' she explained, 'comes into being when someone dies, someone who is so attached to life or to somebody that they take a corporeal form. This ghost then stays with the person they were attached to – they become a ghostly companion.'

'This is because they love someone?'

'Sometimes.' She shrugged. 'It could be hate, too. Both passions are attachments, of a kind.'

'You mean they . . . haunt you?'

She met my question with the same calm face, but then rubbed her nose as if to wipe away an unpleasant smell.

'Yes. Some ghosts are benevolent. Deceased lovers sometimes stay close by their loved ones, awaiting their time to be reunited. Others are malevolent, forever shadowing you, forever trying to cause harm.' My stomach had tightened in a knot as she spoke. The rank smell reminded me of something.

'What happens to them?' I dared to ask.

'Often they end up just drifting off when their loved one finds someone else. Such ghosts are harmless.' She got up and went to fill a glass with water. 'But of all the ghosts to fear, the evil, carnal companion ghost is the worst. They stay close by you waiting for every opportunity to harm you with endless mishaps. People come to me with a run of bad luck or outright disaster, their lives twisted beyond recognition.'

'I see . . .' There was something about the smell that was familiar. 'This ghost, is he here now? Where?'

'Just behind you, by your shoulder.'

I sensed a sudden clamminess and shuddered. Maybe, I told myself, it was just the heat and my fear that were making me damp. Who could have been thinking of me when he had died? Dior had died the year before, but he was my friend. Who hated me enough to expire with me in their last thoughts?

'What does he look like?' I asked.

She hesitated. 'It is more that I have a sense of him than can see him. If you ask, it becomes clearer.'

I paused. Maybe Thomas had been killed in the war, that's why he had never come back? 'Is he young?'

She shook her head.

'Is he thin?'

Another shake.

'Is he big?'

'Very,' she said.

My heart beat faster. The foul smell made me wretch. 'Is he ugly?'

'Very.' She nodded.

'Are his hands small and fat?' My voice shook now.

She peered and nodded again.

'*Schämst Du Dich!*' I screamed, jumping up and spinning round. For so many years I would suddenly feel my buttocks squeezed, my breasts grabbed, and I would jump and look, and see no one. I used to think I was going crazy but now I knew it was him: Schleich. It wasn't enough that he had raped me in life, no, his sticky hands had to reach out, groping from hell itself. When he had disappeared, ma chère, in my naivety it had never crossed my mind that he had died. You must remember that I didn't find out about the murder until long after this visit to Dona Aparecida. I had blocked him from my thoughts. But now I knew it was him.

All at once I could see him right in front of me, the whole, swirling mass of a lost and blighted soul. I knew he could see that I had seen him, and I fixed my eyes on the densest spot, the vortex of this shimmering, ghostly whirlpool. I thought of his hands, his searching fingers, reaching for me through the maestro's pathetic attempts in the Paris attic, and all my pain and fear over the years, losing Thomas and Laurin, and now Charles's illness. Then, like bile rising, a wave of anger overwhelmed me and a rage that I had never expressed erupted from me as I spat dead into the centre of the apparition.

'To hell with you,' I hurled at him, and then turned my back on him for good.

That afternoon, Graça took me to the cobbled backstreets of the city centre to the shops of the *macumbeiras* – the white-dressed spiritualists we saw on the beach every New Year's Eve. Dona Aparecida had given me a shopping list. After Schleich's appearance and dissolution I was willing to try anything she suggested. When we got home we fumigated the house with bundles of herbs and sandalwood. Graça helped me recite incantations in alien words and I made offerings to the motley collection of statues of *orixas*, saints and old slaves that Graça had insisted on buying. That evening, I ran the bath for Charles and was pouring a special potion into the water when he came in.

'What's that?' he said, taking the small glass bottle from me. He held it to his nose and grimaced. 'You did not buy it for its aroma. Is it medicinal?'

I hesitated. I didn't want to lie but I knew he wouldn't approve. In the end, I went for honesty. 'I went to see someone today. To get help for you.'

'Someone?'

I watched as he stiffly removed his clothes. When we had met it had been hard to detect his bones, his body had been so heavily muscled, but now he looked angular.

'Yes. You know those beautiful *candomblistas* we see on New Year's Eve? I went to one for help.'

He grinned at me. 'Go on.'

'Well,' I said, 'it's not science but she is powerful and she said this would help. And she told me to make you drink this.' I held out another tiny brown bottle.

'What is it?'

I hesitated again. 'It was very expensive.'

He took it from me and sniffed it, wrinkling his nose, perplexed. 'Well,' he said, 'we can't waste money, can we.' He tipped the amber fluid into his mouth and grimaced. 'What was it?'

'Essence of boto.'

'Amazonian dolphin!' he spluttered. 'You made me drink that?'

'The essence of the male is meant to be life-saving!'

He fell silent as he stepped into the bath and submerged himself. When he emerged pink and steaming from the hot water he took a big gulp of air.

'Rosa, I know you don't want me to die. But no amount of Hail Marys in whatever language – or any amount of dolphin essence – is going to save me. I'm dying.' He sighed. 'We both need to learn to live with that. And please don't waste any more time or money on this nonsense. Not even your love could save me.'

And then he took a breath and slipped under the water again.

He lost weight, he lost vigour. But still, every day, although later and later, he got up and went to work; every weekend we managed to walk on the beach and visit our friends. The walks and the social calls simply got later and shorter.

When swimming in the sea became impossible for him, without any discussion, we changed to going to the swimming pool at the Copacabana Palace Hotel, where we had first stayed after our arrival in Brazil. He would recline on a lounge chair reading the morning paper while I swam.

One morning, I was swimming up and down the pool, my mind awash with fear. I forced myself to keep going, as if each length I swam would somehow make Charles healthier. I was and still am a poor swimmer – I only learnt as an adult in Brazil – so I stopped often in the shallow end, in part to glance over and see if Charles was alright, in part to take a breath. On one such pause, Charles was not sitting on the lounger where I had left him. I stood taller, my top half shivering in the wintry late-July air. I turned around scanning each chair, each towel-covered guest, each lounger; he was not sitting by the pool. Trying not to worry, I heaved myself up out of the water and glanced towards the bar thinking I would ask Alessandre, the barman, where he had gone. And there was Charles, sitting on a stool by the bar. I turned and went to fetch my towel, walking the long way round; I did not want Charles to notice my panic.

He was holding a glass half-filled with pale, lime-green fluid and shattered ice.

'You look like you need something strong, too,' he called as I approached him.

I half-smiled and shook my head.

'You do.' He turned to the barman. 'Alessandre, two more caipirinhas, please.'

We watched the barman make the drinks, not talking, just listening to the music that was coming from the speakers behind. Alessandre filled two glasses to the brim and pushed them towards us. I breathed in the sweet toffee smell of the cachaça. Charles drained his first glass, the crushed lime skins swirling in the fractured ice. He reached for the fresh caipirinha.

'How come you wanted a drink at 9:30 in the morning?' I asked, struggling to keep my voice light.

'Amour, I just realised that I don't have to worry about my health anymore. It's not going to kill me.' He laughed. 'And I've almost never been drunk and, I don't know, it seemed like a good idea.'

It was true, he drank socially but never much. Reluctantly, I took a sip of mine. One glass relaxed me, two made me tipsy and after three, I couldn't stand. I felt a chill run through me.

'I'll be back,' I said, putting down my glass. 'I'm just going to get dressed.' I needed a moment to pull myself together.

When I returned, Charles had drunk half of his second drink. He had not been joking, he was determined to get drunk. As I settled down next to him and picked up my glass, a new song started on the radio – a trumpet started the melody, then a wistful flute took it up before a woman's honeyed voice floated over the rhythmic strumming of a guitar and soft drums.

'*Vai minha tristeza . . .*' sang the woman. *Go my sadness.* Charles sat up.

'*Oi*, Alessandre,' he called to the barman. 'Turn it up, please.'

Straining forward, Charles listened to the bittersweet singing against the up-beat. We had never heard music like it, with its gentle syncopated rhythm, the soft languorous pain. The guitar suggested a dance, but it was the words that transfixed me.

Enough longing, in reality
There can be no peace nor beauty without her,
Just sadness and melancholy
Which won't ever leave me

Charles pushed his glass away. I floated my hand over the countertop and rested it on his. He grabbed it and pulled it on to his lap, clasping mine between both of his, his face turned away from me towards the big, wide ocean.

'Who was that?' he asked Alessandre as the music tailed off.

'João Gilberto. It's called "Chega de Saudade".'

'Chega de Saudade,' Charles repeated. His French accent softened the already soft 'd' the Brazilians made: sow-da-jee. Brazilians claim that it is a uniquely Brazilian word that compounds longing, aching for something or someone. The title meant 'enough of longing, no more missing her'.

We sat at the bar and our drinks stood untouched as the next few songs washed over us. The ice had melted by the time Charles stirred and turned towards me.

'When I'm gone, you mustn't give in to the *saudade*,' he said, drawing out the Brazilian word.

'Don't tell me how to be when you're—' I started angrily but he lifted up his finger to my lips.

'Shh, mon amour.' He leaned over and kissed me. Then he announced loudly, 'I want to hear this Gilberto guy.'

It is hard to imagine now, but at that time João Gilberto was unknown. Ipanema was still just the beach between Leblon, where we lived, and Copacabana, where we were sitting at the bar. A few years later his soft voice was heard all over the world when

'A Garota de Ipanema', 'The Girl from Ipanema', became a global hit. Without knowing it, we had listened to the birth of bossa nova. Charles recognised something great in this new sound and in the weeks before he died it became a singular passion.

The song propelled João Gilberto into the Rio limelight. Every club in the Zona Sul wanted him to play, everyone who had heard the record wanted to see him for themselves. It was impossible to get tickets, even with my name and half my office staff on the case. I rang everyone who was anyone that I knew, I pulled all the strings I could but there were no tickets to be had. But Rio was full of gossip and my desperation must have been commented on because in the end someone who I knew only by name rang me and told me that her boyfriend was a close friend of Gilberto and kept a guitar in his house just for when Gilberto dropped by. An idea came to me.

About three nights later, just before midnight, the doorbell rang and I raced down before Graça could even get out of bed. Five young people were standing on the porch and I could see some more disgorging from a taxi in front of the house, as an empty taxi drove away.

'I've brought him,' the young woman announced triumphantly as she stepped into the house, followed by the guitar and the guitarist.

João Gilberto sat down immediately and started strumming and tuning his guitar while I busied myself with finding drinks. Gilberto opened his mouth and began to sing. Graça arrived unbidden and, taking in the scene, gently took the tray from my hands.

'Go and get him,' she urged.

By the time I had started up the stairs, Charles was already halfway down, rapidly tucking his shirt into the trousers he had just hitched on.

'Is this magic your doing?' he asked.

I nodded, smiling up at him as tears ran down my face.

He took me in his bony arms and pulled me into a tight embrace. 'I'm so lucky to have found you.'

All night João Gilberto played. Song after song, taking classics from the samba tradition and teasing them out into his new sound; the syncopation, the disintegration of word and beat, the dislocation of rhythm. Apart from jokes and laughter between songs, the young people who had come with him sat silently drinking and smoking in our living room, listening. Charles and I huddled up on the armchair. Charles barely spoke but at the end he got up as the crowd tumbled into the street and dawn was beginning to ease the depth of the tropical night and walked over to Gilberto.

'You can have no idea what this evening has meant to me. Thank you.' He shook the guitarist's hands. Then he leaned forward closer to the musician. They shared a brief, intense conversation before the guitarist departed.

Time passed slowly as his illness progressed. One night we made love, for the first time in weeks. Clasping each other, I was shocked to feel how thin and weak he had become. He seemed to savour every moment; each movement seemed like a prolonged wave of intense pleasure or pain. He was slower and more focused than almost any time since our first and I mistook his mood for fatigue. After we had come, I could feel him diminishing inside of me and realised that he had not withdrawn and spilled his seed. He knew my menstrual cycle better than even I did and never took risks, but he chose this night to come inside me, to make our love complete.

For some time he lay on top of me, breathing heavily. He was so light that I did not need to push him off as I had used to. He kissed me firmly on the mouth and then groaned.

'Are you alright?' I asked. He slid out of me and rolled on to the bed, leaving his hand on my breast.

'No.' He winced. 'Rosa, the pain has become unbearable.'

'Do you need more medication?'

'Of course, but it's not enough. Rosa—' He broke off and grimaced again. 'It's just a matter of weeks, if not days, now.'

'Don't say that, we can—'

'Shh.' He brushed his fingers over my mouth.

We lay together in silence until my tears abated and my fevered breathing slowed.

'I've finished my notebooks,' he said. Since his diagnosis, he had spent every free evening and the nights he could not sleep writing down his memories of his time in captivity during the war. He had filled two notebooks with his neat, precise prose.

'Can I read them now?' I asked.

'No. I've packed them up ready to send to Yad Vashem.'

I propped myself up on my elbow. 'Where?'

'The Holocaust Museum in Jerusalem.'

I stared at him. 'Why? Why can't I see them? Your memories are mine; you're part of me.'

He rolled on to his back so that I couldn't see his face. 'We've had a good ten years, haven't we, my love?'

I nodded. The tears started again. I wiped my face.

'That's what I want you to remember,' he said. 'Not what happened during the war, before we even met. I've written my testimony because I want this to be on the record, as evidence, but it is not how I want you to remember me.'

I stifled a sob.

'Rosa, come here,' he whispered. He had turned back on to his side and was facing me. 'You're indomitable. You will bounce back. Treasure me in your memories, but you must go on living. And loving.'

'It's not too late,' I begged through my tears. 'We could go to New York tomorrow, or Paris. The doctors there could save you.'

'We've been through this. I'm beyond help, no one could save me. There is no cure for this cancer. You must promise to live, live for both of us.'

He kissed me slowly, languidly, and collapsed back on to the pillow. 'After the war, when I went back to Paris, I was so angry, so sad, I never thought I could be happy again. And look – we've had ten years of heaven on earth. Don't give up now, Rosa.'

He folded me in his arms and we stayed like that, clinging to each other. Gradually I became aware that sweat was pouring off him and little tremors were shooting through his body. He was breathing rapidly. There was nothing I could do to ease his suffering and I had never felt so helpless.

'Rosa,' he panted, 'would you get me the whisky? You know, the one that Jorge brought back from London.'

I was surprised to find him sitting up in bed when I came back with the bottle and a tumbler. He poured himself a large measure and I nestled up against him. I had taken my sleeping pill before I had gone downstairs and fell asleep curled in his lap.

When I woke the next morning facing him, my hand draped over his arm, it was as cold as stone. My eyes focused slowly on the blotched, pale skin of his chest, which was not moving; there was no rise and fall of any breath. I scrambled up, my heart racing as though to make up for the fact that his would never beat again. He was lying on his back, one arm hanging off the bed, the other reached out towards me. The empty whisky bottle stood next to the box of sleeping pills on the bedside table.

14

Potpourri

Ah, I must give my potpourri a stir. I try to shake it up once a day to encourage the release of the fragrance. There! Can you smell that, ma chère? The sudden rush of rose, the aroma of a summer evening? The essence of a potpourri – a rotten pot. The trick is to allow the petals or bark and herbs, whatever your choice, to decay gracefully. Originally in France they would layer the petals with coarse salt as the summer months passed, throwing in other fragrant herbs, leaves or flowers. When everyone moved back indoors to escape the wintery cold, and the stench of too many unwashed bodies ripened the atmosphere, they just had to take off the lid, and the smell of the now preserved rose petals would burst from the pot. For myself, I have always liked to have flowers around, but this bathroom is windowless and no flower should have to endure a lack of light. So, I make do with this heap of papery, dead petals. There was a time after Charles's death that Graça and I hid all the vases and pots away in cupboards; I could not bear to see any flowers.

I still cannot quite understand how I reacted when I woke to find myself lying next to Charles's cold body. It was very early, just gone six. I got up and got dressed, choosing a cheery, colourful suit, ready for a new day, a new life, and went downstairs. Graça was up but had not even begun to prepare breakfast.

'I want to go back to Dona Aparecida,' I began, my voice sounding odd to me, too breezy. 'For one last time.'

Graça was not taken aback by my sudden request, she just nodded.

★

Dona Aparecida seemed a little surprised by our early appearance. 'I don't understand,' she said. 'You can't be here about the ghost?'

'The ghost? Oh, no, not that one, he's gone. But I am hoping there might be another, now. My husband . . . he died last night.'

'Senhora Rosa!' Graça cried, leaping up from the bed. 'Why didn't you say? He's alone in the house. We have to go back.' She had opened the door and was ready to leave when she realised that I had not moved.

'He's fine, Graça, he can't go anywhere, he doesn't need anything. But I . . .' I gulped. 'I need to speak to him again. I have to say goodbye.' My voice cracked. 'He didn't give me the chance.'

'I am sorry, senhora,' Dona Aparecida said solemnly. 'But tell me, was he at peace when he died?'

I closed my eyes. The moment had been of his choosing. 'He wanted to live, but yes, he was ready. He was at peace.'

'What did he look like?' asked the medium.

'Did . . .' She had used the past tense. 'What does it matter?'

'It's just that I don't think he's here,' she said apologetically.

And then I could not stop myself. I cried. I cried and cried. Graça came and stood by me, her hand resting on my shoulder as I sobbed.

It was nearly ten by the time we got home. I collapsed on the armchair Charles and I had sat on listening to João Gilberto. Ten minutes later, Graça returned with a sheaf of notes she had found on Charles's desk. It was a series of lists: short lists of people to ring, in what order and for what purpose, and then longer lists of friends and colleagues to notify and invite to his funeral. I felt incapable of talking, let alone ringing anyone, but if this is what he wanted then I would do it. The first name was one that I did not recognise, Ernst Hoffman. Charles had underlined it and noted RING FIRST next to it. I dialled the number and hoped that it would not ring, that I would not need to explain.

'Ernesto Hoffman. Good day.' A Germanic accent clipped the elongated Brazilian vowels.

'Hello. My name is Rosa Dumarais. My husband Charles . . .'
I tailed off, unable to finish.

'Frau Dumarais?'

I tried to speak again, to say the words, but only a strangled
sob came out.

'I'm so sorry,' said the man, his voice softening and slipping
into gentle Viennese. 'Charles said that you would ring when he
died. I'll be with you in half an hour. I'm truly sorry. He was a
good man.'

'That's kind, Herr Hoffman,' I replied, 'but who are you?'

There was a long silence on the end of the phone. 'He didn't
tell you?' he asked at last.

'Nothing.'

'I'm from the Chevra Kadisha. We'll look after him for you
now. You must ring the doctors at once, though.'

The doctor had been a good friend of Charles and came as
soon as I rang him. He did not take long to sign the death certif-
icate, confirming that heart failure and other complications from
cancer were causes. We had all known that it was coming. Not
long after he left, the doorbell rang again and I opened the door
to find a short, balding man in a beige linen suit.

'Ernesto Hoffman,' he said delicately, bowing his head to me.

'Herr Hoffman.' I held out my hand to him, but he kept his
firmly holding the brim of his straw hat in front of his round
stomach, and I let my hand fall, feeling foolish.

'Frau Dumarais,' he said, bowing again. 'I wish you comfort.'
He paused and looked uncertain, then ploughed on. 'I am sorry,
but time is of the essence. Can I see him?'

I spluttered, unable to speak, so instead just turned and started
towards the stairs, indicating that he should follow. Halfway up
I stopped and turned to him. 'What is this Chevra Kadisha?'

'It is something we do – we Jews, that is. It is like a burial
society. It means the Holy Friends. We will do everything for
you.' He took a step up.

'Everything?'

'Yes,' he said, taking another step so he was close behind me, gently propelling me forward. I turned and carried on up the stairs as he explained, 'We clean, prepare and dress the body and place it in the coffin.'

'This is what Charles wanted?' I was flabbergasted. There had been nothing in our lives that was shaped by his heritage, yet he wanted a Jewish burial. It was as if he had blocked me from his core, his inner being.

'Yes.'

'He never said anything.' Herr Hoffman did not reply and his silence made me feel even sadder. We were standing over the bed now where I had left Charles. Herr Hoffman nodded his head and muttered a prayer in a guttural language I did not recognise – I guessed Hebrew.

'How did you know him?' I asked.

'May I?' He indicated the chair by the window. I nodded and sat down at the foot of the bed near Charles's feet.

'We met twice. I was in Auschwitz – in the hut next to his. We played chess once or twice; he beat me. We were not friends as such, but we knew each other there and we both survived.' He looked at Charles with a pained expression. 'That is a special bond.'

'I can only imagine.' I tried to imagine this podgy middle-aged man in the camp with Charles, but it was impossible. Charles had always been firm and muscular but now his insentient body was as skeletal as he must have been then. I was seized by a desire to know everything he knew, about the past that Charles had kept from me.

'When was the second time?' I asked.

'That was a few years ago. We bumped into each other in the street, in Lapa. We had coffee, exchanged addresses.'

'He never mentioned it, I don't understand.' Lapa was a down-town neighbourhood; Charles rarely went there. It was one thing that Charles had kept me from his past, but it hurt to know that he had hid this from me when we were together . . . I thought we had shared everything.

Herr Hoffman fixed his gentle eyes on me. 'To be frank we

had little in common other than our time in the *Lager*, which we both cared not to dwell on.' He sighed. 'Frau Dumarais, please don't be upset. When you rebuild your life on the ashes of the dead you can't look back. He didn't tell you because he didn't want to taint his happiness.'

'It's hard to understand,' I said, failing absolutely. 'But if you didn't see him again, how come he left a note to ring you?'

'When he fell ill, he called me again. I know Charles was not religious, but he wanted a Jewish burial. We survivors, we saw too many of our tribe burnt unceremoniously, their ashes scattered to the wind, or shot and buried half alive in pits of lime. He wanted to be buried with all the rites – for his son and wife, and mother and sister – for those who died before, as much as for himself.'

The pain went deep. Just as his decision not to have children was presented to me as absolute, he had chosen what his death would be like. I could overrule him (Dona Aparecida had convinced me that he was not about to protest) but I knew I had no choice. Charles had never compromised in anything. And I loved him for that.

'If that was his wish,' I said with resignation, 'then I accept it. But why the rush?'

'We have to bury him today, if we can. Within twenty-four hours.'

'Twenty-four hours?' I exploded, forgetting all decorum. 'That's mad. You can't do that.' I stood up, sat down, reached for Charles's cold hand but let go immediately. It did not feel like him. The doorbell rang.

'I am sorry that Charles did not forewarn you, but these were his wishes.'

'Do I have any choice?'

'Frau Dumarais, none of us would have chosen this, but it is our custom, and this is what he wanted.'

I closed my eyes. It was all too soon, too rushed, and none of it was what I wanted. I forced myself to look at Charles's body, which had not moved. It would never move, not today, nor tomorrow; another hour, another day would not change that. 'You're right,' I said. 'Of course.' The doorbell rang again.

'That will be one of my colleagues,' he said as he got up. 'In order to fulfil Charles's wishes we have to work quickly. I shall leave you now to say goodbye and come back in a few minutes.'

I stayed on the bed and regarded Charles's inert form. It resembled a display dummy more than my husband. Barely twelve hours ago, we had mixed our saliva, heat and sweat, I had fallen asleep with his warm arm wrapped round me. I wanted to be able to kiss and nuzzle him again and soak up his scent, but it was futile. This was a corpse. It was not him.

After Herr Hoffman had ushered me out of the bedroom, I showered in Graça's bathroom. She brought me a simple black silk dress to wear and then I sat at Charles's desk making the phone calls he had prescribed, crossing out names in the order that he had written them. When the calls were made there was nothing to do but wait for the hearse. The funeral would be at four o'clock. I joined Graça in the kitchen and toyed with the glass of water she put in front of me.

At some point, Herr Hoffman came into the kitchen.

'Frau Dumarais,' he said, and his quiet voice made me jump. 'He is ready. Perhaps you would like to see him before we close the coffin.'

A rough, unvarnished wooden coffin was perched on portable stands next to our bed. I took one step into the bedroom then stopped. Graça came up beside me, put her hand on my elbow and guided me in. There was a pale effigy with the semblance of my Charles inside the coffin. They had dressed him in unfamiliar, shapeless white linen clothes – they were not what I would have chosen. The grey silk and linen suit had been his favourite. His hair had been combed too neatly and his eyes were shut. It looked so much like him, but it was not him.

'This isn't right,' Graça said.

For the most part Graça was obliging but in the eight years she had been with us, Charles and I had learnt that some things fell into her category of right and wrong. And this was clearly wrong. There was a note of determination in her voice that should have made Charles smile and sigh, but his lips remained still. She turned and left the room and I reached out to touch his cold skin, but my fingers recoiled. I knew I should kiss him one final time but I could not. I wanted his tender kiss the night before to be the last one that I remembered.

Graça came back with an armful of flowers. She must have swept through the house gathering up every bouquet from all the vases and cutting off all the flowers from their pots. She thrust them into my arms and began to take the flower heads and place them in the coffin.

'Ahem. Senhora, this is not customary,' Herr Hoffman said, reaching out as though to stop her.

She paid him no heed. 'It may not have been Senhor Charles's custom but it is mine and I am still here,' she said with that resolute certainty Charles had loved. 'I won't take long.' She plucked a snowy orchid tinged with red from my arms and returned to her work.

I nodded and Herr Hoffman sighed. We stood and watched while Graça made a halo of blossoms, petals and orchids around his head. Then she leaned into the coffin and did what I could not.

'*Tchau*, Senhor Charles. You were like an older brother to me.' She planted her lips firmly on his forehead. 'Until the next time.'

She stepped back and reached for my hand.

Herr Hoffman and the three men who had been helping him came forward, lifted up the lid and closed it over my love, bedded down in flowers.

Later that afternoon, we followed the coffin as it was wheeled down to the grave in the Jewish cemetery of Inhaúma. During the short service in the funeral chapel, a sense of unreality took hold of me. The prayers were chanted in Hebrew. The men wore skullcaps and boots, the women stood to one side facing them, and the rabbi delivered a meaningless eulogy about a man he had never met.

We left the chapel to be confronted by row upon row of plain, pale grey tombs, arrayed under the unblemished sky. At the grave site, the men who had washed and prepared Charles's body lifted the coffin off the trolley and put it down next to the grave on thick bands of tape, ready to lower it in. I wanted to believe that it was a dream.

And then I understood I was awake, this was real. 'No! No! I have to see him,' I cried, stepping forward. 'I didn't kiss him goodbye.'

Herr Hoffman and the rabbi exchanged a few words, then someone came forward and opened the coffin. I stepped up, steeling myself for my last sight of him – but I was met with a nightmare vision. In the heat and darkness of the closed coffin, Charles's pale, dead face had come alive with a swarm of tiny black insects that must have crawled out of the flowers that Graça had arranged around him. Tiny creatures were scuttling up his nostrils and running in and out of his insensate mouth. I screamed and collapsed in a faint.

As my senses returned to me, minutes or hours later, I heard an erratic thudding rhythm. I staggered to my feet and saw that the men in their boots were shovelling in the mud, a thud sounding as each shovelful of earth fell on to the wooden casket. It was too late.

It was years before I had flowers in my house again, and when I started it was with clean, desiccated petals, just like these in this crystal bowl.

15

Mirror

You've never commented on my mirror, ma chère, nor on the number of other ones in the apartment. Have you any idea how expensive a good mirror is? But I don't suppose you even realise that there are differences in mirrors. On the shop floor, the mirrors must ever so slightly slim and elongate the customer. In a gym, the mirrors enhance the bulk that men are sweating to achieve. Such mirrors subtly manipulate reality. I first noticed the importance of a good mirror when I was working with Dior.

Here, in my home, I want clarity and cruel truth. This mirror is the most expensive thing in my bathroom. The cost of the marble floor and vanity units are mere trifles in comparison. When I took this apartment, the first thing I made sure of was that the corridor allowed me to hang the four full-length mirrors by the door. How else is a woman to pass muster before she steps out into the world?

The first thing I noticed when we returned from the cemetery was that the mirrors in the hallway had been covered with thick calico. I reached to remove it.

'Frau Dumarais, *bitte nicht*,' Herr Hoffman implored. 'During shiva, the first week of mourning, we cover up our mirrors. Let's go inside.' He steered me into the salon.

'What is "shiva"?' was all I could say. I felt stupefied, like a fly I might have struck down without a second thought.

'Shiva means seven. We observe seven days of mourning. For the next seven days, Frau Dumarais, you should wear torn clothes and no shoes; you should sit low, close to the ground. We cover the mirrors because the last thing you need is to worry about the way you look.'

He led me to the single low chair that someone had placed on the far side of the room.

'This is where you should sit,' he said. As I settled on to the seat, it dawned on me that he was right. I did not care how I looked, nor could I imagine that I ever would again. He stood over me for a moment then explained, 'Just as the world was created in seven days, we take seven days to mourn a death.' He took a step back and then said, 'I wish you long life.'

Long life! Nothing could have been further from my thoughts.

Soon night fell and the people who had attended the funeral started arriving at the house. The rabbi led the prayers; the men all chanted along with him, the women stood to one side. One of Charles's colleagues delivered a eulogy. The low stool gave me a vista of a forest of legs. I closed my eyes, but all I could see were the insects swarming into Charles's unmoving nostrils and parted lips. I clenched my fists and ground them into the jacaranda tiles of the floor.

A sound started – the strumming of a guitar. Then a whispery voice imbued with languorous pain began singing 'Chega de Saudade'. It was João Gilberto. I lifted my head, wondering if I was hallucinating, but a hush descended on everyone as if this were a prayer. I closed my eyes tightly. Charles must have asked João to come back, that night when they had spoken so intently. I recognised it as his last embrace and gift to me. As the song wrapped itself around me, I let the tears flow, washing away the foul image of the scuttling insects from my eyes. But I did not want to banish my sadness; it was the only way I could feel Charles. I wanted to wear my grief close to me like my clothes. I lifted my hand to the golden brooch that I was wearing and unpinned it. I flexed the pin and thrust it into the black fabric and started to jab and pull until the silk began to tear.

People started to file past me one by one, shaking my hand, some bending to embrace me. And then it was just Graça and me. The house seemed dark and silent. Finally, I got up from my low chair and climbed the stairs.

I stopped on the threshold of what was my room now, not ours, and stared at the bed. Somehow Graça had found the time to strip it and remake it with fresh, crisp linen. I braced myself and walked past the empty bed and into the bathroom. Instead of seeing my reflection in the wall-to-wall mirror, I found myself staring at a sheet that had been taped across it. I realised dimly that the house *was* darker. It was not just my mood, it was a fact; all the mirrors in the house had been covered.

The Austrian and a host of other Jewish refugees from Europe came five more times to say prayers for Charles. Had I had my wits about me I might have been baffled by this kindness but instead, I just accepted it as another incomprehensible wish of Charles's, who had become more Jewish in death than life. During these nightly prayers I had time to consider why Charles had chosen this exit, these rites, this unintelligible language. There had been nothing about our life that was Jewish. But perhaps that was the point; being Jewish had only meant death to him. Jewishness had caused his family's death. He wanted to live free of that burden, but in dying he wanted to return to the fold, to bear witness to his survival. In a strange way I felt he was making his presence felt, even in his absence. Rather than being angry, I welcomed this strange intrusion from his will.

Despite most of the visitors being strangers to Charles, as well as to me, I found I liked having people around. These strange women brought more food than Graça and I could eat, as well as words of comfort and kindness. Both of us had lost our appetite, so Graça gave most of the food to her church to pass on to the poor. During the day I stayed in the house; I did not even call my office. My assistant brought letters, cheques and money orders for me to sign and for the only time in my career I signed without reading, checking and rereading. I would have signed anything at that point.

The day after the shiva ended the house fell silent. Outside, the waves continued to crash on the shore and the cars screeched unceasingly up and down the Avenida Atlântica, but inside all was quiet. In the evening, no one came. I suspect that people thought they were leaving me in peace. But there was no peace. In the tomblike quiet, I heard only the roar of my grief and terror. Since the first evening we had met at that dinner party with Dior, Charles had invaded my head and suffused my life. We had never separated, never spent a night apart after our first time together – except when I had gone in search of Laurin – and now I had only myself and his absence.

I sat still until my limbs ached and I had to move. As the sun began to set and the shadows spread into every room, I walked through our home touching his things: his jackets in the cupboard, his shoes and clothes, his shaving brush and razor. I stroked my finger down the sharp edge of the blade and remembered his plea: 'live for me'.

As I looked up and saw the sheet taped to the wall, I realised that the shiva was over, the mirrors could be uncovered. I reached for the cotton sheet and pulled hard. It flapped down and I jumped back from the mirror, horrified. I did not recognise the stark face with the hollowed, bloodshot eyes. This was not the face that Charles had loved; this was not my face. I climbed on to the marble countertop and fixed the sheet back up.

The next day I asked Graça to have all the mirrors taken down. She refused to throw them out and had them stashed in Charles's study. Despite Graça's protest, I insisted on the mirror behind the countertop in my bathroom being wallpapered over. For years to come the empty spaces on the walls reminded me of what I had lost.

Of course, ma chère, I could not stay a recluse for long and I had to step back into the world. Herr Hoffman told me that after the shiva, Jews should refuse invitations for entertainment for a month, but after that they should start going out again.

I had a business to run; many people's livelihoods depended on me. I accepted enough invitations to parties and functions to keep myself afloat and maintain my business contacts. But I had no wish to go out and make small talk. I narrowed my wardrobe down to black, choosing between silk, cotton, linen and wool, but always black. It was not that I ceased to sparkle, but just as diamond and graphite are both made out of carbon, for some time I chose this more sombre aspect of myself. It gave a new rigour to my designs, a clarity to my lines and cut that helped my business grow as my look became sparse and more elegant.

Without any discussion, in the absence of Charles, the relationship between Graça and me changed. It started with breakfast, which we started eating together. And after a few nights of sitting down to dinner at the table on my own, I picked up my plate and joined Graça in the kitchen. Neither of us wanted to be alone – she, too, was suffering her own grief. She had become embedded in the fabric of our lives, and now this pain was something else we shared. Slowly, she became my friend and companion. Before long, unless we had guests, we were always together.

Ten months after Charles's death – I never considered it a suicide, he merely precipitated nature's own timetable – Graça summoned me to the lounge. Herr Hoffman was standing looking out to sea over the veranda with his back towards me. He was wearing the same suit and had his hat clutched in his hands, just as he had the first time that we had met on the doorstep.

We exchanged greetings and, again, he did not take my hand to shake nor kiss as most Viennese men would. I had learnt enough about Judaism since Charles's death to understand that Orthodox Jewish men never touched women outside their own family.

When we were both sitting facing each other in the salon, he said in his lilting German, 'I came about the stone-setting. It is time.'

'Oh.' I had not even begun to think about a tombstone.

'Have you set one already?'

'No.' I took a deep breath in before I admitted, 'I haven't even

been back to the cemetery. I couldn't – I know I should, but—'
I broke off, feeling guilty. A good widow was meant to tend the
grave, and I had failed.

'No, that's fine. We don't return, not before the stone-setting.'
'Oh,' I said with some relief. 'And when is that meant to be?'
'At eleven months.'

I envied him the simplicity and surety of his rituals, and by
now I was happy to accept the guidance. 'I suppose I should
design something for him?'

'There are customs for this too; something simple. A plain slab
and headstone.'

He pushed his hat away from him on the sofa and looked at
the reddish sheen of the polished jacaranda parquet floor.

'Rosa,' he said, using my first name for the first time. 'I can't
help noticing that your mirrors are still missing.' He had said *Du*,
the informal version of 'you', and such a great leap of intimacy
emphasised his sincerity and made me pay attention.

'Our customs are wise. They have a purpose and help us
through mourning. After the stone-setting, the mourning should
be over. You can mark the anniversary of his death and light a
candle for him, and do this every year. But,' he said, observing
me closely, 'when this first year is concluded, it is forbidden to
mourn. It is a damaging extravagance, and we believe in living.
Rosa,' he said, 'you should rehang the mirrors and get on with
your life.'

The next day, by the time I had finished my breakfast, I had
completed my plan for Charles's grave. Even a plain slab can be
well-designed – the proportions, the headstone, the edge: detail
is everything. I arranged everything but did not go to the stone-
setting. That was too much to ask of me.

I tried to take Herr Hoffman's advice, however, and get on
with life, or at least with work. Fashion was about to undergo
another seismic shift. Dior's New Look had spearheaded the
post-war drive to return women to domesticity, femininity and
the kitchen. But now it was 1958 and we could feel a new wave

of energy surging as the generation that grew up in the aftermath of the war began to reach their maturity. My first trip to Dona Aparecida had an unexpected but lasting influence. I had once crossed a mountain pass while pregnant, yet I had barely been able to negotiate the fetid puddles down the alleyway to the medium's house in my high-heeled shoes. Never again, I determined, would my clothes impede me. I focused on silhouettes that followed the body's contours. I dispensed with folds and gathering, cutting clean A-lines that darted for curves and gave a generous fit. My clothes became more wearable. The more I worked, the more work there was to focus on. I worked to keep the grief at bay. Sometimes it succeeded.

Over the next two years I expanded the business into perfumery and cosmetics. Ever since I had painted Graça's nails before going to Senhor Maluf's, my interest in and understanding of make-up had become a passion, and inevitably that fed into my business. The affluent Brazilians that were my target clientele had been westward-looking. They had always hankered after goods from Paris, London, New York and, to a lesser extent, Lisbon, but I had a feeling that times were changing. As an immigrant the intense colours of the birds and flowers and heady tropical scents had continued to enthral me, so I took them as the inspiration and basis for my range. I started with cosmetics, using cocoa and Brazil-nut cream as a base and naming them after native flowers, birds and gemstones: aquamarine, emerald and jacaranda eyeshadow, hibiscus and *ciriguela* and *tucano* lipstick. My hunch was right, and I tapped into a voracious appetite for well-packaged, beautiful products that had the quality of imported goods but not the price. I focused on marketing them, visiting every major city in Brazil, Chile, Argentina, Venezuela and Colombia.

Whether it was my fierce focus on work or the final vanquishing of Schleich I can't say, but my business grew and grew. Within three years I had become the figurehead of an empire as I hired more and more managers, marketing staff and designers to keep up with the volume of work.

Every day began and ended with the same ritual that you see now, ma chère, getting ready to greet the world. For three years I worked so hard that I barely had time to breathe, let alone cry. Even while I designed clothes and cosmetics using the flamboyant tropical palate of intense shimmering colour, I continued to wear only black, like an Italian widow. I thanked Coco Chanel for her invention of the little black dress.

Still avoiding mirrors even at work (I used a small compact to make myself up), I relied on touch and feel to gauge the fit of a dress. This too informed my design style as comfort and movement became a greater focus. By this point it was not that I did not care how I looked, but I was fearful of seeing what Charles's absence meant in my face. I looked at the definition of the eyeliner, the smoothness of the powder, the edge of the lipstick, but with the compact I managed to avoid seeing my whole face.

And then one day, peering into the small round mirror, it seemed to show only a distorted, blotchy image. Tears I could no longer suppress kept welling up, blurring my vision and making it impossible to see clearly, smudging every attempt. Since I could not go out without make-up, I became increasingly desperate until I finally sank to the marble floor of the bathroom, the same floor where Charles had stood when he took my box of sleeping pills from the cabinet. I wailed and howled like one of those possessed *macumbeiras* on the beach on New Year's Eve. Graça must have heard me – the people in the street passing my house must have heard me – but she did not come. I only stopped when I became aware of how cold and hard the bathroom floor was. I hauled myself up, bathed my raw face in cold water, and went downstairs.

In the kitchen Graça was waiting for me, sitting at the table drinking a glass of water. She had laid a setting for me. She got up and placed a warm brioche on my plate (since Charles had taught her to make brioche and croissants, they were her favourites) and handed me a large bowl of café au lait.

'I thought you might be hungry, Senhora Rosa.'

I was famished. She watched me eat and when I was finished, she said, 'I think you need a holiday.' She stretched out a dish towards me, two slices of cucumber. 'For your eyes.'

When we arrived at the Ritz in Paris, the concierge told me that my booking had been cancelled by a Madame Fournel. I smiled and paid the porter a handsome tip for taking all my bags straight out to another taxi.

'How could you think of staying anywhere else?' she admonished me, leaning over the banister at the top of the stairs as we spiralled up to meet her. As I climbed the last step, she held out her arms to receive me and I fell into them. Her once ample form had shrunk, three or four sizes I estimated. She had become so fragile I felt as if I was holding her up. As we relinquished our embrace, I found my hand in hers. Graça stood back. But, unlike the customs officers and the taxi driver who had treated Graça as if she were contaminated, Madame Fournel smiled warmly at her.

'Madeleine, Graça,' I said, regarding them both solemnly. 'You two are my best and dearest friends.'

Without hesitating, Madame Fournel let my hand go and took Graça's brown one and kissed her on both cheeks. I slept in my old bed and Graça on the chaise longue in the salon. I was home.

The Paris I had known had been through the lens of work, but with Graça I discovered the galleries and shops. Dior had died the year before Charles and despite the many people he had introduced me to, none were friends. Of course, I arranged to meet Yves Saint-Laurent – such a talented young man, who had, undoubtedly, taken what would have been my position had I not gone to Brazil. But apart from him, I did not meet with anyone else. Instead, when we were not shopping and eating out, we stayed at home with Madeleine. Although I had bought some clothes for Graça for the trip and given her some of my old ones, it was only in the Paris shops that I understood what an innate sense of style she had, quite different from my own. Hers was more classic and chic; she was a natural Chanel devotee. By then I was thirty-three years old and Graça was twenty-eight, but I had the younger style. We walked the boulevards, buying clothes in shops which luckily were too expensive to have price tags – otherwise Graça would have refused to leave with anything. She chose pared-down shift dresses, pencil skirts and simple jackets in muted roses, sky blues and camel. When heads turned at our progress, I wondered – with pride and amusement – who it was they were admiring.

One day at the end of such a trip we were sitting in the Jardin des Tuileries when Graça asked what the big building was. Once she had discovered the Louvre, she went back there every day for two weeks until she had walked through every room and taken in every picture, statue or drawing. That's when her lifetime obsession with art began.

After three weeks in Paris, she was beginning to speak a little French so I was unsurprised one morning to find her talking tentatively with Madeleine over breakfast.

'Ah, ma chère, you look rested.' Madeleine smiled, reaching up to bestow my cheek with her customary morning kiss. 'Graça and I have been talking.'

'I can see.' I took a pain au chocolat from the basket and reached for the coffee pot.

'And we've decided that we are going to visit St. Gallen and Oberfals,' Graça said.

I put the coffee pot down, harder than I meant to. Graça picked it up and poured in the coffee and hot milk for me.

'I can't.'

'You must,' Madeleine said, taking my hand. 'Losing Charles doesn't have to mean that you should lose everything.'

I stirred my coffee. I had blocked any notion of seeing Laurin. I had not thought I could bear to see him and walk away again. But the more I considered it, the more pleasing the idea of finding him happy and content with Ida seemed. Perhaps it would help to fill the black hole that ached in my chest. It could not cause any more pain, I reasoned; that was impossible. But nothing would induce me to travel to Oberfals.

'Madeleine,' I said, 'you've been more of a mother to me than my own mother ever was. And I never want to see my father ever again.'

'What about your sister?'

I shrugged. 'It's not as if any of them tried to find me, and I'm not exactly hard to find.'

My clothes had never crossed the ocean but my cosmetics line *Beija Flor* – hummingbird or, literally, flower kisser – was enjoying success throughout Latin America. I was not unknown, and even in the hidden valley of Oberfals I was certain they would have read about me. In fact, I had given an interview the year before to an Italian journalist. They could find me if they wanted to.

'Perhaps it is shame that keeps them silent,' Graça said. 'But sometimes it is better to leave family behind.' She got up and left the room. She had not seen her cousin, Gabriela, since our showdown with Sé at Senhor Maluf's.

Two days later, the three of us were standing outside the old Schurter house. I had rung from Paris, sent a telegram and tried telephoning again from the hotel in St. Gallen but had failed to get a response. When I got to the house, I saw why. Laurin's home was empty and had been boarded up. I knocked on the neighbours' doors. The neighbour on the left-hand side had recently moved in and knew nothing, and there was no one at home on the right or the next house. Three doors along, an old man was in his front garden snipping off dead flower heads and collecting them in a basket.

'Oh, Family Schurter, yes,' he said, peering at us through his thick lenses. 'They're gone.' He clipped off another rose head with his secateurs.

I felt the blood drain from me; I felt faint. 'Do you know where they went?' I asked, suddenly as desperate to see Laurin as the last time I had stood there.

'Away, I'm not sure. Let me see.' He stood up. 'Mr Schurter

died, oh, ten, fifteen years ago, shortly after the war. I'm not sure. Yes, the boys were about four or five, and the little one was still a toddler. It was awful. Poor Frau Schurter was so brave.'

'How did Herr Schurter die? He wasn't so old.'

'Heart attack. Too much work, they said. And she, all alone in that big house with the kids. I think she was alright for money, though. And then one day, about a year later, she packed everything up and moved.' He bent down to another rose bush, then stood up again. 'Some people said she had a new man, but I don't believe it – he would have come to fetch her if that were the case. No, she packed it all up and left.'

My heart fluttered with hope. 'Where did they go?'

'I didn't ask.'

They were gone. I had lost him.

As a last resort, I visited the lawyers the Schurters had used for the adoption process, but they told me that they could not help. Frau Schurter had indeed remarried and moved to Germany, and they had no forwarding address. The house had been sold at the time but was up for sale again.

I bought it that afternoon, ma chère. When I had left St. Gallen fifteen years before, I had been penniless; now it was just a technicality to get the money wired over. During the time it took to arrange I went to the nearby church and found and installed a housekeeper. Frau Wegelin was a war widow with two teenage children. She seemed shell-shocked as I walked her round the shops, buying furniture and fittings. She was used to hardship, could not comprehend my wealth, and insisted on taking me to second-hand stores.

A few days later, once everything was sorted, we were standing on the platform waiting for the train that would take us to Zurich. According to the timetable we were nearly half an hour early. Waiting on the platform was like a needle in my heart. This was precisely where I had seen Laurin for the last time. I had less hope now than ever of finding him again. As my eyes filled with tears, I was glad that the light was poor under the arched steel roof span. As if playing with my memories, a boy and a girl ran along the platform, waving to get our attention.

'It's the Wegelin children,' Graça said.

I waved to let them know I had seen them. They signalled to me not to move, turned and then returned with their mother.

'Frau Dumarais.' Frau Wegelin puffed, red-faced from exertion.

'Is there anything wrong?' I asked her.

'No, but I just had to ask again.' She bit her lip nervously. 'It just doesn't seem real.'

'What?'

'There is nothing else you want?' She stared at me. 'Just live there, me and my children, look after the house for you and open the door to any passing stranger who knocks?'

'That's it,' I said, smiling as reassuringly as I could. 'Just open the door, find out who they are and let me know.'

'I don't understand. You've given us a home.' Her eyes were welling with tears.

'You don't need to understand,' I said. I had no intention of telling her about my desperation or rationale. 'Just do as I ask. Please.'

It was a desperate, costly strategy, but I could not think of a better plan. Maybe one day either Laurin or Frau Schurter would turn up. It was the only thing I could do.

The morning after our return to Rio I found myself staring at the wallpaper covering my bathroom mirror. Something in me had shifted. I still missed Charles like a lost limb, I still longed to find Laurin, but there was something else inside me now. I leaned forward and tried to pull the paper at the seams but it wouldn't budge. Nothing is permanent, I thought, as I climbed up on to the marble countertop and started wiping the wallpaper with a soaking flannel. I never asked what made Graça come, but when she popped her head round through the door she disappeared before immediately returning with two flat knives and her window-washing kit. We worked wordlessly, soaking, stripping and scraping. We did not stop until it was completely exposed.

I scrutinised myself thoroughly for the first time in three years. In the mirror an older, thinner woman, whose face was determined and knowing, stared back at me with a trace of hope in her eyes.

16

Eyeliner

When I make up my face, I always begin and end with eyeliner. In fact, I don't even consider tracing the outline of my eyes as make-up. It is merely a question of definition. Women have been using it for a long, long time. Modern-day Egyptian women wear kohl, as did their foremothers in the time of the pyramids and the pharaohs. When Mary Quant startled the world in the 1960s – she was the next person after Dior to single-handedly launch a new look – I dramatically thickened the line I painted around my eyes. These days I use kohl and crayons, preferring to smudge and blend, either around the rim of my eyes or under the lashes, depending on the image I choose to project. Even if I am just staying at home, I trace a line over my lashes. But on the day of the funeral and the following weeks my eyes were ringed with the darkness of grief, which I wore like a face mask. It was only after I peeled the wallpaper from my bathroom mirror that I began to line my eyes again.

In business I have learnt that the riskiest undertakings, when they come off, can be the most profitable. Two years after my trip to St. Gallen, in September 1963, I received a phone call. The international operator connected Frau Wegelin to me over a crackling line.

'Frau Dumarais,' her tinny voice said, 'he came.'

'Who?' My heart pounded. Laurin would be nineteen. Had he come to find me?

'A young man,' Frau Wegelin continued.

'Did he say his name?'

'He said something about Laurin.'

I gripped the receiver so hard it hurt. 'How old is he? Is it Laurin?'

'He's twenty-five. His name is Dov. He's from Israel. He wants to speak to you. He said something about a professor.'

She put the young Israeli man on the phone. After an absurd conversation I established that he was a relative of Professor Goldfarb. The young man was studying in Zurich and the professor had asked him to see if he could find what had happened to a boy called Laurin, who lived with the Schurters. The next day, Graça packed my bags and accompanied me to Galeão airport.

A day later, I stood jet-lagged and dazed, knocking on the door of an apartment on a hill in Jerusalem. I was still knocking when a little girl opened it. A few minutes later a gaunt, white-haired man emerged from within the apartment and stopped still, his bony hand gripping the door so tightly that his knuckles went white.

'Saba.' The girl spoke to him in a guttural language.

He bent down and whispered something to her and she disappeared into the apartment.

'Professor?' The last time I had seen him he had not turned fifty, now he was old, nearly seventy. Time had been cruel to him.

He just looked at me. There was no warmth in his stern expression. He did not welcome me. We stood either side of the threshold, all my excitement draining away like a flood down a storm drain.

'I've come a long way to see you, Herr Professor,' I said finally.

'I suppose I should invite you in.' His voice was neutral, the voice he might have used to address a shopkeeper in St. Gallen.

When I had turned up frozen and desperate at the university, twenty years before, he had taken me into the home and made me hot milk and honey in his kitchen. This time he led me into his study and sat behind his desk, one finger flexed stiffly towards a chair. I lifted the pile of books off and put them on the rug.

I eyed the threadbare linen seat where the books had been, and wondered if it was safe to sit there, before I lowered myself down.

I looked around, intrigued. If I had accepted his proposal this might have been my home. The flat was small but in a lovely tree-lined street with a view over stony hills rolling towards the sea. He had made a new life for himself, assuming the little girl was his granddaughter or even daughter. That was good to see. But I would never have let him live like this, nor look like that. He had shrunk; his clothes hung on him loosely, failing to mask the angularity of his bones. He was as thin as when I had first met him. His hair and long beard were white over a threadbare collar, his jacket shabby. He looked how I had imagined a professor should, but not like the man I had known.

'So, Rosa Kusstatscher, what brings you here?'

'I – my name is Dumarais now. I married a long time ago.'

'Married.' He moved some paper around on his desk. 'How many children?' He would not look at me.

'He died. I'm a widow. We never had any.'

'I see,' he said, lifting his eyes towards me for the first time. 'Are you alone?'

It would have been impossible to explain my relationship with Graça, so I simply said, 'Yes.'

He nodded and I felt like he was judging me. 'You look good, as if you made something of yourself.'

'I did,' I replied. 'I built a fashion house. Not just clothes but cosmetics, perfume and jewellery. In Brazil,' I added as an afterthought.

'I thought you just wanted your own shop – at least, that is what you wrote in your letter. Ida Schurter tried to explain it to me. You were going to make something of yourself and then come back for Laurin?'

'That was my plan.'

'And all because I offered you a home and a father for your child?'

My recollection was that he had offered slightly more, but I have learnt that it is best to choose the moment to make a point, and this was not then.

'No, not at all,' I said, choosing my words carefully. 'I panicked.'

'Was it such a bad idea?' he said, catching me in his penetrating gaze.

'No. No,' I said. 'It was kind of you.'

'Kind?' he scoffed, then sighed heavily. He picked up a book from one of the many piles cluttering the floor and turned a few pages before putting it down. He had always sought refuge in books. People don't change, I thought, not really.

'I loved you,' I said and waited for him to meet my gaze before continuing, 'but like a father, not a husband.'

'That,' he said, his voice clipped, 'is what I deduced from your fleeing.'

'It is not something we can choose,' I said.

He leaned forward and rested his chin on his fists. 'Have you any idea how much Laurin cried? Every time I went to see him at Ida Schurter's – and that was every day, because I loved him like a son – he was beside himself when I left.'

I raised my hand to my mouth to stifle a sob.

'How could you do that to your own child?' he asked and I realised that for him, who had lost both his children, what I had done was unforgivable.

The door opened and the little girl scampered in. She whispered something in his ear and he replied, then she trotted out again.

'Is she your daughter?'

'No, my granddaughter,' he said, proud and defiant.

I could see that in his eyes I had abandoned my only child. He had offered me a chance to stay with Laurin; he had created a second family as he had promised, and I was still alone. I could see no chance of ever regaining his respect or affections.

'It was a mistake coming.' I stood up. 'I'll leave.'

He looked down at the floor, avoiding my eyes.

'It was just such a shock to see you. You should have warned me. Write down your hotel details.' He thrust a pen and paper into my hands. 'We'll talk.'

The next day, Friday, he rang me. He invited me round for dinner to meet his family.

'This is Rosa,' he told the group. 'She was a refugee from the Tyrol, whom I gave shelter to during the war.'

I shook hands with each person as he introduced me.

'This is Agnieska, my Polish daughter,' he said of a squat, dark-haired woman in her mid-twenties, 'her husband, Samuel, and their daughter, Rahel, whom you met yesterday.'

The little girl smiled and said, '*Shabbat shalom*,' her voice loud and clear in the presence of her parents.

'This is Ármin,' he continued, 'my Romanian son.' A tall, lanky youth of about twenty stood up and shook my hand.

'And their mother, my wife, Judith, is Austrian.' He put his hand on the shoulder of the tired-looking woman in her fifties, who greeted me with a charming Viennese accent.

The family settled down to the Friday night dinner. Judith lit some candles, the professor read some prayers and then they blessed and shared wine. He picked up a loaf of plaited bread from a decorative platter.

'When I came here,' he told me, looking around the table, 'I found that many people had lost their families; there were many orphans. I witnessed the pain and fear of abandoned children.' He paused and continued deliberately, 'So, I made a new family. Like bread, family is the stuff of life.'

I wanted to say something, anything, to defend myself, but this was neither the time nor place to start.

He blessed the bread in Hebrew then tore off seven pieces and doused them with salt. I could not remember the last time I had eaten with a family. I knew what he was doing; he was showing me what a family life meant, what I had forfeited: the noise, the bustle, the company.

'You have a lovely family,' I said at the door after we had eaten, drunk coffee, and stuffed ourselves with baclava.

'It's what I wanted.'

'I wanted it too,' I said, no longer able to fight the need to justify myself. 'I went back for him, when I got engaged, but it was too late.'

He gripped my arm. 'Too late? Had he died?'

'No, he had forgotten me. He thought Ida Schurter was his mummy.'

'Oh.' He exhaled and something shifted in his expression; his face softened.

'I could not wrench him from his mother again. Even I could not be that selfish,' I said, trying to keep the anger out of my voice.

He relaxed his grip on my arm. 'Ahh,' he breathed out.

'You see?'

He nodded and let go of me. I stepped on to the landing. He came out and without saying anything strode towards the staircase and started the descent. I trod after him, my heels clacking on the tiles. He had nearly twenty years of resentment and judgement to dispel, years of thinking of me as utterly selfish. He needed a few moments to remember what good friends we had been. He was waiting for me at the bottom. He opened the door to the street for me and I stopped in front of him.

'When are you leaving?' he asked, his voice gentler now.

'Sunday,' I said. 'I've done what I came to do.'

'There are things to say before you go. Can I come to your hotel tomorrow afternoon?'

The spread of cakes served to us on the terrace of the rebuilt King David Hotel would have fed his whole family, yet the professor refused to eat even one. He sat back in his chair and looked out over the old city, which glowed gold in the late afternoon sun, while I poured milk into my coffee.

'I need to know, Rosa, why you have come?'

I paused for a moment, considering. Why had I come? 'When my husband died,' I said eventually, 'I fell apart. Two years ago, I returned to Europe for a visit. I wanted to stop running away.'

I put down my cup and spread my hands on my lap, smoothing down the linen.

'I went back to St. Gallen. I wanted to see Laurin, just to know he was alright, but they were gone. Ottmar was dead; Ida had remarried and moved to Germany. I didn't know what to do. Then, I figured that if I bought the Schurters' house, one day someone might come looking for them, or they might visit.'

'You bought it?'

I shrugged. 'I ran away to make my fortune so I could look after Laurin properly. Half of the plan worked.'

He stared at me for a long time. 'Was it always your plan to go back?'

I met his gaze, trying to convey the truth in me, the pain of all these years, my constant regret at losing my little boy. 'Always.'

'My cousin was going to go there. Is that why you are here?'

'Yes. The housekeeper rang me when he turned up and I spoke to him on Tuesday.'

'Two days ago?'

I nodded.

Below our terrace there was a dusty lane lined with tall, dark cedars. I rested my hand on the hot stone parapet; in the late afternoon it was still charged with the sun's heat. The mood had changed.

'Did you adopt Ármin and Agnieska?' I asked, just as intrigued by his life as he was by mine.

'Yes. I wanted another family, Rosa, and Laurin was like my son.'

I looked away. 'No, he was like your grandson, I was like your daughter. Or I should have been.'

The professor took up his coffee. He drank, stopping and starting, sip by sip, staring out over the city until the cup was drained.

'Maybe.' He put it down and leaned back into the white iron-work chair. 'I don't know. We were like a family. They are complicated things.' He paused. 'What will you do now?' he asked, and I recognised his question as an olive branch.

'Wait.' I sighed. 'There is nothing else I can do. I don't even know Ida's new surname. She would be impossible to find.'

He helped himself to a slice of cake, took a bite and stared out at the gold-drenched hills. 'And Thomas?' He fixed his eyes on me, watching my reaction closely.

'What about Thomas?' There was something in his eyes that flustered me. 'He's dead, isn't he? I've not heard from or of him since I left him in Oberfals in 1944. It's been nearly twenty years.'

The professor shook his head, and said, 'He's not dead.'

'What?' The news winded me and I gasped for breath.

He registered my shock then continued. 'At least, he didn't die in the war.'

'Have you seen him?'

'No. In 1948 he wrote to me. He'd gone to St. Gallen to find you.'

'I went to Brazil at the end of '47.'

'We'd both left by then but the Hochschule gave him my address.'

'And you wrote back?' I asked, desperate to know all he could tell me.

'I told him what I knew,' he said and I sighed: knowing what the professor thought of me back then, I would not have had a good report.

'Where was he?'

'He was in Berlin.'

'Have you heard from him since?'

'No.'

The next morning, standing in front of the hotel bathroom mirror, my feet resting on the cool tiles, I stopped and examined myself. I had been fifteen when I met Thomas, sixteen when we fell in love. Eighteen when I had left Laurin and the professor in St. Gallen. I had not known it then but I had been a great unadorned beauty; fresh, vibrant and wild like the perfume Charles had created for me. Now, bare before my toilette, at thirty-five, lines were beginning to play around my eyes and mouth and my skin had lost some of its radiance. The girl Thomas had known was gone.

However, when I had fled over the mountains to St. Gallen, I had been young, penniless and helpless. I had abandoned my child. Now I was a designer and businesswoman. I had worked and grafted, was a woman of note. I could fly around the world at the drop of a hat to see my friends. I was a success. I had made something of myself.

I picked up my eyeliner and leaned forward, ready to apply it. A tear welled up in the corner of my eye. I dabbed my eyes and drew a line under my lashes. Another tear spilled out and smudged the wet eyeliner. It ran in a darkening streak down my cheek. I had seen what it was the professor had offered me, what I had rejected. He had a family.

I leaned forward again but I could not focus; my vision was blurred, dark droplets falling steadily into the basin below.

For years my isolation continued; I lived a half life. The demands of my business kept me going but it was only in music, Charles's last gift to me, that I found any pleasure. The year after my trip to Paris, in 1962, Stan Getz released his interpretation of the bossa nova classics and from then on, American jazz musicians streamed into the Rio nightlife desperate to play cool jazz, their interpretation of Brazilian music. Charles had missed this musical explosion by so few years; he would have loved it. Brazil was becoming a cultural hub; people were excited by the new socialist president João Goulart, and the sense of optimism combined with my trip to Paris had shifted something in me. I started going to the dark jazz clubs alone to listen to bossa nova. Although I was going out, I was not, as you say, 'making an effort', but even so, at first, men would try and join me. But soon enough they gave up and I became a regular fixture, the sombre, black widow sitting on her own. The music transported me. It lifted my spirits in the way it had reached Charles and lifted him out of his pain those last weeks. It both took me to him and lifted me out of my *saudade* for him.

Graça had spent the years since Charles's death turning away a steady stream of suitors and callers, answering the phone and saying I was out or indisposed. After I came back from visiting the professor in Israel, she began to write down the names of the men who had called and asked after me. She left little notes for me on the phone table by the front door in the hall so that I could not fail to see them.

It was only on the last night of 1963, New Year's Eve, nearly six years since Charles had died, that I resolved to finally listen to him. He had told me that I had to live for him – but I was not alive, I was just going through the motions. I had to do better, for both of us. So, I told the next man to invite me out that if he could get front-of-house tickets for the three-night run of Isaiah Harris, the New York jazz saxophonist, I would accompany him. It was just before carnival, the summer air was hot and sticky and Rio was in its Golden Age. The city was effervescent. Bossa nova was drawing in the best musicians in the world to come and play with the Brazilian masters. Isaiah Harris was one of the most celebrated jazz musicians of the decade. The tickets were all gone by the time I had tried to buy even one and I was not prepared to pay the bribes required to secure the seats that I had demanded of this optimistic suitor, so I was confident that I wouldn't have to go out with him.

The Count of Sabará's third, much younger wife had just run off with a mustachioed Argentinian journalist. He was clearly not a man who learnt from experience – three failed marriages and he was still wooing by spending – and now I sat with him at the central table in front of the stage. The count had, as I had asked, obtained the best seats in the house for all three nights.

'Senhora Rosa,' he said after helping me into my seat and settling opposite me. 'You look ravishing; such class and poise.'

'Why, count, thank you.' I smiled sweetly.

'Yes, I see now, a man like me needs a mature, refined woman in his life. I am done with youth and beauty.'

Little did he realise, as I sat bejewelled in Victorian jet, a tight black-sequined bodice pushing my breasts up decorously into an inviting cleavage, that his back-handed compliment meant that the bribe that he had offered to get the table for me was money ill-spent.

So I sat regally, drinking champagne and smiling. For once I was excited – not because of my date, of course, I had never intended anything to come from that – but to see Isaiah Harris play. The count was sufficiently charmed and flattered by my polished small talk, something I had had years to perfect. The music from the supporting act drifted over my head and then the announcer clapped wildly as Isaiah Harris walked onstage.

He was a tight, wired man, bursting with energy and moving stealthily like a cat about to spring. He stopped and stood square in front of me. Thin, taut and dressed head-to-toe in black, we mirrored each other – even his shirt was unbuttoned, like my deep cleavage. He raised his saxophone to his lips and took a breath.

After his initial sweep of the audience, his eyes remained trapped in mine. He played with wild abandon, his improvisations unrestrained and swooping. I was entranced and he held my gaze for the whole set.

The next night, the count should have known better. He had secured the same centre-front table, and Harris looked for and nodded at me as he came onstage. He bowed to the applause and stood with his eyes closed as the drummer and bass player started to play. From his first notes I could see he was in a different mood; he seemed lost in the music, which was calmer, more melodic, and glanced out at the audience unseeingly. It was only during his solo that he gazed at me, and I stared back into his dark brown eyes. He turned to the pianist and did not look at me again until the moment after he had bowed. His hands cradled his instrument.

On the third night the count gave up the game, complaining of a headache, and I was delighted to find myself alone. I told the waiter to take a lager backstage to Mr Harris, along with a request that he join me for a drink afterwards. Isaiah Harris nodded to me when he came onstage and then played with the same intense energy of the first night, his virtuosity making me hold my breath more than once. And all his efforts seemed to be directed towards me. At the end of the set I sat and waited.

I was nervous. Not a single man had interested me since Charles's death, but the saxophonist played with a passionate physicality that reminded me of Charles, and in his mellower mood with exquisite tenderness. I felt intoxicated by the most intense *saudade*, a feeling that was neither pain nor pleasure, but revitalising. I had had enough of missing and mourning. As Charles had said, I needed to live.

From the front the dress that I had chosen seemed demure, with a high neckline, but at the back it plunged open down to my waist. It was daring and modest at once. Isaiah Harris appeared at a doorway to the side of the stage. He was carrying his saxophone in a black, battered case. The audience had begun to go home, although some people were still drinking. If they noticed him, they did not show it. He lowered the case on to the chair next to mine. His pale pink fingernails, with their big, creamy half moons, caught my attention as his long fingers grasped the top of the chair. He was standing over me, even taller off stage.

'Senhora Dumarais?' he said in a deep, melodious voice.

'Good evening, Mr Harris,' I said, hoping my accent was not too strong. My English in those days was awkward but passable; after I had left Paris and stopped dining with Dior's American friends, my only practice had been with American and British expatriates who seemed to struggle picking up Portuguese. 'Sit down, please.' I indicated the chair on my other side as I wanted him to take in my naked back as he passed behind me.

There was a curious look on his face as he pulled out his chair to sit down. 'You seemed moved by my music?'

'I was.'

'Forgive me, but I guess you're not Brazilian?'

'No, Italian.'

'But your accent . . . the cadence?'

'Is German.'

He looked at me with the same slow, thoughtful intensity I had seen in his playing.

'My life has been – how should I say? – complicated.'

A waiter arrived.

'Do you want a drink, Mr Harris? A caipirinha, perhaps? It is the national drink here in Brazil.'

He shook his head and smiled. 'Thank you but I don't drink.'

'Oh,' I said, 'forgive me for sending you the *chopp*.'

'Not a problem, my bass player likes a cold beer. I'll take . . . what do they call passion fruit here?'

'*Maracujá*,' I said, blushing. 'The English name is not correct, did you know? It makes you sleepy, not passionate.'

'That's disappointing,' he replied.

He handed the drinks menu to the waiter, stowed his hands under the table and sat up with the erect posture of a musician and regarded me. I thanked the waiter with a smile and then aimed it at Mr Harris.

'So where is your husband tonight, Mrs Dumarais?' He cocked his head to one side, a smile playing on his lips.

'My husband?' For a moment I was baffled, then laughed. 'Oh, the count! I barely know him. I'm a widow.' It had not occurred to me that anyone could have thought I was attached to the count – but what did it say about Mr Harris that he agreed to meet me anyway?

'I'm sorry,' he said, and the smile vanished from his face.

'My husband died nearly six years ago.' To my surprise it caused me no pain to say this; his death was now as much a part of me as his presence once was.

'I see,' he said, sounding much less assured.

'Let me introduce myself properly: I'm Rosa Dumarais.' I held out my hand. 'I'm a fashion designer.'

He took my hand in his. 'I'm Isaiah Harris. I play the sax.' His hand was so warm, the skin so soft; mine looked so small in his. I shivered.

The waiter returned with our drinks. He was almost reverential as he placed them on the table.

Isaiah Harris raised his glass to mine and drank his *suco de maracujá* in one, finishing by tipping up the glass so that the last drops slid into his mouth. His fingers traced the outline of his lips before he returned the empty glass to the table.

'Brazilian nectar. The thing is, Mrs Dumarais, after a gig I'm not one for drinks. But I am famished. I have quite an appetite.'

'In that case, Mr Harris,' I said, 'do you like Italian food?'

'I'm American – of course I like Italian.'

'There is an excellent trattoria just a short walk away.'

I excused myself and asked him to wait while I powdered my nose. The lighting in the ladies' room was poor but, somehow, I seemed spotlit in the mirror. The woman staring back at me reminded me of the radiant, vibrant creature who had once lit up Paris. But something was amiss; my eyeliner was smudged. My make-up had run when I had cried tears of joy as Isaiah Harris's music had embraced me. I inspected it more closely before fixing it with powder and drawing a new, clear line around my lower lashes.

17

Bidet

A young woman I was interviewing for a job as my business assistant once told me that whenever she visited a man's home for the first time, she always pretended to need to visit his bathroom within the first five minutes. She argued that you learnt more about a man's life from the innards of his medicine cabinet than from anything he said or did. Too many sleeping pills or razor blades, drugs that had uses other than their prescriptive purpose – or once, as she told me, a surgical kit complete with scalpels and suturing equipment – would suffice to make her find an excuse and take her leave. It was sound advice and she got the job. I think her approach was correct but limited. It is not just what is hidden away in the cabinets and drawers but the bathroom itself that can be read for clues. There is one thing in here, my marble refuge, that is commonplace in Brazil and France but unusual in this otherwise godly country. Yes, you are right, ma chère, I am talking about the bidet.

There are certain questions of hygiene that are determined by national practice and are incomprehensible to foreigners. Americans like to make endless jokes about the poverty of British dental hygiene, yet I cannot fathom how a nation obsessed with cleanliness and bodily odours does not install bidets as standard. In Brazil, it is not unheard of to find bidets in office toilets – very civilised. The first time I went to Cairo and Istanbul, I was surprised by the tiny pipes inside the toilet bowls there. Each toilet was equipped with its own mini-bidet function. As I said, it is cultural. The Ottoman Empire ruled a vast swathe of countries bordering the Mediterranean and Black Sea and inculcated in its colonies an interest in having a clean derrière. Americans obsess about white teeth, underarm smells and daily, if not more frequent, showers, but seem oblivious to what lies between their legs.

When I finished adjusting my make-up in the shabby bathroom of the jazz club, I led the saxophonist to an Italian restaurant that Charles and I used to frequent. This was the first time I had been back since his death and the owner rushed over to greet me.

'Signora Rosa,' he cried, beaming. *'Come stai?'*

Signor Lorenzo nodded politely at Isaiah but did not offer his hand when I introduced them. I was surprised when he led us to the back of the restaurant, as the table I had always taken before, with a view of the road, was unoccupied.

I was dumbfounded. Normally restaurateurs would try their utmost to have me sit near the windows like a shop dummy. Signor Lorenzo must have seen my displeasure because he said, with an air of polite apology, 'It's more private here,' as he pulled out a chair in the silent back room. I opened my mouth to complain but Isaiah raised his finger to his lips and shook his head.

When Signor Lorenzo had left, he said, 'You don't understand, do you?'

'Understand what?'

'Your friend can't seat us at the front without losing all his custom.' His tone was matter-of-fact. I stopped playing with the grissini that I had unthinkingly taken from the breadbasket.

'Because you're not white?'

'Now you're getting the picture.' This time the smile on his face was wry and challenging.

I was as shocked by my own naivety as Signor Lorenzo's behaviour. In Brazil, it was easy to pretend racial segregation was an unhappy outcome of history and economic circumstance. I knew it was different in the USA. The challenge was still in Isaiah's eyes but he was calm.

'How come you're not angry?' I asked him.

Georgia Kaufmann

He shrugged. 'I'm not surprised or angry. Unlike you, this is not the first time for me.'

When I said nothing, he laughed. 'Experience is a good teacher,' he said, his face relaxing as if I had passed some kind of test. 'Anger can be most unhelpful.'

Isaiah ate every scrap on the three plates that were presented to him, pausing to talk and drink water between mouthfuls. I toyed with my carpaccio and then the scampi while I sipped my Argentinian wine. In those days it was barely palatable without ice in it.

'The only thing I knew about Rio, before I came, was bossa nova and that movie, the one about the bus conductor and that girl during carnival.'

'*Orfeu do Carnaval?*'

'That's it, *Orfeu Negro* – *Black Orpheus*. It won an Oscar, didn't it?'

'Yes,' I said after a pause. The film was a riff on the legend of Orpheus and Eurydice, about the impossibility of bringing back a dead lover. I had found it difficult to watch. 'It is a famous film here.'

'It made me think that things wouldn't be that different here from at home.' He gestured at our empty segregated dining space. 'I was right.'

'I'm sorry,' I said, and my outrage was mixed with shame at my own ignorance. 'I should have known.'

'Well, you do now,' he said generously. 'And you are still here.'

'I am.' I gave him my most dazzling smile. So,' I said, casting around for a change in subject. 'Where is home? Where do you live?'

'I live in New York, in Harlem.'

'Oh. From what I've read, I thought all the musicians lived in SoHo and Greenwich Village?'

He shook his head. 'It's just about OK for a Negro like me – a well-known jazz musician – to live in the Village, but it ain't normal. I want to relax when I walk around my neighbourhood.

Home is North Carolina. It is beautiful, but not somewhere I wanted to stay.'

I took another sip of wine, feeling a little light-headed.

'So where is home for you?' he asked me, leaning back in his chair and resting his forensic gaze on me.

'I like it here, but it is not home.' I picked up my glass and sipped some more wine then pursed my lips. 'I don't belong. I don't know.'

'Was your husband Brazilian?'

'No, he was French,' I said, then added, 'and Jewish.'

He raised his eyebrows. 'And you are a German-speaking Italian?'

I opened my arms in a shrug. 'So, you can see that I am homeless.'

He nodded sympathetically. 'And your husband died six years ago?'

'Almost.'

'Have you been seeing anyone?'

'No,' I said.

'What about the count?'

'He was the first man I have allowed to escort me,' I said with a dismissive wave. 'But it was the only way I could get tickets to hear you play. I love jazz.'

He laughed. It was a warm, big laugh. He cast his eyes down and I could see him turning the situation over. 'Six years is a long time.'

I guessed that he had begun the evening imagining it would be a discreet assignation with a married woman. 'Yes. Perhaps too long – at least, that is what my friend Graça says.'

'Well, if the count was your first date, no wonder you could not take your eyes off me.' He laughed again and leaned towards me with his generous grin. My stomach flipped.

'Your playing is intoxicating,' I conceded. 'That's why I kept coming back.'

'Just my playing?' It really was a dazzling smile.

When the plates were scraped bare and our glasses emptied,

Georgia Kaufmann

I paid the bill. I made my frosty farewells with Signor Lorenzo, speaking in Portuguese not our familiar Italian, and stepped with Isaiah Harris out on to the dark, glistening pavement. It had been raining. We stood in the thick, humid air, which I could feel caressing my back while the doorman hailed a taxi. There was a long wait: carnival had begun and most of the taxi drivers were probably dancing behind an *escola de samba* – a samba school. Eventually a car drew up and for the briefest of moments the saxophonist looked uncertain.

'Where are you staying?' I asked.

'Hotel Regina.'

'The politicians' hotel.' I gave the taxi driver directions. Isaiah Harris opened the door for me then walked round to the other side and got in next to me.

We drove in silence. The night air carried the sound of drums, music and distant voices from a samba parade somewhere nearby.

'You should call me Izzy.'

'I'm Rosa.'

He started drumming a rhythm on the metal panel of the car's roof as his arm rested on the open window frame. I would come to know that making music and rhythms was like breathing for him. At one junction we could see a samba school one block away, parallel to us. Izzy craned to see the dancing people, the drums, the parading festival.

I had no idea what would happen when we arrived at his hotel and I became nervous. Delay suddenly seemed like a good idea. 'Do you want to go to the *carnaval*?' I asked him.

'And lose you like Eurydice? No. I have no intention of losing you.'

His hand reached for mine across the car in the darkness and I curled my fingers tightly round his. I remembered how I had felt when I had first made love to Charles; our belonging had felt inevitable and total. It was much simpler now: I wanted to touch and be touched, to feel him, to feel again. The uncertainty ebbed away as our fingers explored each other's.

The silence followed us into the hotel lobby, where Izzy took the key from the reception then told the bellboy which floor. I followed him from the lift along the marble-floored corridor, the syncopated rhythm of his footfall and the clack of my heels breaking the silence. There was a double bed, a small lounge area with a sofa, two chairs and a coffee table, and a balcony giving on to the sea. I went straight on to the balcony.

'Would you like a drink?' Izzy called from behind me.

'No, thank you, I've had enough.'

'Here.' He offered me a glass of water. He was sipping from one too. I drank it and turned back to the sea. The road in front of me seemed distant and the sounds of the late-night traffic and carnival drumming remote. All my senses were concentrated on him; I could feel him standing behind me. He kissed the nape of my neck then traced his fingers across my naked back.

He had a flight to Buenos Aires booked for the next day and as I left him at dawn, he had already started packing. It was six o'clock when I turned the key in the door and stepped into my house. I glanced at myself in the mirror and smiled. Thin wisps of hair had already escaped from my hasty chignon. My lips were swollen and my chin was rubbed raw by Izzy's early-morning stubble. I removed my shoes as I wanted to avoid click-clacking over the marble and waking Graça, but after two steps I heard the sound of a coffee pot being slammed on to the stove. I forgot my notion of a bath and sleep. Isaiah was scheduled to come back to Rio on his return to New York in two days' time and he said he would extend his stop-over. I had to prepare Graça and, I realised, I had to confess to her.

She was squeezing an orange for me when I walked into the kitchen. Her face was intent.

'Good morning, Graça,' I said, trying to sound as casual as any other day.

'Good morning, senhora, I thought you might be hungry.' The table was laid with fruit, bread and jam. She was right. I was starving.

'You didn't wait up for me all night, did you?'

'No, senhora, I did not,' she said, avoiding my eyes. 'But when I knew you had not come home, I was so excited for you that I woke early.' She handed me the orange juice.

'Excited? You're not angry?' I was so relieved.

She raised her own glass of juice like champagne and eyed me to follow. I clinked my glass against hers. She smiled and took a sip. 'Senhor Charles would have been angry at you wasting your life.' She drained her glass. 'It's been too long.'

'He is coming in two days, to stay for a short visit,' I said tentatively.

She picked up the coffee pot and poured some for me then herself. She was trying not to laugh.

'He's that musician,' I said. 'He's American.'

'I see, senhora. I'll have to go shopping.'

Graça did not comment when I asked her to put the extra set of towels in my bathroom, just smiled and closed the door to the guest room. She bought in huge quantities of food and spent the day before he arrived cooking. The smell of coconut and spices wafted through the house as she made *vatapá de galinha*, a Bahian shrimp and chicken stew, and stewed milk to make a *pudim*. I got dressed and redressed three times as I waited for him to arrive in the late afternoon, and I was changing again when the doorbell rang.

When I came down, Izzy was smiling and sipping a glass of freshly made *maracujá* squash, standing next to Graça, who seemed frozen with her hand extended holding a bowl of Brazil nuts. Izzy took me in his arms and kissed me right in front of her. Then he lifted his battered case on to the table and extracted his saxophone, fitting it together. He started to play. Graça did not move.

When Izzy was finished, he bowed to Graça and then to me. She looked astonished.

'Tell her that's what I do,' he said. 'I make music.'

I translated.

Graça's face remained glazed. 'You didn't tell me that he was black, senhora. He is darker than me.'

She made herself scarce during his visit. She cooked meals, which she served in the dining room, but she did not join us or solicit my company. We lost ourselves in my room, emerging punctually for mealtimes and occasional excursions to the beach or music clubs at night. By the end of that second weekend I had licked, kissed, felt and probed every inch of his skin, just as he had mine. We had mapped each other's bodies and the secrets of our pleasure. Our intimacy was complete and utterly physical. And then he left, and I worked with new zeal. We managed to meet three more times over the following months: once in Chile, then Venezuela, then a trip to New York.

When I came back, I looked around me and realised it was time to leave. Rio was no longer the same place as when I had arrived. When I met Izzy in February 1964, much of Brazil was in the throes of a love affair with João Goulart, a president with socialist credentials, but the rich did not like him, the military took against him and the American big brothers wanted him gone. The Cold War was extending its sticky, paranoid fingers down from the northern hemisphere into South America. One democracy after another toppled and came under military dictatorship, and juntas spread like a malign contagion. On March 31st there was a coup and by the end of the year a military dictator, Castelo Branco, was presiding over the country. He lost no time in flexing his muscles and closing down democracy; all but two political parties were banned and even then, the new official opposition was a lame duck. People began to disappear. Seemingly overnight, the happy-go-lucky atmosphere evaporated and democracy became every bit as insubstantial as a ghost. As a child, I had suffered from the cruel absurdities of Mussolini's fascism, then I had lived through the Nazi occupation. I had no intention of enduring another ruthless regime. I had no reason to stay in Brazil. Izzy merely provided me with a destination.

Selling my house was easy. The other villas lining the Avenida Atlântica had already been torn down and replaced with high-rise apartment blocks. Our home was prime for redevelopment. The one reservation I had was my business: I had too many employees who depended on the company. In the end, I decided to appoint a managing director and head of design and keep it. It would mean starting with less capital in New York, but on the other hand I would still have a successful, ongoing concern to my name. By the end of July, I was ready to book my flight. It was only then that I addressed the most important question of all.

'Graça?' I ventured over breakfast the day after I had decided not to sell the business. 'I know you don't approve of him.'

'Who?' She frowned, feigning ignorance.

'And you know I am going to New York,' I continued as though she hadn't spoken. 'I just wondered if you would come with me?'

'Senhora, do you really think I disapprove of him?' She sighed and shook her head.

'Yes. Well, maybe not him, but—'

'I'm not used to seeing black men with white women. I was surprised.' She sighed again. 'But not being ordinary does not mean it's wrong.'

'Exactly. I want to live in a world where what we have is not extraordinary but normal.' It wasn't clear even to me if I was referring to her or Izzy or both.

She nodded her head. 'I just thought you could do better. The count—'

'—is a vain, tired old man.'

'But he is a count. You could be a countess,' she said, and I realised she was teasing me.

'I didn't realise you were such a snob,' I said, grinning.

'I'm black and poor, I can't afford to be otherwise.' She pursed her lips trying not to laugh.

'Izzy is a genius.'

'What matters to me is that he makes you happy.' She reached across the table and took my hands in hers. 'And that is so good to see again.'

'So, will you come with me?' I asked, with hope this time.

'Before I answer,' she continued, serious now, 'I want to know why you are not going back to Europe. If you leave here, isn't that home?'

I examined the coffee cup. 'There is nothing for me in Europe, just bad memories. I would like to go back if things were different but . . .' Laurin would be nineteen; he would remember nothing of me. It would be pointless. I had no idea if he even knew of me, or that I was his mother. 'Izzy is offering me a future, something different beyond the shadows of the past.'

'Those are good reasons. It's not just some madness, then.'

'No, it's just time. So?'

'Oh, Rosa.' She sighed. The moment she called me that I began to celebrate; it was rare for her to drop the 'senhora'; she saved my name for our most intimate conversations. 'How could you ever think I would not? If I didn't like him, I would come anyway to take care of you, but like this I'll go gladly with you.' And then that stubborn look crossed her face, and I braced myself. 'Of course, I'll have to have English lessons. And he won't mind me listening to him practise, will he?'

I grabbed her hands and squeezed them. 'He'll have to play just for you every day.'

I sold the household contents. Graça tried to stop me, but I wanted to begin again. I remembered how I had left Oberfals, and then Laurin in St. Gallen, with just a suitcase, and now I got the same one out once more. It was battered and worn and I filled it with the mementos, letters and photos that I could not part with. We packed a few trunks of clothes, books and music and sent them on ships ahead of us while I auctioned the furniture and some unwanted clothes. It was as if Senhora Dumarais had died and her house was being cleared. I was leaving all that behind me. A new country and life lay ahead of me.

We left the winter in Brazil to arrive in New York at the tail end of summer. Everything felt back to front. The waterfronts and beaches of New York and New Jersey paled in comparison to the dense tropical forest tumbling down the granite cliffs into the blue of the South Atlantic that I had grown accustomed to. The lucrative sale of my house to developers had enabled me to purchase a decent if somewhat smaller apartment in Greenwich

Village. That fall I wondered, on more than one occasion, if I had been foolish as I craned my neck to glimpse the small sliver of sky above a narrow street and brick building that formed my Manhattan view, and compared it to the view of the shimmering sea and huge blue dome of southern sky I had enjoyed from my by then demolished villa.

The apartment was, at least, the penthouse of a 1930s mansion block. The rooms, though not huge, were well-proportioned and airy. Everything, except housing, was available in huge sizes in this crowded city and I ordered the largest sleigh bed I had ever seen and moored it on a thick marine-blue carpet. For the first few months I spent my days with Graça, walking the grand avenues in search of the perfect furnishings, and coming home forever empty-handed. When the shopping exhausted us, we would explore museums and galleries.

At night if Izzy was in town I either watched him playing in the Village or stayed at home with him. He kept his place in Harlem but stayed with me most nights. I did not know it was possible to be so open, so carnal. Don't give me that look, ma chère, you don't think I have not noticed how much time you and your man spend 'studying'. We both know that in the beginning it is like an insatiable hunger. And I had endured years of famine. I had mourned for almost six years. Now, at thirty-six my appetite for life had been rekindled.

That first week as I walked 5th and 6th Avenues rooting around for the objects that would make me a home, I felt I was missing something. And then I knew what it was. It was as essential as a basin, a bath, a toilet. Once I realised what was missing, it became a matter of urgency and, within a week of arriving, I located a plumber and a decorator. In ordinary times it was something that I considered as basic as washing my hands; in the extraordinary hedonism of the early days of our relationship, I needed one. It took the tradesmen ten days working round the clock to rebuild the bathroom and install a bidet.

18

The Pill

You're right. It is strange that I keep so many useless or out-of-date ointments, creams and remedies in this cupboard. It makes no sense. Look, ma chère, this is ridiculous. Do you know what this is? Yes, the pill – a month's prescription.

It changed my life. I don't believe that young women growing up today will ever appreciate to what extent these little gems transformed our opportunities. At sixteen, I had learnt the hard way the importance of contraception. More than anything else (and I include the vote and education) this is what put women on a level playing field. 1960. People don't think of it as a watershed, men don't really appreciate it (they could always get sex one way or another) but for women there are two epochs, one before and one after the pill. It is not surprising to me that it took two women of independent means, Margaret Sanger and Katharine McCormick, to push and then fund the research for the pill – yet you never hear their names proclaimed as saints. Men complain that women 'catch' them by getting pregnant, but it is the other way around: men enslave women by inseminating them. Unless the women are independent. Although the pill was available from 1960, in New York and about half the states men prevented us from using it until 1965 – if you were married – and until 1972 if you were single.

Can you imagine your life without it? Do you think for one moment that I could have had my success in building a lucrative design house with my hands tied to the kitchen sink? Yes, ma chère, I know the opportunities are there for women now, but even so they are hindered by children in a way that men simply are not. It was the reason I had to leave Laurin behind. I could work harder and earn more for him if he was being well cared for in St. Gallen. Brazil is a different country; the pill was available for those who could pay from as early as 1962. I had watched my friends using it, complaining of headaches and weight gain, of loss in libido or excessive desire – but I had also seen them mutate into more independent creatures. I don't even know if I would have been with Izzy without it. If I could not be with Laurin, nor have Charles's child, then I did not ever want to be pregnant again.

When I moved here, I came with a stockpile of pills wrapped in the sexiest lingerie I had. In those days the customs officers would not rifle through a lady's silk undergarments. Of course, I have not needed to use the pill for a long time now but I keep it here, just in case, like a Band-Aid or surgical spirit. They are evidence of different times. Archaeologists would enshrine the first wheel if they found it. This little packet is as important. In any case, it is better to be prepared. There are always other people to think of, ma chère.

I quickly discovered that the life of an itinerant musician is hard, especially when they have to leave loved ones behind. However, since I was in control of my life and looking for new markets, I would often go on tour with Izzy. He took me back to Europe, providing me with a different trajectory. It meant that I was leaving Graça behind on her own more and more. This proved to be a mistake.

It's hard to remember now which trip it was, but I knew the moment that I walked back into the apartment that something had changed, that there was someone new in our lives. It was the unmistakeable thick, sweet aroma of garlic and beans that assailed me as I opened the door. It had taken years to wean Graça off *feijão*, the Brazilian national dish. It is not that I didn't like it, but I preferred to vary my diet rather than have the same meal twice every day. I knew she indulged in my absence but it was unusual for her to cook it for my return. I found her in the kitchen, hovering over the stove, a man's jacket over the back of a chair.

'Olá, Graça.'

'Senhora Rosa!' She spun around, startled, waving a wooden spoon.

'I can see you've been busy,' I said in English. I was thrilled for her. She needed romance in her life. She spent too much time reading art history books.

'It's not the way it looks,' she said, looking mortified. 'I met him in the church. You'll like him.'

'In church? He must be nice.'

'I hope so,' said a man as he sauntered into the kitchen. He was tall, wiry, dressed in a simple white shirt and slacks. He was not as dark as Izzy; his complexion was more like white coffee, his hazel eyes luminous. There were traces of Indian in his chiselled cheekbones – whether Guarani or Tupi or an Amazonian tribe would be a fact lost in his family history. I could see why she had fallen for him.

'You must be Senhora Rosa. I am Luiz Nonato Moraes.' He spoke in English too, and his accent was good. He glanced at Graça before adding in Portuguese, '*Sou o noivo de Graça.*' He dipped his head in a slight bow.

I stared at him, stunned. 'What?' Graça was beaming with pleasure.

'I'm Graça's fiancé,' he proclaimed again, going to stand by her side and taking her hand. He looked like the proverbial cat with a bowl of cream.

I struggled for words. 'Isn't this a bit sudden,' I faltered, wondering if I had missed something. 'When did you meet?'

'Five weeks ago, senhora.' Graça returned to peeling and pulping the garlic. Of course the rice was for him, not for me. She had forgotten that I was due back.

'We met the Sunday before you left,' Luiz said. 'So we've known each other nearly two months.'

'Six weeks,' I said, going to the tap and filling a glass. I sipped the water and looked at him. Graça had had boyfriends in our time together, but he was unlike any of the quiet, timid men she had brought home before. He was assertive and confident.

He might be good for her but I didn't want her to hurry into anything.

'When are you going to get married?' I asked her.

'Next month,' he replied.

'Why the rush?' I looked at Graça and flicked my eyes down to her stomach. She looked blankly at me then put her hands over her belly.

'Oh, no, senhora, it's not that,' she said, laughing away my concern.

'Well, then,' I said firmly, 'that doesn't give me time to make you a dress or prepare the feast. You can't just get married; you'll have to have a wedding. We'll have to invite your family, and they'll need to acclimatise. No, no, four months at least.'

Graça hugged me. 'You'll make my dress?' she exclaimed, beaming at Luiz. 'See, I told you she would be happy for me.' Then she frowned. 'But my mother won't come.'

'You'll have to go down and get her.' I smiled as another delaying tactic occurred to me. 'Or should we do it in Brazil?'

'Oh, senhora, thank you,' she cried, hugging me again.

I glanced at Luiz over her shoulder. His eyes were aflame. 'No,' he said with an edge to his voice. 'We'll do it here. In three months.'

It took some adjusting to having Luiz around. He was clean, tidy and polite. When he brought Graça flowers, he always pulled out a single bloom and bowed and presented it to me. He did not put one foot wrong, but I had a growing sense of disquiet. The flourish as he handed me the flower was too grand, his politeness almost excessive. I felt like he was playing a game, mocking me. But there was nothing I could say to Graça; she was in love and my unease was based on nothing tangible.

At thirty-four, she was a strikingly beautiful woman. Ever since our trip to Paris she had dressed well in an elegant, minimalist way. She wore her hair short and her features had become finer with age. Luiz could not stop himself from touching her, holding her hand, settling his fingers on her back or arm as he passed or stood beside her. And her hands reached out to him equally.

I understood that hunger well. We had been living in New York for two and a half years and although the initial intensity of the passion between Izzy and me had faded to something more sustainable, I still shared my bed with him most nights. It was just the pattern that had changed. At the beginning, we had spent most of our time together in bed. After a time, Izzy would stay in the morning and practise for hours or read while I worked, designing my collections or planning.

To my surprise, moving to New York had helped my business grow. Whether it was the added cachet of having Rio de Janeiro and New York on my company logo or the fresh impetus and inspiration that moving had given me, but my sales in Brazil and South America were growing. I launched my new American business by retailing the Beija Flor cosmetics range to high-end department stores. The cosmetics were easier and cheaper to ship and were less of a risk than the clothing. The second year I was in New York, Neiman Marcus took my clothing for the summer, and by the following season I had sold the range to seven department stores. By the time Luiz came into our world, I was looking for a vacant store to take over.

However intensely I was working, whenever Izzy practised, sooner or later I would rest my pencil unmoving on the paper. His music always had the same effect on me. He had a fast track into my soul. It was only in his company that I would allow memories of Charles to surface, or wonder where Laurin was, who he had become. And sometimes I would even think of Oberfals: of Thomas, my first love, wondering what had happened to him, and Herr Maier, the postman and my sister but never of my parents – I had dismissed their ghosts as completely as the sergeant's.

Then Izzy would get fidgety and want to go out. We would listen to other musicians playing, hide ourselves in cinemas, trail around artists' studios buying canvases still wet with paint, or watch his friends' latest shows, eating out with the actors after hours. The sex, though less frequent, continued to be as charged.

Which made my own annoyance at the sounds of pleasure that came from Graça's room all the more disconcerting. I knew I should have been pleased for her, and it troubled me that I wasn't. I was sure that it was not jealousy. Luiz had given me no cause, but – call it instinct or intuition – whenever we exchanged pleasantries, I bristled. I simply did not trust him, but I could find no solid reason why. Nevertheless, I was fearful. But this did not bother me as much as the growing friendship between Luiz and Izzy.

One Sunday, Izzy was sleeping late after a gig. It was one of those days when New York tosses off the winter gloom and biting cold and shifts into springtime gear. The sky was a sharp blue and the air warm and breezy, with none of the summer humidity that would later slow us down with its molten weight. I went out to buy fresh brioche and croissant – the availability of such pastries in New York was something I loved. I dawdled, stopping for a coffee, enjoying the holiday ambiance created by this first burst of warmth.

When I came home, I found Izzy and Luiz playing cards. It was not the first time. Luiz had persuaded him to play several times after we had come home from clubs late at night. Those games had been brief but, judging from the extinguished butts in the ashtray and Luiz's whisky glass, they must have started the game soon after I had wandered out. I had never seen Izzy drink, but his hand was resting by an empty tumbler. The dregs had an amber sheen.

Luiz jumped up as soon as I came in and made to clear the bottle and glasses. While he was out of the room, Izzy came over and kissed me, his breath sour from the whisky and tobacco.

'I've got to go.' He kissed me again, lifting his hands to squeeze my breasts. This was not an affectionate caress; he pinched my flesh, like a dog casually marking its territory.

He nodded at Luiz, who had returned soundlessly, and left. A smirk flashed over Luiz's face as he picked up the ashtray.

Fifteen minutes later Luiz knocked on the living room door. I was curled up on the sofa enjoying the pastries and a coffee and working my way through the Sunday edition of the *New York Times*. Reading had become an important part of my morning ritual, something that I had learnt from Izzy – 'How can you respond to the world if you don't know what is going on?' he would say.

'Senhora,' he said, his voice uncharacteristically quiet. 'May I have a word?'

'Of course,' I said, making an effort to appear welcoming. 'Come in, sit down.' I gestured to the easy chair at the end of the coffee table.

He ignored me and sat down next to me on the sofa.

'Senhora.' He sighed. 'I wanted to thank you for allowing me into your home and for giving us your blessing.' There was nothing suggestive in his tone, nothing to be faulted in expressing his gratitude but I bridled. He was assuming an intimacy that he had no right to. He cast his eyes quickly over me, then lowered his gaze down into his lap.

'Well,' I said, smoothing my short plaid skirt down, suddenly conscious of how much leg miniskirts exposed, 'you seem to make Graça happy and that is what I want.'

'Thank you.' He settled against the sofa and spread his arm over the back towards me.

I uncurled my legs and shifted forward.

'Graça is a wonderful woman,' he said. I could feel his eyes on me. I picked up my newspaper again, hoping he would take it as a hint. 'She has all the virtues a man could hope for in his wife.' His hand inched closer along the cream leather.

I opened my newspaper. 'Yes. She is good, strong, steadfast and loving.'

He was so close I could smell the burnt tobacco on him. 'Exactly,' he said.

I was wedged against the arm of the sofa. 'You will look after her?'

'Of course.' The contrast between the correctness of what he said, and the wrongness of his presence was unsettling. I wanted the best for Graça; I wanted to be misreading the situation. Had he been anyone but her prospective husband I would have long since evicted him.

'I mean, treat her right,' I said, keeping my eyes on the newspaper. I could feel him staring at me, contemplating me.

'The only flaw with Graça,' he said, examining his nails, 'is that she has no flaws. Sometimes men like a woman – how do they say here in America? – to be trashy.' There was a hint of a smirk lifting the corners of his mouth.

I met his gaze. 'You could never call Graça that.'

'No, I wasn't talking about her.' He grinned. I was stunned at his audacity in thinking that he could toy with me.

'You're telling me that you like trashy women?' I asked, masking my annoyance. I was not going to take his bait.

'Just one.' He leered at me. He let his meaning sink in. I felt my body stiffen, like a cat ready to spring. 'I thought you would understand. A high-class woman like you with a man like Senhor Isaiah.' He leaned back against the sofa and closed his eyes and sighed. 'I can see you like a real man. You have a taste for black cock.' He flicked up his eyelids, capturing me in his gaze.

That look felt like a slap. All my distrust for him was justified in an instant but I kept my mouth shut. This was a dangerous man.

Business had taught me that it was best to let the opposition lay their cards on the table before showing mine. I managed to return his lascivious gaze with a blank stare, despite how furious I was.

'You know how noise travels at night?' he asked nonchalantly, his fingers stroking the cream leather. 'I try and work out what he is doing to you by the sounds you make.' He smacked the sofa lightly. 'You would make other music with me.'

I slapped my newspaper down between us. 'What I like is none of your business, but Graça is mine. I thought you loved her.'

'I do. I'm talking about gratification, not love. I just thought that, since we're alone, I could offer you some new pleasures.' He bared his teeth in a jackal's grin.

I had what I wanted: an outright proposition, proof that he

was no good for her. 'Get out,' I spat. 'Graça deserves better than this.'

'Of course, I'm so sorry. I would never do anything to harm her,' he said, the usual obsequiousness returning to his voice. He sprang up, but then continued in an altogether different tone, 'And I would not forgive anyone who hurt her.' He took a step towards me so that he was looking down at me with the same cruel smile that had flashed across his face when he had seen Izzy fondling me. 'I think you understand me now, senhora. Don't underestimate me.'

He turned to go and called out as he walked away, 'Don't upset Graça and I won't upset Izzy.'

Three days later, when Izzy was still asleep, I settled down to breakfast. Luiz was not around; I had not seen him since our conversation. Graça said he was at work, but it was never clear to me what 'work' was. He claimed that he worked as a waiter but I had never heard of the restaurant that he mentioned.

'Senhora, I have some news,' Graça said, and something in her tone made me look up from the *Times* spread out on the table. 'My period is late. Two weeks. I think I may be pregnant.' Her face was full of eager expectation.

Despite my carefully fixed smile, my heart sank. Now she would be tied to that snake for good. 'Why, that's wonderful, Graça. Just wonderful,' I said. 'Luiz must be pleased?'

'Oh, he doesn't know yet. I want to be sure before I tell him.'

Later that morning, the obstetrician shuffled through the papers on his polished mahogany desk after we had sat for forty-five minutes on the orange velvet easy chairs in his waiting room, watching the tropical fish swim around the aquarium.

'Mrs Dumarais, I can confirm that Miss Mendes is expecting a baby.' If he had not looked down at his paperwork, he might have seen the smile that lit up Graça's face. 'This is just conjecture, but would I be right in thinking that you may be wanting to remove your maid's . . . inconvenience?' He struggled over the last word, looking up at me only as he finished speaking.

There have been few times in my life when I have been made speechless, and this was one. It took a moment for me to even compute what he was saying but Graça understood immediately. She stood up at once and made the sign of the cross.

'*Graças a Deus*, Dr Brown,' she said coldly. 'Until now I thought you rude, but now I see that you are racist. Come, Rosa, let us go.' She turned and walked out of the room with dignity.

'Send me your invoice,' I said, fixing the blushing man with a cold stare. 'We won't be requiring your services for the obstetric care.'

Half an hour later, we were standing in the lobby of a building reading the large board that displayed the different offices in the building, looking for the Brazilian consulate.

'Graça, you really don't need to register that you're pregnant.'

'I know, but I just want to find out everything I can about getting citizenship for the baby.' She was so excited, so full of plans and dreams, she could not stop talking. 'I don't want him to miss out, not on anything. And then we have to register the wedding – we have to find out about that, anyway.'

'Luiz said that he would look into that,' I said, turning away. I was still wrestling with myself about telling her about the incident on the sofa, but I so wanted her to be happy. She scanned the board while I looked around. It was a busy lobby, full of people streaming in and out of the lifts that served the many floors. I stared blindly at the scurrying swarm and then at the pattern of elevator doors opening and closing.

'Do you think he's going to be excited?' She looped her arm through mine.

'Of course,' I said, patting her hand.

An elevator disgorged another torrent of workers and visitors and as the flood abated, one final passenger stepped out. Luiz stopped and scanned the lobby. His eyes met mine. He slowly flicked his tongue over his lips and then strode out into the street. She did not see him and I said nothing.

★

'I'm worried about Graça.'

I was lying with my head resting on Izzy's chest and he was stroking my back.

'Why? She's found herself a capable man who wants to marry her. And it's good that she's pregnant.'

'Yes, I know she's pleased to be expecting but . . . Oh, Izzy, I don't trust him.'

His hand stopped caressing me. 'You're not her mother. You're being overprotective.'

'No,' I said, propping myself up on my elbow. 'It's more than that . . . I just know he's up to no good.'

'How? Give me an example.'

I hesitated. I didn't want to tell him about the pass Luiz had made nor his veiled threat. Luiz's words had cut deep. I thought that Thomas's and Charles's love had cured the feeling that I was trashy and dirty, stained by Schleich, yet Luiz's ostentatious lack of respect had unleashed something. And if I was honest with myself, I did not know how Izzy would react. His abstinence from alcohol had ended and his moods were unpredictable. He was changing.

'I don't know,' I said eventually, my frustration leaking into my voice. 'It's just a feeling. But look at the way he's got you playing cards – ' I paused, knowing that if I continued I would be opening a can of worms. I took a breath – 'and drinking. I know I haven't seen it, but I've smelt it on your breath.' Izzy withdrew his hand. I should have stopped then but I couldn't. 'I'm worried. I'm sure that you've been seeing him when you're not here. And you don't look well; you look pale and you're losing weight.'

'I never thought I would accuse you of this but,' he said, turning on his side to face me, 'you're a hypocrite.'

'What?' I was stunned.

'It's fine for you to have a man to yourself and to enjoy Graça's love and loyalty but the moment she gets something for herself, you're put out.' He had never been so angry. 'You can't bear the fact that he's only attracted to her, not you.'

'That's not true!' I protested before I had the sense to stop myself.

'What, you think he fancies you, too? Does everyone? Even men who are in love with other women?' He turned away, swung his legs over the bed and sat with his back towards me.

'Look, I just know he's not what he seems.' I touched the base of his spine, where he loved to be stroked. He shifted away.

'He said that women are like dogs. Some need a long lead, some a short, but as long as you master them, they're happy.' He stood up. His face was drawn in an ugly, angry snarl. 'He says your problem is that you think you're top dog and I need to remind you of what you are: just a bitch.' He took a breath. He looked as shocked as me.

'Izzy!' I cried.

'Come on, face it, you rule the roost here and that's what all this is about,' he said with less ire. He seemed a bit remorseful but didn't stop. 'Graça is getting more attention than you. Don't start crying, it won't work.'

I couldn't stop the tears. 'That's nonsense.'

'No, what's nonsense is that I'm not enough and you want another man in your bed.'

'That's not fair.' The tears were coming thick and fast now. 'And it's not true.'

'What's not fair is that once in a while I play cards with Luiz and just because I'm having fun that doesn't involve you, you want me to stop?'

'It's not that at all. It's because you don't look right. In nearly three years you've not touched a drop and now all of a sudden—'

He stepped towards the bed, leaning over me.

'Face it, Rosa, you're just spoilt and jealous.' His hand was rising in a tight fist ready to strike me as he shouted, 'I'm not your boy to order around.'

I gasped and held my hand to my mouth. He froze in his fighter's stance as if he had suddenly become aware of what he was doing. His beautiful hand fell gracelessly to his side. Neither of us said another word as he picked up his clothes off the floor and pulled them on. He left without saying goodbye.

I've often wondered if it would have made a difference if I had told him that Luiz had made a pass at me. But I did not. Even though I did not agree with Izzy, I did not want to be the one to ruin it for Graça. Luiz had warned me not to underestimate him, and I should have listened. I made such a mess of my early life that I can't presume to give you advice, ma chère, but I think what happened next might have been avoided if I had spoken out. I just wasn't sure that anyone would have believed my motives. And to be frank, even I wasn't sure. I had to consider that there might be some uncomfortable truth in what Izzy had said.

When I came back without Izzy later the same evening, I found Graça sitting alone in the kitchen, crying at the table.

'What happened?' I asked, sitting down next to her and taking her hands in mine.

'I told him,' she said, her voice hoarse.

I paused to formulate my words. 'And wasn't he pleased?'

'He said it was too soon.'

'Is that all?'

'No, he said that he didn't want children,' she splurted in a rush, 'that he loved me and wanted me all to himself and that I was selfish if I thought he would share me with my rotten baby.' There was a look of confusion and disbelief on her tear-stained face.

'He must have been surprised,' I said finally.

'I don't understand. He was so kind to me until today. It was as if he was another person, so hard, so cruel.'

I bit my tongue. I thought I was helping by keeping my counsel.

The next morning, when it was barely light, some strange sounds filtered into my sleep and woke me. It took a while to work out what it was and when I realised that it was Graça retching, I got up. She was in her cream cotton dressing gown, slumped over the toilet in her bathroom, sweat glistening on her forehead.

I touched her brow. 'You're ill. I'll ring for a doctor.' I started back out into the hallway.

'No. No,' she called after me. 'It's too late.'

'What do you mean?' I stopped but did not turn back to face her.

'Last night, before he went, he made me take these.'

'What?' I asked, kneeling down beside her.

She pulled something out of her pocket. A white, narrow box.

'They're yours, I'm sorry, he made me take them.' She put the box in my hand.

'How many?' I asked in a whisper.

'He made me swallow the whole pack.'

I closed my eyes to take it in. Her teary red eyes were fixed on me when I opened mine again. 'The whole pack?'

She nodded then turned to vomit again.

I drove her to a hospital, where she stayed for a few days. She lost the baby and needed time to recover from the overdose. The next time Luiz called round, I told him that he was not welcome anymore.

We learnt the hard way that the pill can be used to terminate pregnancies. What we did not appreciate then was the depth of Luiz's pharmacological knowledge.

19

Syringes

Sometimes I think the modern world is crazy. Look at this. The gauze, antiseptic wipes, a vial of blood serum and a few syringes. What do you think it is, ma chère? It's an emergency travel pack for AIDS. It may seem irrational but I still take it whenever I visit Brazil. About five years ago, Dr Michaels insisted that I carry it in case of an accident. I thought he was just being overcautious until I had lunch with an old friend in Rio. She had discovered that her boyfriend had been sleeping with men as well as her – apparently, he did not think of that as infidelity, as with another woman would have been. She had dragged him to the STD clinic in the local hospital. She was first in line for the automatic jab of penicillin that they were given even before his syphilis had been confirmed, and then she watched in disbelief as the nurse wiped the syringe before refilling it and plunging it back into her lover's arm. 'Syringes,' she told me, 'are like your keys, money and lipstick. Don't leave the house without them.'

But I'm jumping ahead of myself – you can tell that I'm still nervous. About tonight, I mean. Talking like this, telling you my story is helping to calm me down, but if I lose the thread I feel as if everything will unravel.

At about the time that Luiz was barred from coming to the apartment, Izzy started drinking heavily. Neither of us commented on Luiz again, but something had shifted. Whether it was the row or the alcohol was unclear. He would arrive at night after a gig with a bottle in his hand and fall asleep in front of the television. His sexual appetites became impulsive, even animalistic. At first these changes disturbed me, but in

some respects it was thrilling. I got used to him satisfying himself
whenever or wherever the need took him. Propriety and courtesy were forgotten. Sometimes it was as mechanical and as
thoughtless as taking a beer from the fridge; other times, it felt
as if he would die if I did not let him in to me immediately.
Being the object of this heady urgency and compulsion was
seductive, even intoxicating. You may think it odd that I am
telling you this, ma chère, but you won't understand unless I
tell you everything. The choices we make are based on earlier
choices, and mistakes.

I never went back to Brazil with Izzy, although I travelled a
lot with him. Whenever he was on tour, if work allowed it, I went
too. We criss-crossed the USA and flew backwards and forwards
across the Atlantic. The travel was not wasted. Wherever I went
I checked out the competition, visiting the high-end retail outlets
of the best designers. I sourced fabrics, patterns and manufac-
turers, and later even went to the graduation shows of the better
fashion schools. And then I expanded: first in LA and San
Francisco, then Boston and Washington DC. Soon I was opening
franchises in department stores. My long-term plan was to build
up to a string of stores in all the major cities. I chose cities with
good jazz scenes and between Isaiah's tours and my business
trips, I was hopping on and off planes almost as often as I took
New York's yellow cabs.

When I travelled I always took account books and novels. Izzy
would beat a rhythm on the tables, read the newspaper or play
chess with his bass player, Greg. They were well-matched and
it passed the time. Izzy always took the white pieces; it was his
joke because Greg lived in Harlem and Izzy with the white folk.
We had routines that were dull and comforting, so it was a
disruption in the monotony of the routine that made me face
up to the gravity of the problem. We were in Rome airport – I
know it was Rome, because I had a momentary lapse of my
lapse of faith and considered returning to the fold – and I was
reading *The Secret of Santa Vittoria*, the book that everyone had
been telling me to read about an Italian village's response to the

Nazi occupation. It was evoking anger and forgotten memories in me in equal measure; I did not find it as amusing as everyone else seemed to. At some point I noticed that Izzy was gone. Greg was staring at the chessboard, his chin resting on his cupped hand. He looked worried.

'What is it?'

Greg sat up straight and began to clear the board. 'He lost again,' he said.

'Again?' I said, my heart sinking. Izzy was usually the stronger player of the two, but a glance at the chessboard showed that Greg's black pieces dominated.

'And not just again, I slaughtered him.' He played with the rook in his hand then dropped it in the box. 'Maybe it's not my place, Rosa, but I have to say something: there's something wrong, seriously wrong.' He picked up the white king, which had been knocked over.

'I know.' I sighed. 'I'm worried.'

'And his sax playing; it's not the same.' Greg hesitated, clearly uncomfortable about criticising his boss and friend. 'Either he goes off into some strange place – it's beautiful and eerie but sometimes I think it unnerves the audience – or he seems so out of it that he can barely blow two notes together. If I hadn't been with him so long . . .' He petered out and finished clearing away the pieces. 'He's just so angry, all the time,' he said, folding the board in half.

Greg had been playing with Izzy for a long time. He was loyal. I knew I could trust him. 'He's drinking.' I had avoided talking about it, even to Graça, as if silence would make things better. It was a relief to admit it to someone else.

'And drugs too?' Greg asked sotto voce.

'I think so.' Saying it made it real. I bit my lip.

The chair between us was pulled back, scraping noisily on the floor, jolting us out of our exchange. Izzy sat down.

'You been telling tales on me to my bass player?' he slurred, putting his hand on my knee. 'Did you know she likes to play dirty, Greg?'

'Izzy!'

'The thing is, Greg, she likes the way I treat her now. It was Luiz who told me that she was no princess.'

'Luiz! You've been seeing Luiz?'

He pushed his hand under my skirt. I clamped my legs together. I spread my hands over the fabric – a bold, black-and-white, oversized houndstooth, very à la mode at the time – making it as taut and impassable as I could. Hitching my skirt up behind the trash cans in a backstreet in the small hours of the morning when we left a jazz club was between us. This was different; it was in daylight, and we were not alone. I had never seen him this drunk in the day. But I would not make a scene, it would help nobody. Izzy had taught me that the first night we had met. His fingers forced their way further up.

'Izzy, don't!' I hissed. He was leaning so close to me that I inhaled the sour scent of whisky on his breath. I stood up. 'I said "don't" and I meant it!'

'And we always do what Rosa wants, don't we?' Izzy smiled and waved his fingers under his nose. 'Ahh, the smell of home.'

I was dumbstruck, ma chère. The man I had fallen in love with was gentle and civil with a beautiful soul, not crude and cruel.

He wiped his fingers on his sleeve. Then turned back to a very uncomfortable-looking Greg and said, 'So, you want another game?'

He turned and picked up the chess pieces and proceeded to set the board up. I needed to calm down so I left to check the departure times. When I returned, Izzy was thrashing Greg.

You look shocked, ma chère, but I am so old now that it could have happened to someone else, and you are just embarking into this world of men; you really do need to know how things can go wrong.

After our return from Rome, I did not see Izzy again for about a month. I thought it was over. I missed the musician and gentleman but not his drunken doppelgänger. I was relieved that he was gone.

Then one night, he crawled into my bed, so late it was nearly morning. He made love to me as he had used to, treating me like an instrument that needed to be played. His lips, tongue and fingers traced every contour of my body, strummed and caressed me until I was spent. In the morning, lying in the low light of my room, the sheet draped over him, he looked dull and skeletal. When he woke, I brought him some coffee and buttered toast glistening with *maracujá* jam – a little luxury I had sent up to me from Brazil whenever they brought in samples. When I put the tray down on the bed, he grabbed my wrist.

'Do you love me?' His voice was rasping and desperate. He had never asked me before, never said it himself, and I had never thought to say so. His eyes were bright and intense, and little beads of sweat were forming on his brow. His irises were wide with fright. For months he had fucked me with the same mindless penetration and thrust as wild animals coupling, but that morning I was soothed by a night of his tender lovemaking. I knew what kindness and music still remained inside him. We stared at each other for a long moment, he looking for his answer, me for a glimmer of what he used to be.

At last I said, 'Yes.'

'Then lock me up in here. Don't let me out, not for anything, and feed me only bread and water – no booze, not even coffee. Will you do that for me?'

'Yes.' I kissed his fingers that were still gripping my wrist tightly. He cocked his head to the side, sighed and released me.

Graça had been inconsolable after she had lost her baby and Luiz had disappeared, but as soon as I explained the plan to her something in her stirred. She prepared plates of sliced fruit and soft white farmhouse bread and cheese and I brought it in to him on trays. We knew about drugs, but not as much as people do now; even the idea of going cold turkey was not well known. For nearly two weeks we kept him prisoner. He sweated, shivered and vomited. He shouted and raged, he shook and trembled, he cried and begged to be let out. At times I was too frightened to go in; other times he slept so heavily that we could creep in and tidy, replace the food thrown on the floor, wipe up the water spilled around him, and change his soiled sheets. After ten days, he fell quiet and started reading the books I had chosen for him, and his appetite returned. After two more days we celebrated by going out for a meal to Chinatown. Izzy opened the cab door for me, pulled out my seat and held my hand.

It was like the beginning all over again.

For a while, we stayed on an even keel. Gradually, the original routine lapsed and Izzy came and went more fluidly; sometimes he would stay over, but not always. It felt more stable. A few times when I travelled for work, I would come back and Graça would tell me that he had waited like an abandoned puppy in my absence.

In the fall of 1967, I opened my first stand-alone retail store in Florida. A new luxury shopping mall had opened a few years before at Bal Harbour and I bet on my tropical, lightweight clothes having year-round sales there. It was a success, but made me realise that I could not just sell for the summer season in New York and Chicago and the other northern states; I had to produce winter collections too. The calm that had descended on Izzy and our household helped me focus. Little by little, Graça had taken to helping me with administrative matters and, partially in order to distract her from her melancholy, I asked her to fly down to Rio as my representative to execute business as needed. She was reluctant at first, feeling that it was above her, but I won by enticing her with visits to her mother, who was growing old. Anyway, I told her, she knew best what foods I missed to bring back for me. A confident businesswoman returned from the first solo visit, bringing with her a suitcase packed with *maracujá* jam and *goiabada*. She knew my business as well as anyone and was a model of efficiency and common sense. Of course, when we hired a new cleaner, it was Graça who took control of the process. She had exacting standards.

And then out of the blue, things went topsy-turvy all again. Bobby Kennedy announced the assassination of Martin Luther King Jr. and riots spread over the country. The gig Izzy was playing in New York that night was cancelled. The next morning Graça did not appear at breakfast; she was too upset. I was pouring the coffee when Izzy read the headline out loud.

'Martin Luther King Jr. is slain in Memphis.' He folded the newspaper and put it down on the table. He pressed down hard and then smoothed out the paper again. 'That's it,' he said. 'They can't even say it.'

'What?'

'What kind of word is "slain"?' He spat out the last word. 'He wasn't "slain", he was murdered, killed, assassinated.' He got up, waving the newspaper wildly.

'It's only a word,' I said soothingly. 'It doesn't mean anything.'

'He wasn't fucking jousting; it was a lynching.' He rammed the newspaper into the garbage can. 'Slain! This is all shit!'

He paced around the kitchen, opened the fridge, took out some milk, put it back. Then he closed the door and leaned heavily against it and folded his arms. His body was tight with rage.

I waited a moment before saying softly, 'Not everything is shit.'

He snorted. 'You and me. There ain't no dream. King was wrong. Black folks and white folks don't get to be the same.' He strode to the door. 'Who were we kidding?' Seconds later the front door slammed shut.

I know it's hard for you to fathom, ma chère, why the murder of a civil rights campaigner could capsize anyone. But back in April 1968, it was literally the end of a dream, a dream he had given us. Five years before, Dr King's famous speech had made it to Brazil and Graça and I had discussed it. It was probably one of the reasons she had agreed to come with me to the US. For the generation that grew up in the Second World War, the future that King and Kennedy imagined for us was intoxicating. You know how excited you were last year when they released

Nelson Mandela? Well, imagine all that emotion, all that hope – and then imagine if he had been shot the next day. That's what it felt like with Dr King's murder.

A few days later, on my way home from the office, I stopped for a coffee in a bar two blocks away from the apartment. Ma chère, taking a few moments to savour a good coffee is as necessary as breathing. I only noticed them when I returned from the bathroom. Izzy was sitting at the bar with Luiz, clutching a half-empty tumbler in front of him.

I froze and watched, my pulse racing. Izzy's whole posture looked wrong; he was hunched forward, talking earnestly, submitting to Luiz's disdain and short rebuffs. Luiz slipped something into Izzy's jacket pocket. Izzy, still hunched over, pulled what I thought was a cigarette out of a box until Luiz unfurled it and counted the notes under the counter. He stuffed them in his pocket and then got up to leave. As he straightened up, he saw me approaching and his lips stretched in a thin, cruel smile.

'Look, your woman is here.'

Izzy turned and looked at me, a peculiar mixture of defiance and guilt on his face.

'Why can't you leave him alone?' I snarled at Luiz. 'Wasn't it enough to make Graça miserable? Why Izzy too?'

'Graça was love,' he said, smooth as silk. 'Mr Isaiah here is business. Very good business.'

I slipped my hand into Izzy's jacket and pulled out the small plastic package. 'Here, take this,' I said, thrusting it back at Luiz. 'Give me his money back.'

'Mr Isaiah man, you going to let this whore treat you like this?' Luiz reached into his inner pocket, took out the wad of notes and waved them in my face, then stuffed them into his front trouser pocket. 'You going to get the money then, *puta?*'

I grimaced. 'Forget the money, but keep your poison too. Come on, Izzy.' I slapped the package on to the bar and grabbed Izzy's arm, which tightened, the bulge of his bicep turning to stone. 'Izzy, let's go.'

'I can't,' he whimpered. The anger and shame had vanished

from his face, replaced with a look of terror. 'You don't get it. I can't.'

'Izzy!'

He swiped the packet off the polished teak and pushed me so hard that I fell sprawling on to the floor. He darted past me and out of the door. Luiz lifted his glass and toasted me silently, smiling while a waiter rushed over to help me up.

The next time Izzy came to the apartment he found all his clothes and music packed in bags by the door, along with a note telling him to leave his keys.

On Sunday July 20th, 1969, Apollo 11 landed on the moon, and I was happy. Izzy had rung me earlier that day. We had not seen each other for over a year and yet he wanted to watch the moon landing with me. His excitement was infectious. I was pleased that he sounded so well.

He came over and sat glued to the TV for hours, the three of us watching the moon's silvery surface come ever closer to the skewed viewing window of the lunar module. We were with Houston when the Apollo landed. We continued watching the hours of preparation that the excited astronauts went through until they opened the hatch and Armstrong descended the ladder. We strained to catch Armstrong's words as he made his small but giant step. Izzy was like a little boy who had just opened all his Christmas presents. We stayed up all night, his euphoria bubbling over as the astronauts orbited us. The views of the earth from the moon were overwhelming. At lunchtime on Monday, Apollo launched back into space and when in the early evening the Eagle recoupled with Columbia, we went to bed. We fell asleep exhausted and happy.

I wasn't surprised to find that Izzy was not in the bed when I awoke the next morning, nor that the TV was already on. Graça was still asleep. I got up, had a shower and pottered into the kitchen, making coffee. I carried the drinks into the lounge and manoeuvred past Izzy's outstretched feet to put the tray down. I was not worried when he didn't respond to my 'good morning'.

I stepped back and yelped as I trod on something sharp and hard. I lifted my foot up and saw an abandoned syringe. My heart froze. Izzy's arm still had the tourniquet on, scarred and puckered from all the abuse. The syringe had fallen from the outstretched hand closest to me, its deadly load spent.

20

False Eyelashes

No, ma chère, I am not going to wear these tonight. I think I must embrace a more natural look, don't you agree? I am so nervous, and although I want to look my best, even the most beautiful women understand that grace and age go hand in hand in the beauty stakes. In my early forties I could still get away with fastening these little spiders to my eyes, but not anymore; it would look rather pathetic. What some women do not understand is that yes, the world is a stage, but there are different theatres and different audiences, and you have to play them appropriately. It would never do to wear the same make-up to a New Year's Eve party in LA as for a Sunday lunch at some mansion on Long Island. Understanding the unwritten rules of make-up, as well as dress, is fundamental to success in society. Just think about it, ma chère: who started to use these fluttering black lashes? Yes, exactly: the silent movie stars like Louise Brooks. We couldn't hear them so we had to see what they felt, they had to talk with their eyes. I realised long ago that men often don't hear women, they see us; they respond to our visual language. Look: if I frame my eyes with these long black lashes, however unreal, any man could understand what I'm trying to tell him. The downside of them is that they make us seem childlike and innocent. I guess that's why they caught on again in the sixties, along with all the flower power. But it wasn't the hippies with their maxi-skirts, naked midriffs and bare feet who wore them; it was modern, miniskirted women like me.

After Izzy died, I went to Vidal Sassoon's salon and asked them to cut my hair and dye it dark brown, and started to wear the cold, sharp look that Mary Quant made her own. I drew dark kohl round my eyes to mask the blue-grey rings from sleepless nights. The invitation to 'turn on, tune in and drop out' palled. The hippies, with their hopeful love, protestations of peace and drug-fuelled lifestyle, seemed naive and foolish. I became harder; I wore miniskirted suits in bold geometric patterns and strong colours. It was a different look for the new me. I was telling the world, as much as myself, that I was done with frivolity – with love.

Even though I had not seen Izzy for the year before he died, I was devastated. On that last night, he was so alive and excited, intoxicated by the progress that a man on the moon signified, that I fell asleep happily imagining that he could return to being the man I knew he was, the man who had pulled me from my grief with his lyrical, passionate playing. I had lost every man I had ever loved: Thomas, Laurin, Charles and now Izzy. After his death the only music that I allowed to move me was the sound of the cash register.

I took stock. What had kept me afloat time after time was my independence and capacity for work. I was in America, ma chère, the Land of Opportunity, and it seemed obvious that the only way forward was to work harder, grow my business and embrace the American dream. And that is what I did, I buried myself in work. I increased the number of outlets I had scattered across the states and grew their floor space. But you can only soak up so many square feet of a department store. Neiman Marcus, Bergdorf Goodman, Saks, Lord & Taylor and Bloomingdale's all carried my Maison Dumarais clothes, jewellery and Beija Flor cosmetics. I travelled to every major city and negotiated good deals on prime positions in all the best department stores, but I heard the same remark again and again: higher profile. The experimental store in Florida was selling better than I had hoped and I reasoned that my sales would flatline if I did not upscale my market position. Having developed winter collections, too, I calculated that it was time to be brave and bold. I needed a flagship store in New York, and then in Paris and London.

So far, I had ploughed most of my profits into expansion. I

had a growing design team and my own manufacturing plant, but apart from the Bal Harbour rental I had kept real estate costs low. If I opened a stand-alone store in New York, it would have to be spectacular to secure against the real estate and rental prices on the desirable blocks in Manhattan. It would be a huge and costly gamble. My store in Rio had been affordable. Here in New York there were no bargains. Investing in real estate in a prime location, which was essential, would leave me very exposed. The paper was full of the exploits of the big developers, their profits, their buildings and their flashy lifestyles. No amount of money seemed to protect them from the mockery of the journalists in the *Times*. And then I hit upon an idea.

Two years had passed since Izzy's death when I arranged to meet Jimmy Mitchell. He was a pre-eminent East Coast property magnate who had carved out a real estate empire with his uncanny ability to see trends and patterns ahead of the game. He had a reputation for not just riding the market but directing it; buying discounted when others were selling at a loss, turning blocks and whole areas around. Jimmy Mitchell was also the talk of the town for his brash lifestyle and string of beautiful girlfriends, a constant feature of the financial pages. He had come from nowhere – or, more precisely, from Monticello, a small town in upstate New York – and had built a business empire from his father's controlling shares in a few local stores and the county newspaper. By the time I met him he was nearly fifty, shiny-faced, his balding head badly covered by thin wisps of brown hair gelled down and a sharp suit hiding his soft belly. He was fabulously rich but known for being unsophisticated and tacky.

I did not walk in any old how to such an important meeting. Making an Entrance is an undervalued art, ma chère. It was when I lived in Paris that I had perfected mine. I had watched the Parisian ladies and Dior's mannequins and learnt exactly how to enter a room. I did not walk, so much as sway in. I do not mean the exaggerated throw of the hips from side to side models use to stalk down catwalks, but an imperceptible balletic gesture – curving, balancing, a gentle shift, as foot and leg step delicately but firmly forward. I was about to enter the inner sanctum of one of the sharpest businessmen in the US with an outrageous plan, and I needed every weapon in my arsenal to win him over.

My latest collection used the tropical palette of Brazil combined with the geometric patterns that were current at the time. I had been careful to choose colours that enhanced my own; the emerald shift dress, the turquoise jacket and shoes with emerald buckles might have been distracting were it not for the effect that they had on my eyes. I had put on large lashes, which framed my blue eyes so that they were unmissable. I took two steps into Mr Mitchell's office on the top floor of his newest building on 5th Avenue, took one look at the thick shag carpet and thanked Roger Vivier and my maître Dior's heir, Yves Saint-Laurent. I could never have crossed the tangled tassels in pointed heels, but mercifully Vivier had introduced solid square heels into the Dior collection. I mustered all my grace and stepped across the twirling mass of wool.

It was a corner office, the glass walls offering a breathtaking view of the city behind a large, old-fashioned mahogany desk that looked out of place on the white carpet. Mr Mitchell sat behind the desk, leaning back on a vast black leather chair. A smaller, matching chair was in front of the desk. In the middle of the room a pair of brown leather two-seater sofas faced each other over a glass table. I could see immediately that there was money but no style in the furnishings; he made gold but surrounded himself with expensive, tasteless trash. I paused short of his desk and extended my hand in greeting, and my gesture forced him to rise and come around to meet me. I took a token step towards him and slipped my hand into his firm shake.

'Mrs Dumarais,' he said, 'a pleasure to meet you.'

I left my hand in his a second more than was natural and smiled before answering, 'The pleasure is all mine.'

He gestured to the sofas and went to sit down without waiting for me. I ignored his command and moved to the window.

'It seems so small from here, Mr Mitchell,' I said, looking out over the city. 'Like a monopoly board. And if I'm right, much of it is yours.'

After a few moments I heard him get up from the sofa, and he came and stood next to me. 'I could show you if you'd like,' he said.

I turned and bestowed him with a gracious smile. 'I'd like that very much.'

He pointed out every building and plot of land that he owned, from Midtown to Lower Manhattan, and the sites he wanted to acquire. I had determined my objectives in advance, but seeing the sprawl of his holdings gave me a moment's pause. There was plenty of evidence to prove he was a good businessman. He returned to the sofas.

He sat down first again and then leant back into the pliant upholstery, before gesturing for me to join him.

'So, Mrs Dumarais, what is it I can do for you?'

I sat down across from him, arranging my legs so that he would not be able to look up my skirt.

'Well,' I began, 'my idea is perhaps a little brazen, but as you are very much aware, nothing ventured—'

'Nothing gained. Shoot,' he interrupted. 'I'm all ears.'

I coughed before recovering my flow. 'The press is full of the new skyscraper you are finishing on 6th Avenue. It will be the jewel in your crown, I believe, and you are looking for good tenants.'

He nodded. 'All true.' His eyes were fixed on me and he was listening intently. I smoothed down my skirt.

'I propose that it is in your interest to give me the ground floor, street-level store on a ten-year lease with the first year rent-free in the new building you're erecting on 6th Avenue.'

He threw back his head and laughed, and settled deep into the cushions.

'I'm not joking,' I said, countering his mirth with my glacial mask. 'It will make good business sense.'

When he realised I was serious, the amusement vanished from his face. He crossed his legs and rested them on the glass coffee table. 'Why would I even consider this?'

I smiled. 'Because you want cachet, because you want the "old money" to accept you, because you are a social climber. And your taste in young girlfriends has made you . . . let me put this delicately . . . not as respected as you could be.' I spoke fast so that he could not break in, but not so fast that I sounded nervous. He watched me but did not interrupt, and I knew how carefully he was listening by the way that his head inclined just an inch towards me. 'You should be the emperor of Manhattan, but you are like a clown, Mr Mitchell. People laugh at you and you know it. I could change all that.'

'You have some gall,' he said, and his face gave nothing away. 'And how would you bring this about?'

'Do you know anything about me?'

'Not much. You're a mid-sized, high-end fashion designer. You built up your business in Brazil and have grown it here.'

'That's only part of the story,' I said. 'Let me tell you the rest.' I spun my story of starting as a seamstress, being discovered by Dior, creating the Maison Dumarais and Beija Flor. I told him that I was growing the business in the US, that Maison Dumarais was poised to take the country by storm, and all I needed was a prestigious flagship store and social prominence.

'So, Mr Mitchell, what I propose is this: that we become engaged.' I paused to let my words sink in. 'As your fiancée, I will accompany you to all social gatherings, openings, parties and dinners. I will teach you how to behave in the higher echelons of society. I will make you "arrive", so to speak. And in return, you will give me the first year rent-free and the next nine years at a commercial rate and, at a mutually agreed time, we can break our engagement.'

He looked long and hard at me. I unravelled my legs and recrossed them in the other direction. He looked at my legs and then got up and went to the window. He stared out at one of the most expensive views in Manhattan. I waited.

'How do you know all this about me?' he asked, his voice flat and unemotional, his back to me so that I could not read his face.

'It's all in the papers, Mr Mitchell, and I recognise a kindred spirit.' I got up and joined him, taking in the view down over Midtown to Wall Street and beyond. The avenues ran through the urban patchwork like rivers seen from a mountaintop. 'You see, like you, I come from a small town and made myself from nothing. I grew up a simple mountain girl, Mr Mitchell, and I've conquered continents. Dior taught me everything I needed to know. And – ' I paused, turned towards him and waited for him to look at me – 'I have class now. I can transform you too, and it will make a difference.'

'So you are like Maria?' His face was unreadable.

'Maria? Oh, von Trapp – because I came from the Alps?' I laughed. 'Not quite.'

'This is an interesting proposal, Mrs Dumarais. I will need to conduct some due diligence.'

'Of course, that's sensible.'

'I'll call you.'

Ma chère, don't look so appalled. I know this was a cold approach but you must understand I was so hurt, so damaged that I had built a carapace of calculation around me, to stop me ever opening myself up again. I was too frightened that I would not survive another blow. The business was the only baby I still had and I wanted to give it my all.

A week later, his secretary rang me and asked if it would be convenient to meet Mr Mitchell at the Four Seasons Restaurant at seven o'clock that evening. I suggested eight; he had to start learning cultivated ways sooner rather than later, and seven was too early. Graça was in a foul mood as I dressed to go out and when I went to put on my Miss Dior, I could not find the bottle. I wore Yves Saint-Laurent's Rive Gauche, instead; it was soft and feminine, and I wanted to disarm him. I slipped on the Yves Saint-Laurent dress that I had bought on my last trip to Paris, a contrasting black and blue silk crêpe de chine with bouffant half-length sleeves and the décolletage plunging into an embroidered corset that girdled me like armour.

The Four Seasons is a grand and classy venue, but not

romantic. It seemed appropriate that we should meet there to discuss my proposition in the company of besuited men talking business, money and golf, with only a few tables decorated with elegant Manhattan wives. Mr Mitchell was waiting for me at the table, the menu open in front of him; not that I was late, he was early. That struck me as odd, a sign of nerves perhaps. For the next hour he led the conversation, describing his latest acquisitions, plans in hand and building nightmares. He pleased and surprised me with his vehement opposition to the Vietnam War. He was no hippy but he was no Republican either. As the waiters cleared the dessert, I was losing patience and took the reins.

'So, Mr Mitchell, have you exercised due diligence?' I tried to look disinterested.

'I believe I have,' he said, regarding me with no hint of a frown nor smirk. For a moment, I had a sudden distant memory of Schleich toying with my father when they played cards. The notion that I was out of my depth terrified me, but I pushed it away. I had learnt the hard way how to play, too. I was a match for Mr Mitchell's poker face.

He pulled his coffee cup towards him across the white linen tablecloth.

'And?'

'You've packed a lot into your life,' he said, still inscrutable.

'Yes,' I said evenly. 'I keep myself busy.'

'Your business acumen is obvious. From the figures I've seen, you are doing very well in Brazil; you created a small empire quickly, and you are on your way to repeating that here.' He dropped a cube of brown sugar into his cup.

'I have a good nose for business, a good eye for fashion and I work hard.' I stirred my mint tea to release some heat.

'And you have an entrepreneurial sense of daring. You're right though: if you got my shop front, you could take America. But the deal involves our relationship so I investigated your personal life too.' He held me in his gaze. 'I think I know everything. The German soldier, Fischer?'

That was unexpected; I thought no one knew about him.

'Thomas. Thomas Fischer,' I said, struggling to keep my voice casual. 'He was my childhood sweetheart. We lost contact twenty-five years ago.'

'Your namesake, Charles Dumarais. I take it you married him for love?'

'Absolutely. I loved him.' I picked up my small glass of Fernet-Branca and swirled the thick dark liquid around.

'And then Isaiah Harris.'

My glass was only halfway to my mouth, but I put it back down. 'He was a brilliant musician.'

'And a drug addict.'

I regarded him, frustrated. He still gave nothing away; we could have been discussing the stock market. 'Mr Mitchell,' I said, by now angry with myself: I should have been prepared. 'It is hard, I know, for a businessman to comprehend the artistic temperament, but genius in any field is compelling and brings its own rewards – and challenges.'

'Well,' he said, sighing, 'as you know from the gutter press, I have been photographed with more than one brilliant young woman.'

I said nothing. I was not going to cheapen my relationship with Izzy by comparing it with the models and starlets he was seen out with.

'What struck me as most strange is that, for a woman of your age and beauty, you have not had many . . . affairs.'

I raised the glass to my lips and downed the Fernet-Branca in one. I tried not to grimace and looked in him the eye. 'I put a high value on myself.'

'Indeed.' He surveyed me. 'Well, that is an important approach to asset management. But the information that has led me to my decision came from a most valued source. And the information that I needed was this: you are reliable, honest and very loyal.'

I took the first sip of my mint tea to rinse away the foul taste of the Fernet. 'Thank you.' I nodded graciously. 'Who was your source?'

'OK, here's the deal,' he said, ignoring my question. 'A short engagement only. You get the store on the terms you proposed, half the street frontage of Mitchell Heights – you can choose which side – and I'll deed you the apartment below my penthouse at the top of the tower as a wedding gift. To—'

'Wedding gift?' I interrupted.

'Yes, the penthouse apartment and the one below it share the same private lift. No one need know that we are not living together. To all intents and purposes, to the outside world, we would be happily married and living the high life.'

I started to speak but he silenced me.

'May I finish? To summarise, I meet all your conditions – with one variance to the deal. Instead of contracting an engagement, we marry. Do you agree?'

I was dumbfounded. 'I suggested only an engagement,' I replied at last. 'Won't a marriage just complicate matters?'

'I know. But,' he said, shaking his head, 'an engagement makes no sense. It's half-baked. Imagine what doors would be opened to us as a married couple. Then we will have truly arrived. I can deed the apartment to you outright. It'll be yours. No strings. It's what you walk away with when we divorce – at a mutually agreed time. It's valuable real estate. And if we draw up a prenuptial arrangement, we'll save long-term lawyers' fees.'

His counterproposal floored me. There was some sense in what he said, but marrying for commercial gain seemed a step too far. My marriage with Charles was sacrosanct, it had been the best thing in my life. Marrying this gauche businessman would be a travesty of that. 'I appreciate that,' I faltered, playing for time. I couldn't escape the sense in what he said. Charles would still be with me in my heart, I reasoned.

'So, do you agree?'

'This is business, not romance, Mr Mitchell.'

'I am well aware of that.'

'No conjugal rights.'

'None, of course not. No conjugal rights – unless you change your mind,' he said, his face still inscrutable. 'Although that would

be subject to further negotiations. And you won't mind my girlfriends?'

I thought for a moment. 'As long as you are discreet.'

'Do we have a deal, Mrs Dumarais?'

I forced myself to wear my warmest smile. 'You can call me
Rosa, Jimmy.'

His poker face finally broke into a broad, boyish grin.

'You will have to excuse my timing and choice of venue, but
I think it will serve our mutually agreed purpose.' He gulped his
coffee down, pushed his chair back and stood up. He came round
the side of the table and sank down on to one knee. 'Rosa
Dumarais, would you marry me?'

He extracted a small blue velvet box from his suit pocket and
offered it to me. For the second time that night, I was completely
wrong-footed. Not only had he changed the deal, he had had the
confidence to assume that he would win the negotiation. I did
not look up, ma chère, but I was aware of a discreet hush around
us, and a sense of being watched. So, concentrating hard, I arched
forward and kissed Mr Mitchell slowly, lingeringly on the lips.

'Of course, Jimmy. Yes.'

The hush in the restaurant was broken by claps and cheers
and there was a flash of bulbs, which continued as I opened the
box. And then I gasped, floored yet again. 'It's beautiful, really.'

'Surprised?'

'Absolutely,' I said, my smile and response genuine. He was a
smart player – I had underestimated him. 'I think you should
put it on my finger.'

He lifted the ring from the box and, taking my hand, slid it
on. I splayed out my fingers and admired the large sapphire
flanked by two smaller diamonds on each side, set in white gold
laced over the rich, warm yellow gold of the band. It fitted
perfectly.

After our public engagement, he had brought me home in his
limousine. I was flustered and excited at what this would mean
for my business, barely able to contain myself in the elevator

rising up to my apartment. Normally, Graça was party to all my schemes and dreams, but after my first encounter with Jimmy, I had not confided in her. I wanted to be certain of the outcome before raising her hopes – or so I told myself.

I found her reading in the living room. Since she had been travelling and running the South American business, and the cleaner looked after the house, whenever she had a spare moment Graça could be found with a book in hand. When we first arrived in New York she had taken English lessons and had discovered an appetite for learning. Over the years she had taken many courses, starting with English Language, then English Literature and from there on to History of Art and Spanish. She was a natural scholar. The transition from maid, to companion, to best friend and trusted employee was now complete. She was the rock in my life, the one who knew me inside out and I was, ma chère, I'm a little ashamed to admit, so proud of having helped polish this diamond in the rough.

She put the book down on the table and smoothed it open, her hand tracing over a colour plate of Leda and the Swan. 'Did you have a nice evening?'

'Oh Graça, I don't know where to begin,' I said as I settled into the armchair.

She folded her hands on her lap.

'I've made a brilliant deal. I'm going to marry Jimmy Mitchell.'

'Congratulations,' she said, switching to English. 'This is a surprise.' Her voice was flat but I was too excited to register her lack of warmth.

'I'm going to get a penthouse apartment and great retail space in his new building. And all I have to do is increase his standing and position in society, using my own social cachet. It'll be easy.'

'Will you be selling this place?'

'I don't know. I hadn't thought about it.' Until an hour ago it had never occurred to me that I would be moving from our home. It had not even crossed my mind since that she might not want to move into the new apartment.

'Perhaps you should keep it as a bolthole.' Her English

vocabulary was precise and cold. Usually we spoke Portuguese to each other, it was part of what we shared. She leaned forward, reaching for her book.

'Graça, aren't you pleased for me?' I asked, like a pathetic child out of favour with her mother.

She looked down at her hands and then up at me.

'No. I don't like it. It doesn't feel right.'

'What do you mean?'

'All your life, you've followed your heart.'

'No,' I said slowly, 'building my business has always come first.' That was a pivotal realisation. Who had I been trying to fool? It was what the professor had tried to tell me in Jerusalem. I had always been selfish; I had never deserved more.

'Really?' Graça said, not trying to hide her contempt.

'Yes, it's what drives me.' I played with the ring. It was true, I had always been motivated by ambition. What love I had had along the way was luck. This decision I had made tonight, I convinced myself, was honest; it reflected who I really was. I was not worthy of true love. I had proven that over and over. My opinion of myself, ma chère, had never been lower.

'If you say so.' She closed the book, picked it up and stood to leave. 'Apart from being surprised, I had no problem when you came home with Mr Isaiah. Even after that first afternoon, when he played his music just to win me over, I could see that although it was not what you had with Senhor Charles, it was some kind of love. But this Jimmy Mitchell, he's . . . tacky, he has money but no taste. Senhora, he's not for you.'

'How do you know?'

'I've . . . read about him.' There was a slight hesitation in her voice. She was a poor, unpractised liar.

Then it dawned on me. 'He tracked you down?'

She stared at me.

'You've met him, haven't you?' I stared back.

'He was very insistent.' She sighed, sitting down again. 'I said no at first, that it was none of my business.'

'But?'

'But he said that, from the little he knew, the man you were about to marry was very much my business.'

'That's what he said?'

'I don't know, Rosa,' she said, gesturing in exasperation. 'Couldn't you have said something to me? What was I to think?' Her face was grim. 'He insisted on having lunch with me.'

'Where did he take you?'

'Lutèce,' she said, smiling reluctantly. 'He thinks he can buy anything.'

I smiled back, relieved that she was thawing. 'What did he ask you?'

'Everything and nothing. He must have hired a private detective. He knew about Senhor Charles and Mr Isaiah. Even about your German soldier boy. He knew about your business, all about Maison Dumarais and Beija Flor, what you are worth. There was nothing I could tell him. I got the feeling that what he really wanted to know was why I had stayed with you.'

I felt a chill at this intrusion. Graça and I shared an intimacy that no one had ever intruded on, not since Charles had died.

'Did he know about Laurin?'

'No, that was strange, he didn't mention him.' She paused. 'It was fun, you know. The fancy restaurant, the car. He sent his chauffeur to pick me up and then came back in the limo with me. But that was just a ploy.'

I looked at her questioningly.

'To get in and see the apartment,' she explained.

'He came in here?'

She shrugged. 'It seemed rude to refuse.'

I wanted to be angry but I had no right. We both knew that I should have told her my plan from the outset. 'What did he say?'

'Not much, he walked around looking and picking things up. He said that you were classy, that he had no style and he needed my help. He persuaded me to get back in the car and took me to the diamond district and got me to choose the ring for you.'

'This!' I gasped, holding up my left hand. 'That explains why it's perfect.' I slipped it off my finger and put it on the table.

'Yes, I had to steer him away from the huge solitaire rocks. Oh, senhora,' she cried, 'he has no idea. How can you consider marrying him?'

Despite her obvious despair, I laughed. 'But Graça, I don't love him. I won't be with him like that.'

'Exactly. You don't love him.' She shook her head. 'You shouldn't marry him.'

'But I'm not deceiving him.'

She raised her eyebrows at me and shrugged. 'I'm not worried about him. I'm worried about you.'

'Me? How can I get hurt?' Even I could hear that my voice sounded whiny and defensive.

'Rosa, this man is used to getting his way. He is smart and powerful. He can outplay you.'

'Oh, I think we're a fair match.'

'You're not,' she scoffed. 'What do you know about him, compared to what he knows about you? What did you offer? What is he taking?' She stared me down.

I had nothing to say.

'Tell me, who got the better deal tonight? And don't say that it was you.'

'Graça, I don't need your help.' My voice was harder now. 'I know how to run my affairs. This will work, believe me. I can outsmart him.'

Graça did not respond for a while, just sat hunched over the table. She played with the ring and then she sat up and handed it to me. I put it back on.

'I learnt about gems when you did that Cintilante collection in Rio,' she said quietly. I was relieved that she seemed to have given up trying to dissuade me.

'At Maluf Gem Exports?' I smiled. 'That's a long time ago. What made you think of that?'

'I thought I would never forgive you for making me confront Sé like that.'

'I just wanted to protect you and your cousin. The police would have done nothing.'

'At the time, I didn't know where you were coming from. I was angry.' She looked up at me, sadness etched on her face. 'This time it is you, Rosa, who needs protecting. You are out of your depth. Laurin came into being because your father gave you up as a plaything to Schleich. Jimmy Mitchell is a playboy – are you really ready to be his latest toy?'

I jumped up. 'I'm nobody's toy, never again.'

'Then don't be played,' she begged.

'I won't. It is a straight up contract. He gets what he wants, I get what I need. It's a good deal.'

'Senhora, you have to listen to me.' She reverted to Portuguese. 'You're deceiving yourself. Come, please.' She took my hand and led me down the corridor towards the entrance where my floor-length mirrors hung.

'Look, what do you see?' she said.

I examined myself, lifting my hand to my face. The blue of the dress enhanced my eyes; Graça had chosen the sapphire to match them. It was a shade darker but not by much. 'Me?'

'No. Many years ago you asked me to look in the mirror. You taught me to look beyond the shabbiness of my clothes, to see who I was, who I could be. Now, I'm asking you the same. What do you see?'

'A woman who still looks good, who looks ten years younger than she is?'

Graça tutted at my vanity. 'I see delusion. Your make-up – the pink lipstick, the blue eyeshadow and those ridiculous eyelashes. Senhora, you are forty-three years old and you are made up like a teenager. If you marry this man and enter into this great sham, I think you may lose sight of who you are. And I would hate that.'

I stared hard into the mirror and saw only the mask I painted every day to face the outside world. Graça was the only person left who knew and loved me.

'You're wrong, but I won't make you move. You can stay here. It's your home as much as mine. In fact, I'll deed it to you. And as for love, I don't have it in me to love again. Business is all that is left for me.'

I stepped closer to the mirror and pulled off the spiky false eyelashes. Graça took them from me and rolled them up in her fist.

'Whatever the truth is,' she said sadly, 'these won't heal the pain. They just cover it.'

And she dropped them into the wastepaper basket under the hall table.

21

Tylenol

You have a headache; it must be the stress of listening to me. Here, I'll just get you some of this. When I was young, the only painkiller I knew of was aspirin, but little by little more choice has become available. Nowadays I don't get so many headaches; the pains I have are different. I do everything I can to keep my joints supple and mobile but arthritis comes from within. Much as I would wish to, much as I fight against it, I cannot stop ageing. I can slow it down but no more. These days I am more likely to use Advil for pain and reserve a low dose of aspirin to keep my blood healthy, but by the late 60s, Tylenol had usurped the place that aspirin had enjoyed as the main analgesic for the masses.

I have never suffered much from headaches, except from this one period in my life. During the engagement, and leading up to this charade of a wedding, I felt at times that my head might crack open. It was as if there were some malevolent beast eating me from the inside, gnawing on my brain. I began popping Tylenol incessantly.

It started with managing the press. Our 'whirlwind' romance was featured in the newspapers and magazines after his proposal at the Four Seasons, and to feed the hunger for column inches, I leaked stories to journalist friends who I knew from the Village about my life in Paris and Rio. Suddenly Jim (I told him that he had to drop the Jimmy; it lacked gravitas) found himself being invited everywhere. We married after six months, during which, ma chère, I designed a new collection to launch the store, and furnished and fitted his penthouse, his office and my apartment. I started by overhauling his office then took over his penthouse apartment, taking him to gallery openings and to meet artists. This kick-started a surprising new passion for him. I had to choose the paintings for his walls because in every gallery we visited he would drift away from the oils, drawings, prints and watercolours and I would find him in front of the sculptures, touching and feeling them as much as viewing. I was pleased to see that he bought good pieces, and even more pleased that he seemed genuinely moved and excited by them. I cancelled all the orders made by his interior designer and started from scratch, focusing on his sculptures rather than showy furniture. And for two months, I forbade his entry.

When I finally let him in to see my work, it surprised me how excited and nervous I was. We were standing at the foot of the staircase he had originally ordered, which swept down from the bedrooms. I had instructed the workmen to take off all the gilt and recover the banisters with white ABS plastic – it was my private joke: the same material used in Lego bricks, it seemed apt for a building magnate's pad. There was little I could do about the brown marble floor so I bought acres of gorgeous silk rugs from Persia. I used the colours from the rugs and had the walls painted in complementary shades of orange, pearl, beige and red. It is not how I would do it now, but then it struck a perfect note of modernism and Eastern mysticism. His two biggest sculptures, a Moore and a Hepworth, stood on either side of the staircase, and on the landing where the stairs bent back on themselves, a large bronze Burmese Buddha that he had not seen before sat in calm meditation. He walked around the lobby, circling each of his statues, and then took the steps up to the Buddha. He did not utter a sound and I could not gauge his reaction – I had realised that much of his business success could be attributed to his perfect poker face. He came down the steps and took my hand and pressed it to his lips.

'If I hadn't already, Rosa, I would propose to you now.'

I could feel a blush running over my face. 'You never did; I suggested our engagement.'

'And I our marriage.' He was still holding my hand. It was the first time he had touched me when there wasn't a horde of press photographers waiting.

I slipped my hand from his grasp and spread my arms. 'Welcome to your home.'

The nature of our arrangement required a grand wedding. I lunched with the social columnists of the major New York newspapers and fashion magazines and studied Forbes, and within two weeks I had a guest list that included all the people who needed to be seen at such an event, and all the people who were never seen but were nonetheless necessary. Then I sprinkled in a few friends I knew from the more bohemian end of town to give it some razzmatazz.

Of course, I had to design a dress and have it made, but that was the least of my worries. I should have hired a wedding planner but I knew too well what I wanted and, frankly, doubted that anyone could accomplish it. I visited stationers, chefs, florists, limousine hire companies, tailors (for Jim); I met with priests and lawyers, I visited churches, hotels and banqueting venues. I had no idea how much organisation went into a wedding; it was a business in itself. And each morning I woke up with a headache that pulsated throughout the day, never so bad as to make me take to bed, but enough for it to be constantly niggling, interfering in my every thought and decision. Somehow, I managed to fit in medical appointments too and was disappointed by my clean bill of health. 'Stress' was the doctors' diagnosis. I was mystified; work pressure had never stressed me before.

Graça and I never revisited the discussion we had had the night I came home with the ring. But on the morning of the wedding we asked Alejandra, the Costa Rican housekeeper, to witness me signing over the apartment to Graça. When we were alone again, Graça looked at me over the kitchen table. Neither of us had managed to eat much in the way of our breakfast.

I put the documents into an envelope and pushed it over the table to Graça.

'These are yours. It's yours now.'

She trapped the manila envelope under her nails that shimmered like pearls; she had grown them longer now that she no longer did housework.

'And you have everything you need for the business?' I asked.

I had appointed Graça acting CEO of Maison Dumarais while I was travelling. She had come to work with me more and more and knew the business inside out, and I had made preliminary sketches for the next season for her to get the design team to work on. We both knew she would take this in her stride.

'You know that is all in hand, and if there is a problem then I will contact you. I have your itinerary; I can always ring or fax you if anything comes up that I can't handle.' She tapped the envelope. 'There is one more thing, Rosa.'

'What?'

'Are you sure?' She fixed her dark eyes on mine. 'It's not too late, we could tear this up and stay as we were. If it is just a matter of pride, better to stop now.'

I reached over the table and grabbed her hand. 'It will work out. We'll be fine.'

She extricated her hands and stood up. 'Then I believe, Senhora Dumarais, it is time for us to get changed into our wedding attire.'

Graça was my maid of honour. She looked exquisite in a simple spaghetti-strap cream silk shift dress that dropped straight to the knees, skimming her lovely figure. The arms and shoulders were draped in a fine silk gauze reaching to her neck and wrists. It was perfect and understated and had been easy to design.

My own outfit had been trickier. I don't know what had become of the Fidelity dress that I had worn when Charles and I married. It captured the romance, the excitement, and excess of the heady love that Charles and I had felt. It had been ridiculous trying to cram it into the small registration office at the mairie in his arrondissement. But now I was faced with a high society wedding, where there would be cameras, press and a host of overdressed guests. I felt exhausted and numb about the upcoming business arrangement, and struggled to be inspired.

Then I hit upon the idea. This was a contractual agreement and in normal circumstances two business partners would be wearing suits to sign a contract. As Graça escorted me up the aisle some photographers mistook her for the bride and assumed I was giving her away, because I was wearing a white silk trouser suit. I had taken the motif of a silk jacket based on the Bar original but brought it up to date: the drape was looser but still accentuated the waist, and it was fastened by two oversized pearl buttons rather than three. It hung over wide-legged, charmeuse sailor trousers. I wanted to remind Jim that this was not a fairy-tale wedding, but a business agreement.

Jim was inflexible about wearing a tux despite it being an afternoon wedding. The only concession he permitted me to negotiate was that it should be white or cream silk. I could not make him understand that a dinner jacket should only be worn in the evening. I have never been one for wearing clothing inappropriately; indeed, I would not have much in the way of sales if people did not purchase pieces for different occasions.

When I reached Jim on the altar dais, he looked a little flushed. We had rehearsed the wedding (in order to plan where the photographers would be stationed) and had already practised the vows, but that had meant nothing. Standing in front of the packed pews, though, staring at Jim's face as he recited the Catholic liturgy, unnerved me. My own voice trembled as I pledged myself to him 'for better, for worse, for richer, for poorer, in sickness and health'. The solemnity of the vows touched me utterly unexpectedly. When the priest invited us to kiss, Jim swept me into a dramatic embrace, bending me over easily and pressing his lips against mine. As the congregation applauded, he pulled me back up.

'I'm a lucky man,' he whispered before he relinquished me and bowed grinning to the pews. I fixed a wide smile on to my face and grasped the bouquet tightly in my shaking hands.

If I had not appreciated how much my life was about to change, I did the moment I entered the first-class cabin of the jumbo jet.

I had never travelled first class before – don't look so surprised, ma chère. As a businesswoman, I never stopped counting each and every cent I spent. In my view, expenses are deducted from profits. That was something Izzy had instilled in me; he was never sure when his bookings might dry up.

All my flying with Izzy was no preparation for the jumbo jet. It had not been flying much over a year when we boarded it and I marvelled at its spaciousness. In the years to come we would take to flying the Concorde over to London for brief trips. It always made me think of the *Titanic* and how its first class was stuffed full of the crème de la crème of New York and London society. The idea of such a concentration of wealth made me nervous. No amount of free caviar and champagne would convince me that I was anything other than another sardine in a tight tin. But that was still in the future; the jumbo was different. In it I felt safe, as if in a cocoon.

A suited, capped chauffeur met us at the VIP arrivals in Heathrow and wheeled our piles of matching luggage. A last-minute trip to Neiman Marcus by Graça had secured me that all-important look of arriving at the airport with matching pyra-mids of his-and-hers Louis Vuitton cases decorated with the recognisable interlocking VL motif. And then we sat alone, screened from the chauffeur by smoked glass in the back of a Rolls-Royce, cutting through the London rush-hour traffic as cars gave way.

Until this point I had never really been alone with Jim. In the jumbo jet he had spent most of the time at the bar in the first-class compartment, drinking champagne and rubbing shoulders with the other men, intent as they were on sizing each other up. We sat in silence. I was sleepy and my head was hurting. It had been a long day: a wedding, a reception and then the flight overnight. We had taken the best suite at the Savoy. I was not used to such luxury, but it was necessary. The point of the honeymoon, in my mind, was to have repositioned ourselves as the newest, most powerful couple to arrive on the New York stage by the time we returned.

The Royal Suite comprised two bedrooms, each with its own pyramid of Louis Vuitton cases and adjoining bathroom, and between the bedrooms was a tastefully furnished sitting room and dining room. The furnishings and fittings came straight from the belle époque. As Jim walked around examining the lamp stands and ashtrays, I looked out at the River Thames. It looked sullen and dark under the flat, grey-white sky, but just in front of me the hotel gardens were full of trees, ornamental shrubs and small rhododendron bushes in flower. The green of the grass was broken up by clumps of daffodils, some white, some yellow. The pain that had been ceaselessly splitting my head seemed to abate.

'Hey, Rosa, this marriage thing is going to be great,' Jim said. 'I'm good at making money and I can see you are going to help me spend it well.'

I still could not read him and was unsure if he was being serious or actually giving his approval. 'We have to stay here, or somewhere like it, to set the right profile,' I said, turning back to the view.

He came up and stood beside me at the window. He grabbed the handle and stepped out on to the balcony.

'Wow,' he said, turning back to me, a grin stretched across his usually expressionless face. He looked younger and wide-eyed. I put it down to the new haircut that I had made him adopt: cropped short all over so that the balding patch on top was part of a stylish whole, rather than hiding under a greasy mop.

'Come on out.'

I grabbed my cardigan and joined him leaning against the stucco balustrade.

'I'm not complaining. I can see now I just had no idea. Fast cars, beautiful women, I get that – but this, London – jeez. It never occurred to me.'

'Not just London, Jim. We're going to do the Grand Tour.'

'What's that?'

'What all rich Americans have been doing for centuries, to get culture and finesse.'

'Hah!' He laughed. 'You've got your work cut out for you.'

I glanced at him. His eyes were fixed on the distance. He was unrecognisable, grinning from ear to ear like an excited boy. His smile was infectious. The tight feeling in my stomach loosened.

'This deal we have, Rosa, it'll be a great investment. I'm sure of it.'

I felt like I had been slapped and turned back to watch the boats moving against the tide of murky brown water. I loved my business but even I did not feel the need to reduce everything to deals and investments.

'Are you going to tell me where we are going?' he asked, his eyes still trained on the Thames.

'Paris, Geneva, Venice, Florence, Rome and Naples.'

'What about Vienna?'

'Vienna's too far.' He could not have everything.

On our first day Jim wanted to walk the streets but I wanted to visit galleries and museums. We compromised. He took a map from the reception and led the way. We stumbled upon Stanfords as we walked up from the Savoy through Covent Garden to the British Museum. Jim dragged me into the cavernous shop. He pored over the array of maps, pulling them open, putting them back, finding the perfect ones. I realised that reading a map, tracing the outline of cities, roads and mountains, was second nature for a man whose wealth was built on land and property. Then he insisted on going up Carnaby Street. I was fascinated by the parade of girls in their tiny mini-skirts, hippies in their maxis and even a few in hot pants. Jim barely noticed them, preferring to look up at the buildings, pointing out the eclectic mix of styles and periods. He tolerated my interest in the shops but after going into one tiny boutique stuffed with Indian skirts, tie-dye tops and fringed jeans he waited outside every time I went in. On the main road, men in well-cut suits sported bowler hats and carried umbrellas; the influence of Mary Quant was still everywhere.

The next morning after breakfast Jim spread a large map of

Europe that he had bought in Stanfords over the table and sat hunched over it drinking his coffee.

'Are we flying?' he enquired, tracing his finger over the British Channel into France.

I considered a moment. 'No, Europe is so small that we're travelling by train. You'll see more.'

'What about driving? We could hire – heck, we could buy – a nice car and travel that way.'

'It's not like America, Jim. The roads aren't as good, they're more crowded. It would take forever.'

'We've got time.' He carried on tracing his finger down the roads marked in red linking the centres of European commerce and culture. 'All that time that other newly-weds spend otherwise engaged, we could drive.' He took a sip of his coffee. 'Unless you have any better ideas?'

I paused, suspicious, but his tone gave nothing away, his face turned down to the map. However clear our arrangement was, now that we were on our honeymoon, it was unsettling. I knew where I stood, but sometimes, for a fleeting moment, I had the distinct impression that he was teasing me. I had to work out a strategy. I was going to prove Graça wrong.

'No, I've already booked everything,' I said eventually. 'It will be a nightmare to reschedule all the hotels. We'll see plenty this way.'

The next day, I left Jim at the tailors on Savile Row. He was being fitted for some sports jackets and work suits, and a proper dinner jacket. He had baulked at the prices but I had insisted, arguing that dress was the key to the social scene and there were enough snobs in the higher echelons of Manhattan society for a new Savile Row wardrobe to make a difference. Like many men, clothes shopping was not his idea of fun, but the tailors and fitters were used to handling their unwilling clients and I left him to their attentions. Meanwhile, I caught a cab to Kings Road. I had to see and feel London fashion for myself.

I was not surprised to find him back in our suite before me.

He was sitting on one of the sofas, his legs crossed, with a smug look on his face.

'How did the fitting go?' I asked as the door closed behind me.

'Fine.' He shrugged. 'The clothes will be ready next week and they'll send them on, or we can pick them up when we get back.' His matter-of-fact tone suggested that it was not the clothes that had made him happy so I glanced around for anything else that had crept into the room.

'I see.' I put my bags down. As well as a few necessary purchases in Mary Quant, I had bought a variety of cashmere sweaters in the Burlington Arcade for the two of us, for the winter. 'And the shirts?'

'I went back to Jermyn Street.' He sighed, not hiding his disinterest. 'Same story.'

My quick survey of the room revealed nothing new except a tray with a silver tea service including a multi-tiered stand with cut sandwiches, cakes and scones on it. 'Is the tea still warm?' I asked.

'Yes, room service just brought it. Join me.' He patted the space next to him.

I sat down.

'Not more maps, Jim?' There was a small pile of them next to the tray. I picked up the largest road map splayed in front of me, and there, underneath, were two sets of car keys. The RR logo was stamped in silver on the black leather tags.

I cancelled our train tickets and we drove to Paris in a convertible two-seater Rolls.

Two days of tourism in Paris was enough for him, and now that Madeleine Fournel had passed away (I had gone to her funeral in '68), there was no reason for me to insist on staying longer. Jim declared that he wanted to open a Swiss bank account so the next day we set off towards Switzerland. Now that he had a taste for driving, I annulled all the hotel reservations as well to give us more flexibility. I faxed Graça to let her know, but I knew she would not be pleased. If she needed to contact me, it would not be so easy now.

It was not so much that Jim dawdled – he drove steadily at the legal limit – but he insisted on stopping the car constantly, to better appreciate a view, or to look at a chateau or church or to find somewhere to eat. Every time we stopped, whether in a small village or a big town, more predictably, he would find a real estate office and scrutinise the shop window, working out land and property value, comparing it to upstate New York and downtown Manhattan. He knew the real estate values everywhere along the East Coast and liked to keep his nose to the ground.

We spent two days in Geneva. I stayed in our hotel room taking Tylenol to quell the knife scything through my brain, while Jim visited the private banks and sat in the room scribbling notes on the leather-bound writing pad, comparing their rates and terms.

I knew that Laurin was no longer in St. Gallen but being back in Switzerland lowered my mood. To be honest, ma chère, I was finding our arrangement a strain. My new husband never hinted at anything untoward, was all consideration, but I was uncomfortable when we were alone. We were, after all, strangers. I felt like I was acting, not living, and it made me ill at ease. Sitting alone in the hotel room in Geneva, I found it hard not to think about the past, about what I had left behind. Jim seemed oblivious to any possible cause of my headaches and sought to comfort me with a trip to Vacheron Constantin, the watchmakers. We both left with a handsome timepiece.

It was easy to sleep in the Rolls; the cream leather upholstery was soft. When I woke, I checked the time on my elegant new watch, admiring the golden frame around a simple white face, tied on with a white leather strap. We had been driving for four hours since we left Zurich (Jim had detoured there for more banking business). I had no idea where we were, but I surmised from the road signs that we were still in Switzerland, not Austria as I had expected.

'Welcome back,' he said, twisting his head to look at me. 'That was a long sleep.'

'Where are we?' I sat up and yawned.

'Well, I took a look at the map and I thought it would be fun to take a shortcut over the mountains rather than going through all those Austrian towns.'

'Shortcut!' I was wide awake now.

'Sure, this was about half the distance.' He was staring straight ahead at the road, his hands on the wheel.

I was annoyed; I had wanted to go to Austria. 'There's no such thing in the mountains,' I said.

'Honestly, I checked the map carefully. This route is more direct and we cut over a pass. It's just a smaller road.'

'It's always quicker to go by the big valleys. Passes can be treacherous and anyway, they are never as direct as they seem after you take the bends into account.'

'What bends?'

'The serpentine bends. They don't show them on the maps.'

The road ahead was wide and straight. I felt a bit foolish. Maybe I was making too much of a fuss.

'Trust me, Mrs Mitchell.' He turned to face me and smiled.

I looked out of the window. I did not like it when he smiled. It made me feel like a mouse in a cat's game.

We were travelling up a flat-bottomed valley. An ice-blue lake filled the basin that a glacier had scooped out millennia ago. We stopped for lunch on the outskirts of Davos. The air was sharp and cold and the sky an utterly clear blue I had not seen for many years. It was June, and the tops of the mountains were still dusted with snow. We ate rösti and sausage and my head seemed to clear.

It was as the car started to climb and climb in the early afternoon that I began to wonder where we were going. I made myself think, to remember what I had put from my mind so many years ago. There are not so many passes from Switzerland into Italy. There were only a handful of passes into Italy, one of which went by Falstal. I glanced at Jim. He was intent on driving. This had to be coincidence, I reasoned. It was the most direct route as the crow flies. The pain struck me across the brow again. I leaned forward to retrieve some more Tylenol. I would sleep, I decided, until we were safely in Vinschgau, the main valley that would lead straight down to Venice.

The sound of Jim's door slamming woke me. The fir trees covering the mountainside in front of me seemed almost black in the shadow that reached all the way down to the valley floor. It was late afternoon. I wondered why we had stopped and got out. Immediately the cold air hit me; we had to be high up. I looked around for Jim. He was standing by a gateway set in a low stone wall, in front of a graveyard. A familiar stone wall, a familiar gate. I spun around just to be certain, to verify what I already knew, to see the painted facades of Oberfals just behind me. It was like an electric shock. Suddenly, I was wide awake.

I stormed over to Jim. I opened my mouth to scream at him but before I could let rip, he lifted his finger to my lips.

'Shh! You can give me hell later. Right now, we are going in here to find out what's what.'

I was trembling and could not move. He took my elbow and eased me forward. The cemetery was fuller than I remembered. I automatically started for my grandparents' graves but could walk no more than a few paces at a time as I noticed the names of people I had known, young and old, engraved on the headstones. The pompous mayor Gruber was under one slab, and the grocers Demetz under another. Here the Ramoser plot was fuller – Rudi had managed to stay out of it, so far, I could see – as were the Holzners', the Mahlknechts' and the Koflers'. Then I came to the Kusstatschers' graves. I stopped. There was a new stone next to my grandparents, which read *Norbert Kusstatscher, born 1904, died 1953.*

'This is your family's?' Jim asked after a while.

'Yes.' I looked up and moved away. 'It's my father.'

'I'm sorry,' he said gently.

I turned round to face him. 'There's nothing to be sorry about.'

I stared straight into his eyes and he met my gaze unflinchingly. 'He wasn't much of a father.'

'So, your mother's still alive,' he continued in the same soothing tone. 'Is there anyone else?'

'Yes. My sister, I suppose.' A small tear slid from the corner of one eye. I ignored it.

We returned to the car. Inside I felt cocooned and safe. Jim made no attempt to drive off.

'So, you really have never been back?' He sounded surprised.

'Not since 1944. Not once.' I closed my eyes. The headache had come back with a vengeance.

'Twenty-seven years!'

'I was very young and very frightened when I left.'

I could feel his eyes on me. 'You were running away?' he asked after a long while.

'Yes, I suppose I was.' I opened my eyes and looked at him. He was wearing an expression I had never seen on him before. 'I thought I was escaping to safety.'

'And you weren't?'

I shook my head. 'Maybe I've been running ever since.' I sighed.

The shadow was stretched across the car now. I remembered how quickly it raced across the valley at dusk. Soon all the trees climbing the sides would take on a blue-green tinge. I glanced at Jim again and saw that it really was concern on his face. He was full of surprises.

'I wondered.' Jim faltered and then continued. He rarely hesitated. 'Because . . .'

'What?'

He sat up straight, smoothed his face and continued in his usual tone, 'Because when I conducted the due diligence there were some questions unanswered, some black holes. And because of our arrangement . . . let us say, I wanted full disclosure.'

I glared at him. 'How dare you?' I said, spitting out the words in a cold fury. I opened the door, got out and slammed it shut, but there was nowhere I could go so I leaned against the car. A few minutes later I heard him opening his door, then the crunch of his shoes on the stony ground.

'You planned this all along,' I said icily. Graça had been right. He was dangerous.

'No,' he stammered. 'No, you've got it wrong.'

'How? We're here, aren't we?'

'That's true,' he conceded, 'but if we hadn't stumbled on the map shop and I hadn't realised how small Europe was, and if the man before me at the tailor's had not bragged incessantly about the Rolls he had just bought on Berkeley Square, and if that hadn't been a block or two away from Savile Row, I'd never have bought this and we wouldn't be here. I was – and I admit this – going to hire a private detective in London or Paris. But this kind of just fell into place.'

The pain inside my head was screeching, deafening his words and my thoughts. I retrieved my bag from the car. I kept the Tylenol in a small middle compartment. I fumbled with the zip to get it out.

'You expect me to believe this just happened?' I said, pouring my scorn into the words. 'Bringing me here, to my hometown, was unplanned?' I took out the bottle of tablets.

'You know, Rosa, the best deals I've ever made have been like this. I research, I get to know all the details, I make plans – but whenever I've made a killing it's when I've followed my gut. And this is like that. I've watched you popping them pills ever since we got engaged. It's stress. You pulled off a big number, sorting out my office, the apartments, your new collection, the store and the wedding in those few months. And then, they started up again as soon as we started getting close to here. You can't run from this, whatever it is, all your life.'

I had managed to unscrew the lid and faced him holding the bottle in one hand and the lid in the other. 'What do you want me to do?' I cried. 'What else can I do?'

'I want you to put that bottle back in your bag and take me into town,' he said in that gentle tone again. 'Let's go and find your mother and sister.'

He walked around to his side and got into the car but I stayed leaning against the cold metal. I was trying not to cry: tears wreak havoc on a made-up face. Towards the end of the valley, even in the darkening light, I could just make out the path where Herr Maier had taken me up over the pass and out into Switzerland, still snaking up under the silver-grey cliffs. It was a long time since I had seen any of this but I knew it better than St. Gallen, or Paris or Rio or New York. Falstal was in my bones. No wonder it hurt so much trying to cut it off from me; it was like being amputated. I opened the car door and got in.

'Two things,' I said, not looking at him.

'Yes.'

'First, I want you to know that I am furious with you.'

I could sense rather than see his nod. 'I thought you might be,' he said quietly. 'And the second?'

I held out the Tylenol towards him.

'I won't be needing them anymore. Turn around and then right, straight into the village.'

22

Sun Cream

You're surprised by my day cream; it's SPF 15, sun protection factor 15. Why, you are wondering, do I need any sun protection in the middle of October? Surely, ma chère, you know about lines, wrinkles and sunlight? Nowadays I never step out of the apartment without sunscreen unless I know that there is heavy cloud cover all day. Better a smooth pale skin than a bronzed leathery hide. The original sun cream, Piz Buin's 'glacier cream', was developed by a student after he was burnt by the sun climbing in the Swiss Alps. As a child I would burn on the first days of summer and then turn a golden shade of bronze. In Rio we rubbed in a thick cream made of cocoa butter and coconut oil to stop our skin drying out after our swim or walks along the beach. Sometimes I rubbed in olive oil blended with carrot juice to speed up, not impede, my tan. By the early 1970s we were not yet paranoid about tanning. In fact, we still tried to spend time in the sun. Since I had not been planning time on a beach, Coppertone was the one thing I had not packed in my toiletries bag. The Alps had not been on my itinerary.

Jim waited before he turned the ignition. I stared straight ahead at the darkening forest and clutched my new Chanel handbag that I had picked up in Paris. This was not how I had imagined the arrangement I had made with Jim. I thought that if I was pleasantly flirtatious but distant, we would resolve into orderly roles quite quickly. But I had not planned that he would get personally involved in my life, and certainly not interfere. It was obvious that Jim was successful in part because he knew how to drive a hard bargain – but his greater skill was that he knew how to play people, how to get the best out of them.

When he drove out of the cemetery and turned left instead of right as I had asked, and took me down the valley to St. Martin, I was not surprised. As we came up to the village, signs directed us to a hotel.

'That is enough for one day. We'll stay here if they have room.'

Italian, Swiss, German and Austrian flags fluttered on poles lining the white pebbled driveway, and window boxes overflowing with red geraniums bordered the balconies. Jim parked the car under a tree.

'I knew the family who used to live here,' I told him quietly, 'the Pernters. They had a boy about my age, Hans. He was always in trouble for not being in school.'

'He was a bad kid?' Jim frowned. 'Maybe we should go somewhere else.'

'No, he had to help on the farm. His parents always had work for him.'

'This was a farm?'

'Yes. You can see how they've built on it.' I pointed out the trace of the original farmhouse and where it had been extended sideways and upwards. On the dark wooden frame above the front door *19*C+M+B+71* was etched in white chalk. A further extension was not complete; the wooded balconies and windows were in place but the roof tiles were not on. A small fir tree balanced on the ridge above the timber rafters. I had forgotten this local custom, forgotten how every January 6th to celebrate the visit of the Three Kings, the initials of Caspar, Melchior and Balthazar were chalked above the front door. The hotel was bigger, newer, smarter than the Pernters' farmhouse but some things had not changed.

The receptionist was a dirndl-clad young woman, with her brown hair plaited over her head. Her eyes were an arrestingly clear blue when she looked up to greet us. She was chocolate-box perfect. I opened then closed my mouth before I spoke in Italian. This was St. Martin but we were still in Falstal and I was not ready yet to be anything but a passing tourist. Even if I used *Hochdeutsch*, High German, rather than the local dialect, my accent would colour my words and I would not be able to safeguard against slipping into the vernacular.

There was a photo of the proprietors behind the reception. An older, rounder Hans Pernter stood with his arm around one of the Stimpfl girls – it looked like my friend Ingrid's little sister. Three grown children stood beside them in the portrait. I glanced back and forth between the receptionist and the photo; she was one of the daughters.

For dinner I dressed up and painted my face with thick, pale make-up. I lined my eyes with kohl and pouted as I layered pale pink on to my lips. I wanted to wear a mask. I looked nothing like my youthful self in my Ossie Clark trouser suit. I asked for seats in the corner alcove – the old-fashioned Tyrolean style created a screened-off place. Jim let me order the food and wine. I was not hungry and played with a *semmelbrot*, breaking it into segments while he ate a minestrone. A well-dressed middle-aged woman in a dirndl with a red bodice, long blue skirt and patterned apron walked through greeting guests. She looked like Ingrid's mother and I realised this was her sister, who had married Hans. I pushed myself into the leather seat, hoping to become invisible. Frau Pernter appeared not to see me and disappeared into the kitchen.

'Irmgard,' I said, suddenly remembering.

'What?' Jim looked at me baffled, his spoon halfway to his mouth.

'Her name is Irmgard, the owner; she was a friend of my sister.'

He nodded and swallowed before saying, 'You could ask her about your sister?'

'No, not now, Jim,' I said. 'Can't you see I'm reeling? Give me some time.'

I could not speak after that but silence did not seem to matter. Jim talked for the two of us. He talked about his idea of buying real estate in Europe, how he was weighing up the pros and cons of London and Paris. I smiled and nodded but barely uttered a word.

I had ordered wild trout for both of us. As I bit into the pale, soft flesh another memory came back unbidden: I had forgotten how this soft white fish somehow tasted of earth. I wondered how much else I had forgotten. When our plates were clear I sipped the thin white wine from the Etschtal and made up my mind.

'I want to stay another night. There's a walk I'd like to do tomorrow.'

'A walk?' He seemed surprised.

'Yes, it would be a sin to be here and not walk. Then tomorrow night, I'll feel more like talking.'

Saying goodnight was awkward. We had taken two adjoining rooms. No one knew us here, we had no pretence to maintain, but as Jim walked me to my door I felt a tug of something. Whether it was gratitude or not, it was some stirring of emotion.

He stood behind me as I searched for my key in my purse.

'Do you know why I took up your offer?' he asked suddenly.

I found my key and looked up. 'Honestly, no,' I said, 'I've no idea.'

'It was what you said about being a kindred spirit,' he said. 'There aren't many people like us. But what no one gets, but I think you do, is that it's not more lonely at the top – at least, no more so than it was where we started.'

I put the key in the lock.

'But you get that, don't you?'

I turned the key and the door swung open.

'This world, this valley, was too small for you. Nothing was going to keep you locked up with these trees. You had to get out. It was the same for me up in Monticello. If I had been born here, I'd have got out too.'

I am not sure who was more surprised when I spun round and kissed him on the cheek.

'Thank you,' I muttered in his ear. Out of the New York press's watchful eye we had not so much as touched since boarding the plane to London. His skin was still soft – maybe he had shaved before going in to dine. He had a new aftershave; he must have bought it in London. His fingers rose towards his face then jerked back down as he turned to his door.

The next morning, I woke early and went out on to the balcony to watch the sun rise. The bright morning light scythed down through the tree-clad slopes, chasing away the shadows. Unlike the slow, soft coastal dawns of Rio and New York, mountain dawn is sharp and sudden. It was already high by the time it emerged from behind the high peaks. I had slept deeply, the first night in months untroubled by the hammering in my head. More than my headache had gone, though; I felt lighter, freer.

When I had left the valley I had walked into an unknown future. The more time I spent with Jim Mitchell the more uncertain I became of what lay ahead. My straightforward arrangement with him seemed less and less straightforward. I could not work out what he hoped to gain by bringing me back to Oberfals, but I suspected there was a price to be paid. It troubled me that I did not understand his motives; it troubled me that I had kissed him at my door the night before; it troubled me that he had walked away so easily. Graça had told me to be careful. I was alone with one of the most successful businessmen in the US – if not the world. I had to watch myself. I pushed open the latch and swung the gate that divided Jim's balcony from mine and banged on the shutters of his window to wake him up.

We drove the car into Oberfals. The square had been turned into a car park. Spaces for cars were marked out in paint and we parked where the Nazi trucks and cars had rolled to a halt that first day when they had driven into Oberfals in 1943. Apart from that, not much had changed in nearly thirty years beyond the odd fresh lick of paint.

I had not packed for mountain hiking and the best I could do was Jaeger trousers, a beige silk twinset top and cardigan and some leather loafers. I looked quite the English lady. I knew that a cream Rolls-Royce with English number plates driving into Oberfals would not go unnoticed and was relieved that Jim, clad in chinos and a check shirt, was so obviously American that we would be taken for nothing other than tourists. I untucked my hair from behind my ears and shook out the bob. I checked my sugar-pink lipstick in the mirror – it was perfect – and then got out of the car.

I led Jim on the route I had always taken, past the faded fresco on the Koflers' house, over the stream where I had felled Rudi Ramoser with a stone, out of the village. We climbed the same path that Thomas and I had climbed so long before. It was much steeper than I remembered, and what had been easy then was now hard. We both had to stop and admire the view often. At last we reached the part where the path snaked horizontally, climbed more gently. I stopped in front of the cave where the Soap Man, Schleich, had been found. The cave entrance was dark, narrow and half obscured by the boulder. We had hidden in it as children but I could no longer picture the inside; I did not want to imagine Schleich's carcass lying in there. There was nothing I could tell Jim, so I carried on walking. We continued as far as the rock where I had sat and waited for Thomas. Where Thomas had given me my first kiss.

'You're crying.'

'No, I'm not.' I wiped a tear from my eye. 'It's just the wind.'

I could feel Jim's eyes on me. He was expecting something.

'Don't you just love this view?' I asked, trying to distract him.

He looked around, taking in the narrow valley, the pass snaking down from Switzerland, the road we had come over, the houses dotted around Oberfals and St. Martin lower down.

'It's very pretty. Does it feel good to be back?'

'Good!' I laughed. 'You said yesterday that there was a black hole in my past?'

'Yes?'

'This is it.'

Jim had said barely a word all morning, but there was nothing grim about his silence. I realised he had just been waiting for me to speak.

Things were not going according to my plan. I had arranged our itinerary with care. The Grand Tour was to be a showpiece

providing enough photos of us at key cultural and tourist desti-
nations that our image would be remoulded by the time we
returned to our separate apartments in Mitchell Heights. But
now I had the feeling that somehow he had all the cards in his
hand and he was changing the game's rules. I wanted to wrest
back control, but I was also glad to be there. Just as I had never
intended to kiss him, but then had done so the previous night,
I did not want to tell him anything, but the words just tumbled
out.

'I had my first kiss here. On this spot. It was Thomas Fischer.'
It was hard to speak but Jim just stood next to me staring out
at the valley. 'I had been raped. I thought I would never recover.
Then, a couple of months later, Thomas took me for a walk up
here and I fell asleep and when I opened my eyes he asked me
if he could kiss me. It was like being woken from a nightmare.
I was in love with Thomas; we had a romance. It was so innocent.'

I paused – all those feelings, all so long ago, seemed still so
real, as real as the hills around me.

'I was pregnant at the time – not from Thomas, but from the
monster who raped me. Herr Maier, the postman and a friend,
took me under his wing. It was bad enough in those days to get
pregnant outside of marriage, but to be the mother of a bastard
Nazi baby was unthinkable. Maier and Thomas decided that I
would be safer in Switzerland and Herr Maier walked me along
this path and up and over the pass.'

'And you've never come back?'

'No.'

After a long silence he asked, 'And the baby?' so quietly that
the wind almost snatched the words away.

I walked away a few steps, then came back to join him. 'It was
boy. I called him Laurin, after Herr Maier. And then when he
was nearly two years old, I left him and went to Paris – to make
my fortune, as they say.'

'And what happened to him?'

'I don't know.' I was staring blindly out at the valley that I
knew so well. I could see here and there new buildings, the odd

large hotel, the beginnings of a ski lift. I could see change. 'I saw him one more time and then I gave him up for adoption. He knew his foster mother better than me and it made sense.'

'That must have been hard,' he said, staring out at the valley, careful to not look at me.

'I was young and selfish.' I shrugged. 'It wasn't easy. I should never have left him behind. And I have never recovered. That is my black hole.'

I sat down on the rock and he perched nearby.

'Let's carry on,' I said eventually and I led him further along the path up towards the pass. I started telling him the names of the mountains and the flowers that I recognised, little by little remembering more. In the end hunger and thirst curtailed our walk and we returned to the valley.

'We'll go to the Gasthaus,' I said, realising I had no choice. 'My mother and sister might be there. We owned it.'

We walked a few paces and then I stopped.

'Jim, I'm frightened.'

'Look, Rosa,' he said, touching my elbow. 'The worst is behind you. You can't move forward until you lay your ghosts to rest.' He gave me a gentle nudge.

Jim pushed open the door and entered ahead of me. The hubbub of voices ebbed as the locals turned to cast their eyes over us. I held on to the doorknob and let Jim pass. People looked at us and then went back to their conversations. It had hardly changed; the only differences were that the tablecloths were red now, not green, and menus were piled on the bar, whereas before we had only had one or two which my mother had jealously guarded by the till. All our regular customers had known the menus as well as their own addresses, anyway.

Jim made for the far side of the bar, where Herr Maier and Thomas used to sit, and pulled out a chair. I had no choice but to sit on the bench against the wall looking out into the room. A young waiter was laying out drinks on a tray and a middle-aged woman was chatting to some of the men sitting at the bar.

After the waiter had delivered the drinks, he offered us the menu. I was so nervous I didn't even look at it – I knew it would be no different – and ordered in Italian.

Oh, ma chère, you think I was foolish to have come so far and not take the opportunity of swanning in and showing myself off. I knew that the villagers must have heard of my success in the intervening years, I remembered well how gossip ran like a steady stream through Oberfals, everyone's every move known and discussed. But I felt like the unconfident young woman who had served beer and *knödel* there many years before. I, who had spent my life polishing an entrance, simply wanted to slip in, eat, and leave unnoticed, incognito.

Jim lifted up the beer glass. 'Cheers.'

'*Zum wohl,*' I replied. 'To health.'

After giving the waiter our orders, I asked him who owned the Gasthaus. He said it was the Demetzes, which explained why my mother and sister were absent. I had always liked the Demetzes. They had owned the grocer's store before the war, before they had been forced to sell it to the Ramosers.

'Your face,' Jim said between mouthfuls of goulash soup. 'You've caught the sun, you're completely red.'

I touched my cheek and felt that it was burning. 'I'll have to get some cream after lunch.'

The Ramosers still owned the grocer's shop – they had done well under the Nazis. I walked around, intoxicated by the familiar scents of caraway and rye coming from the *schüttelbrot*, the local bread that was dried in racks hung from the ceiling, and the smoky smell of *speck*, the spiced and seasoned air-dried ham with thick white fat under the dark purple crust. I went up to the counter.

'*Guten Tag,*' I said, then winced. I had not intended to speak German but the words slid out of my mouth instinctively, and now I had no choice but to continue. 'Three hundred grams of *speck*, the same of the Falser cheese and a pack of *schüttelbrot*, please.'

The door creaked behind me as a young woman and child left and a tall old man entered the shop. He had a newspaper in his hand. Jim was walking around the shop, checking prices and goods.

'Heh, I've never seen so many pickled foods anywhere in my life,' Jim said.

I turned back to the woman behind the counter as she took a heavy knife to the block of *speck* and looked at me, her eyebrows raised in a question. I nodded. We would slice it with a penknife later.

'What happened to the Kusstatschers in the Gasthaus?' I asked as I watched her push the knife down through the meat.

'Oh, they died. A long time ago,' she said.

Perhaps she was a granddaughter of the old Ramosers, or even the daughter of the bully, Rudi.

'All of them?'

'Let me see,' she said, pausing to tear off some greaseproof paper to wrap the *speck* in. 'The father went first.'

'Oh. What did he die of?'

'I don't rightly know.'

'He had an accident,' interjected the old man with the news-paper. He was bending over the glass-fronted chiller cabinet looking at the salami, *speck* and cheese. I knew that voice and felt a deep thrill of recognition. 'He was an old drunk, it was an accident waiting to happen.' The man continued as he straight-ened up, just as tall and massive as I remembered. His watery blue eyes met mine. I began to see beyond the wind-weathered features, beyond the crow's feet around the eyes and the sun-polished skin. I felt butterflies in my stomach.

'And Frau Kusstatscher?' I whispered.

'She wasn't a widow for long. I married her.' Herr Maier smiled at me, but then his lips turned down at the corners.

'That's wonderful,' I cried. 'So, she's with you?'

He took my hand. 'I'm sorry. She had a hard life and in '66 she had a massive heart attack.'

'She was barely sixty,' I said, wiping an unexpected tear from my eye. 'And Christl?'

'She stayed, became a schoolteacher and married a Meraner. She lives down there. She has three girls and a grandson. You're an auntie – a great-aunt, even.'

I turned back to the shop girl who was standing in silence, her jaw slack, her hands immobile on the wrapped pack of *speck*.

'Don't forget the cheese,' I said pointedly. 'Three hundred grams, please.'

'So, you've come back at last.' Laurin Maier wiped another tear from my burning cheek. I turned his mottled and lined hand in mine and pressed my lips into the soft, cool hollow of his palm. I saw Jim watching from the aisle, a jar of cherries in his hand.

'But I thought you would know how to protect yourself by now,' he remonstrated. He turned to the shop assistant, still holding my hand. 'Johanna Ramoser, you can stop staring and pack all this in one bag. We'll need some Piz Buin too. Rosa Kusstatscher has forgotten how to use it. Put it on my account.'

'Let me—'

'Absolutely not, no question. Shh! Enough.' He turned to the girl. 'And Johanna, clean your ears out and do not even think about spreading tittle-tattle over the whole village. I'll know where it's come from, mark my words.' He gave her a fierce stare. Then, still holding my hand, he nodded at Jim and grinned. 'And you, *Mister James Mitchell*,' he enunciated the English words with care, 'you come to my house with my friend, Rosa. Is good?'

23

Moisturiser

S unburn is a disaster in the beauty stakes. No beautician would smear the face with rouge from hairline to chin, yet this is what nature does. After a real burn, there is nothing to be done. Normally moisturisers keep the skin soft and supple, but none of these, with all their active ingredients like crushed sea pearls or silk, have any effect on burnt skin, and in 1971 the science of beauty was rudimentary. There was nothing I could do. Today I might have smeared on some aloe vera. Graça makes me keep a plant in the kitchen for scalds. It is so effective that it has made her complacent. As you know, she seems to be constantly smearing on the gel that she squeezes from the succulent leaves after she has been splattered by oil or accidentally brushed the oven tray with her arm. She never burns or blisters. But as it was, after Laurin Maier had frog-marched Jim and me back to his house, he pushed me towards the bathroom, thrust a blue tin of Nivea into my hands and told me to smear it on thick.

Some moisturisers soak into the skin almost instantly whereas others sit on the surface. Feeling oddly carefree, I slapped so much on that I left the bathroom looking like an iced cake. I found Jim and Laurin sitting at the table drinking coffee, a fat strüdel dusted with icing sugar resting on a plate between them, waiting to be cut. Next to it was a bottle of schnapps and three glasses. Herr Maier filled the three glasses and passed one to Jim, another to me. He raised his own.

'Rosa Kusstatscher, I've known you since before you were born. I married your mother, I've been a father to your sister, I've worried about you for nearly thirty years and, even though you are Mrs Mitchell, I would like us to *duzen*.'

I raised my glass to him. 'Yes, I'd love that.'

'Rosa, don't cry,' he said, leaning forward over the table and linking his arm through mine. We lifted our glasses to our mouths and drank the schnapps. The taste hit me immediately.

'Raspberries,' I gasped.

'Yes, I made it myself.' He smiled then turned to Jim. 'You too, Mr Mitchell,' he said in his awkward English before refilling his own glass. 'My name is Laurin, I call you James.'

They clinked their glasses and downed the shots.

'*Danke*,' Jim said. 'Please, call me Jim.'

I closed my eyes and opened them again. I was tempted to pinch my arms. This had to be a dream. I was sitting back where I had started, with the man who had been my guardian angel, but with Jim from New York, a man whom my best friend did not trust.

'I'll cut the strüdel. I bought it from the bakery this morning.'

Laurin picked up the cake knife. It was my mother's, had been a wedding present from her godmother. I felt I was swimming in a sea of memories. I had thought they were all long gone.

'What was that about?' Jim asked.

'He's just told us to call him by his first name and to use *du*, the familiar form of you, like *tu* in French.'

'It's a big deal, I guess?'

'It's a really big deal,' I confirmed. 'We call him Laurin from now on.'

'Does he always have cake at home?'

'No, he said he bought it this morning.' I realised as I said this that he had not happened on me in the shop by accident. He knew I would be there. I smiled. 'He was always one step ahead of me.'

Laurin passed a plate to Jim, then to me. And then, ma chère, I had what I can only describe as a Proustian moment; the sharp taste of apples, the sweet raisins and hint of cinnamon plunged me back into my childhood. I was overwhelmed.

'This is good,' Jim said.

'Dank you.'

'My mother used to make a strüdel every day for the Gasthaus,' I told Jim, closing my eyes. I could picture my mother in the kitchen spooning the cinnamon and sugar into the bowl with the peeled and sliced apples, taking a handful of raisins. She never had time to measure or weigh but used instinct to guide her. Her cakes were never consistent, but sometimes they were perfect, as this one was.

'So, what I want to know is: how come Laurin knew we were here?' Jim asked.

I translated.

Laurin sipped his coffee then smiled, and his teeth still looked good for a man in his seventies. He poured a coffee for me.

'Milk? Sugar?' I shook my head, impatient for his answer. 'People were misled by the English number plate, but when I heard that a Rolls-Royce had pulled into the cemetery yesterday, I was pretty sure.'

'It was just the Rolls?' Jim asked after I had translated. Laurin looked at him and answered, leaving long pauses after every phrase or sentence so that I could translate.

'Of course not. Rosa spoke in Italian at the Pernters' but even in Italian, her South Tyrolean accent is strong. They might have pretended not to notice, but Irmgard recognised her. By the time you came into the Gasthaus this morning, Hans Pernter had already rung me.'

'Why didn't anyone say anything?' I asked, blushing as I realised how dumb I had been – and how rude.

'Well, *Mrs Mitchell*, it was clear you did not want them to.'

Jim was watching me closely. 'What did he say?'

I lifted my finger and continued in German.

'Everyone knew who we were, right from the start?' I said.

'Of course,' Laurin said.

'How?'

He sighed. 'I know this is a small village high in the Alps, but we do read newspapers and have televisions now.' He raised his eyebrows theatrically. 'How many international jet-setters has the South Tyrol produced?'

I could not answer him. This was before Reinhold Messner had become known as one of the best mountaineers of the late twentieth century; Giorgio Moroder had not yet helped Donna Summer to feel love. Gilbert (a Tyrolean) and George had only just started their collaboration.

Laurin got up and turned to a stack of newspapers on the sideboard.

'What just happened?' Jim asked.

'Oh.' I shook my head again. 'I just made a fool of myself – everyone in the hotel and the Gasthaus knew who we were from the beginning. So much for being anonymous.'

Jim looked at me thoughtfully. 'Heh, it doesn't matter,' he said. 'This is what matters.' He pointed at Laurin, who was leafing through the heap of papers.

Laurin pulled out an old copy of the *Dolomitten* and came back to the table, unfolded it and put it down in front of me. On the front page there was a picture of Jim and me standing on the steps of the church after our wedding ceremony. The headline read 'Rosa Remarries', and the legend under the picture explained, 'After many years in mourning, Rosa Dumarais (born Kusstatscher in Oberfals) finds love again with business icon Jim Mitchell.' I read the article, which briefly outlined my career and life. There was more inside and a further picture of us in Heathrow airport standing next to the matching Louis Vuitton luggage that Graça had bought.

'So, you know everything?' I asked.

'No, not everything, although I do have this.' He returned to the dresser and opened a door. He moved vases, jugs and candle-sticks around before he extricated a faded, hessian-covered scrapbook. He handed it to me. The book was well-used and fragile. The black card pages inside were faded to brown around the edges and the newspaper clippings were yellowing and coming unstuck. 'It was your mother's.'

The earliest articles and photos were of Dior and myself. I was stunned. It never occurred to me that my mother would even miss me, let alone try and keep track of me. It made no sense. She never tried to find me, never wrote to me. I glanced at Laurin. If this wonderful man had seen good in her, had loved her, she could not have been entirely without heart. Then a tragic idea crossed my mind: was it possible that she had never tried to get in touch because she thought I was better off without her, just as I had abandoned my own child for the same reason? I pushed it away.

'You were so young, Rosa, so young,' Jim said from over my shoulder, startling me. I had not been aware that he had come to stand behind me, his hand gripping the back of my chair as he leaned over my shoulder to see. He knew the bare facts of my life from his due diligence, but seeing the photos must have been another thing. 'And very beautiful.'

I looked ridiculous, the young woman swamped by metres of cloth hanging on the arm of the much older man.

'We were such good friends and colleagues,' I said. 'I was the only person who could really argue with him, although it wasn't often necessary.'

And then we turned the pages to Brazil. There were fewer pictures but some smaller clippings reporting the growth of my business, the international expansion, and even a photo of me looking grief-stricken, leaning on Graça coming from Charles's funeral. I could not even remember the press being there, but then I had to be almost carried back to the car after I had fainted over his opened casket.

I was grateful that there was just one photo of me in a smoky jazz club with sharp, sophisticated lipstick, gazing languorously at the stage. The caption wondered if I would be marrying into music. Then there were a few small cuttings mentioning the growth of my American business. None of the New York articles were pasted in.

'After your mother died, I cut them out, but then . . .' Laurin trailed off. 'But maybe you could do it yourself now.'

I closed the book and pushed it away. Jim sat down and reached for it.

'I don't know.' I met Laurin's gaze. 'I don't know how long we'll stay.'

'You must have been very hurt. Your mother always hoped you would come back. She never forgave herself about Schleich. Never.'

I could find no words. I fiddled with the empty shot glass and tipped it up to see if there were any drops left. Jim was absorbed by the old cuttings but Laurin watched me.

'I read about the Soap Man,' I managed finally. 'Did she know?'

'No. She died before.' He looked down. I had never seen him look uncertain.

'Laurin, it was the war,' I exclaimed, shocked that he should feel guilty. 'You saved me.'

'That's not what I feel bad about,' he said, looking at Jim.

I was perplexed. 'What, then?'

'It should have been me who did it,' he said softly.

'It wasn't you? I thought . . .'

'Thomas insisted he should be the one. He said it was a matter of military discipline.'

I put my hand up to my mouth. 'What happened?'

'I got Schleich into the cave. I said you were waiting for him in there. He was too greedy to think. Thomas was waiting inside with his gun and a rope. It was almost too easy. Once Thomas had the rope around his neck, I held him by his wrists while Thomas strangled him.'

'Maybe I could use the bathroom?' Jim said. We had been speaking in German and his question intruded like a knife into the dark scene we had in our minds. Laurin stood up, led him out and came back alone.

'Thank you,' I said. 'I owe everything I am to you.'

He looked at his hands.

'It might not have been me who pulled the rope, but I helped and I watched him die.'

I took his hands in mine and pressed them to my lips. 'Sometimes the right thing to do is not a good thing. I've learnt that myself.'

'That's why we did it.'

'You saved my life. I've never forgotten that.'

We stared at each other. He nodded, then got up, cleared away the cakes and coffee and brought a pack of cards. 'Now, Rosa, we can catch up slowly, but we are neglecting your husband.'

When Jim came back in, Laurin said in thickly accented English, 'We play rummy, yes?'

We spent the next hour playing cards. It didn't take long for Jim to get the hang of it and by the second game he was swapping and trading happily. A smile creased his face as he revelled in the points he made. He failed to beat the old man but trounced me.

Laurin stacked the cards into a neat pack and looked at his watch. 'Jim, go hotel and get bags. Stay *mit* me. This house.'

'We can't stay here, it's too much trouble for you,' Jim said.

'You stay here,' he said, and his tone brooked no argument. 'This also Rosa's home is.'

'I can't. All our things are unpacked,' I said. I always unpacked as soon as I arrived in a hotel; clothes always benefited from being hung up.

Laurin rolled his eyes. 'Jim – Rosa you translate this properly – Jim, I have not seen my friend for over thirty years, I am over seventy. Who knows if I will ever see her again? You are both staying here. Understood?'

I translated his plea with a smile of surrender.

'The old man has a point, Rosa,' Jim said, smiling as he stood up and pulled the car keys from his jacket.

Laurin handed me some glue and scissors and told me to tidy up my mother's album while he made dinner. He moved more slowly than he used to but steadily, his movements still precise and deft. I turned the pages and re-stuck loosened cuttings, sticking in for the first time the New York and wedding stories and photos while he set the table around me. He put out the slab of *speck* and some cheese on wooden platters, bread rolls, the *schüttelbrot*, glasses, plates, cutlery and a bottle of red wine. He sat down, took two glasses and poured wine into them.

'The scrapbook tells some of your story,' he said, hesitating as he handed me a glass, 'but there is an important episode missing.'

'Yes.' I loved this man all the more for his delicacy. He had waited so long not knowing and still he was not rushing me.

'What happened in St. Gallen? To your baby?' He revolved his glass in his hands, swishing the ruby liquid around, the only sign of his agitation.

I took a deep breath. 'I had a son. His name is Laurin.'

He jolted up, his eyes wide, a look of amazement on his face. 'Laurin?'

'I named him after you because I thought you were the best man I ever met.' I reached over the tabletop and placed my hand on his, still holding his wine glass. 'I still do. You did more for me than my parents ever did.'

He shook his head. 'Your mother, she blamed herself.' He sighed. 'She was just so busy.'

'I hated her for it,' I said. But even as I gave voice to the feeling, something shifted in me and I realised that the hate was gone. 'But maybe I've been no different.' Maybe I could forgive her, but perhaps never myself.

I took a sip of the wine and then I started to talk. I told him everything about old Professor Goldfarb, about the dressmaking, about little Laurin, about Frau Schurter and running away to Paris to make my fortune. Then meeting Madeleine, Dior and Charles, how when I had gone back to get little Laurin he hadn't known me; the adoption and then my desperate search for him later, finding out no more than that he had a new stepfather and had been moved to Germany. How I had bought the house hoping one day that he would come back.

Laurin did not interrupt me, nor did he say anything for a while after I had finished. Then he got up and took the scrapbook from me.

'That's quite a story.' He pushed the book back into the recesses of the cupboard and cleared away the glue, newspapers and scissors.

I rested my head in my hands, exhausted. 'I'll never know if I did the right thing. Having made the first mistake of leaving him, did I compound it by giving him up to the Schurters so completely?'

Laurin rested his hand on my shoulder lightly and it felt like a benediction or forgiveness. 'And what about Thomas?' he asked, sitting down again.

'I assumed he was dead for a long time.' I closed my eyes, trying to cast back to how I had felt. 'I just could not believe that he would not come looking for me.'

'Do you mean he isn't dead – he's alive?' The old man smiled. They had been strange companions but they really liked each other.

'I don't know,' I continued reluctantly, not wanting to shatter his new-found hope. 'In 1963 when I went to see Professor Goldfarb in Israel, he told me that Thomas had come looking for me, but that was in 1948. Anything might have happened in the meantime.'

'At least he survived the war. That's good.' He tapped the table. 'Did he never come back here?'

'No. Why would he, if you had gone?' Laurin raised his eyebrows. 'He would never have known what kind of welcome to expect.'

'I guess not,' I said. 'I never think of him as a Nazi.'

'That's because he wasn't. You could sense that.' Laurin looked down at his hands on the table. 'He had to pretend to be, in order to survive.'

I nodded.

'So his trail ran cold?'

'Yes. All I know was that he was in Berlin in '48.'

When Jim had returned with our bags, we carried on playing cards and drinking wine. After a few rounds I put my cards down and declared fatigue. Laurin smiled.

'Tell your whizz-kid husband here that I shall beat him at chess. That's if he plays.'

When I'd translated for Jim, he grinned and responded, 'Tell the old man that he has no chance, my dad schooled me well.'

I tried not to smile. There had never been anyone in the valley who could beat Laurin Maier, but I had no doubt that Jim would not be anything other than a sharp player. I sipped the wine and watched their faces growing taut and concentrated as the quick start slowed down. They were both men accustomed to winning in their own different ways. I was a little bit drunk and thoughtful.

With hindsight, it was obvious that Laurin had always been in love with my mother. But he was not one for an affair. He had just bided his time. What is that saying, ma chère, about the tortoise? Ah yes, slow and steady wins the race. Even now, he took his time pondering the board. He was unrushed, his hands placed on the table either side of it, impassive until the moment of decision when his hand moved with careful precision and repositioned a piece. Those same hands would have held Schleich's wrists as he struggled, as Thomas had squeezed the air from him. I got up and filled a glass with water at the sink.

I turned around and rested against the sink. It was not often that I had the opportunity to watch Jim unawares. He was hunched over, surveying the territory of each and every piece. His hand moved over a bishop, hovered, then retracted, and then moved towards a knight, then a rook, as if each thought should be executed as and when it came into his head. Thought and action were almost one with him. In chess he seemed so instinctive. He said that it was impulse, not premeditation, that had brought us to Oberfals, but I felt uncertain. There was a contradiction between the way he seemed to live in the moment, in this very game, and the premeditation and planning behind him driving us from Paris through Switzerland, to my hometown without giving anything away. I was beginning to realise that he could play the long game as well as the short one.

It is not like me not to consider sleeping arrangements, and looking back on it, ma chère, I can only deduce that I was in some kind of denial. In the hotel we'd had two adjoining rooms and now when I climbed the soft wooden stairs polished smooth by the years of footfall, I took the first door on the left as Herr Maier had told me. One small double bed had been made up.

I sneaked across the corridor and opened the opposing door and gasped. It was Laurin Maier's room, it was furnished with my mother's wedding bedroom suite. My mother had received a wardrobe, dressing table, dresser and bed all painted the same olive green with whirls and flourishes highlighted in gold. She had been so proud of it. I sat down on the hard mattress, overwhelmed. I had probably been conceived on this very bed – this is where my story began. Sometimes on Sunday mornings, when I was very little, I had climbed in beside my mother. As I was only just beginning to realise, maybe she had in her own way tried to love me, but there had been so much work and the hell of living with my loutish father to contend with.

Laurin had a picture of himself and my mother on their wedding day in a frame by the bedside. She looked thin and pinched, about fifty, but beaming in Laurin's protective embrace. I took the picture in my hands. I was glad that she had found some happiness. I stretched out on the bed and held the framed photo up, hovering it over my face. 'I forgive you, Mother,' I told her image before kissing it and placing it back on the table.

The other two bedrooms had single beds that were stripped bare and smelt musty. Laurin must have made up our bed and aired the room as soon as he had heard of my arrival. I could go downstairs and explain about our arrangement, but I felt too ashamed. I returned to our room, opened my suitcase, took out my toiletries then went to the bathroom and washed.

I dipped my finger into the tin of Nivea, scooping up a thick globule of white cream. I spread it all over my body, barely rubbing it in. When I was greased all over I opened the door, checked that it was clear and darted back into the bedroom. I was not prepared to ruin my silk nightdresses, so I opened Jim's case and rummaged around until I found a pair of navy pyjamas (I had to tighten the drawstring to keep them up). Then I got into bed and waited, thoughts and memories buzzing around my mind.

I did not know what I wanted. I was grateful that Jim had brought me here. He had made me happy. It was more than I had expected or imagined in our arrangement. Yet here I was, about to share a bed with my nominal husband, and I was frightened. I had only ever shared my bed with three men and Jim was about to climb in with me. I had no idea what he was hoping for, what he was planning, where his impulses lay or his long-term strategy. Nor did I know how I would react. I reached my hands to my face; the moisturiser was so thick, I felt clammy and greasy to touch. Maybe, I thought as I closed my eyes, I would just slip out of his hands if he tried to touch me.

24

Lipstick

After eyeliner, lipstick is the next essential piece in my reper-
toire. Since antiquity, women have used it to adorn their
mouths. Cleopatra smeared a paste of crushed up beetles and
ants on hers. Queen Elizabeth I of England tinted her lips with
rose and carnation petals, ground and mixed in beeswax. Women
have smeared red lead, henna, mulberries and strawberries on
their mouths, trying to imitate the flush of arousal.

Until the 1920s, only red lipstick was worn and it was considered to be a sign of a loose woman, a prostitute. The cinema
changed all that. With the advent of moving pictures and the
exaggerated make-up of the starlets in the early black-and-white
films, lipstick crossed into popular use. Even so, for years it was
limited to shades of red. In the sixties that all changed; pink
arrived and got paler by the day. We wore pale grape and frosted
sugar pink, pearl and beige, and other so-called natural shades
– and then in the mid-seventies with the explosion of punk, the
colours rioted and any colour became possible, from black to
green to blue. But when I married Jim, I was still using the pale
pinks.

I drifted off to sleep before Jim came up to bed. It was his
breathing that woke me in the morning. He was lying on his side
next to me, his closed eyes fluttering under his lids, his breathing
rhythmic and slow. Without the fixed, blank look he wore all day,
his face was soft. He was lying on top of the bed, his coat draped
over his fully clothed body.

I slipped out from under the duvet and went into the bathroom.
My face was bare and stripped of any make-up, my skin still
glowing red. I examined the thin white lines around my eyes, the

traces of folds that were beginning to carve their way over my forehead. I was ageing. I had spent the night with a man, my husband, and he had not touched me. It was years since I had last had sex, with Izzy. Was I no longer attractive? My skin felt too tender to cover with make-up and the fake pink pigment of my lipstick looked ridiculous against my burning red face. I rubbed in the moisturiser and, for the first time in years, if not decades, I applied no make-up at all, not even eyeliner nor lipstick. I had nothing to prove to either Laurin Maier or Mr James Mitchell.

We stayed another night with Laurin and then drove down into Meran, the beautiful spa town nestling at the confluence of two river valleys. We stayed at the Palace Hotel overlooking the palm-tree-filled park and a short walk from the Passer river that bubbled over the rocks as it carved its way through the town. I stood for a while under the white statue of Empress Sisi, the beautiful, exquisitely dressed princess forced into an unhappy, arranged marriage. The most famous, beloved woman in the vast Austro-Hungarian empire, the statue captured her sitting demurely, passive and constrained. She was trapped.

'Who's she?' Jim asked. 'Elisabeth who?'

'She was a woman who had it all,' I said and led him over the river into the town centre.

Reconnecting with my little sister Christl was an emotional affair. It was not easy after the initial excitement; she had felt abandoned. After our reunion it took years for her to understand and forgive me before we rebuilt a sense of family.

Jim and I stayed a few days in Meran, taking the cable cars up into the mountains, walking on Halfling and Vigiljoch in the cooler air, resting by the hotel pool in the early summer heat. Jim was unintrusive, seemingly happy reading books or walking ahead carrying the rucksack with our water bottle and some chocolate as my sister and I walked behind. We stopped for lunches in the high Gasthauses overlooking the valleys, eating *kaiserschmarrn*, frothy blueberry omelettes, and *pfifferling* and *steinpilze*, on noodles or in *knödel*. On the last day Jim told me he wanted to work and I spent the day wandering under the *Lauben*, the shady colonnades that sheltered the shoppers from both the winter snow and the summer sun, flitting in and out of stores buying clothes and table linen, and in a bookshop a biography of Sisi, photographic books of the mountains and maps for Jim. Christl tried to talk me into buying a dirndl, but I refused – nostalgia has its limits. Jim and I arranged to meet in Café König in front of the Art Nouveau Kurhaus that afternoon and I ordered a slice of *dobos torte* while I waited. I realised that this had been my mother's dream, her fantasy of the good life: to have enough time to go Meran, the big town, to shop and stop for a cake in Café König. I lost my appetite and offered Jim the untouched slice when he arrived.

After that we headed down to Rome, stopping first in Venice and Florence. On the last day Jim drove us down to Pompeii. I felt uncomfortable walking through the fossilised city, the scene of all that catastrophic death. At one point, Jim asked me to pose in front of a villa with Vesuvius in the background. His face was hidden by the camera.

'That's it.' He clicked and wound on to the next shot. I didn't move; I was already accustomed to his extravagance with film; he had a bag full of the rolls he had used up ever since he had bought a Leica camera in Switzerland. Like the Rolls, he was enjoying his new toy. He played around with the lens.

'The thing is, Rosa – yes, that's good.'

Click.

'Look a bit to your left – the thing is that I can't remember when I had such a good time.'

Click.

'Could you sit on that pillar? This is meant to be a business deal – '

Click.

'and I'll honour my side.'

Click.
'But I just want you to know – '
Click.
'from an investment perspective – '
Click.
'that it was a good deal – '
Click.
'an excellent deal.'
Click.
'Maybe – '
Click.
'sometime – '
Click.
'we could renegotiate the terms.'
Click.
'Heh, look at the time. We've got to get the car to the docks tonight if we're going to get it on that ship.'

His face had been masked by the camera as he spoke and then he turned and began to clamber back over the rubble that we had scrabbled through to get his shot. Even if I had seen his face, I knew I would not have been able to read it. There was nothing in his tone of voice to suggest that he had said anything of consequence.

When we got back to America, he honoured our deal to the letter. I moved into the apartment below him and worked hard at my business and he lived in the home I had designed for him. We would meet sometimes in the lift, but otherwise his secretary would ring me with the dates for any social event that we had to attend together and we adopted, at his suggestion, a weekly lunch meeting on Mondays where we would plan our social programme and exchange news. Once or twice a week I would go downtown to see Graça. She had taken my room and was slowly putting her own stamp on the apartment. When I came back she had proved such a good manager that I officially made her the CEO of the South American business, but she decided to remain living in New York. She still insisted on overseeing my household, hiring and firing the staff, making sure it ran smoothly. As you know, ma chère, she has no faith in my competence in these matters.

'What I don't get,' she said one day, pushing the empty plate away from her (she still cooked rice and beans every lunchtime unless she knew I was coming), 'is that everything is going well. The store has been a success, you've got offers from all over the country for subsidiaries and outlets, your designs have never been so successful, you're back in contact with your sister and the postman and yet you're – oh, I don't know how to describe it . . . you're *flat*. There is something missing.'

I considered a moment. She was right. I had everything I wanted. The business was roaring. Jim and I were the toast of the town. The publicity was beneficial for us both. I lived in a fabulous apartment. I had confronted my past. But, there was a but and I didn't know what it was. 'Maybe it was churning up all that history?'

'No, that's been good. Being in contact with Christl has been good, it's been a balm. Same with the postman.'

'Laurin.' Saying his name always made me smile.

'He's always going to be the postman in my mind,' she said, teasing me. 'He writes to you regularly. It has filled a void.'

'Well, almost.'

'I know there is the boy. But that's nothing new. There is something else.' She got up and took the plates to the sink. Then she turned around and folded her arms. 'Is it Mr Mitchell?' She singularly refused to become familiar with him. 'Is he behaving badly? Is he putting any pressure on you?'

'No. Not at all, he's behaved . . . impeccably.'

She looked fierce and feline as she stared at me, weighing my words. 'Just take care.'

Some mornings there would be a cloying scent of perfume in our private elevator or a bottle of champagne tottering in the corner, and once there was even a pair of high-heeled strappy sandals lying abandoned on the thick brown carpet, but otherwise Jim was discreet. The press never got wind of his dalliances and apart from these few signs, he never let me know what was going on in his private life.

But I found it impossible to have a relationship. Two kinds of men tried to woo me. Pretty young men I met at parties or through business who saw me as a rich older woman in need of a . . . what is it that you young people call them – a toy boy, ma chère? But I am no fool and I had no time for idle pleasures, nor did I want to risk cracking the facade that Jim and I had so carefully constructed. And, in truth, the idea of loveless sex did not appeal to me. The second kind of man was the powerful and power-hungry kind, men who would have liked to have bedded me either as a trophy or because they wanted to attack Jim in some way. I was not going to be anyone's pawn – not since my father and Schleich had played for me.

Our public life was determined by the inexorable demands of the hidden rules of high society: where to go, whom to be seen with. These were not our choices but, like deus ex machina, inevitable as fate. Consequently, on our first wedding anniversary, Jim took me out for dinner to the latest culinary addition to the jet-setter's list of places to be seen. His secretary had alerted the press so that light bulbs flashed when he held my hand as I stepped out from his Cadillac Limousine. (The Rolls had taken months to arrive, but he used it as his runaround. His chauffeur objected to the right-hand drive.) It was the first time that we had been alone without an agenda to discuss since we got back from the Continent. Conducting a conversation was usually no effort for me, but I felt constrained, even a little nervous.

After the main course the waiters brought back a smaller menu card. I scanned it and then put it down and watched Jim studying his. From the look of earnest concentration in his face, it could have been a real estate contract. I think, ma chère, that is when I realised that it bothered me that he turned his forensic inspection on everything but me. Since the day we had stepped off the plane at JFK airport, he had been polite and civil, but it was as if he did not see me. I never felt that I was under his scrutiny. It was not my intention ever to be invisible.

I drew myself up, straightened my already straight back and pushed out my chest. Jim laid his menu down on the linen table-cloth but when he glanced at me, I realised that he did not take in my beauty. He did not notice my dress, which was modest in coverage but clingy enough to enhance my curvature. I had wed myself to a man who was blind to my charms, who used me as a front and employed expensive call girls to meet his needs.

'So, Rosa,' he said as he summoned the waiter, not even looking at me as he spoke. 'It's been a year. A good year?' The waiter arrived. 'Just the crêpe Suzette for me, please,' he said. He knew by now that I never had dessert.

When the waiter had gone, he leaned back in his chair and fixed his eyes on me. I could not meet his gaze.

'It hasn't been a good year, then?' he asked, shedding his formal tone, using the voice that had opened me like a nut in Oberfals.

'Don't be ridiculous,' I said defensively. 'It's been marvellous. You know how well the Dumarais ranges have grown, and the stores – they are opening faster than I can handle.'

'I keep on telling you to delegate more, take on even more management.' He switched back to his usual mode.

'It's nothing I can't handle.' I told him what I kept telling myself, wanting to believe it.

'But Rosa, you look – ' he hesitated before he inflicted his wound on me – 'tired.'

Ma chère, it was like a slap in the face – not a compliment or even an untoward remark in a year and now this: my new image was fatigue.

He went on, 'I can tell from your face that I've hit a nerve, but you know you're overdoing it.'

'I feel fine,' I fired back.

'If you say so.' He shrugged.

He looked around and almost as if it was rehearsed, Randall, his chauffeur, approached the table carrying Jim's suitcase. 'Ah, thank you, we'll be another half-hour.'

I shifted in my seat uneasily. Anything unexpected with Jim made me wary.

'Thank you, Mr Mitchell,' Randall said and retreated.

Jim bent over, unfastened the case and pulled something out. 'It being our wedding anniversary,' he said, 'I thought I should get you something special. I have been reliably informed by all my secretaries that the first anniversary is the paper anniversary. So, my dear wife, here is some paper.'

He pushed a large manila envelope across the table to me and I picked it up. It was addressed to Jim and postmarked Merano over the Italian stamps. Jim had crossed out his name and written 'To Rosa Mitchell' across the top in his thick scrawl. My stomach clenched. He knew that I was still Rosa Dumarais; we had agreed I would keep it for business purposes. The name he had written was the opening gambit of one of his games.

'Shall I open it now?' I asked, trying to sound calm.

'That would be usual in these circumstances,' he said flatly.

I extracted a wad of crisp white paper held together with a thick bulldog clip. The waiter presented Jim with his dessert.

'You won't mind if I eat while you examine your present?'

I was furious – it was just sport for him. But I forced myself to say, 'No, not at all.'

There was a covering letter in German but the rest of the documents were in Italian. I flicked through them and then read them again. There was a long, complicated letter from Jim's lawyer; the title deeds for the Oberfals Gasthaus where I had grown up and a property in Meran; employment contracts for the managers of the Gasthaus (the erstwhile owners). The deeds were in the name of Rosemarie Edith Kusstatscher Dumarais Mitchell. Only my sister would have known my middle name.

I read the papers through a third time. It did not make sense, there had to be a trap. On the surface this was a lovely gift. The property in Meran was a villa on Schafferstrasse, a quiet road in green and leafy Obermais; my sister Christl, who had been living in a small flat in Untermais, was to live there. The house was divided into three apartments. There was a tenancy agreement for the ground-floor flat with my sister, who had committed to a nominal monthly rent of a thousand Italian lira (not quite two dollars) in perpetuity; the second floor was for the use of Signora Mitchell on her visits. A local architect's proposals for the rooms in the mansard roof were also included. There was one last white envelope, which contained a travel itinerary detailing flights to Rome, trains to Venice, Meran and Milan, and a return flight to New York. The hotel reservations and tickets were all duplicated, one set with my name, the other with Graça's. I was overwhelmed and unnerved in equal measure.

By the time I had finished reading, his dessert plate had been removed and he was fiddling with his wine glass, observing me closely.

'Well?'

'I don't know what to say, it's very thoughtful.' I reached across the table and squeezed his hand. 'Thank you.'

He turned my hand over in his and then lifted it to his lips. 'Happy anniversary.'

Randall let us out of the car just after eleven at the base of Mitchell Heights. I automatically walked the length of my storefront, just checking that everything was as it should be. Jim went straight in. He always stopped to chat with whichever concierge was on duty – he knew the names of almost everyone he came in regular contact with and often their wives' and children's; it was one of his charms. A woman strutted towards me. She was wearing a clingy polyester, scarlet, bell-bottomed catsuit with deep cleavage and platform sandals. Her eyes looked stark from lashings of thick mascara and her lips were scarred the same red as her outfit. I watched as she went in the lobby ahead of me. There were no other apartments in the whole building other than ours; the rest was office space. She was not visiting me, and there was only one other person there.

I turned and walked back along the store windows. The displays were well-lit so it was hard to discern my reflection but I could clearly see the sheaf of papers in my hand shaking against the midnight blue woman's tuxedo in front of me (inspired, of course, by my wedding outfit). It was not an hour since Jim had moved me by his apparent and extravagant thoughtfulness, yet he was no doubt taking this gaudy woman into his – no, our – lift at this very moment. I clutched the wad of documents to my chest to stop my trembling. I made myself examine the display as I tried to compose myself. A carmine silk blouse on one of the mannequins was unbuttoned. I made a mental note to tell the window dresser the next morning.

Jim was standing in the lobby alone, waiting for me. There was no sign of the woman anywhere. We rode the lift in silence up to my floor, standing side by side. My nose was irritated by the faint smell of musk and patchouli. The steel door opened into my mirrored entrance; the light from the lift lit up a path into my dark apartment.

'Thank you again. It was a wonderful gift,' I muttered, not looking at him before stepping out.

The lift doors closed with a sigh and I was alone with an infinite number of my reflections on either side of the elevator. Misery was painted over my face. Oh, ma chère, in that moment I felt so lonely.

I made myself a tisane then went into my bathroom. Removing my make-up is a slow process. I always begin with my eyes (mascara smudges everywhere if you don't start with it), then do the face and, last of all, the mouth. I soaked the cotton wool in make-up remover and then rubbed my lipstick off. I held up the white ball, which I had stained pink, and imagined that red mouth kissing Jim upstairs, his face smeared by that whore's fiery lipstick. My blanched, clean face stared back at me from the mirror. My breasts were no longer as firm and high as they had been. I was forty-four and, unvarnished, my age showed.

I pulled my nightdress on over my head and slid into my negligee, then marched back to the elevator. I pressed the button for his floor. I had never gone up without being invited before.

The doors slid open and I found myself standing near his Hepworth and Moore in the marble space I had created for him. There was no sign of him.

'Jim! Jim!' My voice echoed in the stony silence. I started towards the staircase, the cream silk of my nightgown flapping as I moved.

'Jim!'

The sound of a door opening and shutting travelled down the marble stairs and I raced up towards the Buddha. Jim emerged from the corridor, his shirt hanging over his trousers, his feet bare. We met at the top.

Under pressure, in meetings, in public, Jim always looked placid but now there was something wild in his eyes. I was too angry to read it – all I could see was the vivid red smeared round his mouth and on his neck like the hungry marks of a vampire.

'What's the matter?' he asked urgently. 'Is there something wrong?'

'I don't understand you,' I shouted.

'What do you mean?' For a moment he wore the open, soft expression I had seen on his sleeping face in Oberfals.

'Why did you marry me?' I could not stop shouting now; months of anxiety and unease were exploding out of me.

His face shut down. 'You know . . . our deal.' His face and tone of voice were blank. It made me more furious.

'I asked for a sham engagement, but you insisted on marrying me. Why?'

'Do you really not know the answer to that?' A flash of anger swept over his face.

He took a step towards me. I thrust my hand up to his face and cupped it over his mouth, smeared the red grease across his cheeks. Even in my fury, I was startled by the softness of his skin under my fingers. He grabbed my wrist and tried to pull me close, but I yanked myself away.

'Your gift,' I said, suppressing a sob. 'For a moment, I thought it meant something.' I took a step back, trying to control myself – I would not cry in front of him. 'But now . . .' I held out the red-besmirched tips of my fingers. 'I can only assume it was meaningless.'

I glanced back before the lift doors shut him from my view. He was still standing at the top of the stairs watching me, rubbing his fingers over the lipstick I had smeared across his face.

25

Make-up Remover

A s you know, ma chère, I have a routine, a very exact routine. I cleanse, always; I never rush this. I apply a base foundation, eyeliner, eyeshadow, mascara, rouge, highlighter, shading, eyeliner again, and finally three layers of lipstick, kissing the first two layers off on to tissue. But today, it's hopeless – look, ma chère, I've done it all wrong. I look like a Disney witch, not at all elegant. Even after all these years of learning different tricks, different styles, I can still make a mess of it. Thank goodness for this little bottle: a generous dab on the cotton ball and then – presto – off it all wipes and I can start again. I think that today I need a simpler look. If you have not seen someone for a long time it is better not to overdo it. Don't you agree, ma chère?

After our anniversary, I succeeded in avoiding Jim for the two weeks before Graça and I left on the 'thoughtful' holiday he had booked for us. In Italy, he was hard to forget – he was like a ghostly guide as his plans and arrangements occupied and shaped our days. Graça is a wonderful travelling companion; she guided me through Rome, Florence and Venice, reading up every night on the history, architecture and art treasures that we would be seeing the next day. The gentle elegance of Meran charmed her. Christl greeted her warmly, which impressed me – in those days it was rare to see anyone who was not white in those parts, and I had been worried about taking Graça there. We stayed only two days, enough time for me to find contractors and begin the overhaul of the villa.

When the car Jim had hired for us rolled up the ever steeper, narrower valley towards Oberfals, Graça was silent. The car pulled up in front of the Gasthaus.

'Home!' I meant it ironically, but was nevertheless moved by
the knowledge that it was mine again.

'You grew up here? Hemmed in by all this darkness!'

I looked around. Seeing it through Graça's eyes, which were
so used to the great vistas of Brazil, this Alpine valley – with
every flat surface put to work, every cultivable inch planted,
bordered by the dark walls of fir reaching up to the rock and sky
– was disconcerting. In all the years I had never stopped thinking
of Falstal as beautiful, and indeed it was; yet she was right, it
was also confining, narrow and dark. No wonder I had left; no
wonder it had taken me so long to come back.

We stayed two nights with Laurin Maier before returning to
Milan. My two dearest friends managed to communicate with a
mishmash of languages, trying out words until a look of comprehension dawned on the other's face. I let them talk through their
excitement and frustration, feeling safe and at home in their
company. On the plane I found myself deliberating over what
home meant: the beautiful villa in Meran that Graça and I had
shared with my sister, the old Gasthaus in Oberfals where the
manager lived, Laurin Maier's house fitted out with my mother's
furniture, Graça's apartment where we had lived together in
Greenwich Village or my apartment below Jim's in Mitchell
Heights?

My confusion continued in New York. Jim was too busy to
meet, his secretary told me each time she rang to cancel our
weekly meetings. With my trip and these cancellations, nearly
two months passed without seeing him. The sudden absence of
pressing social engagements, the clearing out of our mutual
calendar, was not plausible; it did not fool me. I just did not
know how long his avoiding me would last. I wondered if the
'mutually agreed' divorce papers were on their way. I was not
sleeping well so I stayed a few nights with Graça downtown. I
told myself that I could not face the humiliation of another similar
encounter but, as Graça had said to me, I had no right to feel
humiliated, it was what I had agreed to.

Then one Tuesday, my secretary put Jim's through to me.

I took a moment before greeting her, determined to sound breezy. 'Jean, hello. You don't need to apologise about cancelling again, I know he is busy.'

'Oh no, Mrs Mitchell – ' his staff were the only people who I allowed to call me that – 'not at all. I mean, he is very busy, of course . . .' She sounded unusually flustered. She paused and then blurted out, 'I am ringing to invite you to join him on a business trip.'

I sighed and opened my work diary. 'When?'

'Tomorrow.'

'Tomorrow?' I dropped my pen. I was relieved that she could not see the look of horror on my face.

'Yes, he has a meeting in Germany and it's very sensitive. He said he needs an interpreter he can trust.'

It made no sense. There had been no communication from him for nearly three months – just a brief note, hoping I had enjoyed myself, left in a bouquet of red roses (red! Ma chère, how could he?) that were waiting for me on my return from Italy. And now he was saying jump, did he really expect me to?

'He knows I'm very busy,' I said, my voice clipped. 'I've just been on a trip.'

'I am so sorry, Mrs Mitchell, but he said I must impress on you that he would not insist on your presence were it not so important.'

Jean sounded nervous. Until then he had always 'invited', 'requested' or 'solicited' my presence but this time she had said 'insist'.

'How important?' I asked with a feeling of dread.

'Oh, Mrs Mitchell,' she said, and I could hear the stress in her voice. 'I have no idea what it is about. I just know that when he took the phone call from Germany, he went as white as a sheet and then told me not to put any calls through for half an hour after.' She dropped her voice. 'He never does that.'

But I felt alarmed; something was troubling him enough to break the silence that had developed between us. Something had made Mr Poker-Face Mitchell turn white. If nothing else, I was intrigued now.

'OK, Jean,' I said. 'How many days must I pack for?'

'His return is for Sunday; that's five nights.'

I frowned. That was a long trip. 'Tell him I'll go.'

'I'm afraid I can't – you see, he's already gone. He'll be on the plane by now. He said I should put you on the next flight. Could you leave tonight?'

I was certain that he would not be waiting for me at the airport. Clearly whatever his business was in Berlin, it was urgent, so I assumed he would be too busy to collect me himself. As the passengers spilled into the arrivals hall, I checked the placards for my name. Yet there he was, standing apart from the horde of taxi drivers, dressed in one of his Savile Row sports jackets and chinos, scanning the surge of arriving passengers. He looked distinguished despite wearing just a jacket. But, I noted, he was not wearing a suit; he was not dressed for work.

I began to head towards him, my porter pushing my trolley for me; without a schedule I had packed for every eventuality and had two heavy suitcases with me. He saw my bags before me and then waved his newspaper at me in greeting. A smile flashed across his face but swiftly vanished at my stony expression.

'Rosa,' he said, leaning towards me but then withdrawing, as though thinking better of greeting me with a kiss. 'Did you have a good flight?'

'Hello.' He was not even wearing a tie. I was fuming.

'I'm glad that you came.'

'Do we have to go straight to the meeting?' I asked pointedly.

'No, we've got a little over an hour. Do you want to stop by the hotel and freshen up?'

'Yes, I'll get changed into something suitable.' He did not seem to notice my irony.

He put his hand on my elbow and steered me through the crowds out to where he had a car waiting. At the hotel he said he would sit at the bar while I went up to my room. I was even more annoyed; he never drank when he had business to attend to. As usual, we had a suite with two bedrooms, and his clothes were scattered around the smaller room with twin beds.

In the taxi going to the meeting, he was quiet and lost in thought. Every so often he turned and glanced at me, though he was so preoccupied I was not convinced that he was even aware of doing it. Each time he turned towards me, I inhaled the sharp smell of whisky on his breath. I had never seen him even slightly worried about anything before. My anger waned and I started to worry about him. The taxi deposited us outside a squat, modest concrete office block.

'Is this what you're buying?' I asked, unable to keep the incredulity out of my voice. It was hard to see any attraction. There was something strange going on.

'What?' he answered, looking vague. I gestured to the building and he gave me a nervous smile. 'No, but our appointment is in here.'

He pressed a button and waited for the buzz and click of the lock opening before going in. I followed him up the bare stairwell to the third floor and then along a corridor of numbered blue doors lining each side. The door he stopped in front of was like all the others on the corridor. The blue paint was chipped and the tarnished brass plaque had number thirty-seven engraved on it. It was depressing.

'This is it.' He shook out his shoulders as if he were gathering strength, knocked on the door and pushed it open.

A fat young man, sitting at a battered desk, jumped up. His suit looked as if he had just taken it off the shop hanger – even his shirt had a crispness about it that suggested factory starch. His tie was loud. He had seemingly bought a whole new outfit for the meeting, but his clothes were the only new things in the shabby office. His desk was clearly second-hand and the metal filing cabinets behind him looked like they had served in both World Wars. He walked around his desk.

'Ah, Mr Mitchell, good day.' He shook hands with Jim and then offered me his hand, which was clammy. 'Mrs Mitchell, good day, a pleasure to meet you.'

'He speaks English!' I said, glowering at Jim.

'Ah, yes. I'm sorry, Mr Thormann, I have not been honest with my wife.'

'Of course.' Thormann turned to me. 'Mrs Mitchell, may I present myself: Karl-Heinz Thormann, private detective.' He made a small bow.

'Private detective?' I rounded on Jim. 'There really is no business deal?'

'Let Mr Thormann speak; you'll be interested in what he has to say.'

I had cleared out my busy diary for a week. I had jumped on the next flight, barely having had time to pack. I had not slept. I was exhausted and Jim had lied to me about his purpose.

'Enough,' I snapped. 'This is too much! First that woman, then three months' silence, then you drag me halfway round the world because . . . oh, I don't know why, but you hire some detective to spy on me? I'm gone.'

I had reached the lift and was pressing the call button repeatedly when Thormann, not Jim, caught up with me.

'*Bitte, Gnädige Frau Mitchell*,' Thormann puffed in German, his Saxon accent harsh but his tone solicitous. 'You misunderstand your husband; he is a good man. Look at this – please.' He held a photo out to me.

He thrust the picture into my hand. The lift clanged as it arrived and the doors opened, the light from it spilling out and illuminating the portrait. It was of a thin, middle-aged man, with greying hair and thick glasses. It took me a while to recognise him. As the lift doors closed I slumped against the cold metal. I was winded.

'Your husband asked me to find this man, Thomas Fischer.' It was indeed Thomas, ma chère, the first man I had loved. 'Perhaps you will come back to my office now? There is more I must show you.'

'More?' The lift rattled as it started to descend.

'Yes, please come with me.'

I followed him back to his office in a daze. Jim was standing looking out of the window. He turned as we came in and then sat down in one of the two Polyside chairs and Thormann collapsed into his own seat behind his desk, which was clear except for a large manila file.

'Sit, please,' he said beseechingly. 'It is better.' He waited while I took my place.

'As I explained, your husband asked me to find this Thomas Fischer.' I looked again at the photo of Thomas. It was a posed, official-looking portrait. He was sitting at a desk surrounded by books, staring straight into the camera. I peeled my eyes off the picture and glanced over at Jim, who was also staring at it. His face was ashen.

'Your husband requested that I should find also this woman,' Thormann said, drawing another photo from the file, this time of a plump, contented hausfrau. This photo had been snatched as she was walking down the street. She was in focus but everything around her was soft and hazy. Clearly, she had not known that a telephoto lens was trained on her. She was carrying a shopping bag and a newspaper and was looking straight ahead, her face relaxed and open.

'Ida Schurter,' I breathed.

'Formerly Ida Schurter,' Thormann said.

I put the photos down and looked at Jim. He was staring straight ahead at Thormann.

'Ahem.' Thormann coughed discreetly. 'And this young man.' He handed me a third photograph.

It was a snapshot of a young man in his twenties, sporting a tie-dye T-shirt and shoulder-length hair. He was a stranger to me. Like the image of Ida, the tell-tale signs of a powerful zoom lens were evident. There was something intrusive about their being unaware that their image was being captured. He too was walking, a patterned woven bag strung over his shoulder, his face empty, expressionless. The more I stared the more my eyes were drawn to the smudge of blue that was his eyes, the same blue as mine.

'It's my son.'

'Yes, it is.'

'He's alive.'

'He is, as you can see, well and alive.'

'You've found him.' The words were mine, but they made no sense to me.

'Mrs Mitchell. I believe this is why your husband sent for you so quick. He did not want to disappoint you if my search was to be unsuccessful, and yet he wanted you here as soon as possible once I told him I had succeeded.'

'What do you know? How did you find them?'

'Well, I thought it was a hard case to solve: three people with just their names and addresses twenty years ago, but it was easy.' Herr Thormann looked smug and confident now. He leaned back in his chair. 'Fischer is too common, there are over two hundred Fischers in the Berlin phone book, and Thomas, that was goose-hunting, not so good. But I know one thing: he studied economics. At first, I went up a dead alley, but then I thought, maybe he is not here.'

'He's not here?'

Thormann shook his head. 'Not here in West Berlin, but there, in East Berlin. Then it was, how do you say, a slice of cake. Over the wall he's the Economics professor at the university and special economics advisor to the Central Committee of the Party, and an old friend of Honecker.'

'That figures,' I said, surprised to feel the smile lifting up my face.

'And then the rest was easy.' Thormann grinned. 'Especially since he is married to Ida Schurter.'

I stood up. A wave of emotion swept over me. 'He married her? Thomas married Ida?'

'Yes,' Thormann said after a pause.

I sat down again and picked up file of photos. There were a few of Thomas and Ida. I looked at her and spite filled me. Not satisfied with stealing my son, she had seduced Thomas, my first love.

'And he legally adopted Laurin,' Thormann told me happily.

Thomas had adopted my son, Schleich's bastard, the son of the man he had killed. I put my hand to my head. It was like a knife was being forced into my skull. 'He adopted him?'

'Yes – and her other children.'

No wonder Ida looked so contented out shopping for her family – my family that should have been. I'd always been too frightened to look, too frightened to find a trail leading to a gravestone, and now I'd found them all. They were all there. What a happy family. Max looked like Ottmar, and Vreni was a slimmer model of her mother. I hated them.

But I had not found them, I realised with a jolt; it was Jim who had accomplished what I had always been too frightened to. The anger bubbled up from my stomach. What did he think he was doing, and by what right? He had not spoken to me since he had insulted me with that red-mouthed slut on our wedding anniversary and now, without consulting me, he had invaded my world. There was nothing he did not know about me. He probably knew more than I did.

I stood up so suddenly that the chair fell over behind me, and I fled from the room.

Berlin is not a big city and, sliced in two as it was in those days, it was even smaller than it is now. I rushed past the chauffeured car waiting for Jim outside and started to walk. I was wearing a beautiful pair of platform shoes, which while not uncomfortable, were not designed for walking. I turned into a commercial street and walked until I found a bank, where I changed $200 before hailing a taxi to the KaDeWe, the most famous department store in Berlin and the only one I knew of. Half an hour later, depressed at the drab and sensible stock of the shop, but more sensibly shod, I caught another cab to Checkpoint Charlie. I was still insensate with rage; all I knew was that I had to keep moving and that I wanted to be in East Berlin, I wanted to be where Laurin was. And I did not want to see Jim.

Crossing the border was long and slow, and took some of the fire out of my anger. I had to change thirty Deutschmark and was told that I could not return until I had spent all of it. Spending money had never been a problem for me, but there it proved difficult. As soon as I crossed over, it was like stepping back in time to the years after the war. I walked up Friedrichstrasse, the edges of the colonnades shattered and worn by decay. I found my way on to the famous Unter den Linden, a long road lined with lime trees, and up to Humboldt University. I stopped outside and wondered if Thomas was in there. Maybe I would see him if I stood there all day. I started to walk again, past the Old and the New National Museums, the Pergamon. The green cupola of the Berliner Dom, the cathedral, rose out of what I took to be a bomb-blasted empty expanse. I realised that I was not ready to see him yet. Like the city, I was shell-shocked.

Hunger, thirst and fatigue led me on. I tried to find cafés where I could spend my money, or even a restaurant for lunch, but had no success. It was only when I wandered beyond the Museum Island into the old quarters behind, with courtyard leading into courtyard, still pockmarked by bullets and rough-edged from shrapnel and explosions, that I found grocery shops. As I walked along in my well-cut suit and tan suede shoes, a crocodile leather bag and KaDeWe carrier, I garnered cold, unwelcoming stares. In the shops the harsh Saxon accent grated against my ears, but the Berliners' hard gaze softened when they heard my Tyrolean sing-song.

It was late when I returned to Checkpoint Charlie carrying a bag of books from the Pergamon. I had left a pile of the worthless aluminium flakes that counted for money on my remaining note as a tip after my evening meal, before crossing back to the West. As I passed Café Adler on the first corner after the checkpoint, a figure came out and crossed the road towards me. It was Jim.

'I'm sorry,' he said immediately. 'I got that wrong.'

I carried on walking and he fell in beside me.

'It was meant to be a surprise, not an ambush.'

We continued in silence. A taxi appeared in the road ahead,

its lights fuzzy in the drizzle that thickened the air. He stepped into the road and hailed the car.

In the taxi, in the hotel lobby, in the lift I did not say a word, nor even look at him, even as he opened the door to the suite and stood back to let me pass inside. I dropped my bags, kicked off my shoes and went straight into the bathroom. I cleaned my face. I removed every trace of make-up and stared at my hard eyes, their usually piercing blue dimmed by the red around them. My skin was pale, the colour bleached away by each pass of the cotton soaked with make-up remover. The weak bathroom light was unforgiving. Only when it was all gone did I return to Jim.

He was sitting on the sofa surveying a map of Berlin, a guide-book at his side. His face was blanched and grim. I did not sit down, but stood facing him.

'I have tried to understand what has just happened but I can't fathom it,' I said, my voice sharp as a knife. 'We made a business deal. This arrangement was not meant to be personal.'

'Things change,' he said weakly.

'Does it amuse you to dig up all my darkest secrets, to drag out what hurts most, what I'm most ashamed of, and just lay it out there for a strange man like that detective to see? Is this your idea of fun?'

'No,' he spluttered, 'that's not what I intended.'

'No, it's not like the fun you had with that woman that night when you had started out playing nice. Paper anniversary! I should have torn those documents up.'

'I wanted you to have those properties.' Mr Poker-Face was losing his cool now.

'I was touched, really touched,' I said coldly, pausing to let my words sink in. 'And then you brought that slut into our elevator.' I fixed my eyes on him. 'I had to ride up with you, smelling her cheap perfume. What did you intend if not to humiliate me?'

His face fell, he looked like a little boy caught out. He rubbed the back of his neck. 'To make you jealous,' he admitted, screwing up his face.

'Jealous?' I scoffed. 'No, I felt ashamed that I had been such a fool. Graça had warned me. I should have listened.'

'I'm sorry, that wasn't what I wanted but—'

'Why?' I shouted. 'Just tell me why. And then we can go home and get that divorce.'

He got up and went into his room with the twin beds, and I could hear him picking things up and dropping them. Then silence. I waited for him to come back into the lounge and spin another story. I sat down on the sofa, which was still warm from him. I flicked through his guidebook and he must have made a noise because I glanced up.

He was standing in the doorway. He looked tentative and his face was white. Jim Mitchell could not hide his agitation.

'You have to believe me. That's the last thing I want.'

'A divorce? It seems to me that's exactly what you want.'

He took a step towards me. 'I thought you would get it by now.'

'Get what?'

He opened his hands in a gesture of defeat. 'I didn't know how else to do it.'

'Do what?'

'I'm lost here. From the moment you walked into my office, everything you've said was right.' He tried to smile. 'I only know how to be trashy and vulgar. All this, here, I've done it again.'

'And—?'

'And . . . I've never said this to anyone before, but . . .' He took another step towards me. 'I love you.'

For a moment I was speechless. Then I laughed. 'That's ridiculous! Is this the best card in your hand? You expect me to believe that. You've never been in love with me. She wasn't the first woman up the elevator.' I stopped to gather myself, and then continued, thinking that my icy words would extinguish his mock ardour, 'You're just used to owning everyone and everything.'

He took a step back, clinging on to the door frame for support. I was panting and he was breathing heavily, his chest heaving up and down. I fixed him with my coldest, most contemptuous stare – and to his credit he met it head-on.

'You're right,' he said eventually. 'I've never had to win a woman before – they throw themselves at me – or my money, at least. But you can't be won or played. And maybe that is why I fell in love, originally. I won't deny it: your being out of my league was appealing.'

'You wanted a trophy,' I said, folding my arms tightly.

'But you – you've found things in me that I didn't know existed. I fell in love with *you*, Rosa, and love you more each day. And I don't know how to make you love me.'

My anger was glacial. His words poured over me like an avalanche but I was so deep in snow that I could not hear them.

I snorted contemptuously.

He knocked his head against the door frame. 'There's nothing you want that you can't buy yourself, and then when I saw you with the old man, Laurin, it dawned on me there were things you needed that you didn't know that you needed. That was the only thing I could give you. I want to give what you lost in that black hole of yours, the tools you need to heal yourself; because you will never be able to love again until you're healed.'

He took a deep breath and his eyes met mine, unblinking. Then he took a step closer, bent down and lifted up the map from the table. Underneath it was the manila folder.

'Herr Thormann is taking us to meet them tomorrow at ten.' He reached the file out towards me.

He turned back into the small bedroom. He looked spent. I was stunned, but a tiny flame of anger still flickered in me.

'You said at the start you wanted to know everything, to exact due diligence,' I called after him. 'Well, there is nothing you don't know now. Take a good look.' He stepped back into the lounge. I tossed my hair and lifted my bare face to him. All my made-up glamour wiped clean. 'You've laid me bare. This is what I really am. I hope you're happy.'

26

Bath Oils

I'm so agitated thinking about tonight it's almost as if I am sabotaging myself, as if I will never get ready. Everything I touch reminds me of something, and I've been standing here so long and trapped you with my reminiscing. Who would have thought I could be so nervous after everything I have lived through? I'm not sure there is time for a bath, ma chère, but you are right, it would calm me, and I can make it quick. Can you turn the taps while I choose which oils would best soothe me? Today, I need to soak in something calming. Look, I keep almond oil in this bottle – a few glugs of that in the bath, and then a few drops of essential oils, depending on my mood. Oh, ma chère, I think I'll use geranium to uplift and bergamot to calm. It's funny to think that when I was a child, the only beauty tip I knew was that a woman should rub almond oil into her skin to avoid stretch marks during pregnancy. It was in short supply during the war and was a cause for concern, yet now I can pour it into my bath liberally as a libation to the gods of beauty and rest. And look what it has done for my skin – not bad for a woman of sixty-three. I want to make a good impression. I wonder if we'll kiss or shake hands?

The last time I felt this nervous was when Herr Thormann pulled up his car on a narrow road lined with tall, dilapidated houses in what used to be the Jewish quarter around Monbijouplatz, near the Great Synagogue in East Berlin. I had come within spitting distance of the same spot the day before. Thormann came around his car and opened the door for me but I couldn't move.

I felt weak. Sitting in the back of his car with the lingering, heavy scent of his Brut cologne, I felt a rising tide of panic come over me and began to feel faint. Ma chère, can you imagine? After all those years. I had been sixteen the last time I had seen Thomas and he had been twenty-three. Now I was forty-four and the man in the photo had grey hair. It was even harder to fathom that Laurin, my son, was eleven years older than I had been when I had given birth to him, nine years older than I was when I left him behind in St Gallen. He was twenty-eight.

When I finally forced myself out of the car, Jim gently steered me up the pavement behind Herr Thormann, who stopped in front of an apartment block. He rang a bell and waited until the buzzer sounded and the door clicked. I watched as Herr Thormann led the way up the spiralling stairs, letting Jim follow before I gripped the tarnished brass Jugendstil banisters. I heard a door opening above.

'Good day, Frau Professor Fischer.' Thormann's voice bounced down the stairwell.

As I climbed up slowly, Ida came into view, standing on the threshold of her home. She was shaking Jim's hand as Thormann introduced them. She had put on weight and was wearing drab clothes. She looked nervous, smiling too much. A tall, lanky man with stooped shoulders, cropped, greying hair and eyes hidden behind thick, rimmed lenses emerged from the door behind her. Thomas.

Jim shook hands with him, and there was a babble of noise and introductions. I stayed at the top of the stairs waiting for Laurin to appear. Ida broke away from the men and came to me with open arms.

'Rosa, at last.'

I did not reply nor move forward. She stopped short of me.

'Frau Professor Fischer, I'm so glad to see you.' This was not my finest hour, ma chère, but I won't keep it from you. I could not help thinking how the last time in St. Gallen she stopped using *Du* and calling me Rosa. Not only had she stolen my son, she had married Thomas too. And now she wanted to be friends.

'Call me Ida, please.' She reached for my hand, with the same hand that Laurin had clung to. The same hand that caressed Thomas at night. I bristled.

'Of course, Ida,' I said frostily. 'I guess we are family.'

She put her arms around me; I kept mine pinioned to my sides, clutching my handbag.

'Come in,' Thomas said, standing at the doorway.

Ida's face showed her hurt as she turned away, but she forced a smile and took Jim by the arm and led him inside, followed by Thormann. Laurin still had not appeared. I stepped into their home and watched as Ida, Jim and Thormann vanished down a long corridor and into a room. I leaned back against the wall. Thomas shut the front door, took a step in and then stopped in front of me. For a moment neither of us moved nor said a word.

'So, Rosa,' he said finally, and hearing him calling my name was like being transported back in time. 'You look well. I see I have grown older than you.'

'You're a professor.' I gave a small smile. 'I guess that was inevitable.'

'Yes,' he said, mirroring my tentative smile. 'I'm not fit for anything else.'

I took a deep breath. I didn't know how much time we would have alone before we would be called to join the others. But there were some things that needed saying.

'I thought you were dead,' I said tentatively. 'I only found out in '63 that you were still alive.'

He nodded, and I could see the cogs whirring behind his eyes, which still gleamed with that same kind intelligence. 'Professor Goldfarb?'

'Yes,' I said. 'I saw him in Jerusalem. But I had no idea, not about this, about you and Ida.'

'I went to St. Gallen to find you. I found Laurin instead.' There was no hostility in his voice, no anger, just the bare facts. 'And,' he continued, 'Ottmar was dead.'

'I waited for two years.' My voice cracked. 'For nearly a year after the war ended . . .' I trailed off. We both knew how much upheaval there had been after the war, how hard it had been to get around, especially in Germany. He could have been posted to Russia for all I knew.

He ignored my defence and went on. 'Ida told me that you had married and gone to Brazil.'

'I thought you were dead,' I repeated dumbly and opened my handbag to take out a handkerchief and soak up a tear before it could ruin my make-up.

'They were uncertain times,' he said, not unkindly.

'I gave up too soon.' I dabbed my other eye.

'After the war it was a mess. I couldn't send word,' he said. Again the hard facts.

I sighed and fiddled around in my bag, stalling for time. The way he was painting it, we were the victims of circumstance, but I knew that was not true. Everyone made choices; I chose to leave. He had come back for me; it was I who had failed him. The least I could do was be honest.

'I couldn't manage alone. I didn't want to leave Laurin behind.' I looked back up into his unblinking eyes. 'I came back for him, but . . .'

'Ida told me about that last time in St. Gallen, how he didn't know you. You did the right thing.'

'I've doubted that all my life.'

'He's been happy. When I found Laurin – he looked so much like you – ' he dropped his eyes – 'and Ida was alone with three fatherless children . . . Well, it was obvious. She is a very good woman.'

'She is.' I let out a deep breath, ashamed of my behaviour on the landing. 'I would never have entrusted him to just anyone.'

'You should remember that.'

It was not twenty-four hours since I had discovered that she had everything I had dreamed of. Perhaps I was unnerved and jet-lagged, or maybe just overwhelmed by so many suppressed feelings, but it had been impossible until now to recall her kindness. It took time and perspective to acknowledge that I only became Rosa Dumarais Mitchell because I had trusted her.

'I love her. I didn't at first – not the way I was in love with you, Rosa – but I love Ida now.'

'I see.'

I put the handkerchief back in my bag and snapped it shut.

'Can you remember that last night?' He dropped his voice.

'Of course I remember,' I whispered back. For a moment I could have been back in my tiny bed with him. His eyes made my stomach flip as it had done all those years before.

He cleared his throat 'The memory of that night . . .' He breathed out heavily. 'It kept me going for the rest of the war. In the end it led me to Laurin and Ida. And if it had just been Laurin, who knows? Maybe we would still be waiting for you.'

'That's ridiculous,' I said, but could not stop smiling coyly like the girl I had been.

He took a step towards me.

'Is it?' He stood so close that if either of us moved, our lips would touch. We were both breathing hard. Our eyes searched each other's. For what – forgotten memories, youthful fantasy – I don't know, ma chère, but this was the moment of danger.

His fingers brushed down my forearms, and I did not move away. He leaned down and I raised up my face to his. His lips felt as soft as they had all those years ago. There was a moment when this chaste kiss could have become something else – our lips quivered on the edge of opening, our tongues ready to dart. I closed my lips and pressed my forehead against his.

'You smell the same!' This realisation seemed to come from deep inside me, something I did not even know I knew, and with it came memories of lying naked, pressed against him, of our limbs entangled.

'So do you,' he gasped.

Then he shook his head, took a step back and leaned against the wall. I knew we were both recalling the same memories; we could have been watching a film together. I locked my eyes on his. Now I could truly see the young man I had loved in the face of this older man. In that moment, I knew that I could take him back from Ida and destroy the happy home she had made. I closed my eyes. I knew there was a choice to make.

It may seem extraordinary, ma chère, but I had pushed Jim's confession out of my mind. I had slept badly and when I woke up I was so anxious about meeting Laurin and Thomas that I had let my anger rule my heart and head. Graça had warned me that I might get hurt, and she had been right. I could escape all that by reaching across the corridor. I just had to lift up my fingers and touch Thomas and he would be mine again; Ida would lose him; he would lose his family. And I would rid myself of Jim.

Thomas sighed. 'It is not hard for me to understand how much Jim Mitchell loves you. He has made such an effort to find us, knowing it would be risky for him.'

I straightened up.

Thomas was right, this was Jim's biggest gamble. Like Graça had said, he had outplayed me. What a fool I had been, oh, ma chère; so blind, so dumb, I had not even understood what game we were playing.

'We should go in,' I said.

Thomas stayed momentarily and gave a slight nod, saying, 'Yes, that's right. Ida has made one of her cakes.'

I don't know if he realised, but he had just saved me for the second time.

I scanned the dining room as soon as I entered, but it was just the five of us. Of course, I reasoned, Laurin no longer lived there; he was an adult, he must be late. Only then did I notice the furniture. It was from Ida's house in St. Gallen. The table was set with the same fine linen that she had ironed so fastidiously while I had sat stitching dresses for her and our babies played on the floor. It was even the same porcelain. The familiarity, the span of years since I had seen them, the reality of who was sitting at the table, was unsettling. I could feel Jim's gaze upon me, reading my face, and I avoided his eye. I might only now be understanding his motives, but I was not yet ready to forgive his tactics. And just because I had decided not to wreck the Fischer home didn't mean I had made my mind up about anything else. I was more interested in where Laurin was.

There was an array of photos arranged on the lace runner that covered the polished mahogany sideboard. I remembered the lacework – Ida had been very proud of this wedding present from Bruges. I recognised the wedding portrait of her and Ottmar Schurter. Next to it was a photo of her and Thomas; she was wearing the Bar suit I had made her, and the only clue that it was their wedding was the small bouquet in her hands. At the time, I thought she was wearing that outfit because it was the best she had, but later I came to think it might have been her way of acknowledging my part in their family. I put the frame down and fingered in turn the pictures of the children – of Laurin, Max and Vreni getting older. Laurin looked like a cuckoo, so different from his siblings, who shared Ottmar's dark hair and Ida's pale eyes. And there was one more girl, one I did not recognise. I examined the photo of her closely. She was standing holding a large paper cone on her first day of school, her pale, thin hair in neat bunches.

'Ah, that's Gabi – Gabriela – our daughter.' Thomas's voice was soft with pride.

'Oh, so you have four?' My heart pumped as I realised how close I had come to stealing him from his daughter, destroying another family and ruining the honour of this most principled of men. My anger was suddenly spent and I felt ashamed. 'That must be a lot of work,' I murmured.

'Not so much anymore.' Ida was slicing the cake. 'Come and sit down, Rosa.'

Jim got up and pulled back the chair next to him and I sat, although I had no appetite. 'Where's Laurin? Is he not here?' I asked.

There was a loud silence, which Ida eventually broke. 'Rosa, what you must understand first is that Laurin remembered nothing about you.' Ida spoke no English, so I translated for Jim. 'And we never told him, we never wanted him to feel less loved.'

'So, he doesn't know about me?' The words came out in English and I gripped Jim's shoulder.

'He found out.' Thomas replied in English, which he spoke with a thick, unyielding accent.

'He was in the army and had come home for the weekend,' Ida continued. 'We were always careful. But one weekend he came home early. Thomas, who gets foreign newspapers at the Central Committee, had brought me a clipping.'

'It was the *New York Times*,' said Thomas. 'An article about Isaiah Harris, and there was a picture of him with his arm round you.'

'He found it on Thomas's desk,' Ida resumed. 'I hadn't had time to hide it away. I don't know what caught his attention. It was pretty rare to see a profile on a black man in the press, even rarer to see a beautiful white woman on his arm. Maybe something about your face – you look so alike. There was one question after another, so we ended up telling him.'

'He said he always felt that there was a secret,' Thomas said, 'but he had never guessed what it was. He had thought that he must have been our love child, that we had had an affair while Ottmar was still alive.'

'Why?' I said, taken aback.

'He looks so different to the others,' Thomas said, shrugging.

'He was shocked and upset to learn that I wasn't his mother, of course. We knew very little about you then, except that you had been in Brazil and then the US. He was angry and confused. He liked jazz – it's very rebellious here to like Western music, but jazz is considered the music of the oppressed, so it's more acceptable. He would read snippets about you and he got this idea that you had abandoned him to lead the good life. He would not believe us when I told him about the time you returned for him, and how it broke your heart. He could not believe that he had forgotten you, and blamed you for leaving him. It was very difficult. And then when you married Mr Mitchell . . . we saw your wedding on the front page. That did it for him.'

'Did what?'

Ida and Thomas exchanged a glance. 'He won't meet you. He says he doesn't need two mothers and that it would be against his party principles to embrace capitalist entrepreneurs like you and your husband.' Thomas looked embarrassed as he spoke; Ida stared into her coffee.

'He won't meet me?' I said, shaking my head in disbelief. 'I won't see him?' I felt as if someone had plunged a shard into my heart again.

'Not this time. I'm sorry,' Thomas said. 'He's very headstrong – that is something he definitely inherited from his mother. Give him time.'

Jim and I barely spoke on the way back to the hotel or on the plane the next day. My head was spinning. It was a relief knowing that Laurin and Thomas were both safe. Ida had cherished them; they were loved. I could not have asked for more. It was also gratifying to know that the feelings that Thomas and I had shared so long ago were not just a childish dream but had been real. I was unsettled and pleased; I felt like I had passed a test. The load of guilt seemed to lift from me and I felt so light that I was almost giddy. This buoyancy was tempered only by my heavy disappointment at Laurin's rejection. Thomas's words 'give him time' became a refrain.

We had been back in New York for a few days when I found myself standing in front of the refrigerator in my kitchen. I opened it as if by instinct, rather than premeditated thought. My hand reached out and grabbed a bottle of champagne – I always have one or two ready and chilled – and two champagne coupes (flutes are a foolish invention). I stood in the hallway waiting for the elevator, examining myself in the mirror, then smiled and looked away from my reflection. It did not matter, not anymore.

For the second time ever, I rode up to his apartment uninvited. I knew that he took a bath after work before going out, and his secretary had arranged for us to dine together that evening. I knocked on his bedroom door but there was no reply. As I crossed the carpet, I could hear the water rumbling into the bath. I waited by the door. The sound of water filling the bath stopped, and I heard Jim splash as he got in. I kicked off my shoes. It had been so long since I had felt this content. Oh, ma chère, I don't mean the kind of ecstasy that I had with Izzy after so much grief or the sweet intoxication that I had felt for Thomas, but the kind of profound contentment that Charles and I had shared for years: being at peace with myself, full of love again. I knocked.

'Who's that?' Jim barked, alarmed.

'Me,' I called. 'Rosa. Can I come in?'

There was the sound of water sloshing around in the bath and then, 'Yes.'

I pushed open the door with my shoulder and hip. A gush of warm air and a familiar scent wafted over me. Jim was sitting up, his back ramrod straight. His face was flushed from the warmth and water was trickling down over his close-cropped head. A small cluster of dark curls nestled in his chest. His arms, resting along the sides of the bath, were strong and well defined. He had lost weight since we had married and was in better shape than I had imagined.

'I thought we should celebrate,' I said, as though it was perfectly normal for me to wander unannounced into his bathroom. I clinked the glasses on to the Breccia Onciata of the countertop, which I had agonised over choosing. For a moment I regretted not selecting the pink champagne; it would have looked marvellous against the beige marble. I wrestled off the cork and poured us both a glass then walked over to the bath and offered him one. He took it from me and then rested back.

'And what are we toasting?' He was trying to compose his face in his usual mask but he was unable to control the smile that was forming. I made it harder by bestowing my warmest grin on him.

'You, Jim, you.' I raised my glass. 'I have everything to thank you for.' He held his glass high enough for us to clink them together, and then we drank. I leaned against the marble top and sipped mine. 'When did it become real, more than a game?'

He sank a bit lower in the bath. 'I was smitten at first sight, the way you prowled around my office like a tiger.'

I laughed. 'That's not what I asked.'

He grinned, then took a moment to consider my question properly. 'In London, I finally got what you are, what you could make me. And if there was a moment, it was standing on the balcony at the Savoy looking out at the Thames.'

We drank, staring into each other's eyes all the while. When our glasses were empty I placed them on the countertop.

'Can you remember the night you proposed to me?' I watched myself in the mirror as I started to unbutton my blouse, and my eyes were excited and sheepish all at once. He submerged himself so only his wide eyes were visible. He blew out some water and pulled himself up as I spun round.

'In the Four Seasons? Yes, of course.' He was trying hard not to smile.

'And can you remember the terms of our agreement?' I said sternly as I pulled my sleeve off.

'Yes, Mrs Mitchell,' he said, mimicking my formality. 'From you: a public display of a marriage, your public companionship, and guidance. From me: the store, half the street frontage and your apartment.'

I hung my blouse over the towel rail and began to unzip my skirt.

'We agreed also to some exclusions, if I recall,' I said as I dropped my skirt and stepped out of it.

'My recollection is a little hazy; I'm having trouble remembering them right now.'

I hung my skirt up, too – whatever the situation, ma chère, good clothes do not deserve poor treatment.

'I believe that the exclusion referred to some rights. Excuse me,' I said and then bent over to pull down my pantyhose. Any self-respecting seductress would never, ma chère, extract herself from pantyhose in front of a man. Being de-hosed has none of the charm that the gradual unclipping of stockings from suspenders has and then letting the silk slide ineluctably down.

When I straightened up, I was wearing nothing but my bra and panties. It was a white, lacy Chantelle Fête matching set – the white, at least, was bridal. The first time I had put on a Fête bra two years before it had seemed life-changing; it was comfortable and the contours looked natural, which was quite revolutionary, ma chère. It is hard for you to understand now but until then any schoolboy could have been forgiven for thinking that breasts naturally came to a conical point. Jim watched and slid lower in the water again.

'These rights you are referring to,' Jim said, lying back with only his head above the bubbles. 'Which ones do you have in mind?'

'Conjugal.'

'Conjugal?'

'Yes. I wondered whether you would consider renegotiating the terms of our agreement.'

He screwed up his face in dramatic deliberation. 'Only from a position of equality. I feel – strictly in the business sense, of course – a little exposed.' These last words barely escaped from the broad grin that had broken over his face; his expressionless face had failed entirely.

'Equal terms?' I unhooked my bra and let it slide down my arms and then fall to the floor as I levered my panties to the cream bathmat under my bare feet. Putting on the Fête bra might have seemed life-changing, but it was taking it off that really was. 'Are the terms equal now?'

'I'd say so,' Jim said.

I took a step towards the bath.

'I'm getting cold.'

'So, are you proposing that we scrap that exclusion?'

'Yes, I don't think it is necessary anymore.'

'No,' he said. 'I guess it's kind of an impediment.'

I took another step. I was standing over him now.

'I do want to introduce a new paragraph, another exclusion,' I said.

'Would that pertain to red lipstick?' He smirked.

'Yes.'

'Agreed. We'll add as a codicil regarding all other such distractions.'

'What did you use for the bubbles?' I leaned over and brushed them to the side. I smiled.

'I don't know . . . that bottle there.'

I glanced over; there was a large green bottle of Badedas at the end of the bath.

'Ah, my favourite.'

'I bought it in Berlin, they had it in the hotel.'

'You wouldn't mind if I joined you?'

'I've been waiting for you to ask.'

'Move forward.'

He sat up and I lowered myself in behind him and sunk into the water. I slid my legs down the side of the bath over his thighs and reached my arms around him, resting my head on the curve of his back. For a while neither of us moved nor spoke.

'I'm sorry that I got it so wrong,' Jim said sincerely.

'I forgive you. If you had told me what you were planning, I would have run away.'

'I'm learning to get things right.'

'Yes – like the Badedas.' I kissed the crest of his shoulder.

He shifted back against me, resting his head on my shoulder, and looked up at me. Oh, ma chère, I was so unused to this beaming smile and the way it made me feel.

'Are you telling me that if I'd got the right bubble bath, I wouldn't have had to go through all this trouble?'

'Exactly.'

27

Naked

I can't believe it. Look at the time. I should be leaving in forty minutes and instead of getting ready I have not stopped talking. It's as if my life has just passed before me. Just look at me. Have you ever seen me this unprepared? You know that my routine takes an hour if I am not rushing, and I cannot rush having already botched it up once. Oh, ma chère, what should I do? This is pathetic. I'm so jittery I can't draw a straight line. I'm worse than you are on a first date. I'm sixty-three, not seventeen, I should be able to do this. I'm going to start with my hair; I'll brush it out. You will? Oh, thank you.

It's strange how things repeat themselves. About eighteen years ago, after the trip to Berlin, after you were conceived, I was surprised to discover that your father liked to brush my hair. Did you know that? People are funny. He said it reminded him of playing with his sister when they were little. I think it was just relaxing – a way to unwind from work, take off the suit and the businessman's face, and dissolve into Jimmy, the boy from Monticello, the boy who had made good. Your father has two sides. There is Jim with the poker face and there is Jimmy, my best friend.

Wheels within wheels. And now you are brushing my hair just like your father used to. These days he claims it hurts his arthritic hand. When I was little my mother used to braid Christl's and my hair. She would have us stand in front of her as she brushed our tangles out. Then she would take our long hair, like bundles of straw, and twist out a small bunch above our temple. She began to plait, bringing in new strands as she worked her way round so that our hair garlanded our own heads. Every Sunday morning, we would go to church in our best dirndls, our white

aprons starched like sheets of cardboard over the bright cotton
pinafores patterned with tiny flowers and our hair braided like
golden halos. Old habits die hard.

Four years after that trip to Berlin, it must have been the summer
of '76 – in any case, you were three years old – we were strolling
through Central Park on our way back from the zoo when your
father bumped into a member of the New York City council. He
was on the planning sub-committee and Jim was not going to miss
the opportunity for an informal chat. We waited for a few minutes,
then you started pestering me for an ice cream from the stall just
a few yards away. We wandered over to the small booth. I'm not
sure at which point you let go of my hand, but by the time I got
to the front of the queue and looked down to ask you what you
wanted – although I knew it would be strawberry or vanilla – I
realised that you were not standing next to me. You were gone.

'Letty! Colette!'

My shrieks brought your father running.

'Where is she?' Oh, ma chère, the way he looked at me as if
I had lost everything.

'She was standing with me, just now,' I gabbled. 'We were
waiting in line for an ice cream and then she was gone.'

We called out your name again and again. Jim told me not to
move just in case you came back. I did not cry. I did not run
around like a mad woman. I simply froze while wave after wave
of fear and nausea swept over me. A crowd gathered around me
like vultures. Jim ran from tree to tree, bench to bench and the
councillor buttonholed a policeman who was patrolling the park.
They all wanted to know what you looked like.

I never put you in dirndls but somehow the same colours
leaked into your wardrobe; that day you were wearing a navy
blue skirt and a red top. All you needed was a white pinafore
and you could have been mistaken for me as a child because I,
like my mother had done to me, plaited your hair on Sundays.
I told them that you had blonde hair up in a braid.

While others ran, I stood still, turning again and again,
scanning the families, the old couples, the young lovers, looking

everywhere for you, a little girl in blue and red. I revolved like the earth pivoting on its axis, unable to stop, my head spinning fast. One thought went round at a rate that dizzied me: I could not lose you too.

'I've found her!'

I'll never forget those words or the face of the person who uttered them. A girl around twelve, her hair in neat, tight corn-rows radiating from her shiny face, was waving, her hand stretched high above her. She was standing next to a large shrub and as I ran towards her I could just make out the halo of your flaxen hair shimmering in the undergrowth. You really don't remember this at all?

Later that evening after your bath you were leaning against me as I sat brushing out your hair. There is a way that a child nestles up against their parents, the complete unselfconsciousness of belonging. You were pushing your little back into my legs, pressing your shoulders against my shins. It was almost if you were reassuring both of us of our insoluble bond. Then you asked me if I was angry, because I had been shouting so much in the park. I told you again that I had not been angry, just upset because we thought that we had lost you. And do you know what you said, ma chère? No? You said that you weren't lost, you were waiting to be found. And then you blamed me and said you had fallen asleep while waiting for me to get the ice cream and find you. We agreed not to play hide-and-seek outside the apartment after that.

Could you pass me that cleansing milk? Yes, that one. You were a funny child. We could never find you. Wherever you hid, you never fidgeted or squeaked or laughed, but always kept stock-still and silent. And each time we played, the dread of losing you hung over me like a pall until I found you, and you would explode in shrieks of mirth and victory.

It wasn't until that day when you were lost in the park that I realised how frightened Laurin must have been, how abandoned he had felt. What we had both lost.

*

When I became pregnant with you, I wrote a letter to Laurin, which I sent care of Ida and Thomas. From then on, Ida and I exchanged letters several times a year – in those days, phone calls were out of the question. Ida told me that Laurin knew about my letter, which they kept in a little metal box with all their important documents, identity cards, certificates and wills. Ida's letters always ended with same answer to my perpetual question: he still had not read it. I decided that I would not suffer the pain of going back again without knowing that he would see me. Once, Thomas came to New York – he was part of an East German mission to the United Nations here – and I managed to 'bump into' him in the lobby of One Dag Hammarskjöld. We couldn't talk for long because he had a posse of minders with him – not that a man with a wife and four children would be likely to abscond and seek asylum in the USA.

I had to keep going. I was pregnant with you, my business was expanding, people depended on me and I was in love with your father. All I could do was push it from my mind, and I had years of practice of that already. I know you've always said that I am overprotective, and maybe I have been, but can you see now why I did not let you out of my sight unless I knew that you were with your father, Graça, or one of your nannies?

Why are you looking at me like that? You look as angry as I used to feel about my mother. You think you should have known about your brother before? No, ma chère, I could not have told you about him before. Isn't it obvious why? I was too ashamed. And frightened. I didn't want you growing up living in fear that I would run away from you too, that one day you would wake up and I would be gone. No, I decided that I would tell you if ever there was a prospect of a reconciliation. And I had no reason to hope for that.

Ah, ma chère, your eyes are glinting in the mirror now. They're the same colour as mine. Now you understand. But wait, I have to finish my story. Pass me the toner, please. Two years ago, everything changed. First the Berlin Wall came down. Remember how I sat watching the television that November, gripped as the crowd destroyed the most potent symbol of the Cold War, clambering over the impregnable icon and tearing it to pieces, rocking it down with their own hands? I was riveted, as were millions; I knew that this would change everything. And it did, but not in the way I had presumed.

Less than two months later, in January 1990, I received a telegram. Ida had died from a heart attack.

I make so many trips for business, so I doubt that you noticed this one, but I packed my bags and left as soon as I received the news. I arrived in the morning and had a few hours to spare before driving to the cemetery. Oh, ma chère, imagine my dilemma. I owed more to Ida than any woman. She had taken my baby and loved him as her own. But Laurin would be there and it would be a disservice to Ida to steal this moment from her. I had to be there, but I had to be invisible and, ma chère, you know how hard that is for me. My clothes are all beautiful. I have perfected my style, I know how to walk, how to look elegant – and yet I had to attend Ida's funeral without being recognisable, or in any way remarkable amongst a crowd of dowdy East Germans. I did the unthinkable. I took a taxi to Ku'damm, walked into the least appealing shop I could see and bought a shapeless skirt, a ghastly thick coat, a hat and flat, sensible boots. All in black, which doesn't even suit me, and no make-up. It was not funny, don't laugh. At least I would be warm, I thought, but I barely had the strength to leave the hotel dressed like that. I caught sight of myself in the elevator mirror before I quickly turned around; it was the first time that I had ever seen an old woman staring back at me. It was frightening.

Berlin looked different in the winter, but even more so with the rubble-strewn band of no man's land where the wall had been, running like an open sore through the city. The cemetery was colder than the streets around it; a thin cover of snow frosted the trees and the grass around the graves. The funeral service was brief and I sat at the rear corner of the church, my hat pulled down over my hair. Thomas was sitting flanked by a man and a woman on each side. Max had the same brown hair and bald patch as his father Ottmar, and he was sitting beside Vreni, who looked much as her mother did the last time we had met in Berlin. On the other side a smaller, slimmer, younger woman sat leaning into Thomas – she had to be Gabriela, Ida and Thomas's daughter. And next to Gabi, holding her hand, was my son, sitting straight-backed and motionless, his head facing forward. Schleich had been a huge man, fat but also tall. Laurin had inherited Schleich's height – he dwarfed Thomas and Gabi – and his shoulders were broad. When the family got up to leave behind the cortège, he was the tallest man there. But he was not obese like Schleich. His hair was still blond like yours and mine, and he has our blue eyes. As Thomas and Ida had said, he was clearly my son.

I followed the procession of mourners through the cemetery to the grave and found a space at the back of the crowd where I watched as they lowered Ida into the ground. Standing on tiptoes, I had a view of Laurin's face. It was blank and taut, etched with grief. At one point he glanced my way, as if he felt me staring at him, and I looked down at the card I had been given when I arrived. The dates of Ida's birth and death were printed under a photo of her. It was the photo from their flat, from the wedding portrait of her marriage to Thomas.

After the final words were uttered over the gaping hole, the family processed back to a path alongside the chapel. They stood in a line as guests formed a queue to offer their condolences. I walked amongst the marble angels that stood like winged sentinels over the many dead, then returned to a tree that stood near Ida's grave. The gravediggers were shovelling the mud back in. The family stood, wearily shaking hands and kissing well-wishers. At one point Thomas, his face ashen and eyes red, looked back to the grave and caught sight of me. I waved, which seemed foolish, and he nodded but then turned to the next in line. I waited until the grave was full and the diggers had left, then put a bouquet of white lilies on the fresh mound of earth. The family and mourners were already gone.

★

That was two years ago, ma chère. You were just sixteen, still a child, whatever you felt. Now you are at least legally an adult and I feel it is time you know. Why today? Just a moment, can you reach for the moisturiser – yes, that one. I said I would only tell you if there was to be a reconciliation. Look, ma chère, have you ever seen me so nervous?

This afternoon, remember when the phone rang and you answered it? My heart stops just thinking about it. You handed the phone to me with a bored look and a shrug. Until then it was a normal day, like any other. You left before I answered, I think, when I said hello. And then there was a long silence.

'Hello,' I said again.

I was about to put the phone down when a clipped man's voice said, 'Rosa Mitchell?'

'Yes,' I said distractedly.

'I read your letter.' The man was speaking German with a Saxon accent.

'My letter?' My heart was pumping hard. The man was using *Sie*, the polite form of 'you', the term of address used for strangers. And yet I knew who it was, from his first words.

'Laurin?'

'Yes.' He hesitated and I could hear him breathing down the line. Then he continued. 'I read it after my mum's funeral. My father told me that you came, all the way from New York, that you kept yourself out of our way. Is that true?'

I pursed my lips, determined not to cry. 'Yes, I came. I owed Ida – ' I hesitated before I corrected myself – 'your mother – everything.'

There was a long silence then.

'From when I found out about you, she always told me that I had two mothers, that I was the luckiest man alive.'

'You must miss her.'

'I do.' There was a long silence. I swear he would have been able to hear my heart racing; I could hear my blood pulsing against the earpiece. 'But now that she's gone, I want to meet you.'

'You do? Of course, I'll get a plane today.'

He laughed. 'You won't need to,' he said. 'I'm in New York.'

A wave of panic rushed over me. 'Here? When did you get here?'

'A month ago.'

'A month ago?' I repeated. I was stupefied. All I could think was 'he's here, he's here'.

'You're quite the star. You're in the newspapers and magazines a lot.'

'That's my job, to keep up our profile. It helps sales.' Oh, I felt sick when I said that given what Thomas had told us of his views when we went to Berlin.

'I applied for a job, after my mum died, after I read your letter. I was in the Foreign Service before reunification and they amalgamated the two services.'

'Oh, so you came for work?'

'No, work is how I got here,' he said emphatically.

Ma chère, you can't imagine how absurd and hard this conversation was. Each word was a struggle. I suddenly thought of Thomas; keep to the facts, I told myself.

'How long will you be here?'

'Three to five years.'

'What's your job?'

'Deputy Permanent Representative to the UN.'

'You're an ambassador?'

'Almost,' he said, and I recognised the same patient tone as Thomas's.

'You read my letter?' I confirmed. 'I wrote it a long time ago, but nothing has changed. Your sister is eighteen now, that is the only difference.'

'No, I understand now. When I was young I was angry, then proud, but I never wanted to hurt my mum.'

'I understand,' I said, trying not to cry.

'But now I want to meet you.' His voice deepened as he let *Du*, the familiar, intimate form of 'you', slip out, before he concluded with, 'Mother.'

★

So, you can see, ma chère, this is no ordinary meeting. I can't wear my business fatigues, or my evening dress. I'm going to meet your brother for the first time in forty-four years. I want to look good, but not artificial; I want him to see beyond my mask. Look at us: I look good for my age, but you are beautiful, as I was when I gave birth to Laurin. I was younger than you, ma chère – can you imagine? You have my blue eyes and blonde hair – of course, mine is dyed now – and the clear complexion that we inherited from my mother. You are so young. And I was not much older the last time he saw me, though he doesn't remember that.

When you were tiny, I often used to cry over you as you suckled at my breast. It reminded me of the way Laurin would sometimes stop mid-feed and stare into my eyes, his hand stroking my face. It was as if a curtain that separated me from the rest of the world had been drawn back, the way he looked into my eyes. Today I feel as exposed and naked again; I want to hold nothing back. This once, I am going to go unguarded, without my armour – no make-up, no lies. I'll wear something simple, a navy suit and cream blouse.

Just me and him, alone.

Acknowledgments

This novel began as a process of almost dictation many years ago when I was visited by Rosa's arch, pink voice as I walked to work in Cambridge, Mass, in the winter of 1995–6. Somewhere into the pot went bits and pieces from family history and Rosa's spirit. The end product is a long way from that rather salacious beginning; the family stories have all been dropped or transformed in the telling, as Rosa's own voice emerged, exemplifying to me how exhilarating the creative process can be. My daughters despair at my clòthing – if I so much as dare to get into the car wearing crocs I hear them wail 'slippery slope' like banshees. This is fiction. There is only one (auto-)biographical scene in the novel and I am confident no one ever will guess which it is.

Over the years I have been nudged and helped by Christina Dunhill, Julie Pickard, Howard Lester, Don Clark and Farah Ahmed. Louise Doughty, Andrew Taylor and Erica Matlow persuaded me to axe the adverbs and save the twins – before their final reincarnation as one. In the early days in Harvard, the most arch Rosa was welcomed by Jim, whose Joycian prose I will never forget, and Raphael Carty in various cafés on Mass. Ave.

Dr Kathryn Meyers Emery explained the difference between saponification and adipocere to me. Sara Cohen and Colin Hall distracted me when I was in Liverpool. Herr Drs Richard Lorenz and Raffael Jovine helped me with South Tyrolean and German references. Reverendo Tarzan Leão de Sousa, who found me in a favela by asking for the blonde, reminded me of Brazilian niceties. My family are always my first readers. India Gurmail Kaufmann, Nick Kaufmann, Paul Brooks, Phillippa Kaufmann, Richard Wolfe, Ruth Kaufmann Wolfe and my friend, Anna

Fairbank, read and commented on the various versions of supposed (but far from) last drafts.

To say that this book had a long gestation would be an understatement, but the final version was coaxed out by the excellent midwifery of my fabulous editor and co-knitter, Thorne Ryan, Sharona Selby's exacting, meticulous attention to detail and my patient agent, Broo Doherty, who did not give up on me.

I owe special thanks to Ruthie and Hannah who put up with varying degrees of neglect throughout the writing and editing of this story. Last but very much not least, I would not be writing at all, let alone have written Rosa's story, without the continuous support of Richard, who – despite being a chemist and businessman – bears no resemblance to any of the characters in these pages. It is a story.

Any typos and punctuation errors I blame on the cat.